Healing an Elvish Heart

Healing an Elvish Heart
Copyright © 2024 by Austin Welch-Brown.

All rights reserved. No part of this book may be used or reproduced in any form whatsoever without written permission except in the case of brief quotations in critical articles or reviews.

Printed in the United States of America.

Cover design by (Mikayla)

ISBN - Hard Cover: 9798331499112
ISBN - Paperback: 9798330493241

Also By Austin Welch-Brown

The Crown's Agent

Acknowledgments

Thank you to my amazing beta reader Jessica.

Special Thanks to my amazing cover artist Mikayla Dubois.

Trigger Warnings

Anxiety
Depression
Suicidal Thoughts
Dubious Consent
Blood And Gore.

YOU HAVE BEEN WARNED!!!

HEALING AN ELVISH HEART

Elvish Blood Series

Austin Welch-Brown

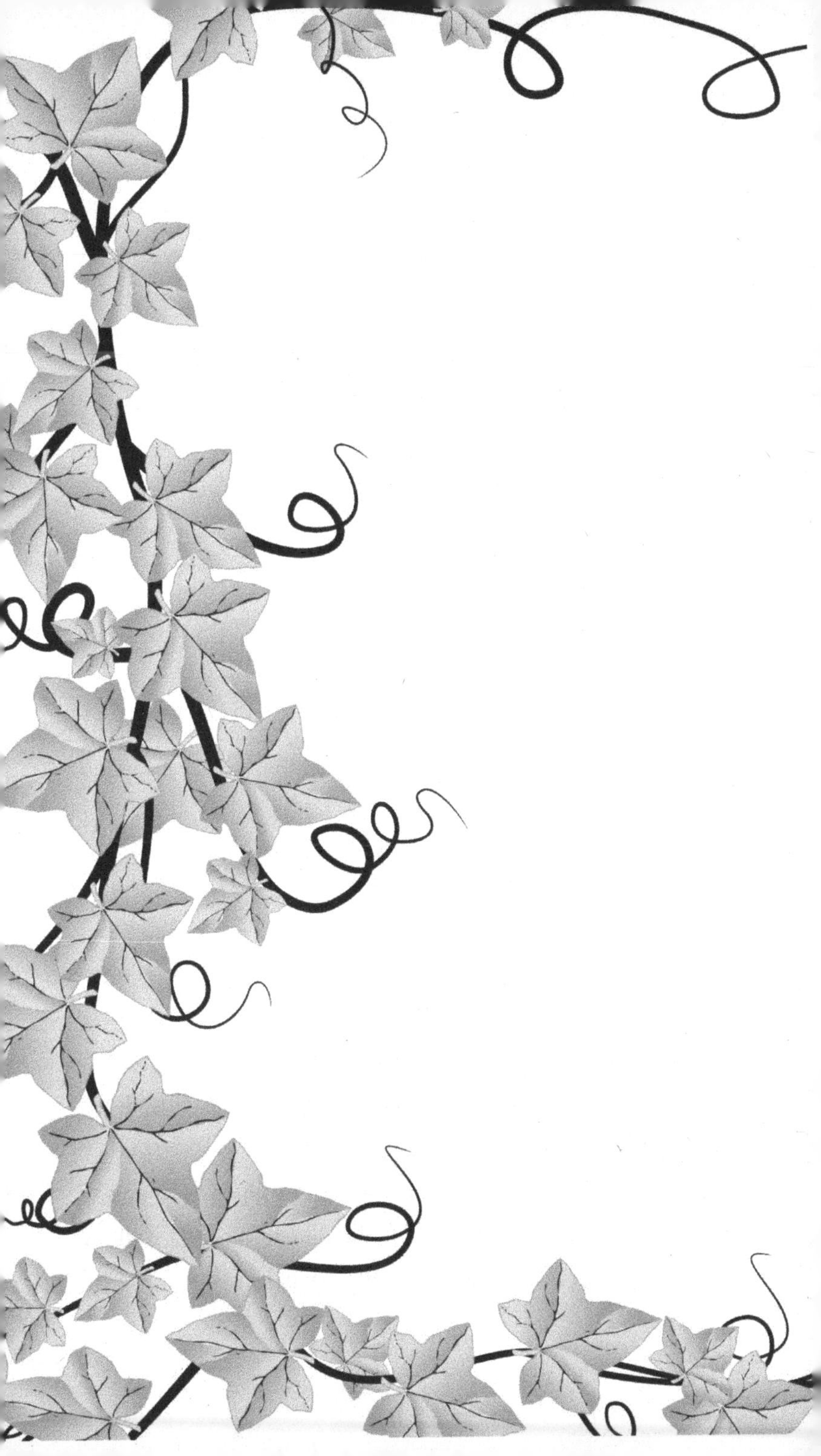

CHAPTER 1:

Aerin

I awoke from another night less slumber and sat up in my wobbling bed. I grabbed my cloak from the hangar and put it on to hide my true identity. Sliding on my fur-trimmed boots, I opened the door that closed my closet-sized room.

I would need to find a job soon if I wanted to be able to afford one more night here, I thought to myself, walking down the creaking stairs to the tavern below.

"Morning Aerin, will it be the usual bowl of oats?" The tall barkeep asked me.

I nodded and watched as the clean-shaven man poured a bowl of oats and hot water into it. He slapped it down, also putting a mug of ale in front of me. I put my hands into my pockets to grab the money.

"It's on the house today…I know you're running low again." He chuckled and handed me a rolled-up piece of parchment.

I smiled and took the paper. I unfolded it and noticed it was another assassination request. There was a man drawn on the paper, and I memorized the picture of his long dark hair, scruffy face and the scar on his neck. I took in every detail and handed him back the parchment. Outside of his physical features, what stood out most to me was the reward: 10,000 pieces of gold. That would keep me happy for a good month.

I downed the oats and had Bill, the owner, return my weapons. I placed two daggers up my sleeves, put another two in my boots, and a fifth inside the quiver I kept around my waist. Bill handed me my bow, which I promptly swung over my shoulder and my two scimitars that went in the pack as well. When I was ready, I turned out of the tavern and headed to the next town over, Morewood.

As I was approaching the town gates, I heard a gallop from behind me and turned to see Alatar, my ivory mare, charging at me. She was right on cue, like always. I held my hand out and grabbed the reins as she stomped past and swung myself onto her saddle in one smooth move. Together, we rode out of the town.

****

We traveled the short distance to Morewood in just over two hours. The gates to the city were closed when we arrived, so I patted Alatar and she galloped off. She would know to come back for me when I completed the assignment. I ducked through a space between the bars of the gates and made my way inside the town, hiding in the shadows and blending into the darkness thanks to my reliable cloak.

The less people who knew I was around, the better.

I scouted the area around the tavern before walking in, sitting at the bar top, and waiting for the barkeep. A man, who looked like he was ready to fall over dead, ambled out of the backroom. He was hunched over and held onto the counter as he made his way over to me.

Humans lived such short lives compared to me, I thought. I have seen friends die and others be born more times than I can count.

"What can I get for you?" He asked, his legs shaking with age.

"A glass of your best wine, and maybe some information?"

"My best wine…"

The old barkeep turned toward the bar behind him and

looked over the options. He bent over and took out a golden bottle with a small elvish decal on it.

"Elvish wine," he unknowingly confirmed for me. "This is the last bottle I have, but it's the best wine you will ever taste." He poured me a glass. "What kind of information are you looking for?"

He was casual, leaning against the counter for support.

"Can you tell me where I can find John Croft?" I asked, whispering his name.

The old man leaned in close to me and pointed a gnarled finger to the corner of the tavern. I turned to see a man sitting in the back corner clutching a bottle of beer. I nodded to the barkeep.

"Go in the back please."

As the old man limped to the back room, obeying my instructions, I walked over to the solitary man and took a seat across from him. I put the bottle of wine on the table after taking a sip from it in a power move.

The old man was right. This was the best wine I ever had.

"Get away from here," the shadowy figure commanded in a drunken slur. He tried to reach across the table and push me away but instead collapsed onto the sturdy wood in a heap.

"You seem to have gotten into some hot water here, John. Whatever did you do?" I was hired to do a job, but I wanted to question him. I hated killing on principle, but I hated killing even more when I didn't know why. John, however, did not answer. Instead, he spat in my face.

"Okay, so it's going to be like that." I stood up and stretched out my arm grabbing a handful of his hair and smacked his face down onto the table. I let the dagger slide down into my hand from up my sleeve and pressed the cold steel onto his neck. John's struggles had stopped when he felt the icy blade on his skin, and he knew if he even moved a single muscle it would pierce him.

"Who the fuck are you?" John screamed at me, fear, anger, and alcohol slurring his words. The bar got quiet, and I could feel the eyes of the other patrons on my back.

"Some call me The Shadow Hunter. Others call me Swift Death. But you can call me by my name because it will not matter if you know it." He turned his head to look up at me. "You can call me Aerin."

I ran the dagger around his throat. A few weak struggles from John as his blood drained onto the floor, and soon he lay lifeless on the table.

I left 500 gold on the table for the barkeep as payment for the wine and the trouble and took the bottle of elvish wine with me as I swept out of the bar. The wine was too good to leave behind for someone else to drink. I played with the chain I had removed from John's neck, embossed with the royal crest, and walked back to the edge of town. It was around noon, but I was in no rush to return home just yet. I decided to walkaround the small town of Morewood to see what they had to offer and ventured into the local blacksmith's shop.

Inside the shop, my nose was instantly assailed by the smell of steel and leather. There was no smell I loved more, except for possibly the smell of freshly baked elvish bread. Now…that was a smell to die for. I walked around the store, admiring the beautiful craftsmanship of the weapons. Nothing stood out too much that I simply had to have, but it was still nice nonetheless.

"Hello?" I called out, hoping there would be some response. I prayed I did not just kill the blacksmith.

"Be with you in a minute!" A deep voice called to me from the back of the shop. Rivertown, where I was from, was too poor and defeated to have a blacksmith, so I had no choice but to wait. I jumped up to take a seat on the counter and waited for the man to leave the back room.

"What can I do for ya?"

The man spoke again, his voice sounding deeper now that he was right behind me. I turned to him and allowed my eyes to drift over his body. Lust for this unknown man quickly shot through my body, and I realized I didn't want to leave Morewood without sampling another delicacy the town had to offer. I sweetened my voice as I responded, adding the magical musicality needed to work my lust charm on him.

"Would a strong man like you be able to sharpen something for me?" I questioned.

The man blinked for a moment, as the magic took hold. He smiled wryly, knowing my ploy. "There is no blade I can't."

I took out my two scimitars and placed them on the counter. He picked them up and took a look over them, twisting them this way and that in the light as he admired the craftsmanship, opening his mouth in awe. "These are elvish. How did you get them?"

I hopped off the counter and walked around to him.

"That is my secret, and if you would like I can be yours," I spoke softly, magic infusing with my voice as I lightly traced my hands down his chest. The man swallowed hard, his subconscious fighting the magic's hold on his motor functions, as I continued weaving my charming spell. Soon he would be nothing more than a puddle of lust at my feet, and ripe for the picking. The blacksmith nodded and started working right away, taking the blades and walking swiftly into the back room. Soon, I could hear the sounds of the grinder melting from the back into the front room where he left me. After a short time, he came back out and returned the scimitars to me.

"That will be 500 gold," he spoke softly, his eyes clouding over.

I thought briefly about paying him the gold, but I couldn't really afford to drop another 500 gold today, and it had been a while since I had a decent release. I grabbed him by the shirt and pulled him close to me, locking his eyes with mine.

"Are you sure I can't pay another way? A strong man like you doesn't come around often." I infused as much magic as I could into the words, and felt his mind capitulate to my will. He swallowed hard, Adam's apple bobbing, and I could feel his heart racing through his dirty shirt. He was now my puppet of lust. I ripped away his clothing, exposing his muscular, hair-covered chest, and allowed him to kiss my neck and undress me. Nothing about this person was attractive to me; I had no feelings about this encounter other than that this was yet another sexual escapade for me. I let him have his way with me on the dirt-encrusted floor of his shop before dressing and leaving him before the spell wore off and he realized what had happened and that I didn't actually pay him for the work he had done for me...

I moved rapidly through the town, sticking to the minimal shadows of back alleys as I closed the distance between myself and the gates. I let outa sharp whistle, and Alatar came galloping to me almost immediately. I jumped on her back once more, and we took off out of Morewood.

Traveling back home, I found myself lost in thought. I had never let myself fall in love or allowed myself to have feelings for someone who would die long before me. I wondered what it would be like to actually be in love; to have a partner, a wedding…all the things I heard about in stories shared around the many taverns I spent my nights in. Yet, I never let myself feel a drop of thee motion.

And why would I? It would result in nothing but hurt in the end.

I learned a long time ago that love is not worth the pain. It is infinitely easier to have sex and move on. Lust is less complicated. More simple. But...I admitted to myself it would be nice to give up this killing; to settle down and have a farm and raise a family. But for that, I would need to find someone of my own kind.

And, thanks to the King, that would never happen.

****

Rivertown was bustling as we rode closer.

I could hear the drunks shouting at each other and watched as the smoke from fires that started out of drunken stupors rose into the late afternoon sky. I made my way through the broken gates and led Alatar back to the stables. It was the only place in the town that was still in great condition, mainly because I was the only one with a horse and I kept up with it for my loyal girl. I removed the saddle and brushed her coat before feeding her and headed back to the tavern.

"Well, how did it go?" The barkeep asked, pausing as he tried to clean a glass with a brown rag.

I slammed the gold chain down on the table, probably with a little more force than necessary. In return, he paid me for my work.

As I pocketed the coins, I handed him the bottle of elvish wine, which he then stored in a secret loose floorboard.

"So? What's next for Aerin?" He asked me, wondering if this was the time I would finally move on.

"A glass of strong ale."

He gave me a look before turning around and pouring me a mug.

"That is not what I meant." He leaned in close to me. "I mean, when are you going to start looking for the elves again? We need them back to help us take down the King."

I shook my head. I had given up on that quest centuries ago, after traveling most of the land and not finding anyone close to my race.

"You know the King purged this land of them," I spoke softly, holding back my emotions.

"Not even the King can eliminate a whole race in one go, Aerin. You know that as well as I do."

I know the barkeep meant well because he always did. But it still hurt thinking about the ounce of hope he was trying to give me. I could feel the fireplace starting to heat up on my back as my rage began to boil thinking about the king's blood lust.

"Hey...cool it before you burn down my place," the barkeep's voice was stronger, the warning tone giving it power. I smiled apologetically. I put my hand out horizontally in the direction of the fire and lowered it until the fire cooled back down.

"Listen, Aerin…you need to keep those eyes of yours in check," the barkeep's tone was more serious than I'd ever heard him as he delivered his warning. "The King's army is here. They arrived shortly after you left. No one knows why they are here, but they know they are not welcome. It's been ten years since they stepped foot in Rivertown, so no one knows what or who they are looking for. All I know is that you need to be careful because they will drag you back to the palace without any thought if they knew about you."

I pulled my hood closer over my head and nodded, understanding the seriousness of the situation.

"Why don't you go relax?" The barkeep placated. "I will bring some soup to your room."

"Thanks Gryphon." I smiled and retreated to my room.

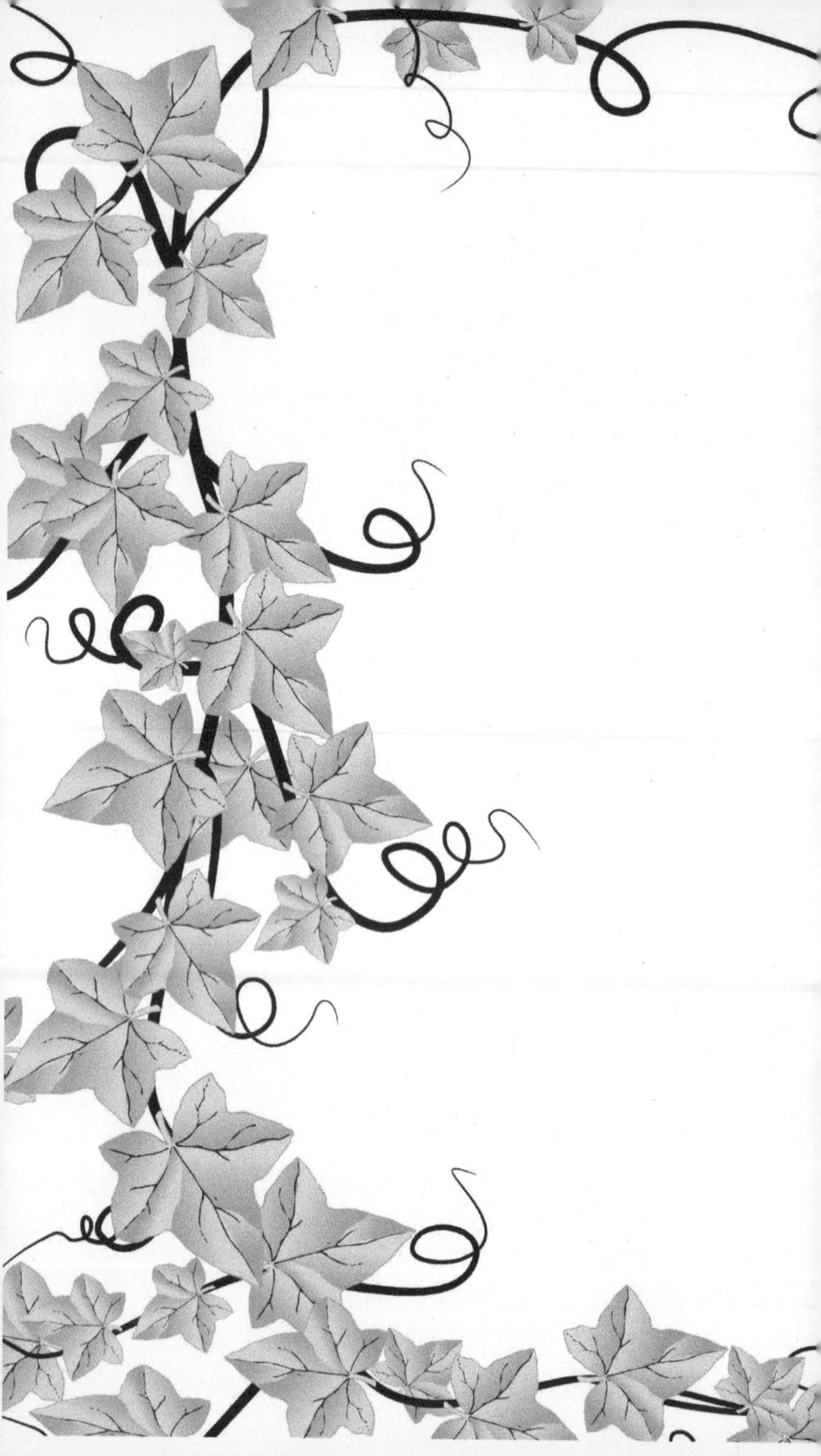

CHAPTER 2:

Aerin

I stayed in my room for a few days, eating soup, and drinking ale to my heart's content. I did not mind the solitude of the dark room. It was like me: empty inside.

Every morning, I woke up with nothing but my armory. Even the memory of my father has started to become foggy. I could remember his blue eyes and blond hair, but nothing more. I couldn't even remember our training… just the blood stained on his hands. I remember the screams the night the king's men charged our home in the Calen <u>Taurë</u>- the Great Green Forest to those who don't know. I remember waking up to the breeze blowing in through my window. The houses were built up in the trees; they overlooked rivers, plains, and more. It was not long after my hundredth birthday when Neo-Quenya was called out by everyone. I rushed to my window and, from my tree topping window, saw a lake of fire engulfing my homeland. I could smell the flesh of my friends, family, and neighbors burning and, before I could move, my house was filled with smoke. My father died fighting the royal guard outside my house. I, however, escaped and took a handful of knights with me.

"Aerin, I brought you your oats."

The barkeep's voice was creaky as he opened the door brought in my food and placed it at the foot of my bed.

"When I said you should lay low, I did not exactly mean staying inside your room all day and night," the barkeep spoke softly, chastising me for my behavior. "It's not good for you. I know you get lost in your mind when you're here."

"You're right." I grabbed my cowl and cloak and set up my armory on myself. "I think these clowns have been here long enough don't you, Gryphon?"

I pushed him to the side and walked out the front door. The sun was just starting to rise as I ventured out into the street. I walked around town hiding in the shadows, watching knights wreak havoc on my town. Despite days of being here, they were still breaking into houses and tossing people out for questioning. I promised myself I would neither be involved nor bring attention to myself.

"Aye! You! Freeze there!"

A knight came up behind me, ordering my compliance. I ignored him and continued walking. With my elvish hearing, I heard his heart quicken as he ran up to me and grabbed my arm. I turned to him and smiled.

"I'm sorry," I smiled sweetly. "I had no idea you were talking to me. Forgive me."

I bowed lowly. As I stood back up, I let my dagger slip from my sleeve and thrust it deep under his helmet and into his neck. I watched as the knight quickly grabbed his neck -- fisting around the dagger -- and dropped the sword in his hand as he tried to stop the blood from flowing out and staining his shiny silver armor as it made its way to the dirt ground. I smiled grimly in satisfaction as I watched this King's bitch bleed out. I had very little respect for humans, and even less for those who serve the King. I turned on my heel and continued on my path, leaving the dagger there in his throat. He was not worth the respect of removing it.

I climbed on top of the alchemist's shop. There, I unsheathed my bow and started raining down arrows upon unsuspecting knights. I fired each arrow carefully, aiming for weak spots in their armor. It seemed they never fixed the weaknesses of the armor in the neck, between the helmet and the underarms being less guarded. I remember hearing my father's voice telling me where to aim when killing enemies.

"HELP ME!"

I heard a child yelling from below. I quickly jumped off the building and raced towards the voice. I found the child and grabbed his tattered shirt as he ran past me and pushed him behind me. I stepped out of the shadows and was met face to face with the 'knight' that was chasing him.

"What kind of knight hunts little children? One that has no honor that's who." I tossed my bow to the floor and pulled out my scimitars. The knight drew his second sword and waited to see my next move. I began chanting in elvish, and my voice echoed through the town. I heard the screams stop and footsteps approaching me. I quickly stopped my chant as I knew I could not fight a whole army, at least not in the open like this. I ran at the knight and jumped over him, turning in the air. As I landed I let my scimitars slice clean through the guard's neck and watched as his head rolled off his shoulders. I turned to the boy and ran over picking him and my bow up. I carried him back to the tavern and slammed the door shut behind me. "Gryphon, get your ass out here," I shouted.

"What is it now, Aerin?" He asked before looking at me and seeing my blood-soaked clothing. "You didn't," he asked, already knowing the answer.

"Take him to my room and keep him safe." I extended my hand and a fireball formed inside it. I watched out the window waiting for the knights as Gryphon took the child upstairs. The knights were hot on my tail when we ran, so they should be here any minute. But there was nothing. No one came in. I left the tavern with the ball of fire still in my hand. I walked through the small town but there was not one guard in sight. They retreated that easily. I knew it was too good to be true. I raced to the stables to check on Alatar.

I made it to the stables and it had been burnt down to the ground. I felt a pain in my chest as I raced to it. I felt tears fall from my eyes as I started to toss the rubble around looking for any sign of her. I found some dead knights, along with dead Rivertown residents. I felt anger brewing inside me. Alatar was the only family I had left. If anything has happened to her, I will go to the King myself and kill him. I continued to push aside the wood chunks and let loose a breath when I saw fresh tracks. They were covered in blood but she was on the move. I whistled but could not hear her. I could feel my heart darkening more. I whistled again, yet there was still no sound. I fell to my knees and covered my eyes.

"Mister, are you hurt?" I dried my eyes and turned to see the young boy I saved. "If you're hurt I can help you."

"I'm hurt but it's not a wound to the flesh." The boy walked over to me and held his hand over my heart. I watched as it flowed yellow, I felt joy radiate over my body and smiled. "You are a faery, aren't you?" The boy smiled and I watched as he shrunk back to his 10-inch size and sprouted wings.

"I am, and you should put back on your hood. You never know who is watching." I quickly put my hood back on, covering my ears. "For saving my life please take this." He handed me a necklace that had a small vile on it. "It can cure anything except death. Keep it safe and one day it will keep you safe." He smiled and waved to me before disappearing. "Your heart is not as black as you think. Open it to love, and let the light inside once more, Aerin. You're a strong elf, and you can change the world," he spoke as he left, and with him so did the feeling of joy I had. I knew I had to find Alatar before it was too late. I stood up and followed the tracks into the forest. They did not go too far, and I whistled from time to time to see if she would come running. I could feel myself falling apart the more I traveled out.

The tracks came to a stop by the river, and Alatar lay next to it. I raced over to her and noticed her breath was short, and I would not have much more time to save her. It has been years since I used my healing powers, or even had the need to. I held my hands over her and calmed myself.

I took a deep breath and began to chant. "Lothron i rod plural rodyn min myself, n- transferred into cin. Sír na- ú- cín anand, hi edr- cín eyes." I closed my eyes and could feel a warmth radiating from my hands as they traveled inside

Alatar. After minutes of chanting I felt myself becoming weaker. I opened my eyes and everything around me was spinning. My vision started to blur as I collapsed on top of Alatar.

****

Alatar licked my face till I woke up. The stars were out and it was time to make my way back home. It took everything in me to stand up and pet her. But the pain did not matter to me, the weakness I was feeling was all worth it. My family was safe. Alatar knelt down and I fell onto her back. She trotted back to Rivertown with me lifeless on her back. She stopped at the tavern where she neighed until Gryphon came out. He fed her an apple and took me off her back. Then carried me into the guild, and sat me on the chair inside.

"How much magic did you use out there, Aerin, you know you still don't have control of it. You hid it for too long and lost touch with the elvish star, draining your life away every time you use magic." I smiled at him and put my hand on his back.

"Shut up Dad, get me an ale," I said, patting his back. Gryphon did as commanded and returned with it.

"The town is very thankful for what you have done. Do you think anyone noticed who you are, I mean who you really are? If they did, you know as well as I do they will be back." I shrugged the statement off and told him the truth.

"I am not sure what they did or did not see Gryphon,

but I do know that I will be ready if they come back."

"You can't fight an army."

"I can die trying though," I spoke with truth in my voice. I would die trying and it would only bring me one more step to my revenge on the King. He would either give me the location where my kin hides out or die by my blade for his sins.

"You need to rest, can you make it up to your room on your own?" Gryphon asked. My legs still felt like puddles of water, as I stood up my legs began to shake from under me and I fell forward onto the table. "So that's a no," Gryphon scoffed and shook his head then carried me over the fireplace and placed me in one of the cushioned chairs. "The guild will be here in a few hours, why don't you try and rest till then." I closed my eyes and drifted off.

****

"Aerin, come on. Keep up with me," a young boy screamed back to me. I ran after him. The trees were bare and snow was falling everywhere. I mumbled under my breath and my pace quickened. I caught up with him and tackled him into the snow. He rolled under me laughing. "You cheated," He spoke between his fits of laughter. I lay over him looking at his beautiful smile. That image was engraved in my mind. His brown hair was a mess and kept short. I leaned down and kissed him. I was nearly 98; a young age for an elf, still a child practically. He was 97.

"Aerin, aren't you forgetting what today is?" I smiled

back at him.

"As if I could ever forget your birthday." I pulled out a necklace and put it around him. It was a shield with my family crest on it.

"It's beautiful."

"Just like you." I stared into his deep blue eyes and saw a life I could have had with him. We could have been happy.

****

My eyes jolted open, and I felt tears forming in my eyes. I remember him so vividly. I can feel his lips on mine. Was this a dream or something more? It felt too real to be a dream. I felt my heart skipping beats as I was reminded of my first and only love. I closed my eyes and I could still see him. I have not felt this way in so long. Although I thought I lost him, he has been with me this whole time. I was knocked back to reality when the door to the tavern was kicked in and the drunks started forming. I closed my eyes again wanting to see him once more but the memory faded.

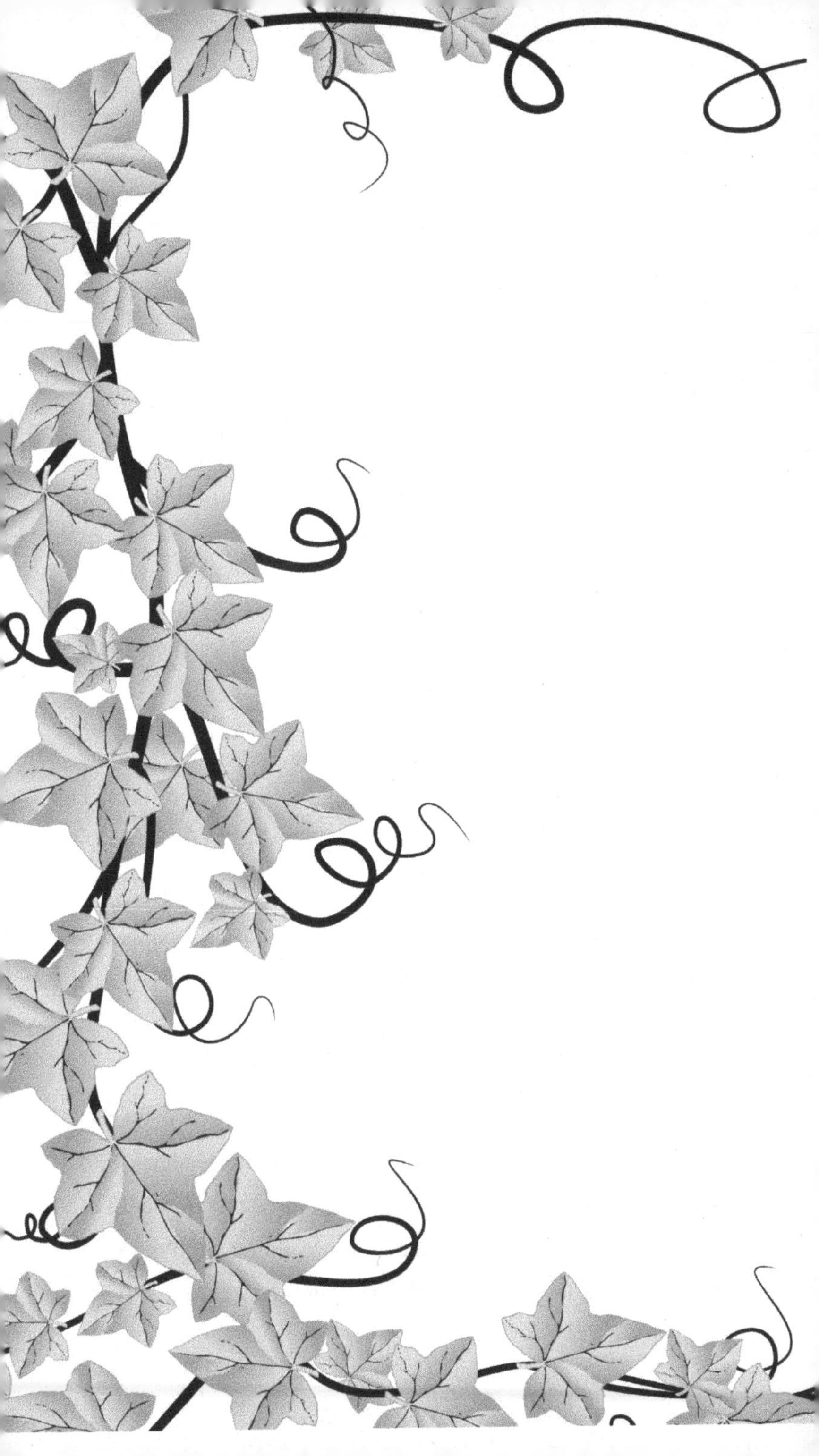

# CHAPTER 3:

Aerin

The assassin's guild tavern was bustling, everyone was inside celebrating my latest kills, treating me as some kind of hero. Men and halflings alike celebrated my victory. Yet it was nothing but more kills, more noted nightmares I would have to struggle with. Although I might have been the best at killing in the guild, there was nothing I hated more. I sat at the head of the table with my glass chalice in hand stirring the poorly made wine in it. Tonight's feast was brought to the table by a bunch of wenches who enjoyed the looks and grins they got from the men. As they placed the roasted pig and sides on the table, the men would pull them on their laps and grope them all they could. It sickened me every time. They left the room and everyone devoured the small portions of food we had. I looked over the table with my cowl covering every part of my face but my eyes. I walked to the stables where I sat on a bale of hay next to my trusted steed. The party continued, and the town could tell they were out of food. Everyone quickly poured out of the run-down tavern and into any place they could find a meal.

    Once the noise settled down I went back into the tavern and took a seat at the bar. I removed my hood exposing my pointed ears and sun-kissed hair. I turned to look at the little fire that was left burning in the fireplace and tossed another log into it. Rivertown was dying. The only money or trade they saw was whatever I would bring back to them. I often dreamed of leaving, but wondered what would happen here if I did, then again would it even matter if they knew what I really was? I walked behind the bar grabbed a bottle of wine that was hidden under a floorboard and sat down by the fireplace with it. I bit onto the cork, pulled it out, and took a sip. It's the last bottle of elvish wine left for miles.

I was about halfway through my bottle when the doors to the tavern swung open. I quickly pulled up my hood and turned to the doors. I saw a halfling there for a moment before he fell to the floor with a knife in his back. I grabbed my bow off the wall and raced out the door. There was screaming as I looked around and saw the town on fire. The fire forever burnt a memory in my mind. The smoke made it hard to see and I had to go on sound alone. I started to the main trail out of town when I was met with a sword against my throat. I froze then gently turned my head to see who was holding me hostage. It was hard to see any details other than the full armor they wore, it looked to be silver and covered the assailant from head to toe.

"By order of the King you are to return with us," the man spoke in a deep voice and took my bow off my person and snapped it like a twig. I put up no resistance, and he pushed me into a carriage. Once I was inside we rode off. I watched out the barred window as my town burnt to ash.

****

We traveled for two days, and I was given no food or water. They wanted to make sure I was weak before we got to the palace. We rode for what felt like a week but it was only three days. I was waiting for the door to open, I knew the minute it did I could make a run for it. I listened as the guards walked to the back of the door and then started to unchain it. They stopped in the process and walked away.

"The King wants to see you guys right away," a small

voice spoke to them. I listened as the men groaned and walked away. The chains outside my prison once again started to rustle. Once I heard the chains fall to the ground, I kicked the door open, sprung out, and landed on top of a small child. My dagger was held against his throat.

"Please don't hurt me," he spoke with tears in his eyes. I could see myself looking back at me. It reminded me of the night I lost my family to the tyrant of a king. I stood up and extended my hand to the young lad. He took it.

"I'm Sylas," he spoke softly, afraid of my next move. "I want to help you," he spoke, choking on his words. I looked him over, he was obviously of some importance here. His clothing was well-tailored, and his hair was kept clean. He was holding onto some kind of book.

"I don't want you to get in trouble," I spoke to him softly, as I looked over the book. It had elvish symbols on it. "You should not have that book out in plain sight, it will lead you to trouble." I gave him my bag to hide his book in. The book was of the old ways of elvish kind with different spells inside it able to take down villages with just one word. The guards raced back out to us and I pushed the kid along. I raised my hands which they grabbed and quickly shackled. They pushed me to the palace doors. I listened as the doors creaked open, they were stone and stood about two stories high. They shoved me through the halls to the throne room and tossed me on the ground. I remained looking down as I listened to the men walk away and the king enter.

The king took his seat and stared down at me. I could feel his gaze through my hood. I looked up at him a bit too fast and my hood fell off. I saw a man with a frail figure in front of me. His long hair had turned gray, he had on only a robe from what I could tell down here. I could tell his body would not handle armor anymore.

"You are the one they call Aerin, correct? The famous killer in the night?" He spoke through a raspy cough.

"I am Aerin, but I serve no man," I spoke as I stood up. I already escaped the shackles that were holding me and grabbed my dagger from my back. I was ready to throw it at him and take revenge for my parent's death when the door behind me opened.

"Sorry I am late, Your Majesty," Sylas spoke from behind me. I quickly sheathed the dagger again. He walked next to me and bowed to the king. "My brother has sent me in his place, as he is currently dealing with matters at the tavern."

"Thank you for joining us, Sylas," the King spoke back to the young boy wholeheartedly. This was not the tyrant killer that killed my parents, something has changed. "Aerin, I wish to provide you with work. The King offered it to me."

"And what is the payment for the task you ask of me?"

"Your life," the King spoke back. "You will accompany Sylas to his house and await my orders." He waved his hand and sent me on my way with Sylas.

Sylas led me through the town and made stops on the way at some vendors. Getting different foods I've never heard of. We finally entered a small cabin. I looked around and there were no royal marks anywhere to be found. There was a fire burning in the center of the room, and two beds to either side of the room.

"Is it just you and your brother who live here?" I asked Sylas who nodded and handed me back my bag. He opened the book and started to read from it. I watched as the knives started to chop the food and prepare the meal. I smiled at the sight of magic. It was banned across the lands but the King, hated anything magic and anything that would outlive him. Sylas smiled at me, and I tousled his hair. "How old are you?"

"I'm 13," he answered quickly.

"Where are your parents?"

"My mom died when I was born and my father, the king sent him on a mission and he never came back." I felt the pain I put behind me come out again, his story was all too similar to mine. "But it's okay, my brother takes care of me and I take care of him." Sylas still smiled as he spoke to me. I nodded to him. He started to read from the book and the food started flying around the kitchen.

"So how old are you again, Sylas?" I asked him as he used elvish magic to prepare the food.

"15," he called back to me, watching closely as the

vegetable started to be cut.

"How old are you really, Sylas?" I asked him and removed my hood to expose my elvish ears.

He looked up at me and smiled. "150 years young," he spoke giddily.

"You're a half-elf?" I asked, looking at him as he smiled and nodded. He continued to chant and the food continued to prep itself. "Why don't we cook the human way in case someone comes by the window?" Sylas nodded in agreement and took out a knife for me. I started cutting some carrots and potatoes.

"Fuck," I called out as I sliced my finger over and over. I still couldn't cook after all these years. I can kill anyone but show me a carrot and I forget how to handle a knife. Sylas laughed and pointed at my cuts and the different-sized vegetables.

"You're not very good at this."

"No, I am not, I have not cooked in a very long time." Sylas walked over to me and showed me how to cut the vegetables.

"You need to slow down. Cooking should be fun, don't make it into a chore." I smiled at him, he sounded like my mother. I looked into his eyes and at his face. He looked so familiar to me. I couldn't shake the feeling. I had never seen him before, but there was something about him.

"I have to go use the bathroom. Can you finish cutting these for me, and keep an eye on the fire? We don't want the soup to boil over." I nodded to him and walked over to the fireplace where a cauldron was hung up. I pushed the vegetables into it and walked around the house. I noticed a lot of elvish items around. There were paintings, maps, and kitchenware. The tables were elvish made as well. Something did not seem right to me, but I couldn't put my finger on it. It reminded me of my old home in the trees. I closed my eyes and took a deep breath. I was able to sense magic around the house, a type of cloaking to it. I remember my mother talking about strong spells that could hide magic from the eyes of mortal men. Was this it, and if it was, how strong was Sylas, let alone his older brother? How have they kept it all a secret from the king for so long? I searched the house more and found some notes hidden behind some books. They were recent notes from Sylas's father, he was alive, and searching the old elvish towns for survivors, for the king. A traitor of his own kind. What kind of elf would even dream of bringing pain to another person, the thought of it made me sick. It is what separates us from the dirty mortals. Even the half-elfs knew it was wrong for pointless bloodshed, and they had the blood of mortal men. They only lived half the lifespan of elves. They wanted our power just as much as the humans did.

I had to get my mind away from all this. I took a deep breath and returned to the kitchen to continue cutting the vegetables. Sylas came back from the bathroom and smiled at me. I smiled back, it was nice to be in his company even if he was half-human. It had been so long since I had seen any elf, and he brought me back something I lost a long time ago. Hope that my kin is still out there somewhere.

"I have to run back out. I forgot to get some meat. I will be right back okay, keep an eye on things."

"I will, don't you worry," I spoke back to him. I put the remainder of the food into the cauldron, gave it a stir, and a little taste. It reminded me of the food my mother used to make. The silkiness of the broth warmed me from the inside out on cold winter nights. I looked out the window and sighed a little. It was nice to be in a real house again. To be in a town filled with people, not just horny drunks. Sure it will be harder to fulfill my needs here, but I have my ways.

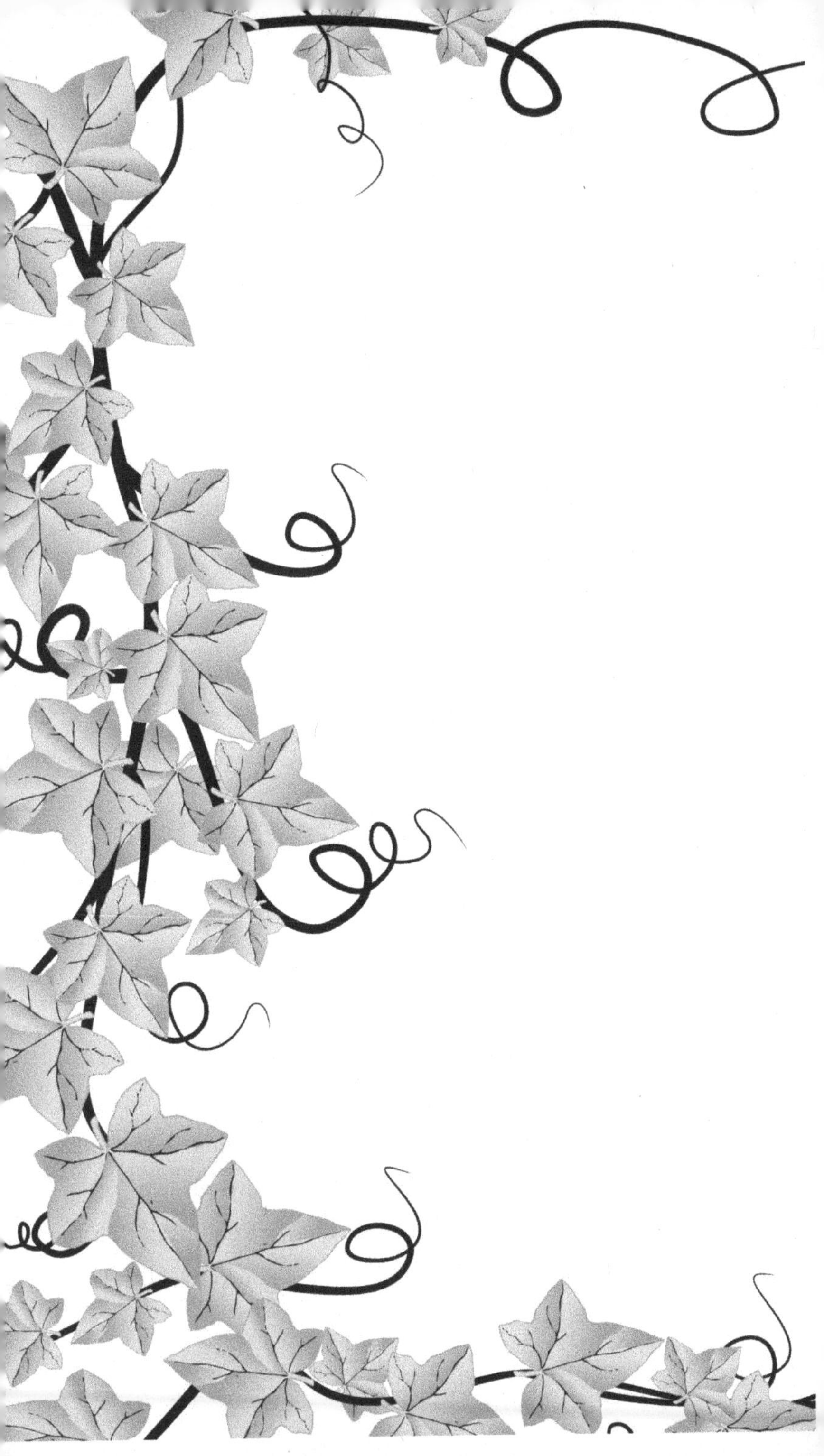

CHAPTER 4:

Thorne

"Thorne, thank god you're here," Sam shouted to me from behind the bar. I looked around and saw two men in the corner shouting and their swords clashing. I walked over to them and pulled out my two short swords.

"Can you two get along or do I have to do this the hard way?" I asked them as I moved closer. "You know I can lay you both out right here." I might have sounded a bit cocky, but it was the truth and they knew it. They both dropped their weapons and went outside. I walked over to the bar and took a seat.

"For you, our brave hero," Sam spoke, handing me a glass of elvish wine. I took it and downed it in one sip. "Care for your other reward?" Sam asked, leaning over the counter.

"Not today. I promised Sylas I would be home for dinner."

"Oh come on, we can make it fast." Sam attempted to seduce me. I pushed him back off the counter, and he fell onto the ground. I got up and tossed a gold coin on the bar. I had another dream last night of my old life, before all this. I dreamt of the old settlement when times were easier and could not get the image out of my head. I made my way to the local blacksmith and dropped off my weapons for their daily sharpening before returning to the palace.

As I walked through the crowded city streets I was able to notice someone stealing from a merchant. I walked over and stood behind them. They turned to run and ran into my chest.

"You were going to stay put, and pay for that, weren't you?" I threatened the man. He raised his fist to hit me but was met with my fist instead. I grabbed the sack of money from his pocket handed it to the merchant and tossed the man to the knights who were close by. They quickly shackled him and I was back on the path to the palace. I walked, watching everyone, my keen eyes picking up on every step and every shady possible outcome. This was my home now and it was my job to protect it.

Outside the gates to the palace, I overheard a few knights talking.

"You should have seen it— the whole town was set ablaze. That ought to show the rebels to think twice before killing the king's men."

"Were there any survivors?" The smaller of the two knights asked.

"Only one, we brought him back. The king wanted him alive for some reason. Something about Thorne."

I made a face at them using my name, but it was not worth the time to put them back in their place. The palace doors creaked open and I reported to the king's dining hall. I bowed upon entering and took a seat next to the King.

"You wanted to see me, Your Majesty?"

"Yes, thank you, Thorne. As you have probably heard, we dealt with Rivertown."

"I have, Your Majesty." I swallowed hard. "But forgive me, did everyone need to die, even the children?"

"That is a matter for the crown, don't you worry about it. I have brought the Shadow Hunter back to your city. I have a special mission for you. I want you and this Shadow Hunter to venture out, in due time and make sure the land in the West is safe still. I have heard rumors of raining fire, and the undead coming back to life. I want you to find out what is causing this."

"What makes you think the Shadow Hunter will work with us?"

"I am pretty sure once you meet him you will understand. Consider this an apology for my stupid younger self. I never knew how much we men depended on your kind. This will be a gift to you, in the end, you will see. For all the hard work you do for me. I am a gracious king after all." I stood and bowed to the King.

"Before you go one more thing. I need you to train the new knights, they are waiting for you at the archery field."

"Yes, Your Majesty."

I left the hall and made my way to the archery field. I walked slowly thinking about how this could be my chance, my real chance to show I can be just as strong as my father. Sure we both made our mistakes, but I can do this. I would travel West, find my father, and bring him home for Sylas. I know how much he misses him. I will find him and the other elves; I will bring them back to the land that I was promised. This is my one chance, and I will not fail.

****

I paced back and forth watching as the archers readied their arrows. They stood with bows drawn back as I walked behind them watching their stances and seeing if their arrows remained level.

"On my command," I shouted and stopped behind one

of the knights. "Bring your elbow up and breathe. If you hold that breath on the battlefield waiting for my order, you will be dead." I walked to the end of the line. "LOOSE," I called out and watched the arrows fly. I made my way to the targets, and they all hit the center. "Great job everyone, that will be all for the day."

I walked away from the archer's range and found myself back at the tavern.

"I decided to take you up on that little offer, Sam." Sam smiled at me and led me into the bedroom he had upstairs. He lit some candles and kissed my neck. "You know the rules about kissing," I said, pushing him down onto the bed. I undid my pants and removed his.

It was just sex I felt nothing for him, and I hoped he felt and knew the same. It was nothing more than a way to release stress. He bent over the bed, waiting for me.

"I'm leaving." I pulled my pants back up and left the room. It did not feel right this time like it was just a waste of time. I left the tavern and returned to the stables. I walked down the long halls and saw a new horse inside there. I opened the gates and stepped in. I held out my hand and she leaned up against it. She had beautiful brown eyes. I saw scars over her neck that were healed by magic. A magic so strong it had to be someone from a fae background. I sat in the stable hiding from the usual evening affairs, with the ivory horse. I was horny as well, so why was I not ready to bed Sam. My heart wanted more. It wanted love, it wanted what it once had. But nothing would ever come close to that. A simple one-night stand would not fill that void, no matter how bad I wanted it to be. I leaned up against the wooden stall, the horse lay next to me, and I fell asleep petting her.

****

"Dad, I don't want to leave. I like it here!" I begged my father to leave me behind. "I don't want to betray them."

"You don't have a choice; we're going to your mother and the King has her, the knights will be here any day and we must go."

"Aerin is here. I can't just leave him behind, he will die," I cried out.

"Then he will die with his family." My father picked me up and carried me out of the house. He used his magic and held my mouth shut so I could not shout for Aerin. My heart still carries the pain of that day. I fear it always will. He shoved me into a carriage and drove off to the palace. He set up the house with a cloaking spell. The King promised him a safe place for his family but found out he killed his wife for mating with an elf. It was a crime against the crown punishable by death at the time.

****

I stretched and reached over to pet the horse, she licked my hand in return. I pulled letters out of my pocket. A stack of them that I wrote to Aerin, but I had nowhere to send them to. I wrote to him every day for years before I just stopped. I tried to put my past behind me. My father betrayed his own kind. My mother would have never wanted that, and now he is out there trying to right the wrong. But after everything he did is there even a single elf left out there?

I got up and left the stables and made my rounds through the merchants. There was nothing out of the ordinary that day. I had nothing left to do but go back to the tavern and see Sam. I walked into the tavern, grabbed Sam, and carried him to the room. I ripped his clothing off, bent him over the bed, and removed my clothing. The tavern emptied out as Sam's moans could be heard from below. I finished with him and dressed. I went back down to the bar and took a seat. I felt empty after, not just physically like last time, but emotionally. Sam, shortly after, joined me at the bar and poured me some ale. I downed the cup.

"Have you heard of the Shadow Hunter?" I questioned Sam.

"I have heard rumors, some say he is a hunter who can kill any man or creature. Others say he is a magic user. I heard the knights that came back from Rivertown were frightened of him. He single-handedly killed 30 of our knights. No one knows his real name either. He tells those he is about to kill but they always die before they can hear it. Some say he has morals though. Something about how he won't hurt children. Others say he is a cold-blooded killer who lurks in the shadows and hunts his prey, even toys with them first. He gets a thrill from the chase," Sam spoke, looking in a spoon to fix his hair. "Why dear, are you worried he is after you? I'm sure my strong Thorne can take him," Sam spoke, trying to pull me into a kiss.

"Enough, I told you it's just sex." I pushed him away.

"Why won't you let me in?" Sam asked, pouring me another drink. "I think you could be happy with me, and I'll help take care of Sylas." I shot him a look that made him stop talking.

"I am not looking for love, the hole in my heart can never be filled. I'm sorry Sam, you are only a hole I use when I see fit."

"Ouch," Sam called back, "Well you can come use me anytime you want. No one treats me like you do." Sam winked at me looking down at my crotch. "What caused this hole in your heart?"

"I did, many years ago, and that is all you're getting out of me."

"Fine, but remember I'm here if you ever need to talk or more," Sam spoke and walked away. I watched as his legs still quivered from our little escapade upstairs. Even if I did not have this hole in my heart I would never be able to love. I have too much responsibility, and being with me would be a death sentence to them. Then there's Sylas. I have to take care of him, he is my first priority right now. The sun was starting to set, and I knew if I was going to make dinner I would need to start heading home.

"Sam, I'm heading out," I called out to him, I knew he

was passed out on the bench back there, he always had to sleep after we were done. He couldn't handle the elven side of me.

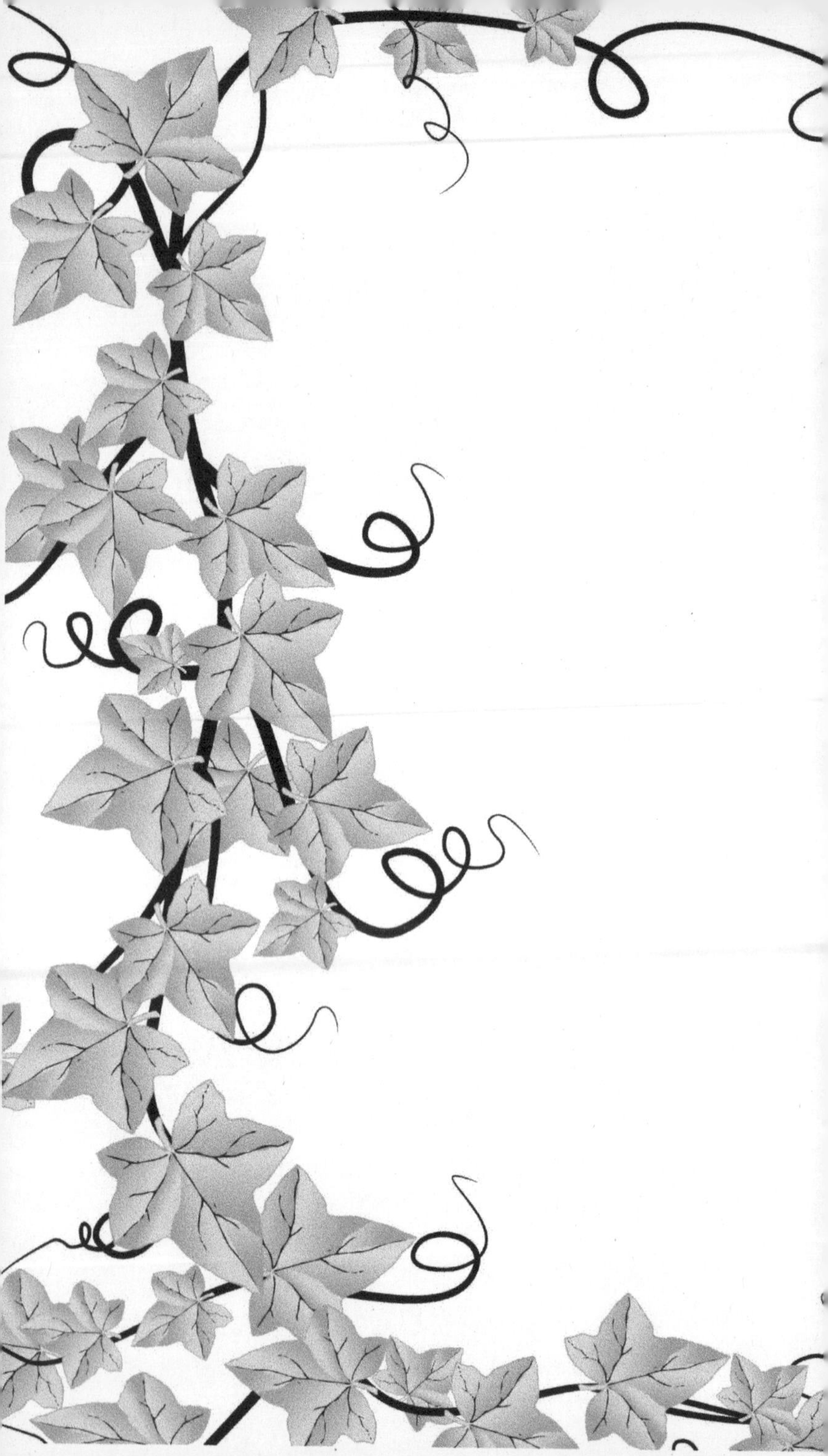

CHAPTER 5:

Thorne

I left the tavern and walked down the road to the local bakery. I went inside and looked around. I wanted to find a nice dessert for Sylas. He always had a sweet tooth. In the window was a tart apple pie next to a chocolate cake. I went inside the store and was greeted by a little old lady. Her clothing was well-worn and covered in flour.

"If it isn't my favorite customer. What can we get for little Sylas today?" I smiled at her.

"I will take the chocolate cake today, June." She

smiled and nodded. She boxed it up and handed it to me.

"Give Sylas a big hug from me," she spoke sweetly. Her old voice had so much wisdom behind it. I smiled at her.

"How much do I owe you?"

"It's for Sylas. No charge today, dear Thorne. You two are so good to me"

"Thank you, he will love this. Can I ask you something?"

"Of course you can," she answered quickly.

"Have you heard of the Shadow Hunter?" Her eyes went wide for a moment before returning to normal. She nodded carefully.

"I haven't heard that name in a long time. When I was a little girl I was about to be attacked by some bandits. I was so scared, but then I watched in the blink of an eye as they all fell to the floor with arrows in them. It looked almost like he danced around in the shadows as he killed them. People say the Shadow Hunter is a bad person, but I think deep down he has a heart of gold. I think there is more to him than we know, Thorne. I hope you get to meet him one day," she spoke softly, remembering the time he saved her. "You know I did catch a glimpse of his eyes. They were green as emeralds. They pierced the night, and have stuck with me to this day." She sighed, "I hope that helps a little, Thorne." I smiled and nodded.

"It certainly helps thank you. Sylas will love the cake

I'm sure." I smiled and left her shop. I started making my way through the city towards our little house. I couldn't wait to get home. Sylas was making our favorite stew that Dad taught him before he left. It was one of the most precious things that reminded me of the simpler days. I continued along my way down Merchant Valley. It was dark out, the only light left was the fires set up around town. I looked up at the stars and found myself daydreaming.

****

"Look there Aerin, it's the Big Dipper," I spoke softly, inching closer to him.

"Where? I don't see anything but stars," he replied. I pointed up and told him to follow my arm. His eyes lit up as he looked. "I can see it, Thorne." He rolled over to look at me and I met his gaze. He draped his arm over me and smiled. "I want to be like this forever. Promise me we will be?" He asked me, smiling his eyes had a glimmer about them.

"I promise, I will always be with you," I spoke back to him. He leaned in and kissed me for the first time. My heart felt like it was going to jump from my chest. It was the happiest I had been in nighty eight years. We sat up and his long sun kissed hair blew gently behind him. This was one of my favorite memories with him. I could stay in this moment forever and never think twice about it. He pulled

out some Lamas bread from his bag and held it for me to take a bite. I laid my head on his lap and looked up at him. The stars made his eyes shine more than normal. There was nothing I wanted more than to go back there. Things are so different now.

"Thorne, one day I will be the leader of the Wood Elves, and I want you to help me along the way," I remembered the fear he had of being the leader, the one who everyone would lookup to for answers.He might have been a great fighter but always had a hard time with words.

"There is nothing I would love more," I spoke back to him meaning every word of it. At the time all I wanted was to be with him, through thick and thin, but that was so long ago.

****

I had to shake my head out of the clouds. That was ages ago, and I knew there was never going back to it. Right now all I need to do is finish this mission and come back home to Sylas. There was so much I still wanted to teach him of the elvish ways. Sure, his magic was already way past anything I could do, but I wanted to keep our traditions alive. He was like our father, a gifted magic wielder and healer, I was the soldier of the group. Together we were a formidable force. I guess that's why the King let us live amongst him, as long as we remained his servants.

I continued along my way home when I came across the butcher shop. I rarely looked inside as I was never going to eat any kind of meat, but I peeked inside this time. I am not sure if it was my curiosity, or just not wanting to go home to meet this Shadow Hunter. Looking in through the window I saw Sylas. I knocked on the window and he turned around. I waved to him, and he quickly ran out holding the sack of meat.

"Are you done with your jobs today?" He asked me, smiling awaiting my answer.

"I am. Is dinner almost ready?" I asked him kneeling down to give him a hug. He jumped into my arms smiling.

"It is, the Shadow Hunter is finishing the food as we speak." I felt a knot in my stomach. There was so much in the house that screamed elves. Sure, we had Dad's charm over the house, but if anyone got too close they would see through it. My face scrunched a bit as I stood up, and took Sylas's hand. We had to keep up the appearance that he was a young 13-year-old boy. We walked back to the house at a slow pace.

"What do you think of this Shadow Hunter?" I asked my younger brother who was humming as we walked.

"I think he is very nice. Offered to help me cook, although he's not that good at it." Sylas laughed, remembering the cuts Aerin had on his hands. "But I still enjoyed the help and it made things go a lot faster so it's good you are off early today."

"Were there any issues that I should know about?"

"Other than me forgetting to get the meat, no. Why, what's wrong?" Sylas stopped moving and asked.

I turned to face him and knelt down. "This person is a killer, Sylas, we have to be on our guard. People like them usually come from a troubled past. They kill for money, sure, but they are twisted, and enjoy the hunt and kill. They savor those moments."

"I don't think he is like that, Thorne. I think he's just misunderstood. You worry too much, you will see when we get home. He is nothing like the King warned me of. It will definitely be a surprise."

I smiled at my younger brother. He was usually a good judge of character, but I have seen the damage this one person is capable of–I have seen the list of names associated with his killings. I wanted to get home fast before the Shadow Hunter learned too much about us. I put my hand on Sylas's back and pushed him towards the house. We were just about home when a knight stopped me.

"Thorne, orders from the King." He handed me a rolled-up parchment and took off. I opened the parchment by one of the fires and took a seat to read it. Sylas joined next to me humming a song Dad used to sing to us.

Thorne,

You are to take the Shadow Hunter out of Lanercost and start your mission as soon as two days' time. You are expected to travel West with him and search the lands. Find any fae creatures you can and bring them back here. Be careful–I have heard of numerous beasts and dark fae out there. Take care not to travel to the far West and end up in Haran. The ruler there will have you both killed. The Shadow Hunter is not welcome in that land, and he still follows my old order of killing any fae that comes close. If you need, I have made connections throughout the land and they will have beds for you. You can entrust Sylas to my care, for the time being.

Entrust Sylas to his care, that would never happen. I put the parchment back in the rolled container and stood up. I looked at Sylas. "Ready to head home? He nodded and I helped him up. I uselessly tried to hide what I was feeling after reading the letter.

"What's wrong, Thorne?" He asked me. Sylas had the gift of an empath and knew something was troubling me.

"The King is sending me and the Shadow Hunter on a mission, I am not sure how long we will be gone for." I watched as his smile faded from existence.

"Like Dad?" He asked, worried that I would not return. I nodded, knowing well that it was just like my father's mission. A mission that would have no end. "What about me?" Sylas asked. I did not answer right away. I thought about the letter, and how the King wants him to remain here, but for what reason? Was it his way of making sure I would return? Did he really think that I would betray him after all he has done for Sylas and me?

"The King wants you to stay here with him." I watched

as Sylas's eyes started to gloss over. He knew that there was a good chance he would lose the rest of the family he had. "But I can't trust you to stay out of trouble so you are coming with us. You will need to follow my every order, and do exactly as I say though." Sylas smiled and saluted me.

"Aye, Captain." He skipped back to the house ahead of me, happy to be going off on his first adventure. I continued to read the letter from the King.

After three months, if you find nothing, return to me as there is a second task I have for you. In my old age, I will need a successor. I will start training you, and you will become my heir. The fae will be able to prolong my life a while longer and I'll be able to make sure you and your family are safe. Thorne, you are the only hope of the kingdom as of right now. Be safe on your travels, and always watch your back. You never know who can trust.

I must have re-read that last part about a hundred times. He wanted me to take over as king when he passed. I didn't think about ever ruling men, it was something that kept me in touch with my elvish side. I wanted everyone to live in peace, yes, but not under my rule. Then again, I could do so much good with that power. I could make sure that Sylas has a good life, and is happy for centuries to come. I could unite everyone again. I was snapped out of my power trip when Sylas kicked me.

"You're getting lost in your head again Thorne. Put a

smile on—we have a guest." I did as he requested and forced myself to smile. My eyes however were still glued to the paper. Sylas opened the door to the house and ran in.

"We are back, how is dinner coming along?" I could hear him talking to the Shadow Hunter. The smell of the stew filled my body with warmth as I entered the house and closed the door.

"Is this the guest you were so happy about?" I looked up and saw a cloaked figure pouring himself a glass of water. He stepped out from behind the kitchen wall and our eyes locked as the glass fell to the floor and shattered.

"Thorne?" I heard him breathe my name. His legs were shaking, and his body froze as if he had seen a ghost. Sylas jumped up and removed his hood. I noticed his long sun-kissed hair, and the green eyes I so desperately longed to see again.

"Aerin," I choked out, holding back my own tears.

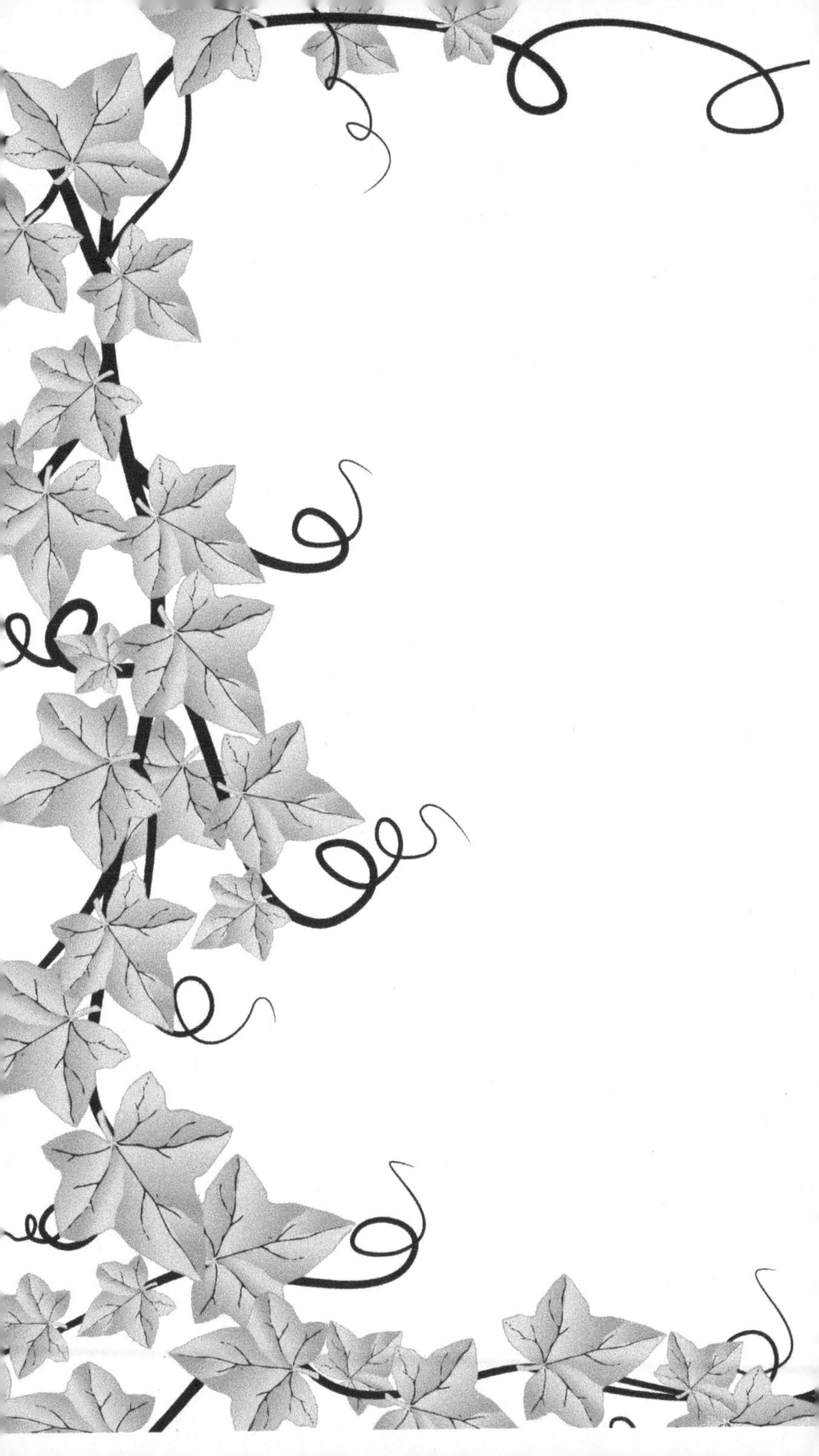

CHAPTER 6:

Thorne

"Aerin," I spoke under my breath. I haven't seen him in so long. He has not aged a bit. I walked closer to him. He did not match my gaze, but I could remember those green eyes anywhere. I thought he died with the rest of the elves during the attack. I spent so many years tearing myself apart for his death. It was like a knife permanently in my chest. I watched as his eyes filled with tears. As I approached, he punched me in the face. I held my cheek and felt the knife be planted right back.

"You left, you never said goodbye. A year later–everything is gone. I had nothing. I thought you were dead," Aerin spoke through his tears. With each word, another knife was speared into my chest.

"I am so sorry. Aerin, my father packed me up and we left in the middle of the night. You know at that age we must do what is asked of us." Aerin punched my chest over and over, I knew that he lost everything in such a short time, in what felt like only days to us. I had to tell him the truth about what happened, he lived so long not knowing. Yet if I told him, would he even look at me the same way?

"You left me alone," Aerin cried out. "You promised me you'd never leave." I hugged him close and he fell to the floor in my arms. I ran my fingers through his hair like I used to.

"I'm so sorry, Aerin." I turned to Sylas, "Can you finish cooking? Aerin and I need to catch up a little, I'm going to show him the town."

Sylas began chopping the meat they picked up and looked at Thorne. "Yeah, I can handle that. Don't be gone too long, I know how you like to stay out late."

"Don't worry, we will be back for dinner." I looked at Aerin hoping he would be too. I stood up and extended my hand to him. He did not take it and pulled his hood back up over his head. We walked out the door and he did not say a word to me. We walked through the city and people parted as we strolled through. There was a mixture of respect and fear for me since I worked so closely with the King. We made our way to the tavern and I opened the door for Aerin.

"Thorne, back so soon?" The man behind the counter called out to me. He was a younger fellow. "Couldn't get enough before? You had to come back for some more?" He called out and I felt my face flush red. I shot him a look with my arm around Aerin. He quickly stopped talking and unlocked the door for me. I escorted Aerin into the room and closed the door behind us. Once the door was shut he turned to me and punched me again.

"You took everything away from me. The hurt is still there, seeing you alive it's even worse again." He punched me again. I let him shout at me, and punch me. Finally, he let out his anger and I held him again.

"Aerin, I am so sorry. I had no idea at the time what my father was planning with the King. He did it to save my mother. I know it's not something you want to hear but it's the truth," I spoke, holding back my tears. He looked at me, his fist still balled up. "There has not been a single day I did not think of you." I pulled down his hood and smiled slightly. His green eyes were still filled to the brim with tears.

"Nothing you say can ever ease this pain I feel. I turned into a killer, I turned into what nightmares are made of. I'm the story parents tell their kids to make sure they don't sneak out at night." I could feel the pain he had felt for centuries, and it was killing me from the inside out.

"I know nothing I say will take away that pain, but if you give me the chance, I will try to ease it," I spoke softly, staring into his eyes. "I want to share that pain with you, Aerin. Can you open back up to me?"

"No. I loved you, nothing has been the same. I've changed, and as bad as I want to let you in again, I can't. What you did, I can't forgive that. Not right now, Thorne." I leaned back against the wall. Hearing him say I loved you, made this all too real. Aerin held his hand against my face and ran his finger over the scar on my eye. I nuzzled slightly into his hand before he pulled it away. "What happened?" He asked, finally looking at me.

"It's a long story." I could not tell him that it was a scar from my own father. He struck me down for trying to run away to him, to find him and get him out once I found out the truth. I reached my hand out and placed it on Aerin's cheek, he closed his eyes and leaned into my hand. "I am so glad you're alive, Aerin." He opened his eyes and hugged me.

"I am glad you are too," he spoke softly through the pain. I reached back and removed the necklace from around my neck that he had given me so many years ago, I placed it into his hands. He looked down and ran his finger over the engraving. He smiled slightly and handed it back to me. "It always did look better on you." He put it back on me and dried his eyes.

"What would the King have me do?" Aerin asked me.

"Can we talk about that tomorrow, for now, I want to just sit with you," I asked him, watching as he paced the floor. I stood up and grabbed his arms, he froze in place. I turned him to face me, still unsure if this was some kind of dream. I knew at that moment I never stopped loving him. His green eyes met with mine, and he started to lean into me. He laid his head on my shoulder. I felt tears fall down his face as they hit my neck.

"I thought for sure this day would never come," he whispered, hoping I would not hear him. I put my arms around him and ran my fingers through his silky hair. I missed this most of all—being close to him, my heart felt complete when we were close. I closed my eyes kissed the top of his head gently, and let my hands continue through his hair.

"We should be heading back, Sylas will have a lot of questions," I suggested, hoping he would join me. "If you don't want to come back I understand. I am not going to hold you prisoner. You can leave whenever." The thought of him leaving broke my spirit. He lifted his head off my shoulder and I wiped away the tears from his cheeks and smiled at him. "It is so good to see you again, Aerin." He shook his head and took a staggered breath in.

"It's a big city, would you escort me back to your house so I don't get lost?" He smiled, looking at me. I put my hand on the doorknob and placed my arm around his waist leading him out the door. As he walked by I could smell the forest, and smiled. It was so long since I had left the city, I almost forgot that smell. I grabbed his hand and pulled him back into the room with me.

"Forgive me, but I have to try." I leaned in and kissed him softly. The spark was still there, I could feel it. I felt Aerin tense up under me and I quickly backed away. I watched as Aerin held his fingers to his lips. "It won't happen again, forgive me." I looked down and he walked over to me. He took my hand and placed it over his heart. I could feel it racing.

"It will take a lot of time, but it hasn't forgotten you." I smiled slightly. "It can't happen again, Thorne, I can't handle the hurt again when you leave." I nodded, I understood what he was saying. We left the room and the tavern. I escorted Aerin back to the house, but before we went inside Aerin stopped me from opening the door. He took off his hood and looked into my eyes. "You really are exactly as I remember. Always a gentleman." He kissed my cheek and let me open the door. He stepped in before me, and I followed shortly behind him.

"Smells amazing, Sylas," Aerin spoke as he entered the house smiling.

"It sure does," I chimed in and set the table for us. I took a seat next to Aerin and Sylas sat on the other side. He dished out heaping's of the stew to us before we started eating.

"It tastes even better than it smells," Aerin spoke,

swallowing the food without eating. I found myself wondering how he survived out there on his own for so long. Sylas finished his food and ran into his room, he wanted to study more magic. It left Aerin and me alone in silence. We finished eating and Aerin washed the plates. He avoided any more eye contact with me. I walked to the fireplace and took a seat in front of it. I held my hands over the unlit wood trying to ignite it. Aerin came over and sat next to me watching.

"You need to hold your hands close to the wood, don't be so afraid of the fire." He put his hands on top of mine. "Close your eyes and picture something that makes you happy. I watched as he closed his eyes. I did not need to close my eyes though, he is all that ever made me happy. The wood quickly caught on fire and I watched as Aerin started to sway back and forth. He started to fall back and I managed to catch him before he fell to the floor.

"Sylas, come out here," I called out to him. He quickly came running in. Sylas looked over at Aerin quickly and looked back at me.

"He lost the grace of the elvish god, Thorne. I read about it before in one of my books. Hang on, I will go get it," Sylas spoke as he darted to his room. I picked up Aerin and carried him to my bed. I laid him down gently and lit the candle next to him.

"Here it is," Sylas spoke, handing me an open book. I read the book carefully.

When one of elvish blood turns his back on his own—the gods forsake them. Using magic of any kind will slowly drain their life energy. Unless they can be brought back to the light, they will live a mortal life.

"It's a punishment for someone who turned their back on their own kind, or whose heart has been blackened," Sylas spoke softly, looking down at Aerin.

"Thank you, Sylas, go back to your room. I will look over Aerin." Sylas nodded and turned for the door.

"He will be okay, right?" Sylas asked, filled with hope. I looked up at him as a tear rolled down my face.

"He has to be." Sylas left and I turned to look at Aerin. "What happened? Why did you give up? Did I cause you this much pain?" I lifted Aerin's head and leaned back against the wall resting it on my lap. "You have to be okay, please?" I found myself begging. I looked up at the ceiling and started to yell. "Take my magic, let me suffer in his place. It is all my fault so stop his suffering." I sat there the rest of the night watching over Aerin as he slept and prayed he would be okay. I spent about 20 minutes removing all the daggers he had on his body so he would not nick himself in his sleep. I couldn't believe the number of blades he had.

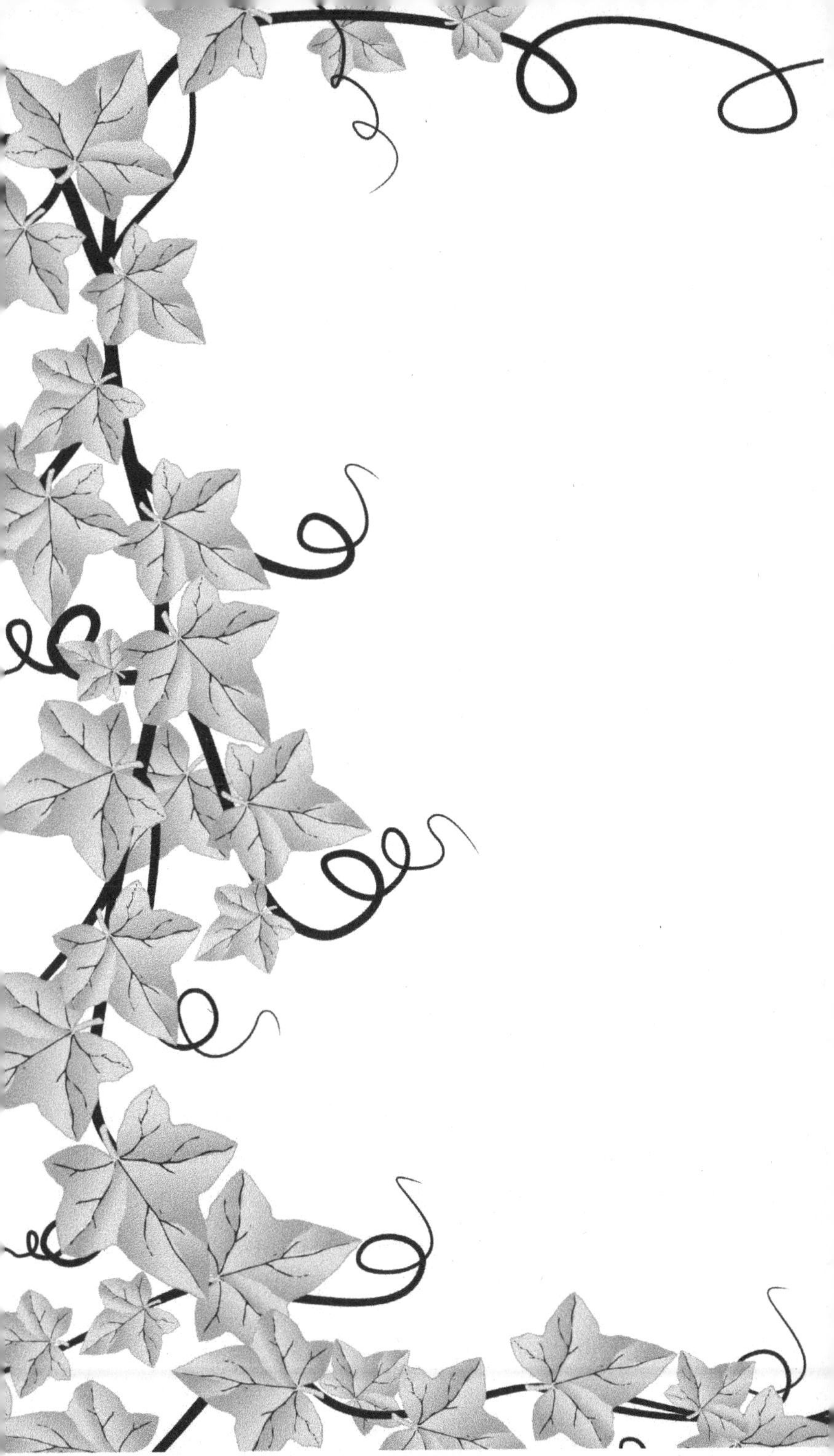

CHAPTER 7:

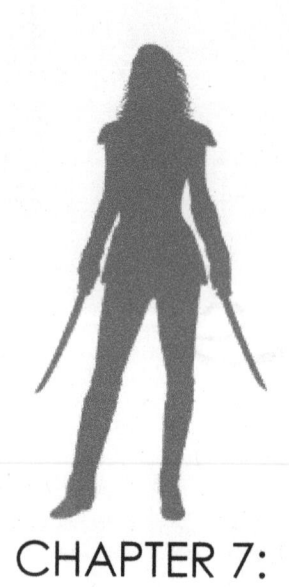

Aerin

The sun was shining through the window, I stretched and opened my eyes. The first thing I saw was Thorne. I felt my heart pound hard as I realized everything from before was not a dream. I was in such a mix of emotions, that I did not know what to do or how to feel. I rolled over to face him and smiled. I noticed I was lying on his lap. It brought back so many memories. The memories I held most dear to me flew through my mind. In some ways, it felt like we just picked up right where we left off, but I knew deep down it was anything but that. I looked up and couldn't help but touch him. I ran my finger over the scar on his eye and felt the pain that it once caused him. I took a deep breath and looked at it. I used my natural gifts and could tell it was a scar from a sword. It was healed by elvish magic, but by a beginner healer and that is why he still had the scar. I could heal it, I could return his face to the perfection it once was.

Then it came back to me, all the hurt and pain. I wanted to punch him again. But honestly, I wanted to be with him again too. I wanted things to go back to how it used to be. Sylas came running into the room and pulled me out of my mind. He walked over to the bed and tapped my back.

"Aerin, I know you're awake." I rolled over and smiled at Sylas. He flagged me to the door. I stood up and laid Thorne down covering him with the blanket he covered me in. I pushed back his hair. I gently caressed his cheek before turning back to Sylas and joining him in the dining room. Sylas was sitting there with a few books open, I took a seat next to him.

"What's all this?" I asked him, examining the books. He smiled, looking up at me.

"I did some research last night, Thorne was very worried about you. He said you passed out after using your magic. I think I found a way for you to keep your magic and your health."

I smiled at him, "Sylas, I've tried everything. I have

come to face the fact that I have to try to avoid using magic, and learn to live like men do," I spoke softly, a little heartbroken.

"I think I found a solution though, something only known to a few people. The faeries have this magical potion that can cure anything, but no one has seen them for a long time." I sat down next to Sylas and smiled, tousling his hair.

"You did all this research for me?" I asked him.

"For you, but mainly for Thorne I can tell he really cares about you." I nodded and looked away from him for a moment. I turned back and looked at the book. "I think I might have something that can help you, but we need to ask Thorne first."

Thorne came out from his room just then and knelt down behind us. "Ask Thorne what?" He questioned.

Sylas turned to him and smiled. "Good morning, did you sleep okay?" He asked softly. Thorne looked over at me and I could not return the gesture.

"I slept better than I have in a long time," he spoke sweetly, hinting that having me back in his life was a blessing. I leaned forward and let my hair cover my face. He was right though, last night was the best sleep I had in centuries. "What did you find out, Sylas?" Thorne broke the silence and looked over the table.

"I found a way that might help Aerin, but it involves a lot of magic and something from Dad's chest." I could hear Thorne's heart quicken, and he swallowed hard before answering.

"Will it work, Sylas?"

"I am not sure if it will work, but it might be his best shot.."

"Is there any risk? To him?" Sylas shook his head.

"Not that has been written down, but you know everything has risks, Thorne." Sylas paused before continuing. "There is just one catch to this."

"And what is that?" I chimed in.

"Once we start this we can't stop no matter what. I am not sure what will happen if we do."

"But as long as we finish the spell Aerin will be able to use his magic? Will it no longer cost him his life?" Sylas nodded.

"I'm sure of it." Thorne looked down at me and smiled.

"What will it cost us, Sylas?"

Sylas swallowed hard and took a deep breath. "The potion dad has been saving. The one the King gave him that the faeries made." Thorne put his hand on my shoulder before walking away. I guess that was a no. He did not say a word, just walked away. I stood up and patted Sylas on the back.

"Thanks for trying." I headed back to the room I woke in and grabbed my daggers. I walked back to the room to find Sylas and Thorne sitting at the table with a big chest on it.

"I couldn't get it open. I think Dad changed the enchantment on it." Thorne told Sylas.

"Let me try." Sylas held out his hand, a pale blue light shone from it, but the chest did not open.

"Together?" Thorne asked and Sylas nodded. They both held their hands out to the chest, a blue light from both shone onto the chest and I could hear clicking from within it. It still did not open though when they tried to pull the lid off. I walked out of the room and headed for the door. I opened it and Thorne quickly slammed it shut.

"Where are you going?" He asked me. I turned to him and looked into his eyes.

"I'm not going to let you risk your lives to save mine, Thorne." Sylas picked up the chest and threw it against the wall and it shattered. A small vial was on the ground within the rubble.

"You never had to. If there is a small chance this can save you, we are doing it," Thorne's voice was deep but he only spoke to me. He used his gift of telepathy to communicate with me. I felt myself smiling as I walked back to the table. Sylas grabbed the vial and pointed to Thorne's room.

"It will take some time, it might be better if you lay down," Sylas suggested, walking to Thorne's room and holding the door open. I nodded and Thorne guided me in. I laid down on his bed and closed my eyes. Sylas put the vial into my hand and I drank the potion. I felt my body start to warm as my mind began to fog. I closed my eyes and tried to calm my nervousness...

"Aerin, are you okay?" Sylas asked but I couldn't hear him.

"Aerin?" Thorne called out to me. His voice echoed in my mind. I smiled a bit, he always got through to me no matter what was going on. I opened my eyes and saw him looking down at me, his hand on my forehead. "Sylas, he's burning up," Thorne told him with worry in his voice.

"We need to start before it's too late," Sylas spoke softly. My vision was starting to blur as I watched Thorne crawl over me. Sylas laid the book on my chest so they both could read it. I turned my head to look at Thorne who met my gaze. I shot him a smile to ease his worry. "You can't worry, not right now, you need to focus." Sylas reminded him of the task at hand. They both looked down at the book. I watched as their eyes changed to deeper shades, and they looked up.

"Sar call teague Tel' gods Ath old. Forgive Tel' ent uannamends. Renew Tel' Faer Ath Tel' Tel' yrrinnam. Restore Tel mil siilen." A ray of purple light shone from each of their chests and down onto me. I looked past Thorne, the window behind him that was once sunny was starting to darken. I startedto squirm a bit on the bed as I could feel my blood starting to heat. Thorne noticed and I could see the pain on his face but he continued with Sylas. "Sar call Quor'She Kyed Al fhaorsaloh-il -iel-ila -lie from

Shee lor nae lar lirrIvae Arta sarenq uessesti Tan. Restore fiaen sienenbe rynfin esslithent faeny athy Arael." The light shining from them changed to red, and I started to scream. The pain was unbearable, I was unable to hide the tears rolling down my face.

"STOP!" I yelled out to them, but they ignored my cries and continued the chant. Thunder started booming from outside, and I could hear lightning crackle as it struck down trees.

"Sar beg va var Quor'She Kyed answer, let Tel' thy Ivae Alet eshaalTel' nevae, ent return Tel' grace siilenva var." The light from their chests went out and a new light beamed through the ceiling, shining down on me. I felt myself lift off the bed and looked around. I was 10 feet off the floor, and felt light as air. I heard screams coming from outside.

"HELP." Thorne and Sylas were in a trance and did not hear the cries. I looked out the window and saw zombies walking around, and dark faeries flying through the town. They were heading towards us. The use of magic this strong was a target for dark fae since the elvish kind were eliminated.

"Quor'She Kyed hin saren cries ent resoshiAl fhaorsaloh-il -iel-ila -lie aulorsiunArael."

I felt myself losing consciousness as a small orb appeared through the light and flew into my chest. As it entered, I passed out. I could still hear everything around me but had no strength to move. I fell hard back onto the bed, and both Thorne and Sylas looked down at me.

"Is he okay? Did it work?" Thorne asked Sylas who shrugged. He held his hands over my chest and felt my heart beating.

"He is alive."

"HELP US." The cries from outside got louder. Thorne turned around to see everyone running and those who were unable to outrun them, falling to their deaths. A purple fog formed over the city, and it became hard to see through it. Thorne went to crawl back over me, I grabbed his arm.

"Don't." It was the only word I was able to get out. My hand was weak and fell from holding him. Thorne looked at Sylas and smirked.

"Protect him." Thorne grabbed his sword from the wall and ran out into the fog. It wasn't long before we could no longer see him. Sylas stood next to the bed holding a fireball in hand. He reminded me of myself, the same magic of choice. A zombie broke in through the door, and Sylas burnt him to a crisp. Using his magic only makes it worse. The fog rolled closer to the house, and all the cries outside died down. We could still hear the sword clashes from the window and I could hear Thorne grunting for a moment before that noise was gone as well.

Sylas turned and shook me. "Aerin, please wake up." Three zombies came in through the sidewall and surprised

Sylas. The fire quickly vanished from his hand. His fear was blocking the fire. A dark faery flew in through the window and Sylas let out a scream.

"AERIN!" My eyes shot open. I felt a power taking control of me. My hair stood on end, and the tips were on fire. I looked at the zombies and they ignited, turning to ash. I grabbed a dagger from my back and threw it at the faery. It soared through her neck.

"Where is Thorne?" I asked Sylas, who was in shock after seeing the zombies self-destruct. He pointed outside but was frozen in place.

"Hide under the bed, okay?" Sylas nodded but did not move. I pushed him over and under the bed, tossing the blanket from the bed in front of him before running outside.

"Thorne!" I called out. There was no answer, I could barely see 10 feet in front of me. I took a breath and ran faster, I had my elven speed back. I darted around the house looking for him. As I ran I used my daggers, throwing them into each zombie I came across taking their heads clean off their shoulders. "Thorne!" I called out again. But there was still no answer. My anger was starting to get the best of me. I should have noticed that this much magic usage would attract dark fae. If I lost Thorne this risk was not worth it.

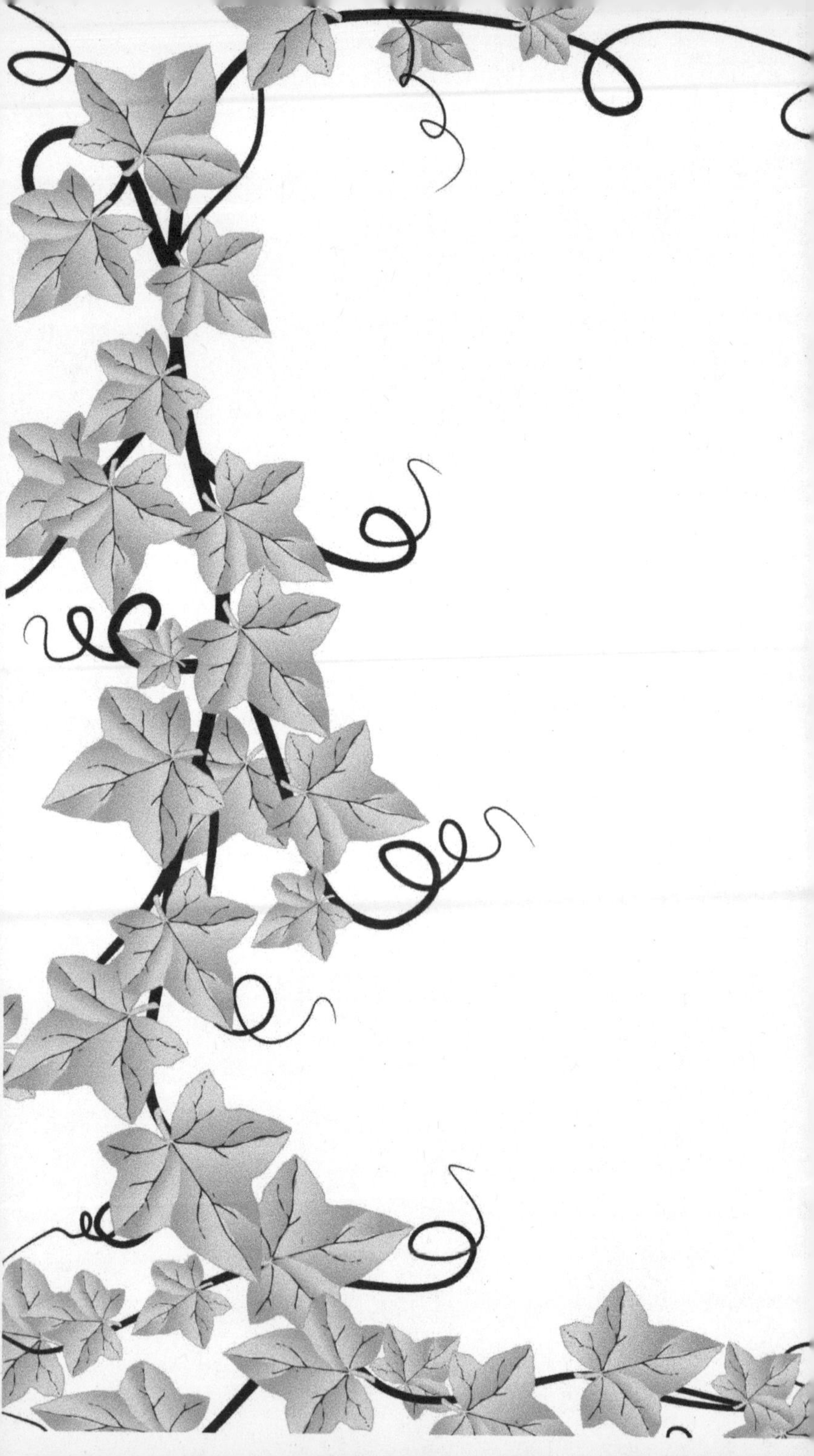

CHAPTER 8:

Thorne

The purple fog was making it hard to breathe, I could feel my breath fading as I was starting to suffocate. My sword was stained black from the blood from zombies, and faeries I killed. My arms were losing their strength, I wasn't sure how much longer I would be able to keep this up. I looked back to where the house would be and hoped that Sylas was okay. I found myself circled by zombies, as they were closing in I could see there were hundreds of them. It looked like a small army starting to form around me. I could feel my heart quickening. Where were the King's men? Why have they not started to fight? I felt anger brewing inside me, and I tried to focus it on the blade of my sword. My father taught me a spell to set my blade on fire, but I couldn't remember the words. Instead, I looked up to the sky and closed my eyes. Lighting started to clash around me, striking a few zombies here and there.

I was no good with magic, that was Sylas's field, I was the brawn of the family. I charged forward with the strength I had left slicing into the enemy. The sound of flesh hitting the ground was the only thing I heard. I let out a blood-curdling scream as one of the dark faeries tore into my back, another dug their dagger into my arm causing me to drop my sword momentarily. Each slash felt like a paper cut from their small daggers. Hundreds of them at one time were the worst pain I have ever felt. I bit my lip and stood back up grabbing my sword. I spun around to kill them but I was too slow from the pain. I might have missed them but it bought some room between us.

I turned back to the house swinging my sword to keep creating the space. I turned my head around and saw them closing in on me again. I took a breath and muttered to myself, the ground started to shake around me and the zombies fell. The faeries, however, continued to close the gap. I turned back around and focused on where I was running. As I got closer to the house I turned to the army to stand my ground. My back was against the house, and I quickly looked into the window searching for Sylas. The room was empty, and my mind started to race. Did they get Sylas, is he even alive? As the army got closer I started swinging my sword blindly due to the fog in my face. I took a deep breath and lowered it ready to accept my fate. There was no way I could fight them all. I closed my eyes as they were an arm's length away, but opened them shortly after when I was not attacked.

As I opened my eyes I was blinded by a red light that shone through the fog. I could hear elvish chants that echoed through the city. The fog started to vanish and I saw Aerin walking towards me, throwing daggers at the zombies. The numbers dwindled as he inched closer to me. I picked up my sword and charged the army from the back. We cleared a path to each other and stood back to back. I felt him take off his bow and start firing it, as I swung my sword.

"Turn," I called to him, and we both rotated, taking out the enemies on the side. Aerin held his hand out to me and I took it spinning him around me. He let loose arrows as he whirled around. He landed, and we waited to see their next move. The purple fog vanished, and the zombies and faeries vanished along with it. I leaned over catching my breath, as the sun started to shine again. I turned to Aerin, who collapsed in my arms. The tips of his hair were still on fire but did not burn my arms as it draped over them. I picked him up and carried him back to the house. I opened the door and dodged a fireball that Sylas threw at me from under the bed.

"It's me, Sy." I walked over to the bed and laid Aerin down. Sylas climbed out and stood next to me. He looked over at Aerin and held his hands over him, checking him for wounds but found none.

"Thorne has his magic back, but it will take time for him to get used to it again. Also, it seems like part of the god's personal magic has entered him. The way he was able to merely look at the zombies and make them self-combust sounded like Rillifane had shown him a favor. The god of the wood elves has blessed him with returning his magic and giving some of his own. It will take a good amount of time for him to get used to that much power. Did he use any magic out there with you?" I nodded and looked down at Aerin.

"Is he going to be okay?" I asked, worried that I might lose him.

"He is going to be okay, he just needs to rest. It is hard to use that much magic, after not using any for so long. What did he do out there?"

"I'm not sure, it was magic I have never seen. A bright red aura shone off him, it looked like it weakened the dark fae, and made the purple haze vanish," I spoke, closing my eyes, remembering the light that brought me out of the darkness.

"That is the power of Rillifane, my book talks about

his power showing itself in the strongest of elves when someone they care about is in danger," Sylas spoke while reading from the book. "How do you know Aerin?" Sylas asked me. I wasn't sure how to answer him. He did not know about the elven village, or what father had done. I didn't want to break his heart by revealing our family's secret.

"We grew up together, a long time ago. We were…" I looked over at Aerin. "We were lovers, he was the only person I really ever opened up to." I sat next to Aerin in bed and looked down over him. "I guess that is all in the past now." I smiled at Sylas and stood back up to walk to the kitchen. I prepared some eggs from Sylas and Aerin before peeking my head into the room. "Sylas, breakfast is on the table, I am going out for a bit," I called to him. I watched as he ran out and grabbed his food. Aerin started to stir and sat up in bed.

"How are you feeling?" I asked him as I took a seat next to him.

"Just tired, I think it worked," Aerin spoke to me as he made a fireball in his hand testing his magic. He clenched his fist and it quickly snuffed out. He stood up and fell back onto the bed. His legs were not ready to hold his weight. I caught him and smiled.

"It really is just like old times," I spoke softly. He pushed off me and stood up holding onto the wall.

"It will never be like old times," Aerin reminded me,

as he pushed off the wall and walked out of the room. I felt my smile fade but followed after him. I walked to the door and turned to Sylas.

"I am going out to see the damage to the city. Do you want to come?" I asked Sylas, but Aerin walked over to me pulling up his hood.

"You might need more protection, so I will come with you," he spoke to me, teasing me that he had to rescue me just like he used to save me from my father. I nodded agreeing to let him tag along.

"Sylas, how about you?"

"I think you two need more time to talk before we get on the road, I will stay here and pack up stuff we need for our trip," Sylas answered, walking to the backroom and grabbing our rucksacks. I held the door open for Aerin, and he walked out. His hair brushed against my face as he walked away, and I found myself smiling. I led Aerin down the merchant path and noticed everything was rubble. There were a few people trying to set up their stands for the day, but it broke my heart to see the remains. I looked over at Aerin who seemed completely unfazed by it. I guess after everything he has been through, this was just another day for him. An older man was cleaning the soot from his table before placing his fruits on it. Aerin stopped and looked at the fruits, picking up a handful of apples.

"These look amazing, sir, I have not seen apples like this in a very long time." The old man smiled at the compliment as Aerin put them in his bag. "How much do I owe you?"

"10 silver," The man spoke. Aerin reached into his bag and handed him 50 gold. Nearly five times the price of the apples. "Sir, this is way too much. I could never accept this." Aerin just smiled at the old man.

"Take it, fix your stand, and feed your family well tonight," Aerin told the old man. He helped him set up his stall and I watched smiling. He was just as sweet as he always was. His heart did not darken like Sylas and I thought. I heard a cracking and saw the oak tree next to Aerin starting to fall.

"Aerin, look out," I called out, he looked up and saw the tree starting to come down. He picked the old man up and moved him just as the tree fell. It would have crushed them both. Aerin put the old man down, and he bent over trying to catch his breath. They moved faster than humanly possible, Aerin tapping into his magic again. I joined them and finished helping the old man set his stall up. He gave me an apple in return and we went on our way.

"Thorne," a deep voice called from behind me. "The King wants to see you," he spoke to me. I nodded and looked at Aerin.

"I shouldn't be long."

"That is fine, but I'm coming along," Aerin demanded. I knew it was not a good idea to let him in the same room as the King, but I couldn't tell him no. I never could and he knew that. I closed my eyes and took a deep breath grounding myself.

"Fine, but no violence." I retorted.

"Would I ever do something like that?" Aerin spoke sarcastically, twirling his hair around his finger. I shook my head and rubbed the back of my neck.

****

We were escorted into the throne room and waited for the King to show up. The doors behind the throne opened, and I quickly knelt on the hard floor. I tugged at Aerin's arm. He looked over at me and huffed before doing the same.

"Thank you," I whispered to him. He shot me a look that screamed at how disgusted he was. The King took his seat, but I remained knelt down in front of him.

"I see you brought the Shadow Hunter with you," the King called down to us.

"Yes, Your Majesty," I replied.

"Do you know what caused the dark fae to attack us this morning? My men say they saw some kind of light shining through your house." I swallowed hard, thinking about my next answer. Before I could speak, I saw Aerin stand up and remove his hood.

"They were after me, one of the elves you happened to miss." His voice echoed through the room, booming as he spoke more, " And now you will answer the questions I have." The King's men barged into the throne room and ran at Aerin.

"Wait, I called out." The men stood waiting for the King's order. Bows were drawn and pointed at Aerin. The King stood up and looked down at him.

"You look so much like your mother," the King spoke softly. I knew it was not a good idea to bring up his parents or the incident."You must forgive me, I was young and stupid," the King spoke softly.I looked at Aerin as his hair started to ignite.

"Aerin, please." I stood up and pulled him into me hugging him close so no one would fire at him. They would not dare to hit me.

"Why should I show him mercy, he showed us none, and you would defend him."

"The king is a changed man, Aerin. Please hear him out." Aerin looked at me and pushed me away.

"You burnt my home to the ground. Your men slaughtered children. They call me the Shadow Hunter, a monster, when in fact it is you that is a monster. You sit in this room while your people suffer, you sip your elvish wine while they eat gruel. You slaughter families for fun."

The King sat back down, he knew Aerin was right. "That was a long time ago, Shadow Hunter. I have spent the last 500 years trying to right that wrong. My city has since felt the pain of losing the elves. I was afraid of the power you possessed, but now I see it was that power that kept everything in line. It helped the earth produce food, it kept the dark fae away. I owe your kind everything," The King spoke with tearful eyes. Aerin's hair returned to normal, and I stood up. I walked over to him, his eyes glued to the king's. "I am dying, Shadow Hunter, and before I go I want to return my kingdom to the peace it used to be in. That is why I have sent it for you, I want you to go out West with Thorne. I want you to find the elves and bring them back to their homeland. I want to welcome back the old ways."

"If you mean that, then I accept your mission." The King stood up and bowed to Aerin.

"I know your bloodline, and I welcome you among the king's table. You will make a great king one day, Aerin son of Elwin."

An arrow was released from one of the bows and I caught it in front of Aerin's face, inches from his nose. The King turned to where the arrow came from and snapped. His men raced towards the archer, but not before I let my anger take over. I turned the arrow and threw it into the man's neck. He dropped his bow and fell to his knees, his hands around the arrow, and I watched as the blood fell down his body.

"There is something you should both know," the King spoke sitting back down. "Morgana, the Queen of the dark fae, made a settlement in the shadows of Amhe Lenora. The light around the area has been tainted and the air is thick. You should avoid it at all costs. We need more elves before we can stand a chance of taking her down."

"Amhe Lenora, that used to be the capital of the elves,"

I spoke quickly, not realizing that Aerin was about to explode. Hearing his sister's name made his blood boil more than the King could imagine. No one but myself knew the truth about her. I took his hand and he started to calm down. He turned to me and took a breath.

"I will kill her myself. She dares to taint the elvish capital, it will be the last time she spits on our kind, Thorne."

"In time, Aerin. Everything will work itself out. Trust me."

"I wanted to bestow you both with a gift for this adventure." The King snapped his fingers and the doors opened from behind his throne. A young boy walked out holding items wrapped in cloth. As I uncovered my gift, a double-edged sword was revealed. The blade was solid gold and inscribed in elvish. It read: The one who wields this sword will forever be blessed by the purest waters. I smiled as I watched the blade become charged with water and lightning. I turned to Aerin who was looking down at the boy. He hesitantly took the clothed item from the young boy. Aerin unwrapped his gift, which was an elvish bow with a spiked curve and blades on both ends. Aerin pulled the bow string back mocking a shot. The bow was elvish and looked like it was lighter than a normal bow. There was a spike on the front of the bow as well.

"Thorne, I give to you the sword Sannoris. It has been blessed by one of your gods to protect its wielder at any cost. Be careful, for I have seen with my own eyes the amount of damage it can do." I nodded and bowed to the king. "For you Aerin, King of the forgotten realm, I have given you the bow your father used in the first war against the dark fae. It is said to be the lightest bow ever created. Arrows fired from this bow are able to pierce the strongest armor. I am not sure how your father did it, but if you can figure out the secrets behind that bow, it can create vines that hold enemies in place or pull them into the bow to be impaled. Your father was an astounding soldier." Aerin smiled, holding the bow that once belonged to his father. We turned from the King and went to leave. The King called down to me, "As for young Sylas?"

"It is my decision that Sylas is to come with us," I spoke, afraid it might anger him.

"In that case take this for him." The King walked down and stood in front of us. He handed me a small necklace. "He will know what to do with it." The King took both of our hands.

"The kingdom of Amenlean and I depend on both of you," the King spoke wholeheartedly and walked back to this throne. I took Aerin's arm and pulled him out of the palace. I could tell he did not fully believe the King, and still wanted his revenge.

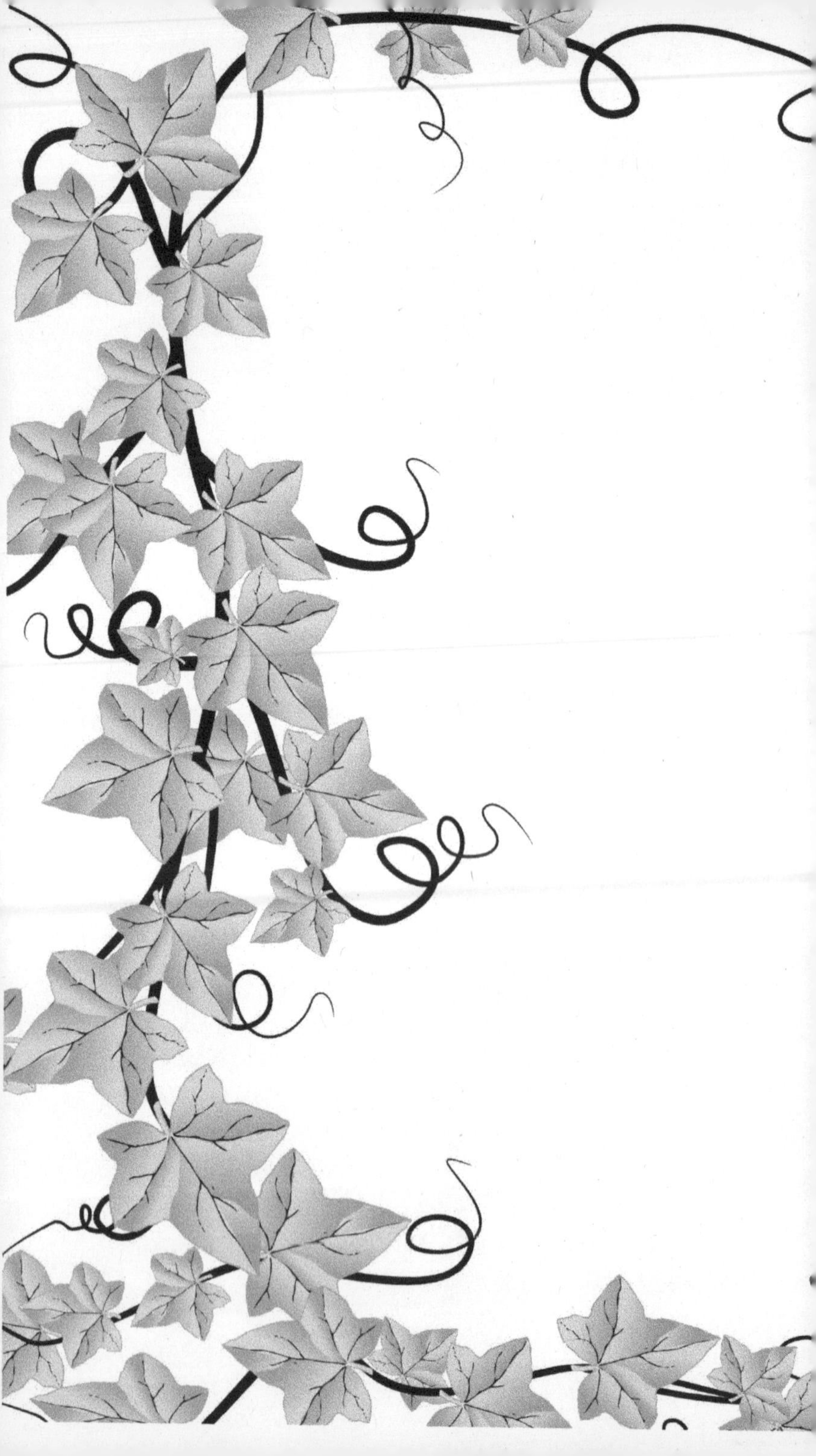

CHAPTER 9:

Aerin

The walk back to Thorne's house was quiet. I was lost in waves of emotions. Could we really trust the King? It seemed too easy for him to change that much. I did not trust him as far as I could throw him and with my new power, that was pretty far. I looked at Thorne, I still trusted him even after everything. I knew I could trust him, but I had to keep my guard up too. I took the bow off my back and admired the woodwork. The engravings of vines made the bow feel unique. My father engraved them, I could feel his magic coursing through the bow. I turned to Thorne and smiled looking at him. Catching a glimpse of him still sent chills down my spine. He was right; it was almost like things never changed.

Thorne held the door open for me, and I walked in to see Sylas sitting by the fireplace. He had two bags packed with bedrolls and cooking supplies hanging from them. I walked over to Sylas and took his bag.

"I hear you are coming along with us?" I asked him. He nodded and took my hand getting up. He put out the fire and walked me to the door after handing Thorne his bag. We walked to the stables where Thorne placed a saddle on a brown horse. He gestured to the horse in the next stall for me to start getting ready. I walked outside the stall and took a deep breath. I whistled and it echoed through the city. Sylas came running out and looked around. Alatar came running to me, her wounds were completely cured. I smiled looking at her and gave her a good pet. I jumped onto her back and rode her over to Thorne's stall. He turned and walked over to Alatar and me. He held his hand out reaching for her and she nuzzled into his hand.

"She remembers you," I spoke softly. I watched as Thorne smiled and looked into her eyes.

"It's been a long time," he said, petting her.

"It's been too long, Thorne. Did you ever even look for me, or go back to the village?" Thorne looked down at

Sylas and back at me.

"Can we talk about this later please?" I looked at Sylas and nodded. Thorne strapped the wagon onto his horse and waited for Sylas to get in. He looked at me with pleading eyes. I smiled and extended my hand. He took it and I pulled him up onto Alatar. He sat in front of me, my arms were around him so he would not fall off. Sylas laughed as Alatar stood on her hind legs. Alatar was more of a showboat than I was, and could tell it would be easy to impress him. Thorne however was not impressed by her.

"Be careful with him, and don't run full speed either." As he was speaking, I smirked and Alatar took off. Sylas was holding on to the reins and laughing. He was having the time of his life. We made it a good distance through the city before we stopped at the gates. I hopped off Alatar and picked Sylas off her. I patted her back end and she took off down the road. Thorne caught up with us after a bit, and we hopped in the back of the wagon. I peeked my head through the canopy to Thorne. I looked at him as he was looking at a map of the kingdom.

"Where are we going first?" Thorne pointed at the map at a small beach. "We can see if the water elves are still around." Thorne had hope that I lost a long time ago.

"Don't get your hopes up, Thorne. I have searched everywhere for our kind. I have not found anyone." I felt myself falling back into the darkness. I pulled myself back into the wagon and sat with Sylas. I handed him the necklace the King gave us. "This is from the King, he said you would know what to do with it." Sylas took it from me and looked down at it. It changed from a small pendant to a shield in his hand. His eyes lit up. The shield sent a pink aura from it and it surrounded the wagon. "What is it?" I asked him.

"A barrier. It should protect us from any non-magic attacks. From a distance, it will keep us invisible as well. If they get close though, they will see right through the spell." He was admiring the shield and smiling as he pretended to fight with it. I took out one of my daggers and handed it to him.

"Only use this if you absolutely need to. Keep it hidden at all times. People attack people holding a weapon and don't think twice. Promise me, you will only use it if you absolutely have to," I whispered to him trying to keep Thorne from hearing me.

"I promise." Sylas took the blade from me and hid it inside his cloak.

"Wanna play a little game?" I asked, reaching into my bag and taking out some dice.

"Yeah, I love games." Sylas sat on the wagon floor with me.

"Do you know how to play Vandl?" I asked, slamming a cup on the table. Sylas shook his head and I laughed. "You mean your brother, the Vandl champion, never taught you how to play the game?" I looked out the window at him and frowned a bit. It was Thorne's favorite game when we were younger. Did he put everything about us behind him as well? I found myself thinking about it and getting sad. I shook it off and turned to Sylas. I faked a smile and picked up the cup. "So we take turns rolling the dice inside the cup." I shook the cup a little and slammed it back on the floor. I peeked under the cup. "You then decide to either tell the truth about the dice under it or lie. For example..." I looked under the cup again. "Three twos and one five." I looked up at Sylas. "Then you decide if I am lying about it." Sylas looked at me and smiled.

"You're lying." I picked up the cup and showed him the dice. They showed two threes, a four, and a five.

"So, in this case, you win the round, now you go." Sylas shook the dice and peeked under the cup.

"Two threes and two sixes," he spoke. His face was a stone, there was no telling if he was lying or not. I thought about the possibilities and squinted looking at him.

"You're lying." Sylas lifted the cup and showed that he was not lying. I smiled and handed him one of the four dice. "So after you win two rounds in a row you take one of the dice as a reward. The winner is decided after all the dice are gone." Sylas nodded and shook the cup again.

****

Time flew by playing with Sylas. It has been so long since I was able to forget all my worries. I looked up at him and he was starting to yawn. Half the day has passed. Sylas laid on the wagon seat and closed his eyes. The shield's pink aura faded as he drifted off to sleep. I turned to the front of the wagon, crawled out, and sat next to Thorne.

"You know he is almost as good as you at Vandl." Thorne smiled. I nudged him a bit and looked over at him. "How are you holding up out here?" I asked him.

"I'm starting to get tired." He looked over to me and I could see his eyes were glossed over. I put my hands over his. I could feel my heart racing as my skin met with his.

"Why don't you let me drive for a bit?" He nodded but didn't take his hands off the reins. I nudged him again and he released his grip.

"Aerin, can I ask you something?" He asked, starting to fall asleep. I watched the road but nodded. "When did you become the Shadow Hunter?" I pulled back on the reins stopping the horse and looked at him. I inched close to him on the seat.

"A hundred years after everyone died. I had no money, and I was barely surviving." I closed my eyes remembering my first kill. "I killed a man who tried to rape me. Turns out there was a bounty on his head. They paid me ten thousand gold for that kill. I knew if I was going to survive I had to keep killing." Thorne's eyes let a tear fall, and he inched closer to me.

"If I hadn't left, that would have never happened," he spoke, holding his hand over his heart. "You know I thought about you every day. I wanted to come back and find you. Without you around the beatings got worse. There were days I could not walk, I couldn't swallow my food. Without you there I was helpless." He held his hand over his eye. "It was right before Sylas was born, I had enough of missing you, I had to know if you were alive. If you somehow escaped. My father caught me packing a bag, and wanting to leave. He tossed his dagger at me, and it stuck into my eye. The King had his best healer take care of me, but you can see how well that worked out." I moved closer to him and held my hand over his eye. A golden ray shone from my hand and over his eye.

"Let me heal you," I whispered to him, I could feel the pain he felt from not only the dagger but the pain he felt from being away from me for so long. Tears started to fall from my face. In order for me to heal something, I had to embrace the pain the person was feeling at the time of the injury. That pain becomes mine to bear instead of theirs. I lowered my hand and Thorne opened his eyes. He placed his hand on my cheek and I nuzzled into it. For a moment I let my guard down, and my heart took the lead. I turned to his hand and kissed it softly. I quickly realized what had happened and shook the reins again and the horse started moving once more. Thorne looked at me and smiled. He inched closer and laid his head on my shoulder.

"I'm sorry about your father, Thorne, I wish I could take away all the pain." He looked up at me and shook his head.

"If you took it all away, I would forget you," he whispered in my ear. Chills traveled down my back. "Aerin, I missed you so much, even if things are different now, it's nice to have you back in my life." He spoke as he drifted off to sleep. Another tear rolled down my cheek, he was right. It was nice to have him back, but I could not ignore all the hurt that was there with it.

****

We rode most of the day and Thorne slept on my lap. I peeked back and looked at Sylas who was waking up and walking towards the front of the carriage. He sat at the window and looked down at his brother.

"Aerin, are we going to stop soon? I have to use the bathroom." I chuckled and shook my head.

"Can you make it a few more minutes? According to Thorne's map, we are approaching a small clearing where we can make camp for the night."

"I can if we talk to make the time go by faster," he said, begging and shaking his leg.

"What do you want to talk about?"

"Are you and my brother back together?" I looked down at Thorne and brushed the hair out of his face.

"No," I spoke softly.

"Then what are you two?"

"We are friends, and always will be no matter what happens. Just like you and me, Sylas."

"He cares a lot about you. He broke Dad's biggest rule

for you. If he finds out, it won't be a pretty sight."

"I care for him too, but there are a lot of things you don't know about, Sylas." I closed my eyes and a tear fell onto Thorne's cheek. I brushed it away and steered us down a small path. Who was I kidding, I still loved him with all my heart. I did not just care about him. I heard Sylas chuckling behind me. I turned to him. "What is your elvish gift, Sylas?" He held out his hand and let a pink aura flow from him to me.

"I am an empath. I can feel what you feel. I know your heart has not stopped racing since you first saw Thorne, and I can tell you want nothing more than to kiss him." I turned around and shot him a look. He quickly pulled away from my mind but smiled. "Don't worry your secret's safe with me."

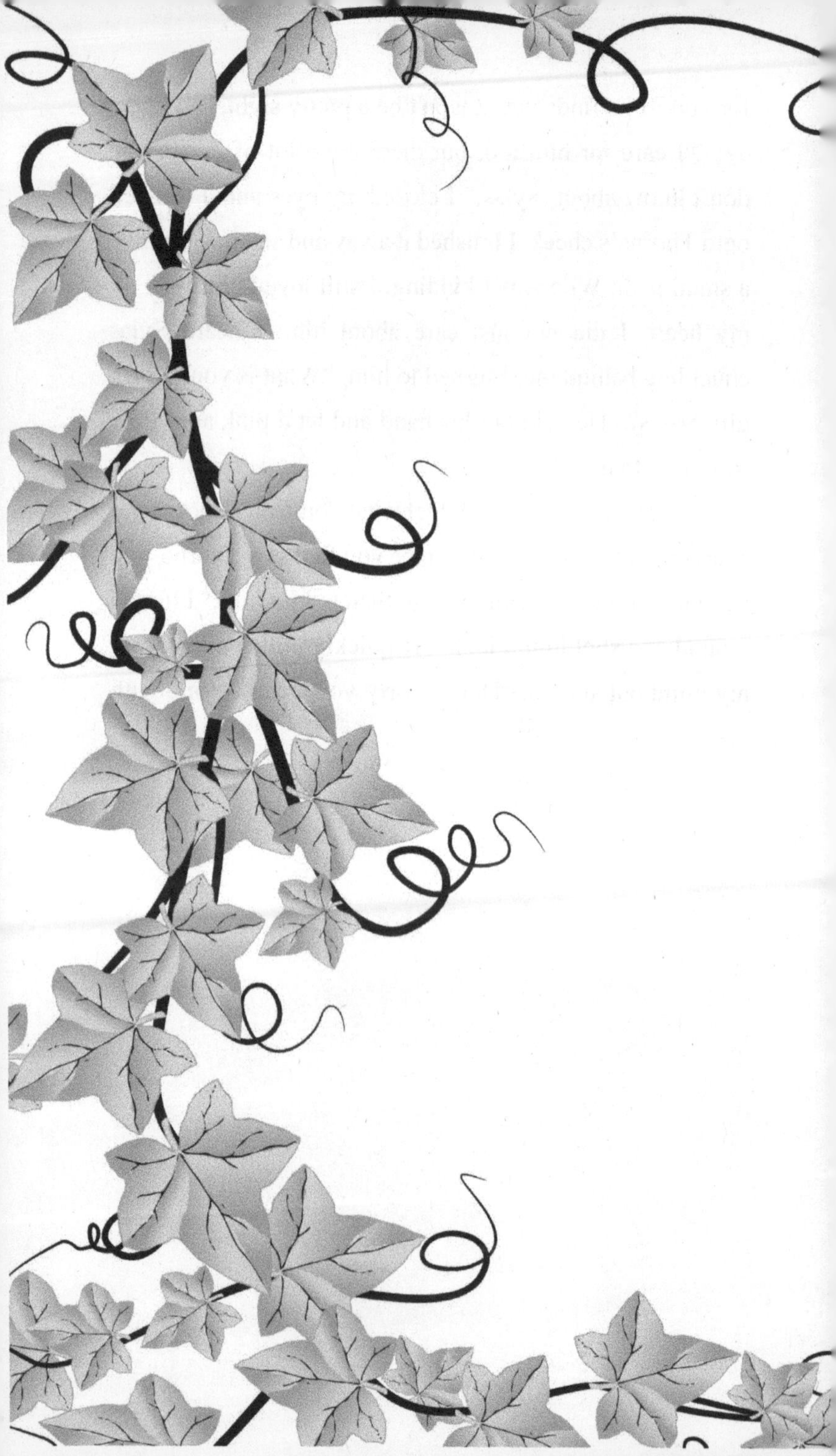

CHAPTER 10:

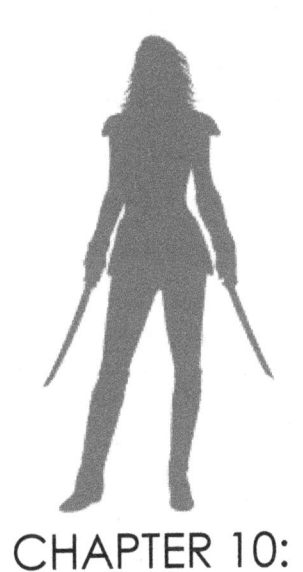

Aerin

I pulled the reins on the horse and it came to a halt. Sylas jumped out of the wagon and raced into the woods. "Don't go too far," I called out after him. Thorne sat up from my lap and rubbed his eyes. He got off the seat and extended his hand to help me off. I did not take his hand and hopped down. I set up the tents Sylas packed while Thorne went out to grab firewood. I tossed the bedrooms into one tent for the two of them. I found myself thinking of the camping nights

Thorne and I used to have together, their bedrolls looked so similar to the ones my mother gave us for our hikes. I walked over to my tent and looked inside. It was a green tent, with nothing inside it. I did not have the luxury of a bedroom, it was always out of the budget. I took off my boots and left them outside of the tent. I crawled into the tent and lay on the hard ground. I listened to my surroundings and heard Sylas's footsteps as he was making his way back to the clearing. He peeked into my tent before crawling inside.

"Where is your bedroll?" He asked me, looking at the bare ground I was lying on.

"I don't have one," I answered, cracking my neck and adjusting from lying on a rock.

"Do you want to use mine?" He asked sweetly. I shook my head and crawled out of the tent. I walked over to the river, filled my waterskin, and tossed it to the side. I removed the rest of my clothing and walked into the river. I let the current flow over me as I looked around. There were birds flying overhead, singing their songs. Fish swam around me as if I was a rock in their path. I looked back at the clearing and saw the trees were swaying in the wind. I watched as their orange and yellow leaves fell gently to the ground. My hair was blowing back and forth, as I crouched down in the water letting it rise up to my neck. I closed my eyes for a moment to dip my head back into the water.

When I picked my head back up, I noticed Thorne

had returned holding some fallen branches and logs. He built a small hut out of the wood and held his hands over it. Sylas stood next to him laughing as he was unable to start the fire. Thorne looked over at me in the river and the fire ignited under his hand. He had not noticed that it lit until the flame rose up and engulfed his hand.

"Shit." I heard him yelling. He stood and made his way over to the river. He dipped his hand into it, and deep blue lines appeared in the water and ran up his arm. He pulled his hand out of the water and the burn was gone. I turned and swam behind a large rock that was in the river to get some distance between us.

Thorne removed his clothing and jumped into the river. I was able to hear the splash and closed my eyes. Part of me praying he would not come over here. I looked down, the water was crystal clear. I felt my breath start to quicken, and I could no longer hear Thorne. My heart raced, and I peered around the rock. I could not see him. I turned to place my back against the rock and found Thorne standing in front of me. I sucked my lips in for a moment and fought the urge to reach for him. I held my hands in front of myself to try and cover up the fact that I was getting hard. I was taken away by his new physique. He was no longer a skinny elf, and I found my eyes glued to his chest. I admired his pecs as I watched them rise and fall with each breath he took. His arms were thicker than I remembered, and every part of me wanted him to throw them around me and pull me in. I glanced into the water hoping he would not notice, and saw that he had grown down there as well. I found myself biting down on my lip as he moved closer to me.

Before he had me completely pinned against the rock, I dove into the water and swam back to shore. I heard him splash behind me and follow. I took my clothing and hid in my tent.

Thorne went to walk over to my tent when Sylas stopped him.

"You should give him a minute." I heard Sylas suggest. I was starting to think Sylas was the older of the two if I didn't know better. Thorne sighed but knew Sylas was right. The two sat by the fire and played Vandl. I, however, sat in my tent starting to shiver. The fall nights were cold, and soon winter would be here. I had to get a bedroll, or some warmer clothing soon. I got up and left the safety net of my tent to join them by the fire.

"Come to join us, Aerin?" Thorne asked, watching as I took a seat next to Sylas. I was trying to keep some distance between Thorne and myself. I knew if I got too close, I would not be able to hold myself back. I held my hands over the fire trying to warm them.

"Three fours and two fives," Thorne called out peeking under the cup.

"He is lying," I spoke softly.

"Truth," Sylas called back. Thorne showed the cup

and won the game.

"Sylas, it's getting pretty late. Why don't you go turn in for the night? We can play more tomorrow," Thorne suggested, as he put the cup and dice back into my bag. He stood up and gave Sylas a hug before he ran into their tent. Thorne sat next to me on the rock they placed next to the fire.

"Aerin," Thorne spoke my name softly. "You can't ignore me the whole time we are out here." I looked at him and saw his brown eyes glowing from the fire. I sighed, looked up at the stars, and I laughed a little.

"Look, Thorne, I can see the big dipper." He looked up and back at me, leaning in closer.

"You still remember that night too?" Thorne asked with so much love and hope in his voice it punched through my heart. I remembered it all too well.

"It was the night you promised to never leave me, and look where we are now," I spoke, standing up and walking away from him. I turned my back on him and the fire and stared at the river. "You're a knight, your life is pretty good. I am the Shadow Hunter, barely surviving. You have a family, and I have–I have nothing." I turned back to Thorne. "Did you ever once try to find me?"

Thorne looked at the ground and refused to look at me. It hurt, but the silence was enough. "I wanted to."

"Well what stopped you, and don't you dare say

your father, you outmatch him."

"Aerin, it's not that easy." He walked to me and put his arms around me. "Listen, every time I left the city to find you I was dragged back by my father or the King's men." I looked him in the eyes, I could see the hurt and believed him. I pulled away and turned back to the water.

"Thorne, I can't be with you again. I thought about it so much for so many years. I can't do it again. I have too much darkness in my heart, it would not be fair to you, and it certainly would not be fair for me to bring that darkness into your family." I held my arms, warming them.

"But what if I am able to bring the light back into your heart, Aerin? I still love you, I never stopped." He walked over to me and wrapped his arms around me pulling me in again. His warmth relaxed me a little, as he rubbed my arms for me. "What if I am willing to sacrifice everything for it?" I turned in his arms.

"Why, why would you sacrifice everything for me?" I asked him.

"Because I made a promise that I broke before, and I will never break it again."

"You can't promise that Thorne, I would never believe it again," I spoke, letting my tears flow. I leaned on my toes and kissed him. As I kissed him I felt my tears flow faster.

"That is the last time we will kiss. From here on out

we are just friends, we have to forget the feelings we have for each other. You will need to in order to protect him," I spoke, looking at their tent. "We will be together still, just not as lovers." I pulled away from him and ran into my tent. I closed the flaps behind me and sat in a ball crying my heart out. I finally said what I wanted to say to him for so many years. I finally got the closure I was denied, but did not feel any better. The fire burnt out, and I heard Thorne walk to his tent. I dried my eyes and lay on the cold ground.

Thorne was pushed awake by Sylas. "Aerin is freezing, go over there with him," he demanded. Thorne grabbed his bedroll and climbed into my tent. I closed my eyes quickly pretending to be asleep. He covered me with the blanket and laid next to me. He kissed my cheek.

"I will win you back, Aerin. I love you, but I will not push you." He turned away from me but still laid close enough that I could feel his back on my own. I took a few short breaths and fell asleep next to Thorne.

****

The next morning I woke up in Thorne's arms. I fell asleep after him, and even in his sleep he still thought about me. I could hear him chanting my name. I rolled over and placed my hand on his chest. He woke up and looked down at me.

"I'm okay," I whispered to him. He hugged me. "Do you want to talk about it?"

"It's the same dream I have had for as long as I can remember seeing our home in flames, and you are trapped inside your house. You're unable to get out, and just as I reach your house, it is swallowed in flames." I nodded and hugged him back.

"You don't need to worry so much, Thorne, I am here with you now." I sat up and cracked my neck before stepping out of the tent. I reached my hand back in to help Thorne to his feet. We walked over to Sylas's tent and found him still asleep. I yawned, walked back to my tent, and laid back down. Thorne entered behind me and sat on the opposite side. I rolled to look at him.

"So, we are going to find our elvish blood, and return to peace? Sounds like a great idea. I guess I can hang up the cloak now."

"It would be nice to have everything back to normal and start a little new village. Sylas can grow up knowing all about our past." Thorne inched over to me and pinned the royal crest on my quiver behind me. "I guess the Shadow Hunter will join me in the royal guard then?"

"I guess he will," I spoke back laughing. I knew that hanging that up would mean that either we finish this mission a success, or I have nothing to return to again. I frowned and Thorne noticed.

"If we don't succeed, you will still be welcome in my home. Sylas would love to have another older brother who can teach him magic." I smiled and took his hand.

"I would be honored to live with you both." I barely knew Sylas, but I already felt like he was a little brother to me. I never had siblings in the village, Morgana was much older than I was and left before I was born. Thorne smiled at me and pulled me into a hug then looked into my eyes.

"Good morning, Aerin." He smiled and squeezed my hand.

"Good morning, Thorne." I squeezed his back harder. We sat hand and hand and talked about the past few hundred years.

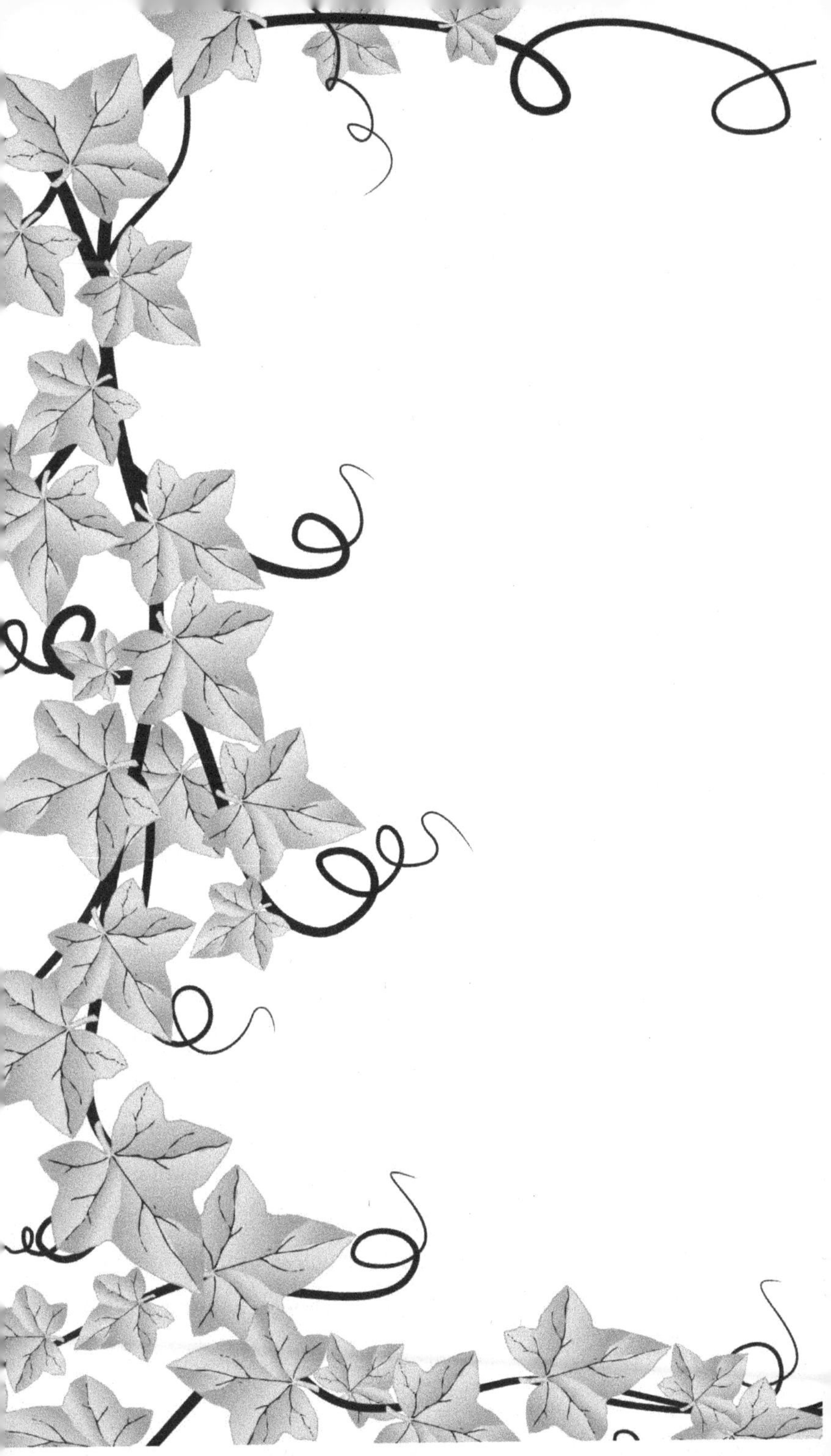

CHAPTER 11:

Thorne

"Help." I heard my brother screaming from the other tent. I grabbed my sword and ran to him. There were five men out there. Their faces had black veins over them. I will be damned if I let them take Sylas. I raced to them and swung my sword. I managed to kill one in the group before they quickly outnumbered me. They had the speed of an elvish knight and circled around me. "Thorne, help," Sylas called out again. I tried to hold back my anger in order to focus on the fight at hand. I was not strong enough and the ground around me started to shake. Aerin flipped over the men and landed next to me.

"Thorne, relax, that will hurt Sylas too." He knew I was about to drag the river over us all. I took a deep breath and charged towards Sylas. Two men ran at me and their arms crossed over my neck knocking me down. I started to choke from the momentary loss of breath. I stood back up and swung my sword at them. I missed them both as they slid under the blade and pulled their daggers out, slicing my legs. I fell back to the floor. I turned to see Aerin fighting the other two. He was managing to win, dancing around them slicing into them over and over again. I watched as one of them fell to the floor. The two men raced at Aerin, and I started to crawl over to the one holding Sylas.

"SY," I shouted, trying to get to him. The purple fog appeared once more. It engulfed the man holding Sylas and just as quickly as it appeared, it vanished along with the man and my brother. I felt my heart rip out of my chest. This anger has given me enough strength to stand. I ran over to where they were standing, but there was nothing. How could they have vanished out of thin air, and left behind no trace of magic? I knelt to the ground looking for anything that would point me to where they went.

"Thorne, I could use some help," Aerin shouted, as he was dodging the three men that remained. I could hear his voice but was frozen to the spot. They took my brother, I will never see him again. My hair turned to water as I grabbed the dirt where they stood. I turned to face the three men that still remained there. I dropped my sword and waved my hands. The river dried as it flowed around the men and Aerin. It created a bubble as it spun around them. The air was being pulled from inside. I watched as the men fell to the floor, and quickly stopped my attack when I noticed Aerin was also on the ground. He was clenching his throat and gasping for air. I lowered my arms and the water returned to the river as if nothing had happened. I fell to my knees, the anger that gave me strength was gone. I crawled to him. I found one of the daggers that were on the ground from Aerin and picked it up. I stabbed each man in the back until I reached the last one.

I sat up and rolled him over. I held the blade to his neck. I could see the tears forming in his eyes as his life started flashing before him.

"Please, I have a family. Show mercy," he cried out.

"So did I. Where was he taken?" The man ignored my question. I felt a fear inside him that paralyzed his tongue. He looked up at me and begged again for his life. "Why did you attack us?"

"We were ordered to. We are not able to refuse commands. If we refuse, we die. It is part of the curse."

"What do you want with Sylas?" I asked, pressing the dagger harder against his neck. "Tell me or you're dead," I commanded.

"I don't know if there has been talk that our leader

needs more power. She talks about spells that will drain us of ours." The man swallowed hard knowing I would not like his answer.

"Who is your leader?" Aerin managed to get to his feet. He grabbed my arm and took the dagger from my hand, and slit the man's throat.

"You are not a killer, Thorne, you do not kill out of revenge. You are better than that," he spoke softly to me. "You already know who the leader is." He was right, the purple fog gave it all away. Morgana was behind this. If she even laid a finger on Sylas, it would be the last thing she did. I tried to stand, but the slashes on my ankles prevented it. Aerin carried me to the water and I healed myself. Before returning to the tent and grabbing my bedroll and bag, Aerin grabbed my arms and forced me to look at him. I finally let my emotions take over.

"We have to find him," I said, falling into his arms.

"We will," Aerin answered, rubbing my back. I took a deep breath grounding myself once more. I started walking to the wagon and preparing the horse for the trip. Aerin looked at me and took my hand.

"It will be faster if we travel light." He whistled and Alatar ran down the path to us. He jumped up and grabbed her reins before reaching down for me. I took his hand and was pulled up behind him. I placed my arms around him as we took off. I watched the surroundings waiting for a surprise attack. "Noro lim." I heard Aerin calling Alatar.

"Noro lim." Alatar started to run faster. He sensed that we were being watched as well, I could tell by the fear in his voice.

****

We traveled for the day on Alatar, her speed did not slow at all. Yet Aerin stopped her.

"Why are you stopping? We have to get to Amhe Lenora," I spoke, wanting to continue on. Aerin hopped off the horse and looked at me.

"We will continue on in a few hours. We are close and can use the night to shield ourselves. You have to trust me, I want to get him back just as badly as you do." I took his hand and he helped me off the horse. We sat against a tree as Alatar ran off. I looked over at Aerin who was sharpening his arrows. I found myself wondering what was happening to Sylas. The King was right, the air around here is thicker, and it took me a bit to get used to breathing it in. We were on the outskirts of Amhe Lenora. I looked up at the tree and climbed it.

I could see tall buildings in the city. A purple fog sat over it but did not cover the tall peaks of the elvish buildings. I could see the stained glass windows and tall statues. I closed my eyes and extended my reach. I called out to Sylas's mind hoping he would answer back. I let my gift connect with people inside the city, and I could see through their eyes. The fog was thick, and rubble from fallen statues cluttered the once-vast city streets. I could not find any signs of Sylas though. As I got closer to the main hall, I saw two purple eyes staring at me. I heard a voice speaking to me in Elvish.

"GET OUT." It echoed so loud I could hear nothing else. I felt a force that was pushed from Amhe Lenora to me. I let go of my gift and returned to my body. The purple ring of force punched me in the stomach. The force was so strong it shoved me out of the tree. I screamed as I landed back down next to Aerin. I held my stomach as I crawled to the tree.

"Aerin, Morgana is there," I spoke to him. "I heard her voice. It echoed through the city, and in my mind." He put the arrows back into his quiver.

"Did you see Sylas?" Aerin asked me, ignoring the fact his sister was only miles away. He was telling the truth, all he wanted to do was save Sylas and get out of there as fast as he could. I shook my head and leaned against the tree. "You should get some rest, we will both need our strength," he whispered to me and closed his eyes. I, however, was unable to rest. I could not just sit here, I could not just sleep. I stood and paced back and forth for a bit.

"At least sit down, Thorne, conserve your strength. We have no idea what we are getting ourselves into," Aerin begged, patting the seat next to him. I walked over and knelt down.

"What if we are too late?" I found myself asking, and fighting the urge to leave.

"You can't cloud your mind with things we do not know," Aerin spoke to me like a wise old man. I laid my head against his shoulder and closed my eyes.

****

I did not dream during the rest we took. I instead found myself projected in Amhe Lenora. I raced around the city, looking for where Sylas might be. I made my way to the great hall and heard Sylas crying. "Throw him in the dungeon." I heard Morgana call to her men. I watched helplessly as they dragged him out of the hall. I followed closely behind them invisible to the naked eye. They crept down a dark alley and opened a cellar door. I watched as they chained my brother in a cell. The guard pulled out a whip and brought it down on Sylas.

"This will teach you to spit at the Queen," he brought it back down again. I winced at the sound of the snap. I mumbled in elvish and the whip flew out of his hand. The man turned and picked it back up. He slammed the gate shut before locking it. Sylas sat in the corner of the cell crying. I wanted to reach out to him, but I knew if I did, he would expose me. I sat against the wall watching him. The guard returned and slid a bowl of some gray liquid into him. Sylas was smart and did not move to it. He kicked the bowl, knocking it over and spilling the contents. The man opened the gate and threw Sylas against the wall, tearing his tunic to shreds. He whipped him again. I watched helplessly as I could only do so much in this state.

I will slit his throat and enjoy watching as every drop spills from him. I watched, unable to look away at the pain my brother was in. His screams echoed in my head even after they stopped. The man whipped him again, but Sylas had grown numb to the pain. The guard walked out and slammed the door shut behind himself. Sylas lay lifeless against the wall and cried in silence. He dared not to make a single peep. I saw blood spewing from the gashes on his back.

I needed Aerin to wake me, I still have not learned how to return to my body. I could no longer stay here, I could not bear the pain Sylas was in. His gift was overwhelming and set me and everyone around him to feel the pain he was in. I could feel each gash as if it had been on my own back. *Fucking hell Aerin, now is not the time to be asleep. Wake the fuck up and bring me back.*

The minute I wake I am coming back here, and the first thing I am doing is bringing that man as much pain as he did Sylas. I will slice into him 1000 times, remove his arms, and the minute he is begging for death I will leave him in a puddle of his own blood. I felt my own heart darkening. Sylas looked back at me and smiled.

"Do not darken your heart, Thorne," he whispered. "Rescue me and show compassion, he is under her control." I knew it was a huge risk walking into the enemy's stronghold, I would pay any price to save my brother. I would do anything to hold him again. I would take his place if I could. I will make sure he is safe. I will ignore the command of the King, and leave behind my mission. My brother's life is worth so much more.

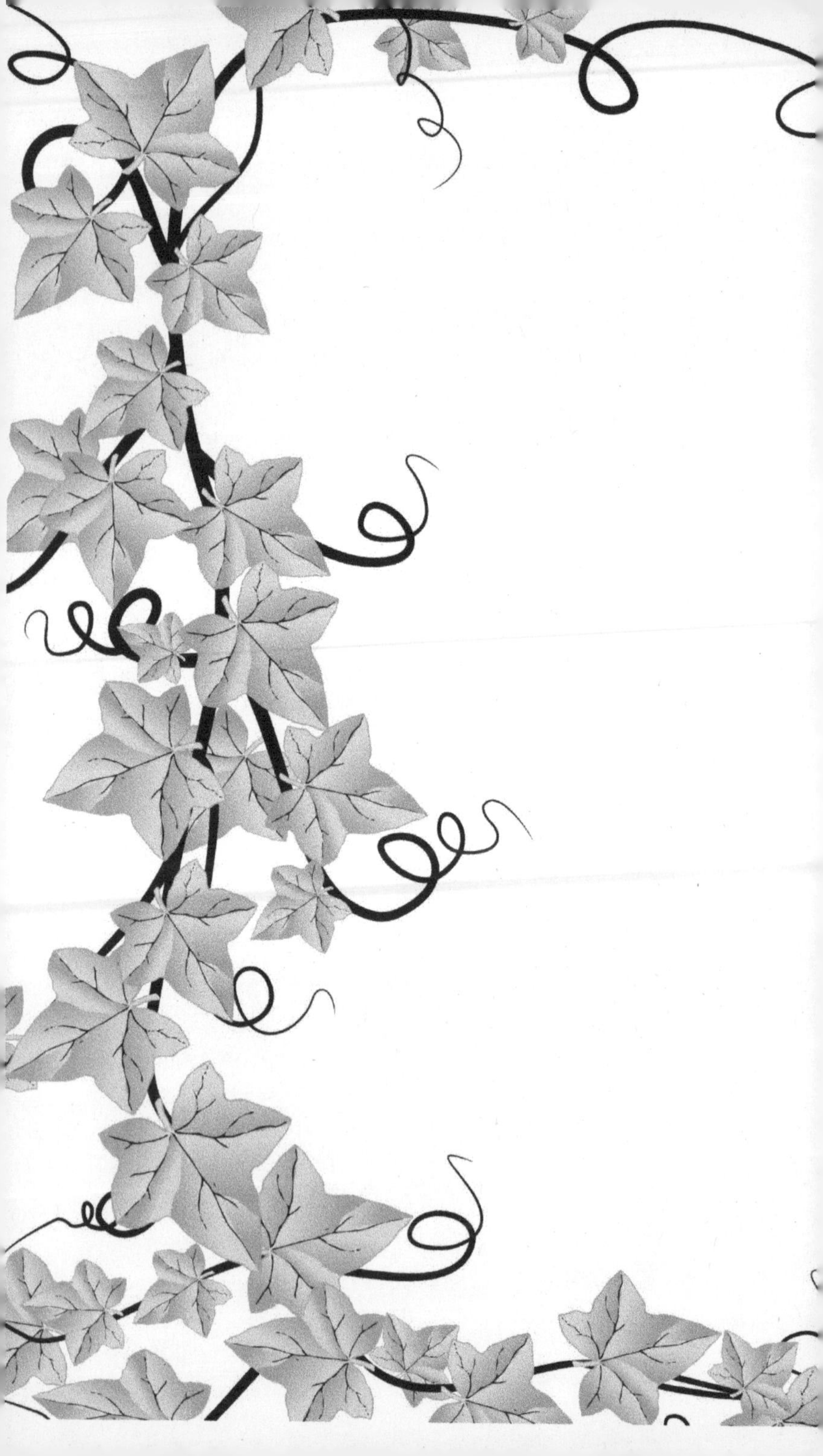

CHAPTER 12:

Aerin

I stood over Thorne shaking him awake. His eyes blinked open and he hugged me.

"Thank you for waking me, I could not bear that anymore."

"Did you find out where he is?" He nodded.

"You knew I would go there, didn't you?" I nodded my head. I knew he would not be able to stay put. We needed to know where he was being held so we were not in the city for longer than we had to be. I know Morgana will sense me the minute I get too close. I pulled up my hood and nodded to Thorne. He knew it was time to go. I climbed the tree watched him fall out and extended my hand to pull him up.

We jumped from branch to branch, inching our way closer. Thanks to our elven speed, it only took thirty minutes for us to arrive. We jumped from the last tree in unison and landed inside the gates. I took Thorne's hand and pulled him into the shadows beside me. The city was covered with all different races. I noticed a few halflings, men, and elves walking around mindlessly. Their faces bore the same black veins as the men we fought earlier. If we found a way to remove these curses, they would be free.

I watched as everyone walked around and pulled Thorne into a dark alley. "Where are they keeping him?" I whispered to Thorne, holding him against the wall. I could tell he was ready to bolt.

"They are keeping him in some kind of dungeon near the city hall." I took his hand and looked him in the eyes.

"You need to follow my steps and keep a level head. Morgana can sense our emotions."

"Find them." A voice boomed across the city. The mindless dwellers started racing around the city looking for us. I pulled my bow out and took an arrow, tying a rope into it. I fired it into the top of a small wooden shack and pushed Thorne to the rope. I waited as he scaled the side of the building. I turned to watch the people running around, I started mumbling and cast a barrier to shield us from peering eyes. I grabbed the rope and climbed up. Thorne stood waiting for me, pulling the rope to him. I took his hand and he fell back pulling me up. I led Thorne to the city hall, and he pointed at a cellar door. I took out my bow and nodded to him. He pulled the doors open, and I held an arrow ready on the string. We slowly made our way down the stairs, and let our eyes adjust to the barley-lit cellar. I sheathed my bow and pushed Thorne against the wall. A man walked by us going to leave. Thorne unsheathed his sword and sliced the man's neck.

We walked into the cellar further and could hear a whip crashing down on flesh. Thorne ran past me. I quickened my pace. We turned the corner and saw Sylas chained and the whip clashing on his back more. We ran into the cell. Thorne grabbed the man's hand and threw him into the bars. I turned to the man and held my dagger to his neck. I checked his clothing and found some keys before tossing them back to Thorne.

"Scream, give me a reason to run my blade across your neck." I let my eyes go black. I could sense the fear in him. I turned back and saw Thorne holding his brother and walking over to me.

"Take him," Thorne demanded of me. I took Sylas's lifeless body and walked out of the cell. I overheard the man inside with Thorne screaming. I put Sylas down for a moment and went back to get Thorne. We had to leave, we had already been here too long.

"We have to go," I yelled at him. I watched as Thorne tortured the man, letting his sword scrape against his flesh in all different positions. Blood was splattered everywhere. His face was coated with the man's blood. I grabbed his arm to pull him out of the cell. He was in complete blood lust and swung his sword at me, cutting my cheek. I quickly turned away and held the gash on my face. Thorne dropped the man and held his hand up at me. I smacked it away and walked back to where I placed Sylas down.

"Aerin," He called out to me. I pointed to his brother.

"Grab him and let's go." I turned away from him and pushed open the doors. There were two halflings waiting for us. They held daggers and pointed them at me. I'll be damned if I get cut again today. I quickly tossed two daggers into them. I flagged Thorne up, and we started running to the gate. We needed to stop, as I could see Thorne was losing his grip on Sylas. I pushed him into a small building where we sat down for a moment to catch our breath. I was unable to look at him, my face burning from the cut that was still bleeding. I searched the small space and it was empty. I found some old clothing and held it to my face. I winced at the pain and knew it would scar me.

Thorne laid Sylas on the bed in the room and stood over him.

"Is he okay?" I asked Thorne, trying to keep a good

amount of space between us.

"He will be," Thorne spoke softly, walking over to me. I backed away from him and found myself backed against the wall. He took the clothing from me and pulled me over to a bucket of water that was in the kitchen. He let the water travel up one hand and over to his other hand as it healed my face. I could feel the water rushing through my skin. He put his hands back down and I felt my cheek. The cut was gone. "Aerin, I'm so sorry." I did not respond, I just nodded at him and walked over to Sylas. Thorne carried the bucket of water over to him. I watched as the gashes on Sylas's back started to close and his eyes opened up.

"Thorne," He called out to his brother, hugging him. "Aerin." He hugged me, and I felt a flutter in my chest. I picked him up and hugged him back fiercely.

"Glad you're okay little man." I put him down and walked to the window of the abandoned house. I looked out and noticed we were cornered. I stood on the table and pulled some of the hay from the ceiling, exposing the outside. I reached for Sylas and held him up so he could climb through the hole. I knelt down with my hands folded and gave Thorne a push-up. He held onto the ceiling as Sylas tried to pull him up. The door was kicked in and the window crashed open. Men, halflings, and elves poured into the room with me. I looked up to Thorne and Sylas. "RUN" I yelled at them.

"Aerin, come on. Take my hand," Thorne called back

to me. "I can't lose you again."

"Get Sylas to safety, that is why we are here. I will buy you time." I was quickly surrounded. While I tried to kill them, I was horribly outnumbered. A heavyset man jumped on my back and I fell to the floor. Purple fog filled the room as they all took turns punching and kicking me. They quickly backed away from me as the purple fog fully filled the room. A woman walked in wearing an amethyst gown, her hair was blacker than a night without the moon or stars. I picked myself up off the floor and spat out the blood from my mouth.

"Morgana," I spoke, hiding the pain and fear from my voice.

"My dear brother, Aerin. Have you finally come to join me?" She asked, mocking me. "Or did you come to complain again about Mom's death?" I wanted to jump at her, to throw a dagger in her neck.

"I have come to save my family," I spoke loudly.

"Your family? But I am right here, I do not need saving. I have everything I need," she spoke, holding out her arms.

"You have never been my family, and never will be," I spoke, in reaction. "You still have nothing, Morgana, Father may be dead but I will live my life to make sure you never rule this land. I will die before I ever let you take another piece of land. I will take back everything you have stolen." Morgana took the bait. She walked to me and the men parted as she inched closer. She slapped me and laughed.

"I have seen your mediocre magic, you are not as strong as our father." Hearing her say that killed me. She said it only to get under my skin and I knew it. I did not let any emotion show on my face, I was not going to let her win. I quickly threw a fireball at her, the short distance should have been enough, but the fog swallowed it whole. She held out her hand and I went flying through the wall. I slowly stood back up. I closed my eyes and took a deep breath.

"Morgana!" My voice boomed through the city and was echoed by the voice of Rillifane. My body lit on fire but I did not feel any pain. I held my palms out and flames flew from my hands, cleansing the building of patrons. I watched as Morgana teleported next to me. She raised her hand again but nothing happened. I stayed exactly where I was. I moved my arms around me in a circular motion and a fireball started to form. With both arms raised, I pushed towards her. She quickly vanished, shouting that this was not over. The fireball flew into one of the statues making it explode. I turned and ran to the gate. I felt Rillifane's power coursing through me. It made me faster and stronger. But it also felt like it was trying to take over me.

I jumped over the gate and took a breath once I was outside Morgana's grip. My hands were on my knees as I hunched over. Morgana was scared, I could feel it. She would be looking for more power now. It feels good, to be able to finally stand up to her. I knew I could get revenge for Mother's death now. She killed her to take her magic, just like she was going to do to Sylas.

I walked away, not looking back. I knew that one day I would stand in the great hall as king. Today is not that day, but it will come. I walked to where Thorne and I were before our daring rescue. Sylas and Thorne were sitting against the tree taking a rest. Rillifane's grace was gone at his point, and I felt myself weakening. I could feel each punch and kick I took in that house. My back was tense and sore from going through the wooden building. I started to fall over as I made it to Sylas and Thorne.

"Are you both okay?" I asked as my eyes started to close.

"Thorne, is he…" Sylas paused, looking down at me. Thorne picked up my head and frowned. I opened my eyes and shot them a smirk.

"I just need to rest a bit." I took a deep breath and nuzzled into Thorne's chest. "We are going to find the elves, and we are going to stop Morgana." I held out my hand to Sylas and he took it. "We will do it together as a family of elves." I looked up at Thorne. I wanted his face to be the last thing I saw as I closed my eyes.

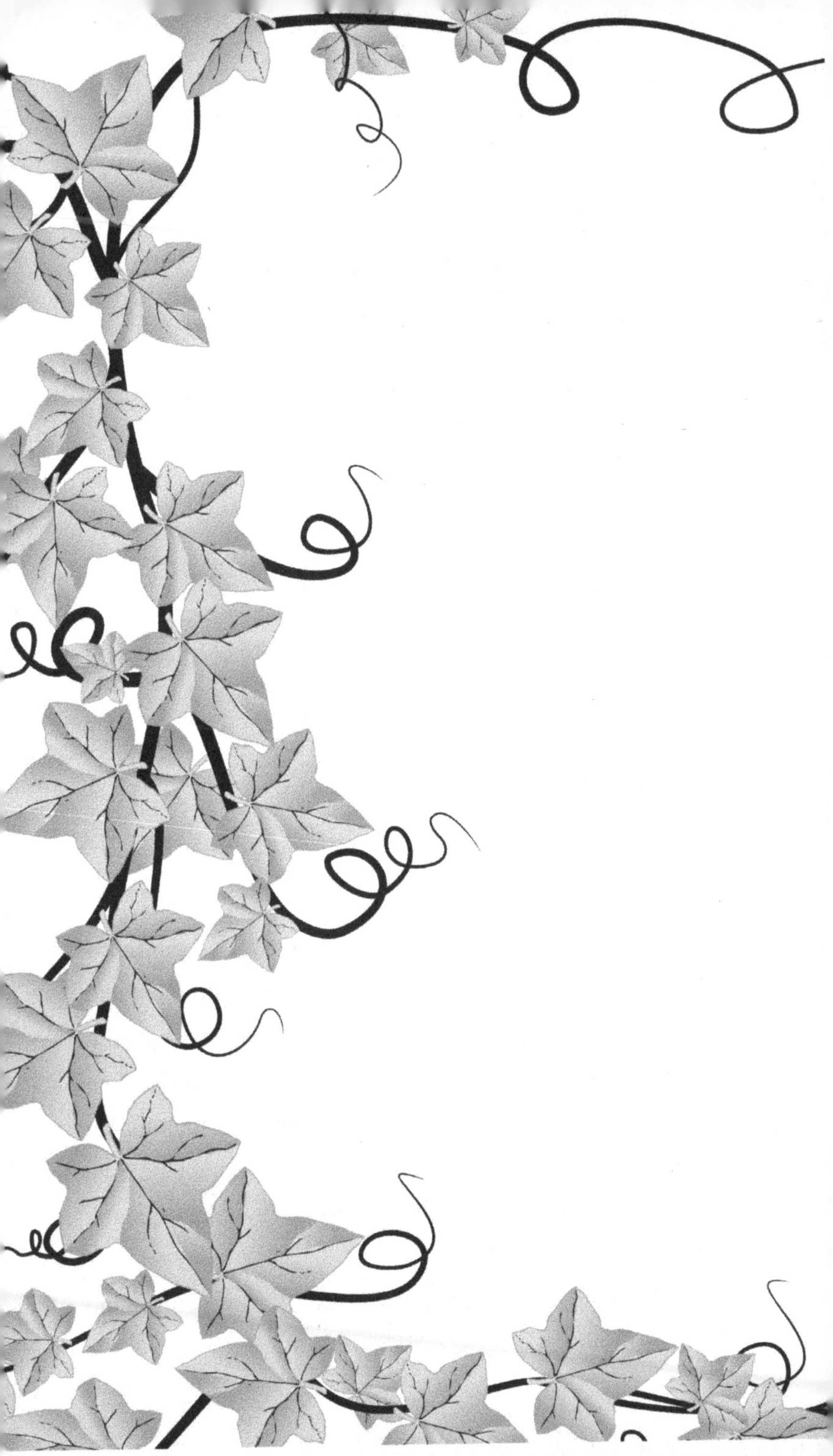

CHAPTER 13:

Thorne

Aerin slept for two days, and I kept a close eye on him. I was worried he would not wake up. Sylas would go in and out of the tent, checking on him. that he purchased from a traveling man. The tree behind the tent had chunks taken out of it from me practicing every day to make the time go by. Aerin had a plan, but he did not tell us about it before he passed out. Did he have a clue about where we can find the elves?

"Thorne, check this out!" Sylas called to me from the

tent. I walked over and peeked my head inside. I saw Aerin still asleep in my bedroll and Sylas sitting beside him with a book on his lap. He turned the book around and showed me an old sword-fighting style from the first Elven war. I took in the images of the twirls and slashes, I smiled at him.

"I will have to try that one day. Let me know if he wakes up soon, we should start moving from here today." Sylas nodded and I went back to my training. Next time Morgana sent someone after us I would be ready. I was a knight, and I will be damned if I let anything happen to Sylas or Aerin again. I pulled my sword from its scabbard and held it in my hand. I spun on my heel and jumped as I whirled around. My sword transformed into a water bow and fired arrows of lightning from it. I watched as the arrow disappeared as it hit the tree leaving a scorch mark.

I spun again on my back heel, jumping and the sword transformed back into its natural state. I gave it a little twirl and smiled. I had no idea the images Sylas showed me would be so easy to imitate. I called Sylas out and showed him the new transformation magic I already mastered. He was very impressed by it. I was too busy showing off to notice that Aerin walked out of the tent with Sylas. He stood there leaning against another tree clapping his hands.

I laughed a bit and ran over to him. "Are you finally awake?" I asked him jokingly.

"Are you done showing off?" He replied. He hugged me and Sylas. "Glad to see you are doing well." Sylas smiled at him and walked over to the tent to start packing everything up.

"So, do you have a plan, Aerin?" I asked, hoping he had dreamt of some way to overcome Morgana's power.

"There is a town nearby, we should go there and get supplies. We left a lot behind at the clearing. We can talk about a plan there," he spoke, shaking his head.

"How are you feeling?" I asked him since he was still leaning on the tree. I watched as he pushed off it and ran over to me. He tackled me to the ground.

"Still strong enough to take you down," he said smiling. I found myself struggling to not kiss him. It felt right to thank him after helping me rescue my brother. I looked him in the eyes as he lay on top of me.

"Thank you for saving him," I spoke softly, finding myself hypnotized by his eyes. It took every ounce of strength I had to not pull him closer. I want his face buried in my neck, I want to feel his lips as they press against my skin. Aerin got off of me once he started getting poked from underneath and helped me to my feet. Sylas walked over to us with the supplies all packed and we started walking to Yellian.

****

The city was booming. I was in awe looking at the gold statues and tall buildings. We approached the entrance and were stopped by soldiers.

"Halt! State your business," they called out to us.

"I am Aerin, king of the wood elves," he spoke to the man, who was not impressed in the slightest.

"I am Thorne, knight of King Abdiel," I spoke, removing a small parchment from my pocket. "The King has promised us safe travels among the land. We are seeking shelter and food." I hated soldiers like him. The ones who think that because they are a soldier they can do what they please, and feel they are better than everyone else. He snatched the paper from my hand and tore it up in front of me. I wanted to slug him one. I swallowed my pride and looked at him. "You will allow us entrance, or report to the King himself." The man laughed.

"The King has not been here in over 100 years, you think he will come just because some lonely knight calls for him?" He asked, barely able to stand straight from laughing so hard. I turned around to walk away but stopped myself. I brought my fist up and whacked him square in the nose. I let my anger take hold as I picked up my foot and held it down on his throat.

"You will grant me entry, you have already received the paperwork, and you will bow to me as the King's successor." Aerin put his hand on my shoulder and pulled me back to him. We walked past the guard and into the city. I watched as Sylas bounced around racing from booth to booth looking at all kinds of jewelry, magical items, and potions. I ended up having to hold his arm or we would get nowhere. I sighed, he always got distracted by anything shiny.

We came across a building that had a sign with a mug on it and entered it.

"Take a seat anywhere." We sat in the back corner. Aerin sat against the wall watching as people came and went from the tavern. My leg was moving a mile a minute as my blood was still boiling. I have never seen so much disrespect from a knight in all the years I have served the King. Were all the knights here like that, would I need to stay here and teach them what respect is? I know when I take over I will sure as hell remind them what authority is. I have no issue running my sword through someone who uses the title as an excuse to be an absolute ass.

I sat at the table in silence while Aerin and Sylas ordered food. I was in no mood to eat and if I dared to drink, I would be marching back down to the gate. The tavern was filled with men and a few halflings who shouted as they drank. I felt myself getting a headache but ignored them. I watched as Aerin and Sylas both ate a salad. Well, Sylas ate it, and Aerin inhaled his food. I guess it would be expected after three days of not eating.

"I'll be back," I told the two as I got up and walked to the barkeep. He slapped a mug of beer in front of me.

"On the house, it is the best beer you will ever have." He spoke with such confidence. I did not want to insult him so I picked it up and raised it to him. I took a sip of the brown substance. I enjoyed the smoothness and hint of maple in it.

"Have you seen any elvish kind around these parts?" I asked him leaning over the bar trying to not catch the attention of the drunks around us. He laughed at my question and just turned away. A cloaked figure walked over to me and took a seat.

"What do you want to do with the elves?" He spoke in a higher-pitched voice, with his back to the patrons, and did not make eye contact with me.

"We need their help," I said calmly to him.

He took a deep breath in response and turned to me. "Meet me back here in one hour, I will take you to them." He stood and walked out the door. I finished the mug of beer before returning to Sylas and Aerin.

"We might have a lead, there is a man who says he will take us to some elves in one hour." Aerin looked up at me, the shock was glued to his face.

"Can we trust him?" Aerin asked, sipping from his glass of wine. We paid for the food and drink before making our way up the back stairs to a room. Sylas was excited and pushed the door open exposing a well-lit room, with two big beds inside. Sylas jumped into the bed and sighed. I could tell how happy he was to sleep in a bed again. He instantly fell asleep. I turned to Aerin.

"It could be a trap," I spoke softly.

"You think?" Aerin called back to me, "And you are ready to walk right into it?" he asked me. I looked at him and shrugged.

"We don't have a choice. Plus I have the Shadow Hunter on my side. He wouldn't stand a chance." I said, nudging him with my shoulder. Aerin shot me a quick smirk in response.

"Should we get some rest before then?" Aerin asked, and I nodded. I stood and saw that Sylas was not fully asleep yet and sprawled himself taking up the whole bed. I turned back to Aerin.

"Seems someone wants us to share a bed instead of sharing his," I said as I walked to the bed. Aerin lay there and invited me to crawl in next to him. I imagined myself pulling him under the blankets and kissing him, undressing him. I wanted it so bad, it's been two weeks since we've been together now, and every day it was getting harder to hold back my feelings for him. I climbed into bed next to him and turned to look at him. He took a deep breath before rolling back to look at me. He nuzzled into my chest and I put my arm over him. It was the closest we've been since we met back up. My heart was racing, and I was worrying about making the wrong move. I tried to think of anything other than Aerin to avoid getting a hard-on.

****

Aerin shook me awake. I blinked, adjusting to the lit room, and sat up. I was glad to see Sylas was still asleep, it would be easier to deal with an ambush without needing to look after him. My eyes met with Aerin's and I nodded. We both carefully got out of bed and left the room. The tavern was crowded as we had to force our way through the drunken men and women. We made it outside and found that it had been snowing. It must have started while we were sleeping because it has painted the ground now. We waited by the door for what seemed to be forever. The person was late, and they better have a good reason for making us freeze.

I looked over at Aerin who was rubbing his arms to keep warm, and frowned. I took off my cloak and draped it around him. He smiled and glanced down the road looking for anyone. I was ready to give up and go back to our room when I heard a long whistle in the distance. It definitely did not feel right, it had to be a trap. I jerked my head, hinting for Aerin to follow me as I walked towards where the whistle came from. We walked to the far end of the tavern and I was met with a blade against my neck.

"We were told to meet someone here," I said, swallowing my momentary fear.

"You were told to come, no one said anything about a spare."

"Hold your tongue," I spoke back, drawing my sword and knocking it out of his hand. "This is Aerin, King of the Wood Elves, and all elvish kind." The man nodded and led us to the back of the tavern and down to the cellar. I made sure that Aerin had a quick escape and walked in front of him. The cellar was deep under the tavern, I noticed, as we walked down four flights of stairs. Inside the cellar, there were hundreds of barrels and a small fire in the middle of the room. Three cloaked men stood around the fire and watched us closely as we walked in. Aerin stood behind me, his cowl still covering his head and face.

"What do you want with the elves?" The man in the center asked us.

"We are planning to take down Morgana and return the nation to them. However, we need their help to do it," I explained, stepping closer to the fire. I found myself starting to freeze due to the room being poorly insulated. The elves on the side created fireballs and held them in their hands.

"We are no match for Morgana, and you dare to mention her name. You must be a servant of her brainwashed like our brethren." They tossed the fireballs at me. One hit me and I flew back to Aerin who quickly put out the fire. I stood back up, and Aerin removed his hood.

"You will help us," he said without a missed step. "Your king demands it."

"We have no king," the man called back to him. Aerin stepped closer and showed his face in the fire.

"I am Aerin, son of Elwin, and you will obey my command."

The three elves quickly dropped to their knees. "Forgive us, we thought the bloodline vanished when your father died."

"How many of you are there?" He asked and they rose

to their feet.

"It's just us since she took over the capital." He paused for a moment. "We were cowards and ran, we left our brethren behind and they were enslaved."

"There is a young half-elf, very smart for his age. You will help in his studies and find a way to cure our brethren. This will grant us the power we need to drive Morgana out."

"Yes, Aerin." The man bowed before him and Aerin turned to me to make sure I was okay from the fire. I nodded to him, and we left the cellar. Before leaving I turned back around.

"His name is Sylas, and if anything happens to him, be my brethren or not, you will find yourself on the edge of my sword. You will meet him here at first light." The elves did not say a word and Aerin turned back to them.

"You will treat Thorne with the same respect you owe me."

"We will be here," they agreed. Aerin led me out of the cellar, and back to our room. Sylas was still asleep so we would need to talk to him the next morning. I climbed into bed and removed my shirt exposing the scorch marks on my chest. Aerin walked over to me and held his hand on it.

"Are you okay?" He asked.

"I will be fine, it's nothing major." He laid his head down next to mine and held onto me.

"Don't get excited now, I just don't want to fall out of

bed tonight," Aerin spoke softly to me. Don't get excited, how could I not? It's been so long since I was able to lay in bed with him and hold him this close to me. If things never changed we would be locked together, our bodies pressing against each other as we kissed. He would be under me begging me to enter him again. I want to feel complete once more, but thanks to my father, that will never happen. I closed my eyes and gently kissed his forehead before falling asleep.

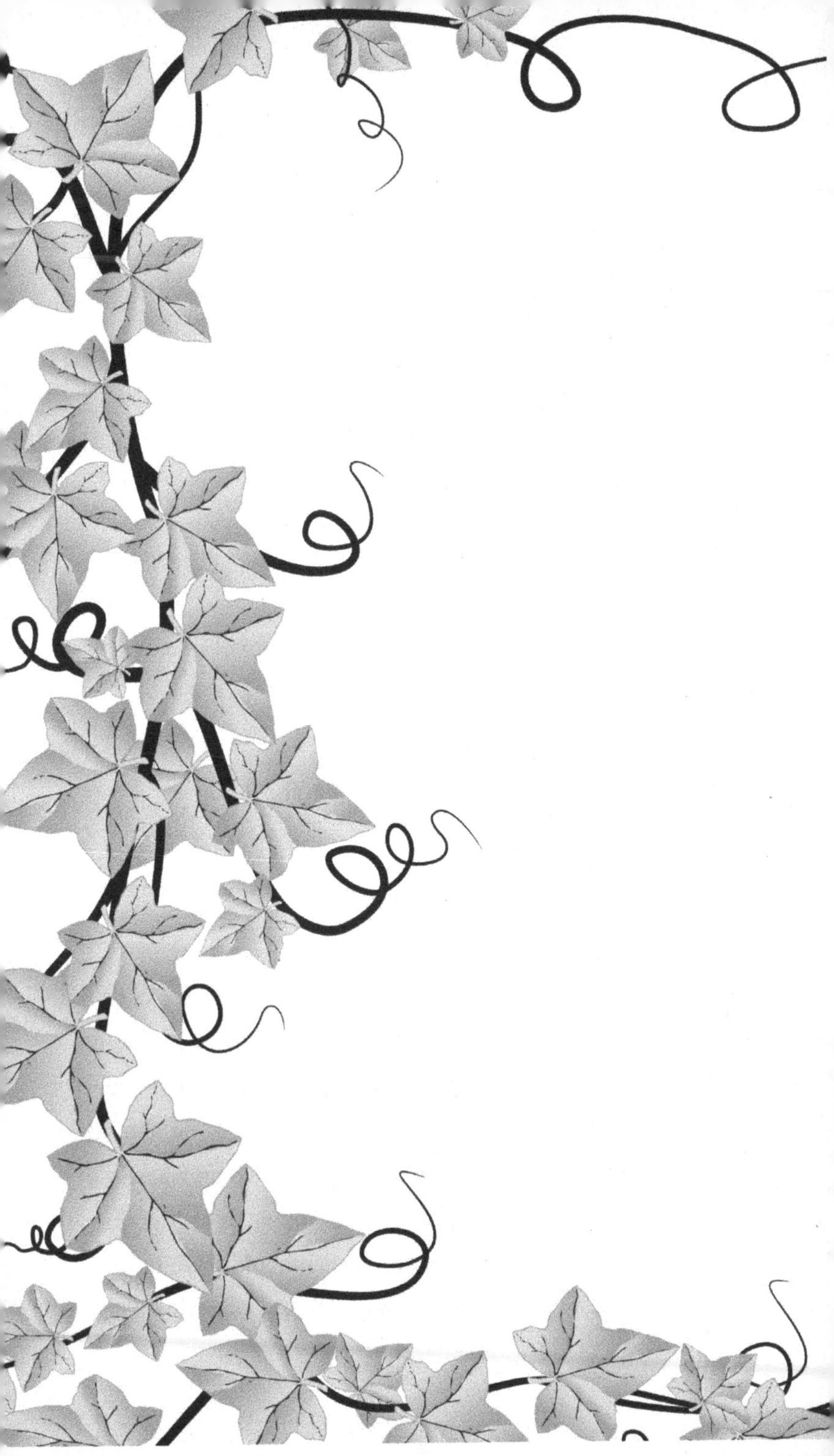

CHAPTER 14:

Thorne

It was hard to stay asleep that night with Aerin so close to me, and I craved to pull him closer. I wanted to forget everything going on and be in the moment with him. I knew my judgment was clouded, I was not going to be able to ignore the fact that Aerin doesn't want to pick up where we left off. I was unable to protect my brother from Morgana because I was with him. I knew that I would have to pick between the two. I could not pretend that everything was okay any longer. I would have to put my feelings for Aerin behind me if I were to protect my brother and it killed me knowing it. I still wanted to hold onto the hope that he would open back up to me. But if it comes to choosing between him and Sylas–I have to protect my brother. Part of me wished it was easier, but the pain reminded me that I was alive. I opened my eyes and kissed Aerin's head before getting up. I moved over to Sylas's bed and shook him gently.

"Sy," I whispered to him. "We need to talk." I watched him rub his eyes as he sat up. I grabbed his books from the bag on the floor next to him.

"Is there anything in these books of yours about breaking curses?"

"There are a few passages, what kind of curse are you looking to break?" I looked him over before answering.

"One that holds the will of the living, and binds them to someone."

"I have not found anything like that in my books."

"Morning," Aerin spoke, walking over to us. He sat next to Sylas on the bed. "If there is nothing we can do from your books, maybe there is a place here with scrolls that can help?" Aerin smiled as he pulled the map of the city from the table next to him. "That might be able to help us." Sylas rolled out of bed and joined me as we walked out of the room. We took our seats in the back corner once more. We ate a platter of fruit that was brought to us by the waitress in silence. I knew that I would have to be returning to the cellar where I was not welcome. They loathed me, I could tell. They had no respect for me either being half man. They still bore the wound of my father's betrayal and I found myself worrying what they would do to me or Sylas if they found out the truth. Better if I keep that between us for now.

The tray was empty, and we made our way down to the cellar where we met with the three elves. They were true to their promise and bowed as we entered the room. Sylas dropped his bag on the floor and smiled. We told the three elves their mission and started going through Sylas's books as well as a stack they brought. Aerin looked over at me and smiled.

"Would you accompany me around the city today?" My heart jumped a few beats, was he finally ready to put the past behind us? Was this his way of asking me on a date? I wanted nothing more but looked over at Sylas and worried that something might happen to him if I was to leave with Aerin. My heart was screaming louder than my brain though.

"I would love to." I walked over to my brother and knelt down beside him. I handed him a leaf and looked at him seriously. "If anything happens and you need me."

"I know, I know, whistle with it. I will be fine, I am among friends here, I can tell. Go have fun with Aerin, and kiss him already." Sylas grinned at me. I felt a knot in my stomach, it was butterflies that I had not felt in forever. I turned to Aerin and we went to walk out of the cellar together.

"If you guys can't find anything, please go to the scroll keeper and ask for any elven scrolls. There has to be something to break the curse," he spoke to them before joining me at the door. We left the cellar not looking back. I took a deep breath before finally breaking the silence.

"Where did you want to go?" I asked Aerin, trying to get inside his head to understand the purpose of this outing. I had to know if was this a date or just work.

"I thought we could start off at the smith, get our blades sharpened, then look into getting new armor and clothing," he responded. They were simple tasks he could have done on his own. Why did he need me to join him?

"Why did you want me to come for some meaningless tasks?" I asked if I was only dragged out to do some menial errands.

"I enjoy your company, is that a crime? Is it so bad to want to be around you?" His questions stabbed through my chest. I did not know how to respond to him. He wanted to be around me, he enjoyed being with me. I looked him up and down, his clothing was torn and smeared with dirt. He did need a new outfit badly.

"I'm sorry," I whispered to him. He took my hand and dragged me into the smiths shop. We met a tall, muscular man who took our weapons to the back room to sharpen them. He told us we had some time to kill and to come back later for them. We were about to leave when Aerin stopped, admiring a dagger. He picked it up and held it to the light seeing if it was straight. The blade had vines along it and the hilt was made from gold and silver.

"How much for the vine dagger?" Aerin called back to the smith.

"500 gold." Aerin put the blade back on the table; it was more than he could afford at the moment. We walked next door and into the armory. I handed them my shoulder guards to polish and straighten while Aerin looked around. He walked over to me holding a pair of arm guards made of leather. He paid the lady 10 silver for them before trying them on. They were a perfect fit, and sexy on him. They both had a spot where he could hold a dagger, no wonder he picked them up with no second thought.

The next store on his list was the clothing shop, and we all needed something from there. I held the door open as Aerin walked through. Two old ladies walked over and greeted us. I was not much for being dolled up and the clothing here was, well let's just say high-end. I knew it was well out of our budget. Aerin, however, decided he wanted to try on the clothing anyway. He grabbed a few outfits before walking to the back corner.

"Thorne, I could use some help here," I walked over to him and folded my arms.

"What do you need help with?"

"I need you to make sure no one looks over here while I try these on," he spoke back to me. I turned my back to him, creating a wall and protecting him from any stray eyes. I grabbed a small mirror and held it up, sneaking a peek for myself. I watched as Aerin removed his shirt and found myself losing the battle of the bulge. I watched as he slid off his pants. He turned his back to me and I could see the muscles in his back. His shoulder blades were pronounced and I found myself angling the mirror, admiring his whole body. His legs shared the same muscular physique. He was not as muscular as I was, but still well in shape. I lost the battle with myself when I caught a glimpse of his perfect, round ass. I wanted to turn around and take him right there in the store. I quickly put the mirror down and tried to think of anything else.

I waited for any cue from Aerin to turn around when he was done. Instead, he put his hands over my eyes and turned me around. He removed them and I was face to face with him. His green eyes looked at me softly, and I could feel my heart fluttering. My breath quickened as our lips were inches apart.

"Well, what do you think?" He asked me while giving me a spin. He had on a crop top that stopped right below his ribcage and showed off his flat stomach. He wore his pants low and they hung on to his hips for dear life. My mind was only thinking about running my fingers along his stomach as I held him by the waist. I moved closer to him and grabbed his chin, pulling his gaze to match mine.

"You look happy, I missed that beautiful smile." Aerin blushed a bit and pulled back his hair, tying it up with a piece of twine he had in his pocket.

"I meant the outfit," he whispered and playfully smacked my chest.

"It looks great on you," I spoke softly, ignoring the thought that was on my mind playing on a loop. I wanted him now more than ever, I wanted his body pressed against mine.

"Thank you, now let's get you something," Aerin spoke, walking away from me and looking through the tunics on the table. He grabbed a green one and a pair of brown pants for me to try on. I started to remove my shirt and felt his fingers against my chest, I froze for a moment with the shirt pulled over my head. My heart was racing. I knew that touch and missed it so damn much.

"When did you get so muscular?" Aerin asked me, quickly taking his hand off my pec. I put on the tunic he picked out and left it untied to show his necklace. The color was so vivid and had golden vines embroidered on it. It reminded me of the clothing we used to wear when we were younger.

"I had to work on my body and get stronger to protect my family," I spoke softly, straightening the tunic. I removed my pants and slipped the new ones on. My face heated up as I felt Aerin's gaze on me when my pants came off. I looked up at him and saw he too was losing the battle of the bulge. He swallowed hard and turned away from me. The pants were a perfect fit. "Well?" I asked, waiting for Aerin to turn back around.

"I have the gift of picking out a great outfit," he spoke, smiling at me. I could not deny that he was right. The clothing not only looked good on me but was an amazing fit.

"Aerin, I can't afford these clothes," I spoke, a tad embarrassed by the lack of money I had. The King supplied Sylas and me with most of our daily needs so he did not pay much for my services.

"It's on me, but let's find something for Sylas, too." I smiled and walked over to the kid's clothing. I found a tunic in his size with stars along the collar. It was deep blue, with different shades that flowed through it to the bottom. I picked it up knowing he would love it, and a matching pair of pants. Aerin was looking at an elvish-style vest and put it on. It had a slit that exposed his naval, It was sliming on him and looked amazing. It had matching golden vines along the collar and the trim towards the bottom. I nodded at him and we walked to one of the women who held out her hand.

"For all that 2000 gold pieces, please." Aerin handed her the money and we left the shop. We returned to the blacksmith and grabbed our weapons. We walked past the front of the tavern and Aerin pulled me inside. We both ordered some hot cider and another for Sylas before going to the cellar.

"Any luck?" I asked them as we entered. Sylas shook his head, looking at the books still.

"Not yet, we might have a hunch but we need to see if they have the scroll." Sylas spoke as he looked up at me, "You look nice." He peeked around me looked at Aerin, and smiled. He grabbed my tunic and pulled me down so he could whisper in my ear. "Did you kiss him yet?" I shook my head and pushed him a little. I handed him his new clothing and he raced to our room to get changed.

"King Aerin, Thorne," one of the elves spoke out. "Sylas is wise for his age. He has answered so many questions and he is right. We have a very strong lead from the book. It seems we can use the light of the elves to cure the capital. But it will take a great deal of power." I looked over at Aerin and worried he would try it on his own. Aerin furrowed his brow, I could tell he was thinking the same. "We need to confer with the scroll to know for sure. Sylas can cast it, he did it here on a small rat. We used the same dark curse she was using and he managed to overpower us and cured it. There did not seem to be any side effects either," he spoke before bowing and leaving the cellar. "We shall return tomorrow for more studying."

"We will go with Sylas to the city scrollkeeper and see if we can find the missing information we need," I spoke as the three elves left the room. I felt hope for the first time since this adventure took off. "So, we can actually do this,"

I let out with a sigh of relief.

"We can, Thorne together we will restore our people to the life they are well owed." He hugged me and my heart fluttered again. "Together, we will have a family again. Bigger than we can imagine. Everything is falling into place, and soon this will all be over." I had no doubt, I believed every word he said. He was right everything is going to fall into place, then maybe I can have back the love I lost.

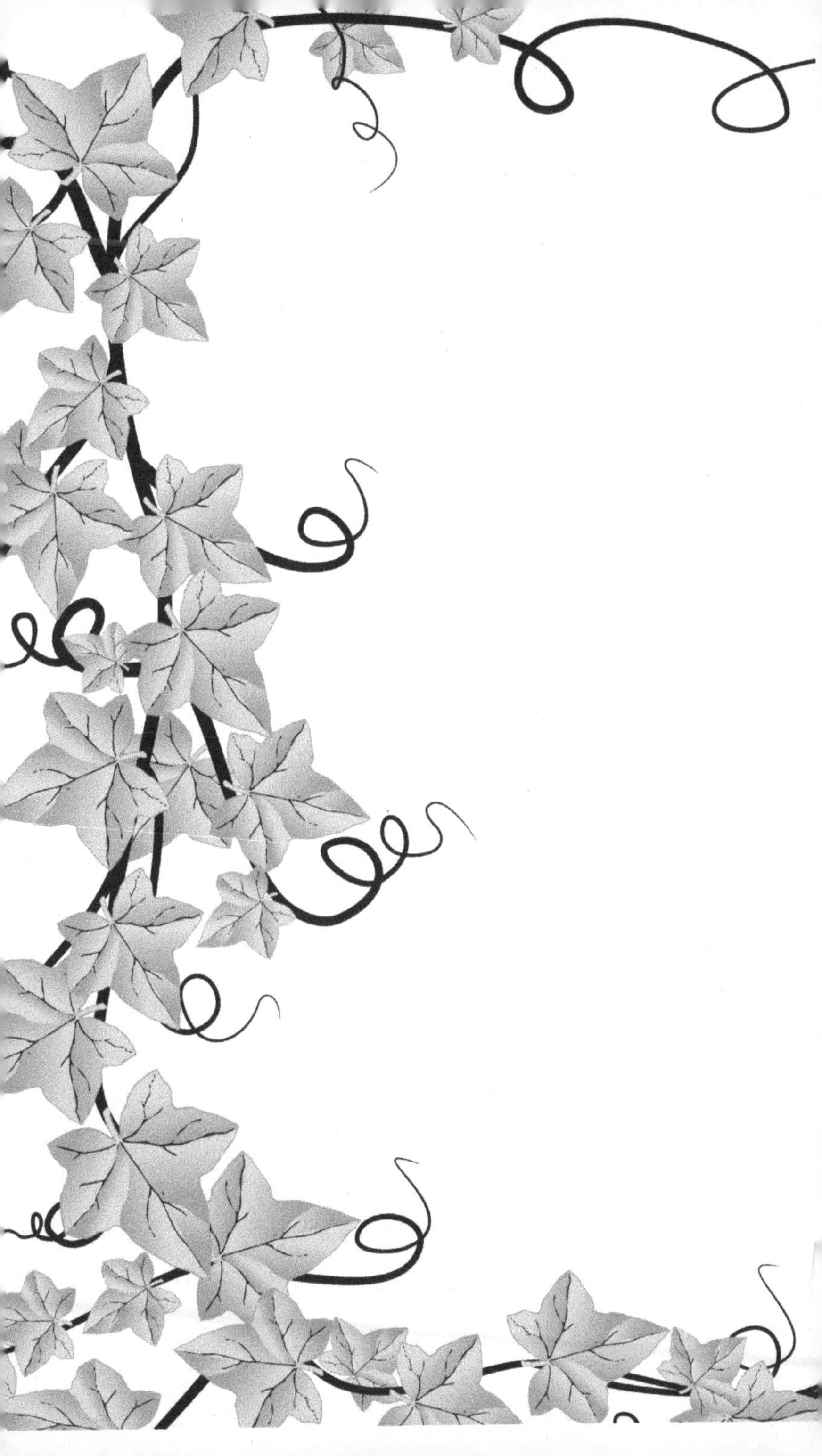

CHAPTER 15:

Aerin

I walked next to Thorne as we followed behind Sylas into the tavern. We walked past the drunks around the bar. I was disgusted by the amount of people that passed out in their own puddles of piss this early in the morning. Thorne knocked on the door before we entered. Sylas was already in his new outfit, and he looked so adorable. The silver stars brightened his blue eyes. "I love the new outfit. Thank you,

Thorne." Thorned stepped aside and looked at Sylas.

"I didn't get you it," Thorne spoke, looking at me. Sylas ran over to me and gave me a hug thanking me. Seeing the smile on his face was worth every cent. Sylas went down to the tavern to place an order for food to be brought to our room, and I plopped on the bed. I patted the spot next to me for Thorne.

"So, we have a plan in action. Sylas looks happy, what about you? Are you happy?" I asked him wanting to hear what was going on in his mind. Thorne turned on the bed and faced me. I noticed the pants I chose cupped him perfectly. He took my hand and looked me in the eyes.

"I… I am content," he spoke back to me. I knew a simple change of clothing would not make him happy. But it still hurt a little hearing that he was only content. I inched closer to him.

"What would make you happy then?" I asked, staring into his eyes. He slid his other hand around my waist and pulled me close to him.

"There is only one thing that would make me happy again." He closed his eyes, and leaned into me. I followed his lead, I let go of any fears and doubts in that moment. I wanted the same thing he did. I hesitated a moment before closing my eyes. One kiss wouldn't kill us, one taste. My mind was cut off when the door slammed open and Sylas came running in.

"The scroll keeper was attacked," he called out. The

townspeople were talking about a purple fog that showed up and covered the tower. No one has seen anyone come in or leave all day." Thorne and I quickly separated, and stood up. Thorne grabbed his sword and I grabbed my daggers then we raced out of the room.

"Stay here Sylas, and lock the door," Thorne called back to him. We sprinted to the tower, when we got there the fog was gone and everything looked normal. The door was not kicked in, and nothing seemed to be broken from the outside. We quietly opened the door and snuck into the tower. I watched Thorne as he circled the room. The tower was one floor with scrolls along the walls. It looked to be about five stories high with ladders along the walls. I circled the other side of the room. We met in the back and found a man who looked like he could be no older than fifty sitting against the desk. His hands were over his eyes as he muttered to himself. I looked at Thorne who ran over to me. The muttering quickly stopped as we kneeled before him. He looked up at us with bloodshot eyes and black veins running through his face.

"Aerin, did you really think that you could get away from me that easily? Dear brother, stop being such a pain and join me. We can have so much fun." The man moved his mouth but we only heard Morgana's voice. I looked over to Thorne and he was ready to behead the man. I shook my head at him, and he connected into my mind.

Get Sylas, let's remove the curse. Thorne understood

and ran outside. I heard him whistle with the leaf and came back standing at the door.

"Morgana, let the man go," I demanded from her, trying to buy time for Sylas to arrive.

"Now why would I do that? What do you want with him?" The man stood up and grabbed me by the neck. "It would be so easy to kill you brother, you're not a fighter like our father." My hair started to ignite as I looked down at the man. His bloodshot eyes started to turn black. I felt my powers being drained from me and I started to gasp for air.

"Thorne." I barely managed to get out as the man was close to snapping my neck like a twig. Thorne charged the man and tackled him to the ground. I fell to the floor gasping for air and Thorne ran over to me. He dropped his sword and held me. I looked up into his eyes and watched as he looked down at me. The man stood back up and walked over to Thorne, he picked him up and tossed him against the stone wall.

"Dear brother, do you really think you can out-power me, your muscles are down now, what is your next move?" She spoke mocking me as I looked at Thorne who had passed out. The man picked me up again by the neck and started to squeeze. The door swung open and Sylas ran in. He saw his brother on the floor and ran to him.

"He is bleeding badly, Aerin," Sylas called over to me. I turned my head through the man's grip.

"Heal him and get out. Forget about me."

"I can't heal this, Aerin, it's too much blood. I haven't mastered it yet." I turned back to the man's black eyes.

"How do I break the spell?" I shouted, gasping still.

"You have to believe that you can, you are stronger than her. Take away her power, and dominate the creature. The only way to break the curse is to have faith in the gods and ask them for help. Show them the light once more of the elvish star" Sylas called out to me while he was pushing down on Thorne's head. Purple fog started to form inside the room and I could no longer see Sylas or Thorne.

"Take him and get out of here Sy. I can't beat her." How could I, I was only a Shadow Hunter. A killer who fights in the night, I am a king with no one to follow me. I was a failure, I ran when my people needed me.

"Yes you can, You are Aerin, son of Elwin, you are king of the elves. You can do this." I felt Sylas tap into my mind. He felt the emotions I was feeling. I felt tears form in my eyes as I was accepting my fate. The only thoughts I let stay in my mind were of Thorne. I closed my eyes and a single tear fell.

"Don't think like that. That is exactly how she wins. She is in your mind, Aerin. You did not run, you survived. You have people who will follow you. I will follow you, my king. You are not just the Shadow Hunter who fights in the night. You are powerful, you are Aerin." I opened my eyes and looked over at Sylas who was crying, feeling what I was. "If you can't do it for yourself do it Thorne. Do it for the man you love, if you don't he will die." I knew he was right, I had to heal him or he would be lost forever. I turned back to the man and looked into his black eyes.

"Morgana, you have no power here!" I shouted and took the man's hand off my neck. The power of Rillifane flowed in my blood now. Sylas was right. I can do this. I closed my eyes and when they opened I saw they were red in the mirror behind the man. "I command you to leave from here, Morgana. You will no longer hold this man prisoner." I felt my body heat up as my hair lit on fire. The man backed away from me, unable to take his eyes off me. I walked to the man and held my hand over his heart. "Let the light back into your life."

"You have not won, Aerin, I will be back. I will take everything from you, then you will join me." The man's eyes returned to blue and he looked at me with fear. I closed my eyes and released the power. The man calmed himself and I ran over to Thorne. I placed my hand over his head and started to heal him.

"Aerin..." Sylas whispered to me pointing behind me. I turned to see the fog appear again and vanish. About 30 zombies appeared in the small room.

"Get Thorne to safety, he will survive but not if you guys stay here. I can't watch you both and fight them." Sylas nodded and started dragging his brother under the desk. The man ran over to them and helped. I pulled out my daggers and charged at them. I danced around the zombies letting my daggers slice into them, I killed about five of them before they cornered me. Outnumbered and I lost my two daggers. I dodged past the zombies that came at me with swords and grabbed Thorne's sword. I spun it around as I whacked two of them on the head, cutting their skulls open. I spun on one foot and kicked another in the chest. I paused for a moment and watched them. I was pinned again, I dodged attacks as they tried to kill me.

The zombies were pushed to the sides and I saw Sylas at the other end of the parted zombies. I nodded and ran to him. I made it behind him and he fell over, that much magic for one small elf is a lot. One of the zombies grabbed my dagger and tossed it at Sylas who was left defenseless. I grabbed him and spun him around. The dagger stuck into my back. I smiled at Sylas.

"Are you okay?" I asked softly. Sylas was hugging me and felt the blood falling from the dagger onto his hand. I reached behind myself and pulled the dagger out, dropping it to the floor. Sylas just shook his head. I stood with him pinned against the wall as more daggers were thrown into my back. I bit back the screams of pain. The fog came back and delivered more zombies. This was it, I did not have the strength to fight them anymore. The cuts and gashes on my back made it hard for me to keep my eyes open. I felt the tip of a sword touch my back as someone banged into me. I turned to see Thorne holding his stomach with his own sword sticking out of him. I could hear Morgana's laugh coming from all the zombies. Thorne fell back into me as I dropped to my knees.

"HIDE!" I demanded of Sylas as my entire body caught fire. Sylas ran for cover. I looked down at Thorne who was holding onto my cheek. "It's going to be okay, Thorne. Keep your eyes open."

"Protect Sylas," he said, coughing up blood. I laid his head down gently and levitated. I let out a blood-curdling scream that echoed through the city. My arms were crossed over my chest then swung down. I let out a shockwave that shook the entire city and probably could be felt in the neighboring ones. I heard Morgana screams each zombie turned to ash and the scrolls caught fire. I floated back down to the ground beside Thorne.

His wound was a mortal wound, and I could not heal it no matter what I did. I picked up Thorne's head and kissed it gently.

"Why would you do that?" I shouted. "I told you not to leave me again," I screamed and again, another shockwave went out from my inner being. I leaned over his body and saw the potion dangling from my neck. I took it off and pulled the sword from Thorne. I held his head up and poured the potion inside his mouth. The wound did not shut. I leaned over and kissed him. "Why couldn't I let you in?" My tears fell and landed on his cheek. My hand was over his wound. "I love you," I whispered. The wound was starting to heal, and I dried my eyes. I took a deep broken breath and picked up Thorne. "Grab his sword, Sy."

I carried Thorne to the tavern and laid him down on the bed. I removed his shirt and cleaned the blood off him. His breathing was soft, but it was there. Sylas sat beside him.

"Is he going to be okay?"

I nodded to him, "He has to be." I looked out the window and the moon was at full peak. I turned back to Sylas. "Why don't you get some sleep, or try to. I will keep an eye on Thorne. Sylas climbed into his bed and rolled away from us.

I crawled next to Thorne and laid my head on his chest. I listened to his heart beating. He would give his life for me. In return, all I did was try to keep him at arm's length. I closed my eyes and a tear hit his bare chest. I felt him run his fingers through my hair.

"Aerin, why are you crying?" I opened my eyes and sat up smiling. I pulled him into a hug. He groaned a bit from the pain. The wound was healed but the pain took longer.

"You're okay," I cried, looking at him. He nodded.

"Thanks to you I'm sure, how did you heal that?"

"Potion from the faeries." I smiled at him. "What were you thinking running in front of that blade?"

"People say you do dumb things when you are in love," he whispered to me. I chuckled with tears still falling from my eyes.

"What if you had died, I can't live without you I nearly destroyed the whole city." I swallowed some air, and he pulled me into him. "I love you, Thorne. You can't just throw your life away."

"I have been waiting for so long to hear you say that." He pulled me into him and kissed me. My tears still fell and I continued to feel the pain of him leaving, but it was not hard to ignore it. It was not hard to let myself enjoy his embrace.

"It will take some time, Thorne, and we will need to start again. We are not picking up where we left off." He nodded in agreement.

"So, I get to make you fall in love with me all over again, sounds fun." He smiled and kissed me again. I laid my head back on his chest and he ran his fingers through my hair till I fell asleep.I listened as his breathing returned to normal, and he stopped moving his hands and fell asleep. I closed my eyes and let myself fall asleep in his arms for the first time again as his new lover.

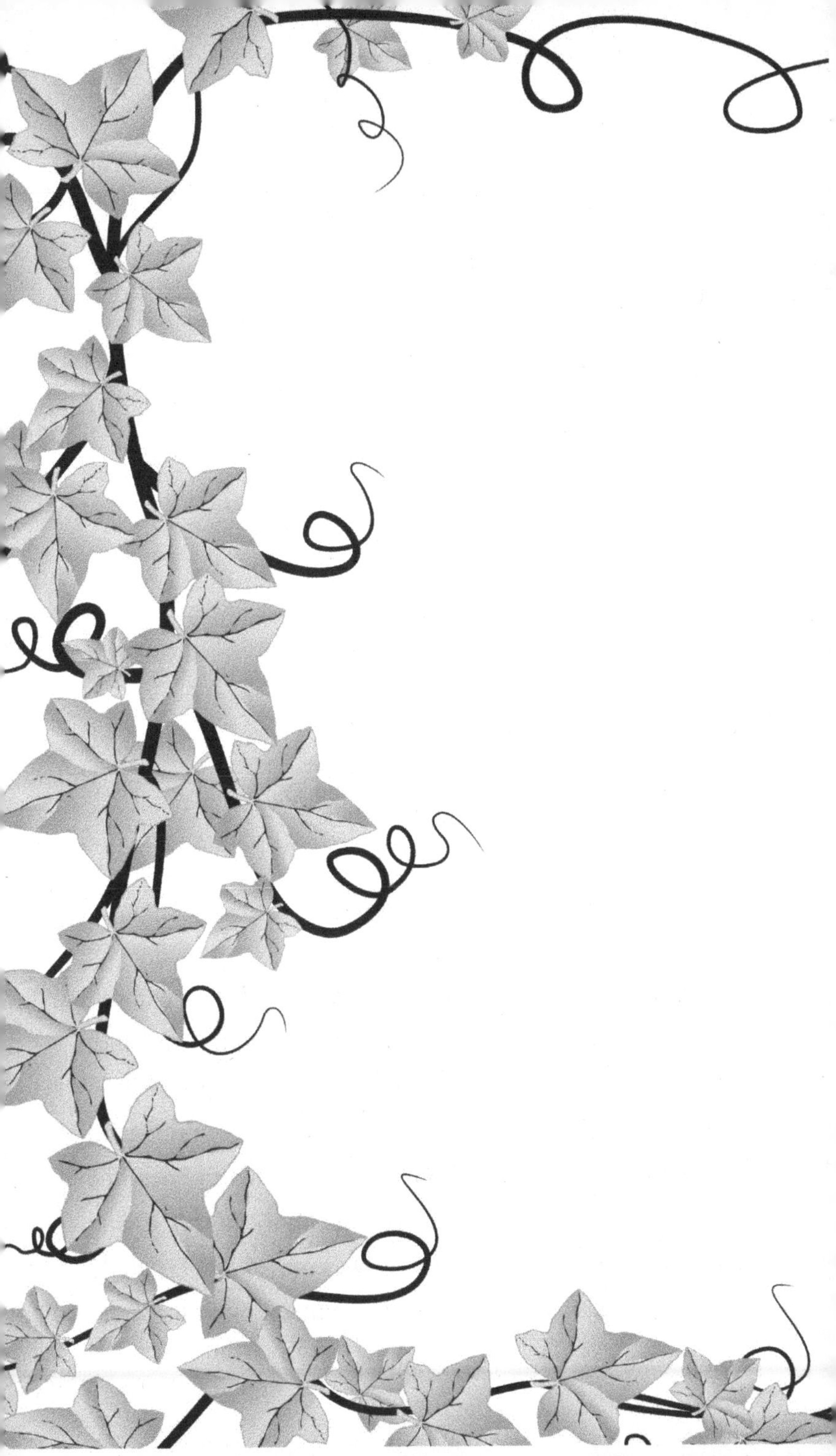

CHAPTER 16:

Thorne

I was getting used to waking up holding Aerin, and enjoyed being smothered by his hair. Things were starting to return to normal for us. Sylas enjoyed seeing how happy I have been over the past few months, and has been working hard on finding the final piece he said we needed to break the curse for good. Until then, we could only hinder it, and weaken its hold on people. Aerin has tapped into his godly powers a number of times at this point and was starting to get stronger. The last fight was easier for him to turn the elves back to our side. The numbers game was starting to finally even out. We had more elves meeting with Sylas every day.

Aerin woke before me and Sylas. I felt him straddle me. His hair tickles my face as he leans over to kiss me awake. I quickly reach up and pull him into me, kissing him back.

"Good morning, my king," I spoke softly, opening my eyes to match his green gaze.

"Morning, my strong man." He called back before leaning in to kiss me again. I enjoyed this morning ritual, of being suffocated by his kiss. I felt alive every time our lips met.

"If you two are going to be having sex at least wait till I leave the room," Sylas spoke half asleep and rubbed his eyes. Aerin grabbed the pillow next to me and tossed it over his shoulder hitting Sylas in the head. Sex is the one thing that has not happened between us. It was far from either of our minds. We wanted to be together, don't get me wrong, in every sense of the word but there was too much going on. Too much on the line to enjoy the pleasure of the flesh.

"Come on, hitting a child while they are still half asleep? Really, Aerin?" Sylas snapped at Aerin.

"Shadow Hunter, in case you forgot," Aerin spoke before returning to kissing me. I had to push him off since today was the day that we returned to the Elvish capital. We agreed to bring the fight to Morgana this time to save the people from any more destruction of their homes. We had a day's ride back to the gates, and we were to be accompanied by the elves. While we had growing numbers I still doubted their ability, being trapped in their minds for so long, could they remember how to fight or use magic? Were they really prepared to die as they told Aerin they were?

Sylas was the first out of bed, he quickly dressed and raced down to the tavern to eat. I stretched before standing up, my morning wood at full attention, and Aerin quickly noticed it. He crawled on the bed to me and gently kissed my abs. His arms wrapped around me as he gently sucked on my hip, leaving a mark. My eyes closed and rolled to the back of my head. I had to fight every urge to not take him right then.

I looked down at him and rested my hand on his chin, picking it up to match my gaze. I leaned over to kiss him before smiling.

"We should be getting ready," I whisper to him before kissing him once more. I wrap my arms around him and pick him up. His legs wrapped around me, and fell gently onto the floor as he stood up. I pushed his hair over his shoulder before kissing his neck. We both dressed and headed down to meet with Sylas.

"What time are we moving out?" Sylas asked, looking at myself and Aerin.

"We are not, you are staying here. Aerin and I are

leaving within the hour." I watched as Sylas's face screamed betrayal, but I did not care. He was safer here than in the battle ground. Plus with him here, I would not need to worry about him and can fight with all my strength. I looked at Sylas and met his frown, "We will be back before you know it." Aerin inhales his food alongside Sylas, before heading to the door.

"Join me for a quick dip in the river, Thorne?" I thought, what the hell, and stood up. It would be nice not to smell the whole duration of the adventure. I followed behind Aerin to the river, admiring his hips that swayed from side to side. He knew I was looking because he was purposely swaying them more than normal. As he got closer to the beach, he removed his shirt and tossed it to the side. I admired his shoulder blades while I picked up my pace. He stretched back pushing his shoulder blades together waiting for me to catch up with him. I let my hands rub against his back as he slowly bent down and removed the rest of his clothing before diving into the water.

This was my domain, I quickly undressed and used my magic to swim up to him. The current formed around me and propelled me to him. I approached behind him, stood up, and placed an arm around his waist. I pulled him back to me with my other hand around his neck. He leaned his head back onto my shoulder as I gently bit down on his neck. Aerin let out a whimper as his eyes rolled back. He was giving in to me, and I knew it. As bad as we both wanted to, we knew that now was not the time. I released his neck and he turned to me draping his arms over my shoulders. I kissed him before he slid his hands down my chest and dipped back into the water. He swam off and sat on a rock, I used my magic and surfed over to him.

He took a deep breath and looked back over at me as I sat next to him.

"Thorne, promise me something," he spoke softly, and I felt the atmosphere change. I felt my heart skip a beat. I could tell by his voice that something was bothering him.

"Depends on what you are asking of me," I spoke, taking his hand in mine. He squeezed it but did not look at me.

"If things turn south today you run. Go back with your brother and take him to safety. Go as far away from Morgana as you can, promise me." He looked at me with tears in his eyes. I could feel the fear of today's mission from him. I squeezed his hand and took a deep breath before answering him.

"I can't promise you that Aerin, I am not leaving without you. We are going in together, and we are leaving together–either in this world or the next. I am not leaving you behind again. I made that mistake once before and I am never doing that again." I felt myself tearing up a bit, I was not going to lose him again. "I will have your back, and you will get out of there with me." Aerin let a single tear fall down his face and rested his head on my shoulder.

****

Aerin and I rode out together shortly after our heart-to-heart at the shore. Aerin nodded and I flagged the elves behind me to follow as I led them to the side. They parted half to the right and half to the left. There were 10 of us, not including me or Aerin. Five on each side hidden in trees and watching as Aerin approached the gates of the capital. My heart began racing a mile per minute and my breaths quickened as he got closer to the gates.

"MORGANA!" Aerin yelled out, his voice echoing through the quiet capital. "Show yourself, face me." I watched closely, waiting for anything to happen. The wind picked up, and clouds started to roll in blocking the sun. I swallowed hard and spun on my heel making my sword into a bow. I was ready, nothing would come close to Aerin as long as I could help it. I drew back my bow and the elves on both sides did the same.

A purple fog formed in front of Aerin, and Morgana appeared. She looked around, and from what I could tell she did not notice us. I wanted to appear in her mind, but was worried if I even attempted she would flee. I was close enough to hear as Morgana started to laugh.

"Brother, have you finally come to your senses? Are you ready to join me and rule by my side?"

"I have come to free my people from your grasp, Morgana," Aerin spoke as he started to glow. His hair was standing up at the sides, and he was ready for any attack she might throw at him. Morgana met this with a deep purple glow of her own. She held a ball of shadows in her hand and threw it at Aerin. It was a direct hit. Aerin flew back a few hundred feet clenching onto his chest. Once he managed to rise he hurled a fireball at her that hit her in the chest, but she did not move. I could tell he was not using all his power, he was waiting for her to summon her army so he could release them. My leg started to shake as I became anxious, waiting to attack.

How long is he going to wait to give the command? I don't want to watch him suffer out there, and I sure as hell don't want him dying on me. Do I make the call myself? I looked around at the small fleet around me. Each watching the fight and waiting for my cue. Purple fog formed behind Aerin and two shadows held his arms out, stopping him from making another fireball. Aerin took a deep breath and breathed out a fire that formed a circle around him and burned the shadows. They were evenly matched. Each attack Morgana threw, Aerin had some kind of answer for. I felt my heart skipping beats as each attack hit him. He was not blocking and was waiting for the right moment to show his cards. My heart ached more and more as each attack hit him. Morgana could see she was getting nowhere.

"Charge," she called out as the capital emptied and charged towards Aerin. However, Aerin did not back down. He held one hand out and started to glow brighter.

"Morgana, let our people go," he demanded as the

elves stopped charging. The rest of the creatures continued to Aerin.

"FIRE," Morgana called out and arrows rained over Aerin, but burned in the thin air making an ash rain.

"LOOSE," I called out and both sides rained arrows at Morgana. I fired along with them and watched as my arrow sliced along her chest, she let out a scream. The elves that were once under Morgana's control were starting to realize what was going on. They made a break for it and raced over to me.

"Don't just stand there, you fools, kill them all," Morgana shouted and the remainder of her army started to charge at us and Aerin. They started killing the elves they thought of as traders, and quickly surrounded Aerin.

I started making my way to him slicing through anyone who stood between us. The elves that made it away from the army were tended to by a handful of our militia. While the ones who could still fight joined me in the charge. I dodged through fireballs, lightning bolts, and water whips making my way to Aerin. Morgana was inching her way closer to him as well. She was hunched over, having lost a great amount of power once the elves turned against her. There was far too much to dodge, and I found myself with cuts and burns. The closer I got to Aerin, the harder it was to move. I felt Morgana's fog tugging at my legs, and squeezing at my lungs.

I watched as the light from Aerin started to dwindle. I could no longer walk from the pain of the attacks but crawled my way to him. I caught him as he gently fell from floating. I brushed his hair back.

"You did it, Aerin, the elves are free." I whistled for Alatar and placed him over her saddle. She took off with him, and I turned to Morgana. I let my bow transform back into a sword and sliced the fog from my legs. The clouds had opened up, and rain formed over me like armor. Morgana let out a blood-curdling screech as she floated over to me. Her hands were around my neck and she started to choke the life out of me. My sword was unable to pierce her. I noticed a bright light from behind her and saw Sylas walking towards us.

"Morgana, you have no power here," He shouted at her. "Put him down and you may get to live." Sylas unfolded his hands and fire spewed from them, tall as pillars. His eyes were completely red, and he was floating like Aerin was. Morgana turned to him and tossed me to the floor. I sat there coughing up blood for a moment before I stood and raced at her. I felt a warmth spray across me as my blade slipped into her stomach.

"You fool, you think something so weak can hurt me?" She spoke, mocking me as she stepped off the sword. The blade was painted black with her blood, but her wound quickly healed. She raised her hand at me, knocking me back hundreds of feet. I looked up from my knees as the fog held my eyes open. A black blade appeared in her hand as she walked closer to Sylas.

"NOOOOOO!" I screamed, unable to protect him. Why did he not stay behind? I found my mind screaming for Aerin's help, but that was all I could do. I watched as the flames vanished, and the battlefield went quiet. The elves cheered thinking they won as Morgana and her army vanished into the night. I ran over to Sylas whose back was to me.

"Sylas!!!" I screamed at him as he turned to look at me with tears flowing freely.

"Thorne, I am so sorry," he spoke softly. As I inched closer I could see Aerin there holding his stomach. His eyes were filled with tears. I dropped down to my knees and took him from Sylas. "Morgana turned to me and went to stab me, but Aerin was so fast. He got between me and the blade moments before it connected with me. Thorne, I'm sorry. I should have stayed behind like you said." I laid Aerin's head down after kissing it. I went to stand and turn to the gates. Sylas grabbed my arm, "Morgana can wait, Aerin can't."

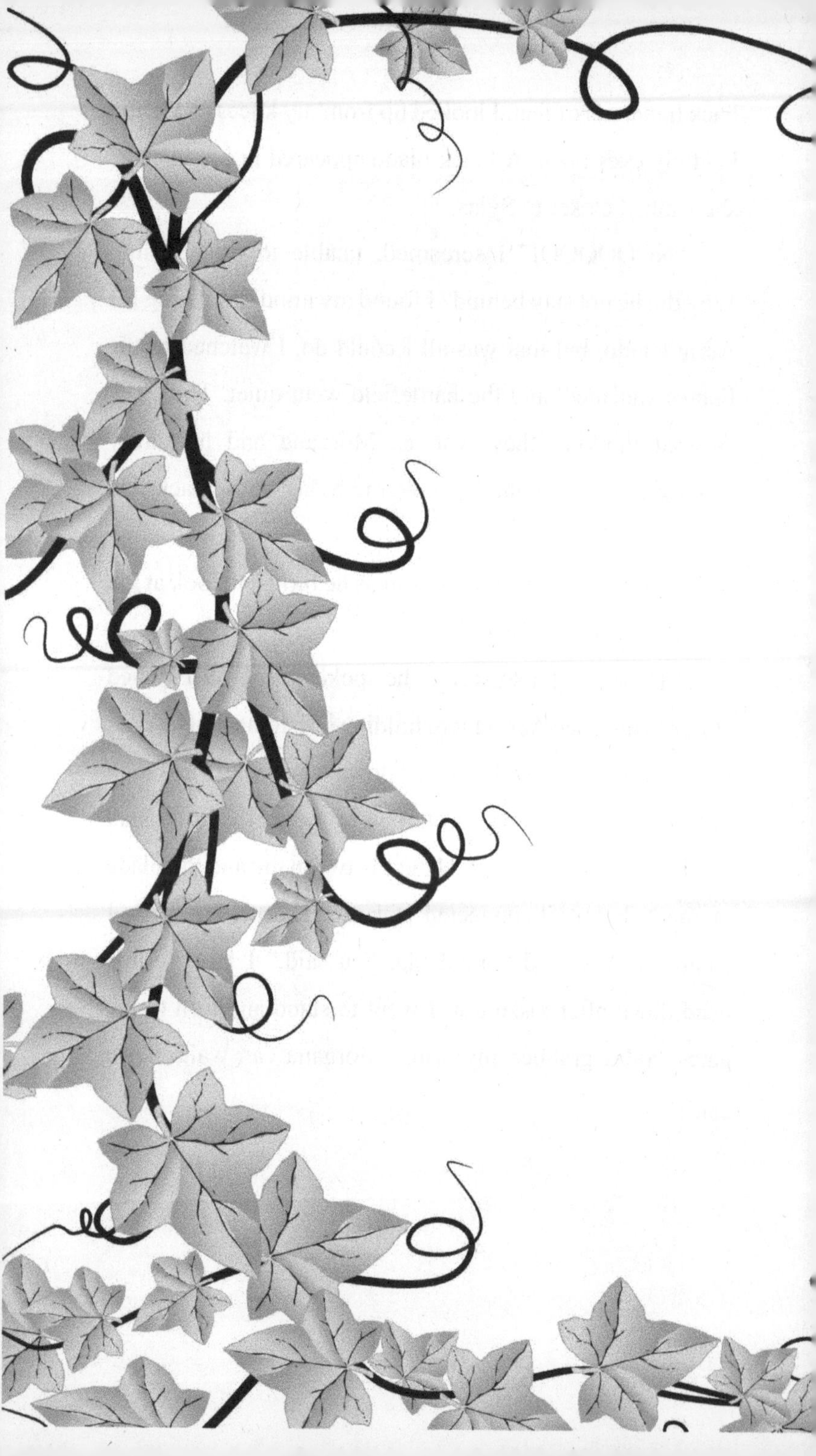

CHAPTER 17:

Thorne

Sylas was right, I turned back and grabbed Aerin, carrying him back to the tavern. His skin was so cold to the touch, his head clammy. I fought back the tears that wanted to fall as I led the small army back to their temporary home. I laid Aerin down on our bed and cleaned the blood from his stomach. Looking down at the wound, I noticed there was black starting to travel in his veins. It needed elvish medicine, but Sylas and I are not healers. Sylas swung the door open and joined next to me. He looked down at the wound and placed a hand on my shoulder.

"It's a shadow blade wound," he whispered to me. We both knew what this wound would do to him. It would darken his soul and make him into a shadow wraith. He would be a servant of Morgana, and forever be lost to us.

"How long, Sy?" I asked, looking up at him. Sylas would not look at me. I turned to him and grabbed his shoulders. "Answer me, Sylas." The amount of pain I was holding back made it hard to speak. My hands started to shake as I looked at Sylas. "HOW LONG?!" I shouted at him. Sylas fell to his knees.

"It should have been me. If I just listened, Aerin would be okay." I realized me yelling at him was not going to solve the issue. I pulled him into a hug, and let a tear roll down my cheek.

"You can't blame yourself." I looked over at Aerin. "He loved you like you were his own brother, Sylas. He would have made the same choice a thousand times over." I took Aerin's hand in one and Sylas's in the other. "We are a family till the very end." I let go of Sylas's hand. "Go see if any of the elves we saved are healers." Sylas nodded and dried his eyes before racing out the door.

I laid my head on Aerin's chest and listened to his heartbeat. It was slow and sounded like it was getting slower. "Aerin, hold on please," I begged him, as my tears covered his top. I squeezed his hand and pulled it to my lips. I needed him to be okay. I know he took the blow for Sylas, and for me. I should have never called for him. This was not Sylas's fault, it was my own. I have never felt more helpless, I needed to do something. I climbed on the bed and picked his head up resting it on my arm. I rocked back and forth, singing to him in elvish. Sylas came back into the room and shook his head. There was not one healer among the elves we saved.

"Find something in your books, Sy," I demanded, pulling Aerin close to my chest. I closed my eyes and remembered Sylas glowing like Aerin did. I looked at him. "Sylas, how were you glowing like that in the battle, what magic did you use?"

"When Aerin fainted, the gift passed from him to me. He no longer has the power of the gods. My books won't help with this." I held his hand and started to cry harder.

"What can we do, Sy?" I asked choking on my words.

"There is nothing we can do but wait. It's up to him, there are stories of people surviving the wound, the curse, but it's not common." I knew he was doing everything he could to bring me hope, but it was not what I wanted. I did not want hope, I wanted Aerin. I leaned over and kissed him gently then laid his head down on the pillows. I covered him with our blanket and took the extra ones in the room as well to cover him. His body was so cold that I had goosebumps just from holding him.

As I laid the final blanket on him, I heard shouts coming from outside. I looked at Sylas who nodded at me and we both ran down the stairs and out of the tavern. The purple fog was forming around the tavern, and everyone ran away. The elves stood beside me holding their new scimitars and bows waiting for my command. Morgana appeared in front of me alone.

"I have come to claim my brother. It should not be much longer before he is ready to join me."

"Over my dead body." I flagged the militia down to lower their weapons. I raised my sword to the sky and lightning struck it. I held it at Morgana firing a bolt at her, she quickly dodged it and I charged her.

"My pleasure," she spoke with a smile as she charged me back. She conjured two scimitars out of the shadows and met my blows with her own. They were not shadow blades, but elvish. I did not know what kind of magic they hid so I had to be on my guard. We were evenly matched as sparks flew from the clashing steel. One of her blades swung up and nicked my chest, slicing through my skin. I did not let her know it hurt, or that I noticed. I pushed off the wall swinging my sword for her stomach, and Morgana pushed her weight onto her back foot, spinning as she swung her scimitars. One slammed into my sword blocking my attack, the other nearly missing my face.

She wheeled on her foot and swung her swords in a circle around her. I dropped to my knees and slid past her blades, stabbing her leg with one of Aerin's daggers. She dropped one of the scimitars and removed the blade then tossed it at me. I deflected the dagger, spinning and jumping off a foot, and my sword transformed into a magic bow. I fired shot after shot before stopping to see if any of them would make a connection. Morgana raised her arm and the fog appeared but the lightning arrows pierced through it from what I could tell. I heard the clashing of them hit something but I could not see through the fog. It was quiet for a moment and I was finally able to catch my breath.

The fog parted and Morgana caught me off guard. The blade was hastily pressed against my neck. She let out blood-curdling laughter as she moved to be in front of me, still holding her blade against me. She used it to lift my head, forcing me to match her gaze.

"I could kill you right now, or," A shadow dagger appeared in her other hand. "I could make you suffer the same fate as Aerin." I swallowed hard and curled my lips. I spit in her face, and she backed up for a moment. She swung her head again looking at me and held her hand out, fog chained me to the wall. "My brother, at least, chose to fall for a fighter but you will still die here." I struggled against the chains binding me, they were draining my magic and I was unable to fight back. I tried to pull myself free, but all that did was send pain shooting down my spine as I was snapped back into the wall. Morgana slowly walked to me smiling. A black fog formed in front of me, and I swallowed even harder. This was the end I knew it.

"You will not lay a finger on him, Sister." The fog

vanished and I saw Aerin standing in front of me. "You have made a great mistake. You have given me the power to truly be the Shadow Hunter." Aerin grabbed my sword off the ground and held it to Morgana's neck. "You will never sleep again, Morgana. Thanks to you I am what nightmares are made of. I will hunt you until the last breath you take." The chains binding me started to loosen enough for me to break free. I fell to the floor and Sylas ran over to heal my minor cuts. My eyes never left Aerin though. His skin was still sun kissed, there were no black veins.

"You are nothing," Morgana called back to him, and she charged him. Her blades swung wildly at Aerin. I watched as he danced around and dipped into the shadows and back out of them. He appeared behind her and shoved her into the wall. She turned back to Aerin frowning. "This is far from over," She screamed and the town was covered in darkness. She vanished but there was no sunlight left. The crops, and wildlife around the area died in an instant as well. Aerin ran over to me and helped me to my feet.

"Are you hurt?" I shook my head, Sylas already healed the minor wounds. I was more worried about him, what was happening?

"Are you... Are you okay?" Aerin smiled at me and nodded.

"I am, but if we are going to defeat her we need a lot more numbers. We need men and the small amount of elves we have. Aerin looked around him. The hundreds of elves bowed to him. Sylas joined them, and I knelt down on one knee.

"We will follow you to the very end, Aerin," I spoke softly. Aerin crouched down and lifted my chin until I stood.

"You kneel before no man, Thorne." He pulled me into a hug. Aerin raised his arms and his eyes went black. He parted the fog that made the land dark. The sun shone down on the land once again. He then turned to the elves. " Together we will defeat Morgana, we will reclaim our land. You will see your family again. Your loyalty to the ways of elves will not be forgotten. Each and every one of you is welcome to join as lords in the new capital." He took my hand. "There will be a new order of men and again, we will all live together in peace." The elves cheered at his promises. He took my hand and turned to the tavern.

"High King Aerin," a voice called from behind us. We stopped and turned back to the voice. "I used to have connections with the elves across the sea. They left before Morgana took over, they wanted to come back home. With your blessing, I will write to them, and see if they will join us in the attack on the capital." Aerin smiled and nodded to the man.

"You have my blessing." The man smiled and kissed Aerin's hand. He ran off and we walked inside the tavern. I sat at the back table and Aerin joined me. I took his hands in my own and squeezed them.

"Don't get me wrong, Aerin, I am glad you're okay, but how?"

"I'm not completely sure. I remember hearing your voice telling me I had to be okay. The next thing I knew I looked out the window and saw you and Morgana fighting." I nodded to him, I was so glad he was okay, yet I felt conflicted. Would the new powers make it easier for Morgana to tempt him? It was like he could read my mind, I watched as his expression changed. "No, Thorne, I will not join her no matter what she tries, clear that thought from your mind. I am here on your side, I always will be." Fuck, that is confirmation that he could clearly read my mind. I smiled, and the barkeep brought us some ale. I chugged the first cup he brought.

"I thought I lost you, Aerin," I said, kissing his hands.

"You almost did."

"What you did for Sylas, I can never thank you enough." I stood up and pulled him out of his chair. "I can start to thank you though." I pulled him into me and kissed him gently. He smiled, looking at me.

"I would do it a thousand times over if I get to kiss you each time." He kissed me again, "But this will have to wait. Right now we need to plan an attack."

"Sylas won't be back for a while still. He went to get a map to help with preparations, I thought maybe we could go upstairs and spend some time together." I proposed, clenching his hand. Aerin smiled and followed my lead up to the bedroom.

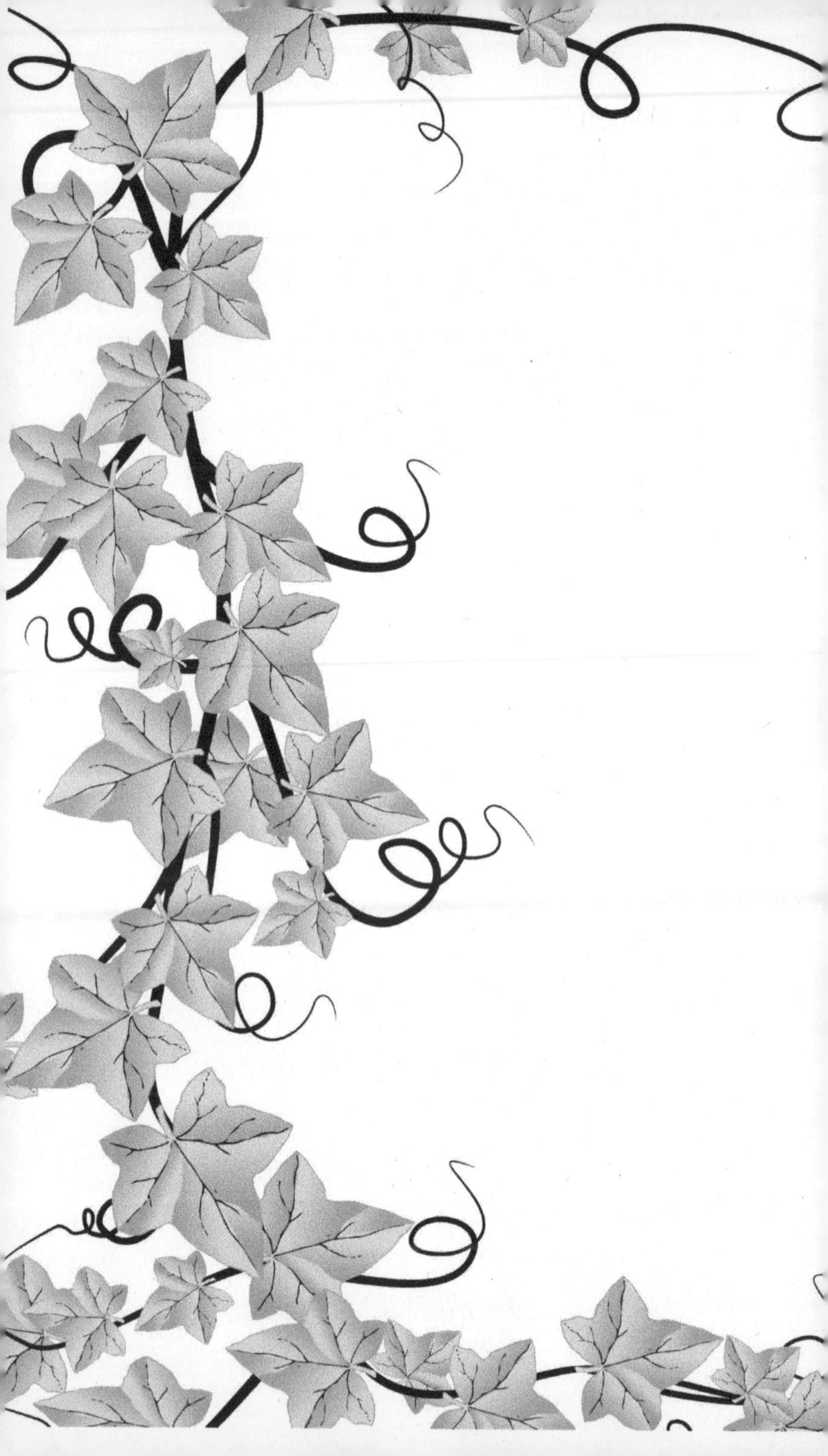

CHAPTER 18:

Aerin

Thorne crashed on the bed ready to fall asleep, and I climbed in next to him. I nuzzled into his chest and sighed. I remembered his scent. I ran my fingers through his hair and leaned up to kiss him. I closed my eyes for a moment and he pulled me into him.

"How long until her next attack?" Thorne broke the silence. I knew he was right, it was only a matter of time before she was to come back. We need to buy time until we hear back from the elves from across the sea. We needed numbers. We also needed men. I looked up into Thorne's eyes.

"If we go to the King, could we gather men to help defend the city?" I asked Thorne, hoping he would have some pull in that department. He nodded.

"I will send word to him at first light," he promised. The King's men would be here within a day's time. We would have forces, and be ready for our attack. Once Sylas got back with the map we could start planning. I looked at Thorne's eyes and shushed my blood-lusting mind. For now, I wanted to be in this moment with him. I was taking in every detail from each freckle on his face to how many times his heart was beating. I inched closer to him, I felt safe in his embrace. It has been so long since I felt this way. I sat up and dragged him onto the roof of the tavern.

"Why are we up here?" Thorne asked as I sat on the floor. He lay down and looked up at the night sky. I laid my head on his chest and pointed up at the stars.

"Look, Thorne, it's the Big Dipper," I whispered to him. He laughed and looked down at me.

"Where? I can't see it," he spoke back. I smiled and felt a tear roll down my face. He remembered the first night we snuck out together. I placed my arm over his neck, pulled him down to me, and kissed him. "I will never forget that night, the stars danced in your eyes, and you were so happy." Thorne started to play with his necklace. "It was exactly three years later you gave me this." I nodded. "Seven hundred years later, and here we are." He reached into his pocket and slid a ring onto my finger. I held it up to the stars looking at it. It was silver and looked like vines, there were moonstones around it tied inside the vines. I could not hide my smile or the emotion I felt.

"It's beautiful," I spoke through the emotion.

"Just like you." He leaned down and kissed me. We both wanted things to be like they once were so badly, and I hoped that once we defeated Morgana we could go back to that peace.

****

Three days have passed and in that time we were greeted by hundreds of the King's men. The tavern was running low on ale, and it was felt among the men. Numerous times Thorne had to step between punches and stop his soldiers from killing each other. Thorne has been distant as well, it was a lot of stress on him having them here. I wanted this fight to be over already. I could not take the stench of the drunks or the amount of time I spent away from Thorne. I barely saw Sylas anymore. He was studying every ounce of elvish magic he could. He was set on joining us on the battlefield this time.

I was sitting in our room staring at the map, with the marks Thorne and I drew for the battle when I heard a pecking at the window. I turned and saw a bluebird pecking at the glass. I opened the window and it landed on the table.

It was holding a letter. I unfolded the parchment and began to read.

We will be there in two days. We are bringing healers and our strongest soldiers. We await your command, High King Aerin.

I looked out the window and saw Thorne walking in front of his troops. He was training them in ways to deal with the shadow fae. It did not matter how much he trained them, I knew that. You can never really be prepared for the dark fae. You never know what kind of magic they are going to use, or what underhanded tricks they will use to mess with someone's head. I had to practice my new magic by myself though. I walked to the mirror in the room and looked deep inside it. I watched as my eyes changed to black and a dark fog formed around me. I thought of Thorne and only of him.

Before I knew it, I was in the archery field. Arrows were fired not knowing I was going to be appearing.

"HOLD," Thorne called out to his men. I managed to use the fog and absorb the arrows. It was far too close for my liking. I should have appeared beside him, not hundreds of feet away from him. I blinked a few times and the fog vanished as my eyes returned to normal. Thorne ran up to me and pulled me in close. "Are you crazy you could have gotten yourself killed," he shouted at me like I was a child. I felt myself brewing with anger. I knew he was only worried and always wore his emotions on his sleeve, but this was ridiculous. I took a deep breath before I handed him the note. "That is great news," he spoke while reading it. I, however, no longer felt the same excitement that I did. I raised my hands, vanishing in the fog.

I reappeared on a rock in the middle of the stream where I stripped and dove into the water. The anger inside me heated the water around me enough that it was steaming. I closed my eyes and sank lower into the water. I knew he meant well, we were both beyond on edge. I calmed my nerves just in time.

"AERIN!" I heard Thorne calling from behind me. He walked over to the rock and sat down. "What's going on?" I pulled myself up onto the rock and sat next to him. I laid my head on his shoulder.

"We are under so much stress. I barely get to see you anymore. You come up to the room barely able to move with exhaustion. Maybe right now..." I started to take off the ring he gave me. "Maybe right now is not the time for us to be trying to make a relationship work." Thorne did not take the ring back, instead, he pulled me into him and kissed me.

"Don't think like that, I am done training for the day, they are ready as they can be. What do you say we spend the rest of the day together?" I dried my eyes and kissed him softly.

"I would really enjoy that." He stood up helping me to my feet. I turned to walk away when he pulled me back into him. He held me, just staring into my eyes. I felt my face flush. My hands rested on his chest as he took breaths in.

"I love you, Aerin, don't ever forget that." My heart melted, and I was basically a puddle of mush at this point. I laid my head onto his chest as his hands traveled down my back, and rested on the top of my ass. "As much as I enjoy the view, Aerin, you might want to get dressed before we head back to the city. I pushed off his chest and gently punched it before dressing. We walked back to the city and he pulled into the smith shop. He told me to turn away from him so I did and admired a scale mail chest plate.

He turned me back around and handed me the two fighting swords I was eyeing up the other day. I spun them in my hands smiling. "My way of saying sorry, Aerin, I will be around more often. I promise." I beamed, holding my fighting blades, and hugged him.

"And I promise to not be such a pain in the ass," I said, kissing him. The smith cleared his throat and we quickly exited the shop.

****

Two days passed and Thorne was true to his word. We spent every moment together; eating, sleeping, and walking the streets. Sylas was dressed and ready to go before Thorne and I were even out of bed. He was excited to meet more elves. We rode out to the coast to greet our new companions. We waited around half a day there, and it was nice. We had a picnic. Sylas packed them with different kinds of fruits and sandwiches. I watched Thorne as he smiled and played with his brother. His brother meant the world to him and I could tell. He would one day make a great father.

"They're here," Sylas called out as he pointed at the ocean. Ten large ships with mermaids on the front sailed towards us. We watched in awe as elves poured off the ships and onto land. They were in formation and walked up to us before stopping. They parted in the middle and a man with brown hair and the bluest eyes walked to us. His cloak was flapping in the wind and showed off his long sword. He stopped and dropped to his knees.

"My King, we have come to serve you in taking back the homeland." I bowed to the man and gestured for him to rise. "I am Lord Thuridan."

"It is an honor to meet you. This is Thorne, my best fighter, and Sylas. One of the smartest elves I know. With you, Lord Thuridan, we have a team Morgana will never see coming. Join us back at Llyn, we have much to discuss before tomorrow." Thuridan nodded and followed us back to the city along with his army of elves.

Back at the tavern, we headed up to our room. Thorne and I walked Thuridan through the plan, and he was immediately on board. "We ride out in one hour." Thuridan nodded and left the room. I turned to Sylas and Thorne and sat on the bed. I let out a sigh of relief. I was starting to see a light at the end of all this. I spent the hour in anything but silence. I wanted to talk to Thorne all I could. I wanted to be inside his mind. The hour went way faster than I would have liked it to. We walked together to the stables and prepared our horses. I watched Thorne closely with tears in my eyes.

He walked over to me and hugged me tight. "Don't do that, it's not goodbye." I laid my head on his chest and closed my eyes. Sylas came over and hugged us both. We both forced a smile on our faces. I picked up Sylas and put him on Alatar, and turned back to Thorne. "You better keep him safe," he spoke, patting Sylas's leg.

"You know I will." Thorne nodded at me.

"And you better be safe too, I will see you at the end of all this. We will meet up together again in the home of our people." I forced a smile on my face, even though my heart was breaking. It was so hard to see him leave. It felt just like the first time, maybe worse. Thorne grabbed me by my waist and pulled me into him. "I love you, I will see you soon." He kissed me and started to cry.

"I love you too." I pulled away from Thorne before any strength I had to do so left my body. Every fiber of my being was telling me to stay with him. I couldn't shake the feeling that something was going to happen to him. I leaped upon to Alatar and rode off, looking back at Thorne until he was out of sight. It felt like my heart was staying there with him, and I was about to lose everything worth living for.

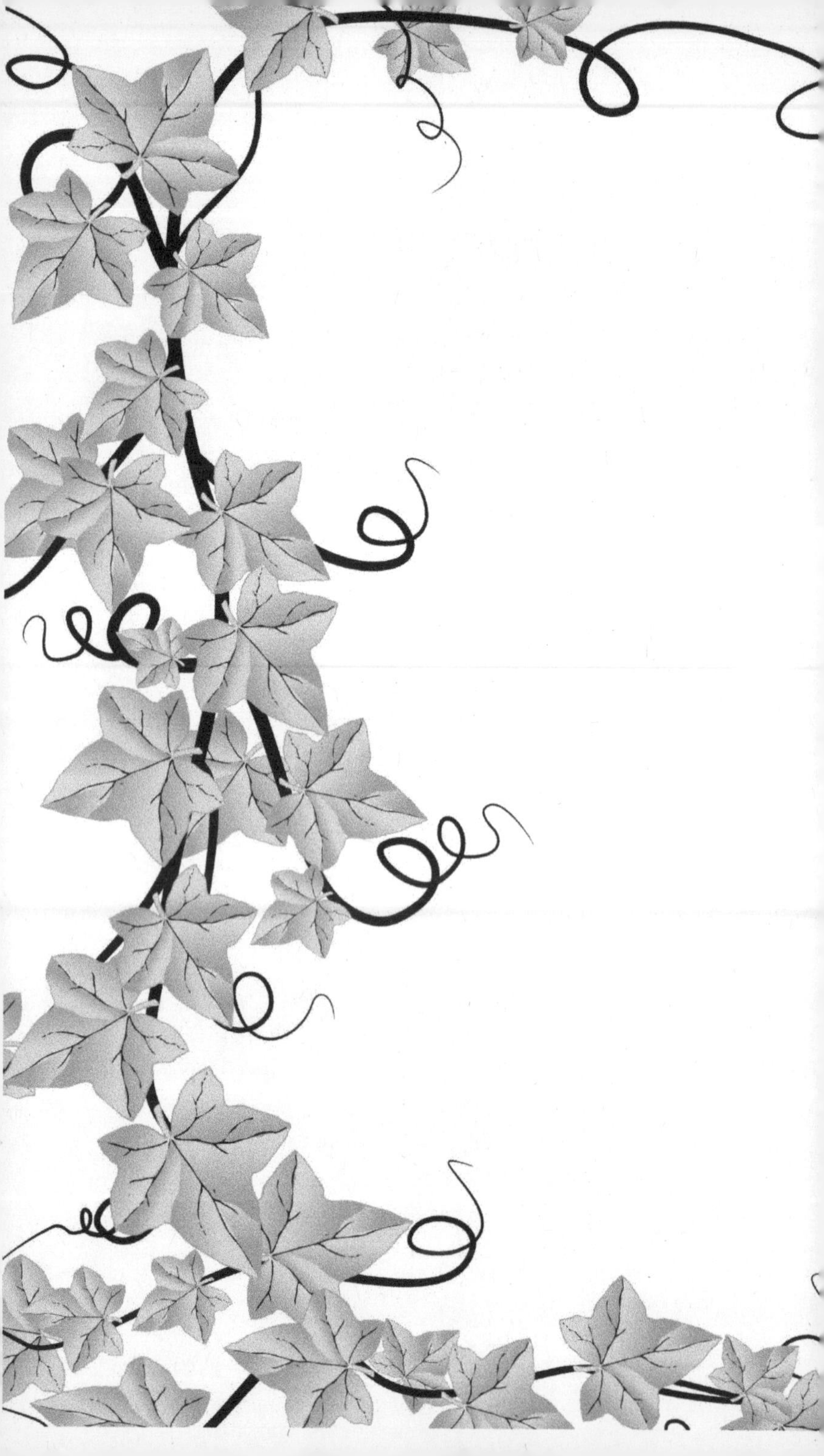

CHAPTER 19:

Aerin

We did not make camp, and the ride seemed to take forever. I watched as the trees we passed were starting to die. Morgana's powers have grown in the few days since our last fight, she must have been draining the powers of the elves that were out of my reach during the rescue. We made it to the back of the capital and waited for the sun to set. As the sky turned to dusk, Sylas looked back at me.

"It's time, I can hear Thorne calling Morgana out." I

nodded to him and my eyes went black once more. The purple fog that was over the city was becoming black as the elves charged into the city. Sylas hopped off Alatar and walked into the city with flames pouring from his hands. We were met by Shadow goblins, but they were an easy defeat for us. Morgana had her attention on Thorne, who was challenging her authority. I let my mind race through the city as Alatar guided herself in the battle. I saw Thorne and his army fighting Morgana and her shadow creations. Thorne was locked in combat with a giant. Where the fuck did she get giants, I thought they were extinct. He needed the elves there faster. I watched as his army was being thrown across the battlefield from one swipe of the giant's club.

I came back to my own body. "Thuridan, bring Sylas to safety, it's worse than we thought." I watched as Thuridan grabbed Sylas and put him behind himself on his horse. The dark fog formed around me and Alatar, and her hair became smoky, and her ebony body turned black. Her eyes were as dark as mine were. She started to gallop at full speed through the city, as we charged I pulled my fighting knives from my back and cut the heads off goblins we rode by.

We made it to the other side of the gate, I found Morgana walking up to Thorne with an evil smirk on her face. I watched as Thorne was hit by one of the giants, and sent flying into a tree. I winced when he fell from it, leaving a dent in the tree. "Noro Lim," I shouted to Alatar, and she took off to Thorne. Morgana disappeared from sight, but I knew exactly where she was going. She came out of the fog in front of Thorne. "Noro Lim, Alatar, Noro Lim," I shouted again. She raised her shadow blade above her head and brought it down with force. I made it just in time and held my fighting knife, blocking the thrust.

Alatar vanished in the fog with Thorne. "Yn him lor nae, Thuridan," I spoke softly to her. I turned to Morgana. "You wanna fight, you fight me," I spoke, twirling my blades. Morgana's smirk vanished as she lunged forward. I pressed my weight onto my toes and just before she hit me, I jumped over her head. I shoved her into the tree with my shoulder. "You die here, Morgana," I spoke to her as a giant started to walk towards us.

"Mai," Morgana shouted, as I turned to see the giant raising his club.

"ELLA, Uskeche viaren elandi." I heard Thuridan call from behind the giant. I watched as arrows rained down on the giants and they fell to the ground. I nearly lost my balance from all the quaking. As they fell to the ground, they turned to fog. I turned back to Morgana but she was gone.

"High King, are you okay?" He called over to me.

"Where are Thorne and Sylas?" I shouted. He looked at me but before he could speak Morgana stabbed him in the back. He fell off his horse and hit a rock. She laughed and it echoed along the battlefield. The elves all turned and saw their leader fall. I teleported over to him,and dropped to my knees. I felt for a pulse but there was none. The elves knelt before me and waited for my command. I could not think of what to do. They needed a commander, Thorne and Sylas needed me as well. I couldn't be in two places at one time. "ELLA, Uskeche viarenelandi," I shouted to them, and they returned to the fight. They laid out all the shadows that stood at the main gate and charged into the city. I followed behind them and watched as the healers started to remove the curse from the inhabitants of the land.

"THORNE... SYLAS..." I called out during the battle. I searched the city the best I could but it was too big for one elf to check.

"High King." I turned to see a battered elf before me. I ran over to him, put his arm around my neck, and led him to a bench. "I am sorry I left them, but I had to come find you." Left who, what the fuck was going on? "In the main hall, Alatar brought Thorne there, I healed him the best I could but Morgana showed up. I am no match for her." I turned to the main hall and saw a thick fog around it. "You can't go in, I barely got out. Sylas helped me, but he is in there fighting her." My heart sank, my family was in there, and no one could get in or out. "The fog drains your magic, and there is some kind of current that burns at your flesh." I did not care about the risks, I was going to save my family one way or another.

I felt my inner rage coming to life as I disappeared into the fog. I was moving faster than the eye could see, and charged through. I did not feel my magic being drained, but I screamed from all the burns. I knew I would almost be unable to match her now, but I would die before she took either of them. I charged through the wall and ended up in the room with them. I did not show myself right away. I saw Sylas holding his own against her. He had some scratches on his face. He stood in front of Thorne's lifeless body.

"You little brat, think you are going to beat me? You think you really stand a chance?" Morgana spoke cockily to him. She tossed balls of shadows at him. Sylas danced around the balls and hurled fireballs back at her.

"You are old, Morgana, you can't keep this up for long," Sylas called back to her. He lowered his hands and let two pillars of flames fly at her. They created a circle of fire around her. They started to move closer to her, cutting off her oxygen. I looked back at Sylas. He was not glowing, this was all him, and this was the power he was capable of. I swallowed hard as Morgana let out a scream. All the stained glass in the room shattered and flew at Sylas. I showed myself, the black fog circled him, and teleported him into my arms. I turned him away from the glass that stabbed me in the back. I grunted from the pain. I looked at Sylas and smiled. I heard Morgana clap her hands and the room was filled with shadow monsters. I pushed Sylas to the side and started to dance around them, taking down as many as I could.

Thorne rose to his feet and joined my back. It was like a hydra, the more we slaughtered the more formed in their place. Thorne and I were quickly surrounded and were eating punches and kicks to the face. I was the first of us to fall. The burns made it hard to raise my arms. The blows were nothing compared to the pain I felt in my chest, listening to the breaking of bones I heard from Thorne. I started to cry, not from the pain but from the broken heart I was already feeling.

I turned my back to the enemies to hold Thorne, he met my gaze. Then the fog vanished from the room. Sylas was glowing a golden hue. The monsters turned to dust and did not reform. I watched as Sylas turned to Morgana. For the first time, she actually looked afraid.

"Your reign of terror ends today," Sylas spoke, but two voices left his mouth. Bright golden lights shone from his eyes and pushed Morgana into the wall. "Your curse is going to be lifted, each person who dwells here is going to be free." He held out his hands and two more lights hit her. I couldn't believe what I was seeing. "You have no power here, Morgana, and you never will again." Sylas crossed his arms charging his powers. When he raised his arms out to his sides a shockwave of golden energy shot out from him. Morgana managed to slip away at the last second, but the air was clean. It was easy to breathe again. I could no longer hear the clashing of steel from outside.

Sylas walked over to me and Thorne and collapsed onto us. I stood up carefully and held onto the wall to leave the main hall. As I walked out, the sun was shining. The battle took all night, and there was not a single cloud in the sky. I watched as the trees started to bloom again, and the grass turned green. The waterfall from the mountain sprung to life and filled the streams in the city once more. There was a rainbow overhead, but it had not rained.

"High King." The same bruised elf ran to me and started to heal me. I stopped him.

"They need it more than I do, hurry." The young elf whistled and a group of healers ran into the main hall. They started healing them, all chanting together. I held the wall and walked back into the room. I sat on the bench in one of the archways and waited for them to finish. They stopped healing Thorne and I walked over to him. I lifted his head and kissed him. His eyes opened up and I smiled looking down at him.

"We have to stop meeting like this," I spoke softly. He raised his hand and wiped some blood off my head and below my eye.

"Why have they not healed you yet?" He questioned me and the healers. They all circled around Sylas. I looked over at them, and Thorne matched my gaze. He stood up and walked over to them. He held out his hands and chanted with the healers. I sat against a column as the room quickly filled with elves and the remaining people from the capital.

"Bren Bhin nha vian savior, su has freed bren town Ath Morgana feer su," I called tothem as they entered. They joined in the circle and placed their hands on the other elves, and the men in front of them started chanting with the elves. A bright light shone through the skylight and landed on him. I heard the chanting stop as Sylas took a deep breath and Thorne fell to the ground holding his brother.

"I'm fine, she couldn't touch me."

"Wutheh Al enial aul salen coraar. Ath amhe lenora. e long e va e, leha thro millentunevaeFae noreshEnt it nha fee ruaulsiin." I spoke to the elves, and they let out a cheer before leaving the room. "Find a home, you are all welcome in my kingdom. Chosen by Amhe Lenora. Stay as long as you like, but know darkness will return one day. And it is us who will stand against her." I repeated in common language for those who remained behind. They followed after the elves. I fell to the ground after the room was clear, and crawled over to Thorne and Sylas.

"He is not wrong, Thorne, Morgana could not hold a candle to him. He is stronger than he lets on. I'm sure he could take us both on." Thorne lowered his hand into the stream that was flowing beside him and healed me. I kissed his hand. "You are the only person I want to heal me." Thorne smiled and pulled me into him with one arm and the other pulled Sylas in.

"We won today and took back our land. We did it as a family." Sylas got up and ran out of the room. "I am going to look around the city. I will be back later." He called out and I heard him gasp as he left the doorway.

"It really is a site to see," I spoke, extending my hand to Thorne who stood up and took it.

"But not nearly as great as the scene I have right here." He placed his arms around me and pulled me into a kiss. We walked to the end of the room that overlooked the water and waterfall, I laid my head on his shoulder and sighed the first sigh of relief in a long time.

"We should go about the city, and see what needs to be worked on, but for right now, King Thorne, I want to be with you."

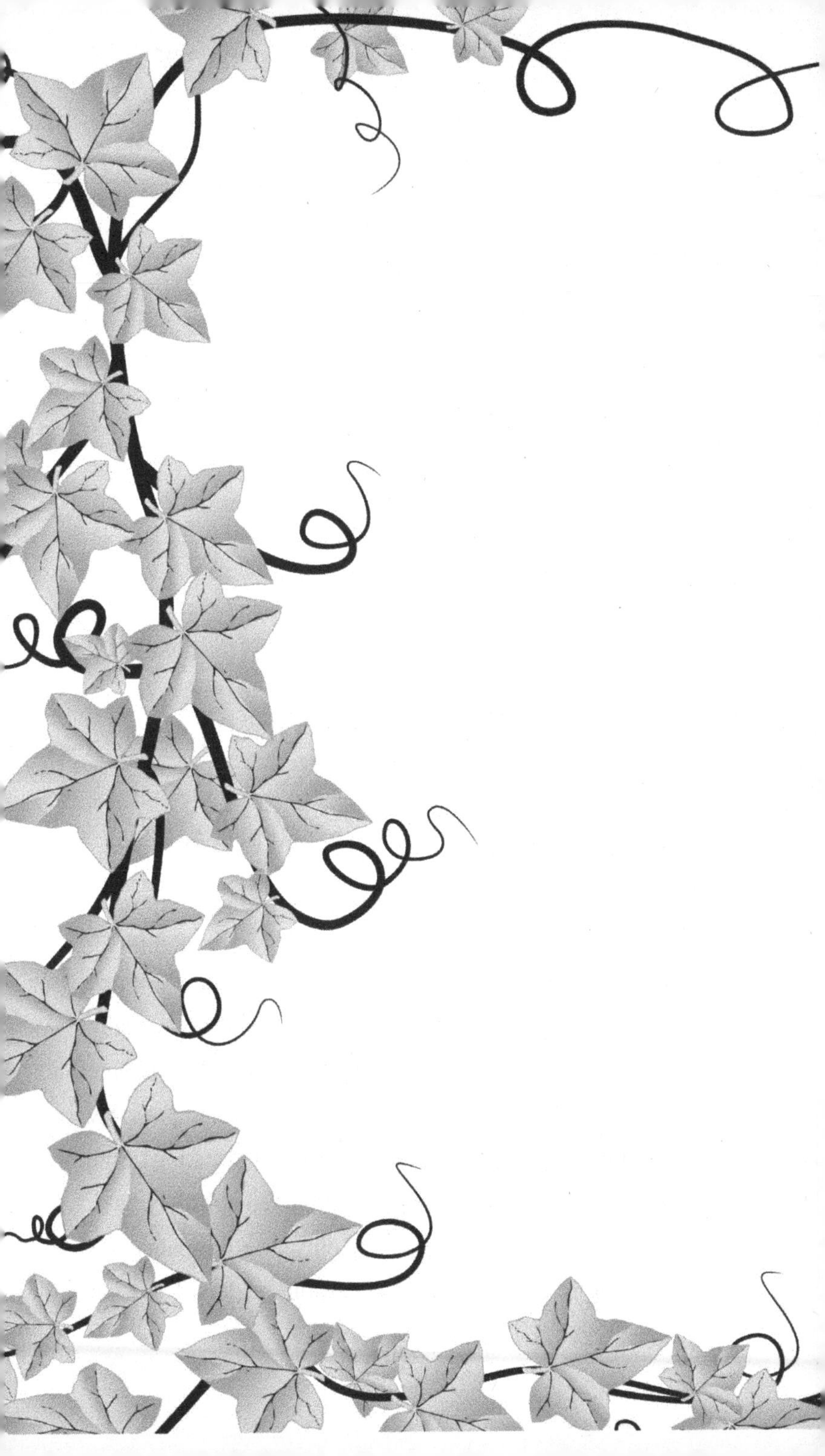

CHAPTER 20:

Thorne

I could not believe that battle was over but looking around, it did not feel like it was the end. Sure it was the close of one chapter, but what have we unleashed? There were too many unknowns with Morgana running free now. The people here still knew it. While they were trying to grow accustomed to their new lives, there was still the sting of the curse. Years for many of them have passed and they have no recollection of it. It has been only one day since we defeated Morgana, and thanks to all the healers, I did not have any pain left. Aerin has been busy as king, trying to make everyone relax and know they are safe. Sylas has spent the past day helping everyone he could in the city. He was playing matchmaker, helping people find their loved ones, and helping others fix up their new or old homes.

I walked down the stairs of the elvish home I lived in with Sylas and Aerin, and to the main hall. Aerin had his hair braided which flowed over his right shoulder. He was reading a book Sylas found in the library about his new powers. He was so buried in it, that he did not look up when I came in. My guess is that he did not hear me. I walked over and took a seat on the bench beside him. He closed the book as I slid my arm around him. The battle was behind us, and it was time for us.

He looked over at me and smiled, his eyes reflected the water from the stream behind us. I took his hand and knelt in front of him.

"Could I steal the King for the day?" I asked bringing his hand up to my lips.

"You can steal your King any day." I stood up and swept him off the bench. He laughed as I ran out of the building holding him. We walked through the village but were blind to everything around us. I put him down and took his hand in my own. We followed the winding paths of the city, stopping to admire some of the statues. We came to the statue of his father, and Aerin stopped. He knelt down in front of it and smiled.

"Do you think he is proud of me?" Aerin asked. I knelt beside him, and put my arm around his shoulders pulling him into me.

"There is no doubt you have made him proud, you took up the crown, and led your people to freedom." I rubbed his shoulder and kissed his cheek. Aerin started praying to the statue before standing back up. He dried his eyes and looked over at me.

"Where to next?" I honestly had no idea, the city was new to us both. To be honest, I did not care as long as I was with Aerin. I took his hand and pulled him along with me. We walked till we came to a small gazebo, and took a seat inside.

"Aerin, I want to talk about it." Aerin looked away from me but nodded. "My father was captured by the King, he had my mother. The King promised her safety if he told him the location of our home." I swallowed hard and took his hands. "He had no idea what the King had planned."

"I don't blame him or you. I think if I was in that situation, I would have done the same to save you, Thorne," Aerin spoke softly. "It just hurts that you never said goodbye. You left, and I spent years thinking you were done with me. That you had forgotten me."

"I know, I spent the same time thinking how much you would hate me. I never lost hope though. I finally got away from my father, but when I went to the woods, there was nothing left but ash. I gave everyone a proper ceremony so they could cross over. I could not tell who was who. Until you showed up at my house, I thought I said goodbye to you."

"I spent years searching the land for you. I never stepped foot into the King's town, I knew it would have been a death sentence." I nodded because at that time he was right. He would have been killed just getting close to the gates.

"It has not been easy for either of us." I looked at him and held back my tears. "My father beat me every day, he blamed me for some reason for my mother's death, for losing our friends. We had nothing left and had to stay with the King and become his servants. It was not until Sylas was born that the beatings slowed down. Without you there to defend me from him, it was worse than ever." I pulled Aerin into me. "I am so glad that we are back together though. I am so glad that the stars aligned and you found me. We have another chance to be together."

"And this time you are not allowed to leave," Aerin spoke sharply at me. He was still dealing with all that hurt. "Is there anything I can do to help ease that pain?"

"The pain will always be there, Thorne, it's not something that will just vanish. I wake up every morning scared to roll over, scared to see if you are going to be there or not." His eyes started to fill with tears once more. I pulled him into a warm embrace and rubbed his back.

"Aerin, I will always be there. I will be by your side till

the very end. I will never make the same mistake. Never." He hugged me back and I kissed his cheek. "I know the pain won't just go away, but I hope it will get easier to deal with." He nodded at me.

"It does get easier to deal with every day that I spend with you." We spent some time there together enjoying the breeze and scent of the blooming flowers. We finally got off the benches after spending an hour there together.

"I could use something to eat, how about you?" I asked him as my stomach started to growl at me. He nodded, I felt like he was thinking the same as me. It did not matter what we did or where we went as long as we did it together. I led Aerin, following my nose to a small place to eat. When we walked in, the place smelt of fresh bread and stew. It reminded me of the old days. Aerin and I sat in the middle of the room and were greeted by an elvish female. She brought us glasses of water. I took his hands in mine on the table and stared into his eyes. His face flushed red.

"Don't just stare at me." I could not help myself though. The sun was shining through the window behind him, and he looked so amazing. His hair was shining and his skin was glowing. I never wanted to forget this moment, I was taking it all in.

"Is it a crime now to admire something so beautiful?" Aerin blushed harder and was saved by the food the lady brought out to us. The bread was warm and soft and it melted in my mouth. I enjoyed the sweetness of it. The stew was golden with vegetables floating in it. I watched as Aerin took a spoonful. "How is it?" He nodded and just stuffed his face full of the stew. I laughed, before joining him. We paid for our meal and shortly left the small diner. We walked for a bit in silence enjoying each other's company before we came across an open meadow. I looked at him and smirked.

"Race you to the other end?" I joked.

"You're on." We both took off, and I looked back at him.

"Come on, Aerin, you're falling behind." It was just like before, he used his powers and caught up to me tackling me to the ground. We lay there together, his head resting on my chest. I brushed his hair gently. "You cheated," I spoke softly. He rolled over to look at me and smiled.

"I love you," he whispered to me, "I think together we can push past our history, and make a new future together."

"I want nothing more than that." He reached into his pocket pulled out a box and handed it to me.

"I saw this earlier this morning, and thought of you." I took the box from him and opened it, inside was a golden ring. It was waves that held a sapphire. I smiled and looked down at him. I held out my hand for him to slip the ring on. I held it up next to his hand and the rings looked great together.

****

We returned to the city capital where Sylas was waiting for

us. He made dinner plans for us that we both knew we better keep or face his wrath. Sylas was standing against the columns with his arms crossed and feet tapping. He looked like a father who was about to discipline his children.

"You are both late. It seems Thorne's horrible timekeeping is rubbing off on you." Aerin smiled at him and bowed.

"Can you ever forgive us, Lord of timekeeping?" Sylas laughed and hugged us both. He led us up the spiral stairs and into a dining room. He had plates all set and a feast laid out for us. The table was way too big for only us three, but it was still nice. We had elvish wine, and a lovely salad before he left to retrieve the main course.

I watched as Sylas and Aerin joked and couldn't help but stare at them. It is like they have known each other their whole lives. I found my guard let down. I knew I no longer had to defend Sylas on my own. Aerin would be there for him if I ever couldn't be. I ate in silence listening to the two of them, as they talked about plans for the city. I nearly choked on a piece of lettuce when Sylas turned to speak to me.

"When are the two of you going to get married?" He asked without a second thought. Aerin's face went as red as the tomatoes on his plate, and I felt like I was not that far behind him. I mean he wasn't completely wrong, it's not like I never thought about it. I used to think about that every day, settling down with Aerin and making him the happiest elf alive. I cleared my throat and looked at the two of them.

"Who said anything about getting married?" I questioned him.

"I am not stupid, or blind, Thorne. I saw the rings."

"They were just gifts, no one is getting married." I saw a slight frown on Aerin's face. "At least not right now." I reached over the table and took his hand. "It's not that I don't want to, it's just not the time–there is too much going on right now." Aerin nodded, and he agreed. I turned back to Sylas and shot him a look.

"Sorry, I just assumed that you two have such a strong history and the rings and all. Can you blame a guy? I see how you two look at each other." He was right, I knew Aerin was the one for me. Sylas knew it, hell, I'm sure every tavern member knew it as well. There is nothing I wanted more than to be with him, and here I finally am. I can now put behind me all fears I had about love, the excuse of protecting Sylas. All of it, I was finally able to open my heart back up. Aerin always brought the best out of me.

We finished eating in silence and helped Sylas clear the table. Aerin and I walked up to our room and crawled into bed together.

"So, are you thinking about marrying me?" Aerin asked, smiling and looking into my eyes. I nodded and told him yes. I wrapped him up and kissed his nose.

"I used to think about it every day before everything happened." I watched as Aerin smiled and closed his eyes. I kissed him and we fell asleep. It was nice and peaceful, it felt meant to be. It felt like we were fated to find each other and rekindle the love we shared.

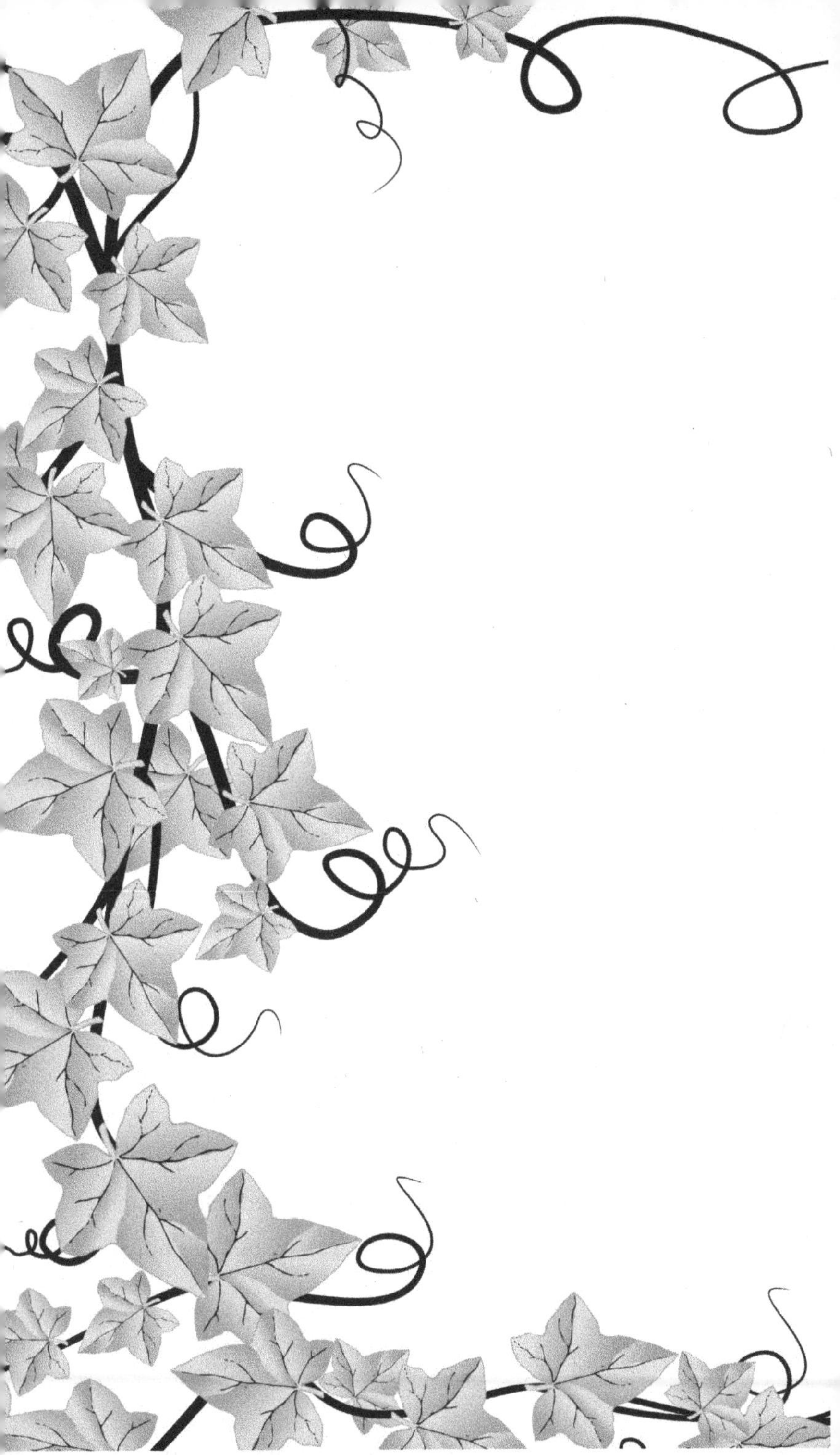

CHAPTER 21:

Aerin

I found myself in a dark castle. I was barely able to see in front of my own face. My hands pressed against the cold concrete as I inched around the building. I heard voices from a distance and made my way to them. As I inched closer I could hear Morgana.

"How could he have that much power? How could I have been so blind." I heard her speaking but was not able to see her.

"Now Morgana, don't fret. You played your part amazingly." A deep manly voice called back to her.

"Played my part, I am weakened. I lost so much power." I could hear the panic in her voice. "All my work and for what? For some child to take it all away."

"Morgana, he had help and you know it. Aerin has defied you every step of the way. And Thorne is too strong-willed for his own good. They care for each other, we can use that. The King is not as guarded now. My men are already on their way. You will have a new kingdom to rule."

"A kingdom of men, what good is that to me?" I had to get closer. I inched my way closer to them and saw Morgana. She was looking down into a scrying bowl. Her hair was now white, and she looked older. Without being able to drain all the elves of their magic, she was losing her youth as well.

"The King will fall and Thorne will be forced to rule over them, it is then we strike." I covered my mouth but not quick enough. The gasp I let out was heard by them both. I backed away hoping they would not see me.

"I want that child, I don't care what happens to Thorne or Aerin. I want his head on a platter. I will kill him for this." I felt my blood starting to boil, I would never let her harm a hair on Sylas's head. "And I know just how to do it." She started laughing. "Thorne will be forced to return to the kingdom, and Sylas will not want to leave. Aerin can't defend everyone at the same time. He will want so badly to be with Thorne. He might even follow him to the kingdom of men. That will leave poor little Sylas all alone." She looked directly at me, and I swallowed hard. I don't even know how I got here. The last thing I remember was lying in bed with Thorne.

"That will not work Morgana, he has already defeated you once before, he can do it again."

"Not after I complete this ritual. I will be even stronger, I will be the ultimate power. There is just one thing I need." She looked over at the man.

"Whatever you need, it's yours." She reached the man and he approached her. She leaned in and kissed him before stabbing him and ripping the blade through his chest. She pulled out his heart and dropped it into a cauldron.

"It was nice having someone so faithful." A green beam shot out of the cauldron, and she laughed harder. "His head will be mine." I will drain every last ounce of magic he has, and make sure he never sees the light of day again. Thorne will never make it to the kingdom. He will die on the path, and my dear brother, he will be alone again." That remark struck me right in the chest. I would be alone. Was this all because of me? Is my being with Thorne going to cost him his life, and the life of Sylas? No, I can protect them both–I will protect them both. "Aerin will be the last after he watches them both die; I will take his heart, his magic, and after he falls–the elves don't stand a chance."

My blood was past the boiling point. I started to run at her, but the whole room became black. I could no longer see anything. I couldn't hear Morgana anymore. Everything was black around me, and the only sound I could hear was my own heartbeat.

****

"Aerin! Aerin," Thorne shouted, shaking me. I opened my eyes and hugged him close. I found myself crying into his chest. The thought of losing him was too much to bear. Even though he was right in front of me, holding me, I could not control myself. The room was filled with black fog, and the bed was shaking. My heart was screaming out for him. He hugged me tighter, lifted my chin, and kissed me. With just one kiss the room cleared and the shaking stopped. My hands however still shook, and I looked into his eyes.

"What happened?" I wanted to tell him, but I didn't even know what happened. I did not know where to start to explain it. Even if I did, I don't think I could stop crying enough to tell him. After a few minutes, I finally settled down enough to breathe normally again. "Was it a nightmare?" I mean I guess you could call it that, but I shook my head no. It felt way too real to only be a nightmare. I was there, I could smell the potion, and I could feel the dampness of the room.

"I think I astrally projected in my sleep." It was new to me, I could never do it when I was awake–I never learned how to do it. That was Thorne's thing. He shook his head, "You did not astral project. You were burning up, and screaming for me."

"It felt so real, Thorne, it couldn't have been a dream." I took a deep breath. "I saw Morgana, I was in some dark building. She is plotting something, she wants revenge badly. She was talking about coming for Sylas."

"Sylas is safe," Thorne spoke as he pointed at his bed. I looked over and Sylas was fast asleep.

"Thorne, it's not over, not by a long shot. Promise you will stay with me no matter what happens." Thorne could tell there was more, but I was not ready or going to talk about it now.

"I promise, Aerin," he whispered, pushing a piece of hair behind my ear. He kissed my cheek and smiled at me. He looked at me, my body was pale and cold to his touch. He wrapped a blanket around me and pulled me into his warm chest. I listened to his heart beating and matched his breaths. He was so warm and so caring just like I remembered from our time together.

"Thorne, I think I was there, it had to have been real." He frowned a bit and kissed me trying to take my mind off it.

"Because you were," Sylas spoke, walking over to us. He placed his hand on my head, and let his gift fill me. He was seeing exactly what I did. His eyes filled with tears. "Your new shadow powers are connected to her, you were there with her. She did not notice you luckily, but you need to control your powers. You might not be as lucky next time." As Sylas spoke, I felt Thorne's arms stiffen around me. I looked at Sylas hoping he would not tell Thorne everything. "At least we know her next move now."

"So, that means she really is after you, Sy?" Thorne asked, still holding onto me. I looked up at him and over to Sylas.

"It doesn't matter if she is, we will find a way to defeat her. I will protect my family at any cost."

"Well on a positive note, I finished the ritual yesterday–the city it protected from any dark fae attacks. They will turn to dust the minute they enter the city," Sylas spoke, trying to lighten the mood of the room. I smiled at him and took his hand.

"You are so gifted for such a young age."

"I am going to go and get some stew, I will meet you guys later." Thorne nodded to him and he left the room. I was still shivering, I felt just as cold as I did in the room with Morgana. Thorne started to rub my arms. He laid me back down and laid over me. I took a deep breath as my troubles left. I found myself turning into a puddle of lust. He was doing this to warm me up, but my body and mind had other ideas.

Thorne knew it too, he knew as he adjusted himself from being poked. He wrapped his arms around me and held me tight.

"Are you still cold?" He asked me.

"Freezing, I think you need to get closer." My legs bent up allowing him to sink into me. He kissed me softly and shook his head.

****

We dressed and made our way out of the main hall and into the city streets. There were people screaming at each other. They were fighting over land and power. Everywhere we looked, people were starting fights among themselves. Thorne stepped between a group of men and elves about to start a civil war.

"We can't live with those stuck-up elves," one of the men shouted.

"If it was not for us, you would all be dead," an elf called back.

I watched as Thorne tried to settle the dispute, but there was no stopping them. This was supposed to be a time of peace, was that too much to ask for? My city was splitting down the middle, and there was nothing I could do. If I stepped in, the men would just accuse me of siding with the elves since I am one of them. I stayed back and watched as Thorne settled the argument. He was a strong leader, and I was so happy he was around to help. The elves went back to their houses and the men followed behind them. He came back to me and took my hand.

"What would I do without my strong handsome right-hand man?" Thorne smiled at me.

"I guess you would use your left." He chuckled and stuck his tongue out at me. I curled my lips at his joke and laid my head on his shoulder as we walked through the town. "I told the men they were not prisoners and could leave whenever they wanted and explain to the King why they have returned before being told. I also told the elves they need to give the men time to adjust, it has been so long since they have been around any kind of fae, that they don't know how to act. They are scared, Aerin." I knew exactly what he meant, I felt that same fear. I knew what Morgana was planning, and that my family was her target. She could strike at any moment and all of this would be lost.

"High King." I stopped and turned to an elf child. I knelt down to him.

"Is everything okay?" I asked, and he handed me a small box. I took the box from him and opened it. It was a bracelet made of different stones. "What is this for?"

"It is for protection, my family has blessed it. We wanted to thank you for saving us, and for bringing us all back together again." I nodded at the boy, and he skipped off. It felt good to finally be the hero and not the thing that nightmares are made of. My heart fluttered a bit. It was something so small, just so heartfelt. I took Thorne's hand and slipped it onto him.

"I can't take that."

"I need you to, please, if it brings protection I want you to wear it. Promise me you will."

He nodded and shook his wrist making sure it would not slip off. We heard a loud crash from down the road and some screams. "HELP," voices called out screaming. Thorne took my hand and we raced down the street to the screams.

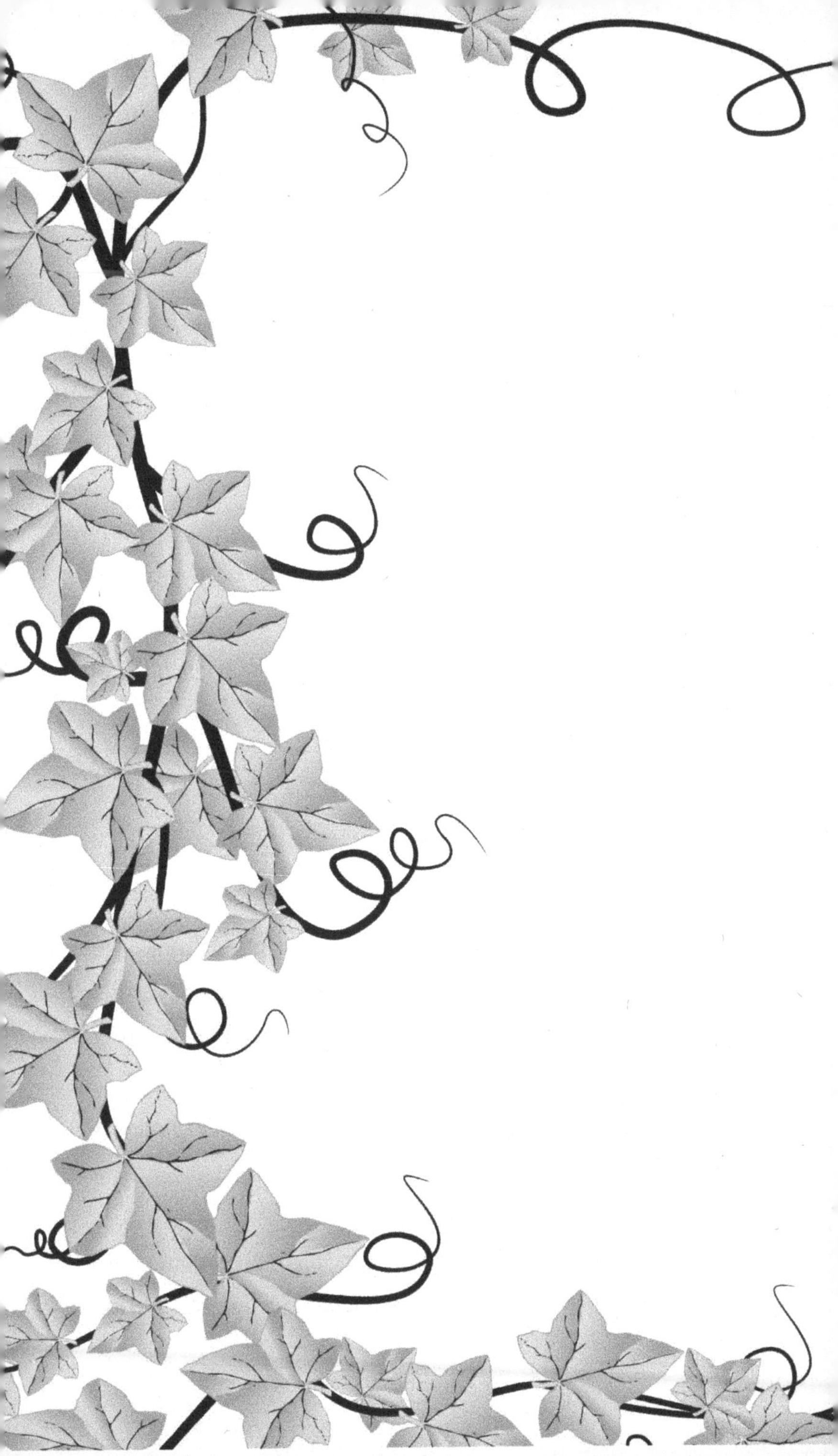

CHAPTER 22:

Thorne

We made it to where the screams were coming from. The library had collapsed. There were pages and scrolls everywhere, and people were crying. I raced to the first person who made eye contact with Aerin and me.

"What happened?" The lady was shaken and had dirt all over her face.

"The building just came down."

"THORNE." I heard a voice crying out from under the rubble. The voice was very airy and sounded hurt. I turned to the rubble and saw Sylas under a pile of debris. Aerin was already there pushing parts of the building off him. I raced over and joined him. We got most of it off him when I noticed a column on him. I knew I could never move that, it would take all of us to get it done. I sat down next to Sylas and took his hand. Aerin was gripping the column and fog appeared around him. Aerin lifted the column on his own and I pulled Sylas out.

"How did you do that?"

"I am not sure, but he is safe now." The healers showed up shortly after we did, and started healing Sylas. I turned back to the rubble and started searching for anyone else.

"Is anyone stuck?" I shouted and listened for anything. Aerin and I helped the remainder of the elves out of the rubble. After making sure there was no one left, I ran over to Sylas.

"What happened?" I asked him, kneeling down.

"The building is old, relax, Thorne it was not an attack." My brother knew me so well. He knew my mind went right to the worst option. "Really Thorne, I am okay. You don't need to worry so much about these things." He stood up and started chanting. He fixed the library back to its original state. It looked way better than it did before and had more sound. "I can handle myself, Thorne, go be with Aerin. He needs you today." I nodded to him and turned around to find Aerin sitting at his father's statue.

"I wish you were here, I could use your guidance. I would give anything to see you again."

I put my hand on his shoulder and he stood up to face me.

"Thanks for saving Sylas again." He kissed me and smiled at me.

"He is not just your brother anymore. It's not just up to you to protect him."

"I know, but old habits die hard." I hugged him again. "I want to be alone with you." I took his hand and pulled him back to our house. I carried him up the stairs and placed him gently onto the bed. I walked over and sat next to him. "Do you remember when we were younger and we used to sneak out late at night? We would meet at the river."

"I would sit by the big oak until you showed up. When you did I would jump into your arms."

"Mhmmm," I groaned as I leaned into him. I have seen him at his lowest points, and he has seen me there too. "Do you think now would be the right time?" He shut me up, pulling me on top of him and kissing me.

"Stop talking, and take me." My hands slid up his shirt removing it and I left his lips. My new target was his neck. I tilted his head and bit down on it. He let out a groan as his hands went up my shirt. His fingers traced over every muscle and sent shivers up my spine. He pushed me over and straddled me. He removed my shirt and smiled as his fingers traced me. He quickly kissed down my chest, and I found my hips bucking up into him. I wanted more, my heart was racing, and it was ready for him. I rested my hands in his hair as he nibbled and kissed my hips.

****

We lay in bed catching our breaths. I found myself in a pool of ecstasy. It was just like I remembered, and even better. We lay under the blanket, Aerin's head on my chest and I played with his hair. I've never felt as good as I did at that moment. It was a feeling that I wanted to have all the time. We lay there in silence, both basking in the moment. It was the first time we climaxed at the same time as well. I could still hear his moans and found myself smiling.

"You were amazing," Aerin panted. "You should pick me up like that more often." I blushed a bit at his statement. I wanted him again. One time was not enough, but I knew everything good has a time and place. I stood up and walked to the window and looked out. The city really was beautiful, and I am glad I got to share it with Aerin. Aerin joined and hugged me from behind, he gently kissed my shoulder. I turned to him and pulled him close to me. Our bodies still warm and pressed together made me want him even more.

I picked him up carried him back to the bed and laid him down. I crawled between his legs and they wrapped around me. I gently thrust up into him and watched as his eyes rolled back. The door flung open and Sylas came in. I fell next to Aerin who hid under the blankets, completely embarrassed.

"Ever hear of knocking, Sy?" I blurted out at him.

"Were you guys?" Sylas started speaking and I shot him a look. He looked around the room and saw our clothing tossed all over it.

"What is so important, Sy?" I asked, searching under the blanket for Aerin's hand. I found it and squeezed.

"I was just wondering if you guys wanted to get lunch? However, I see you both skipped right to dessert." Sylas laughed and left the room. Aerin uncovered his head and looked at me.

"You didn't think to lock the door?" He scolded me. To be fair, that was far from the first thought I had. I looked down at him and smiled.

"I had no time to lock it." We both let out a small chuckle before standing up to get dressed. We walked down the stairs and followed our noses to the dining hall. The elves had prepared a large feast for us. We took our seats and my mouth started to water. There were platters of deer that looked amazingly cooked, a pile of all different steamed vegetables, and desserts laid out as far as the eye could see. Aerin took the lead and started filling his plate with all the food. I found myself smiling and chuckling to myself knowing how much of an appetite we worked up.

I filled my plate with some vegetables and began to try each when one of the elves came in with a letter. He handed it to Aerin who read it, frowning.

"It seems there is more discourse between the men and elves. Sylas managed to keep peace between them, it says he has a way with words. I think one day he will make a great leader." It filled my heart with joy knowing that one day he could see Sylas as king. The only question is of what group? Would he be king of the men or of the elves? I continued to eat with Aerin. "What do you think we should do about the civil disputes? I wanted this land to be a home for all, not only for the elves."

"I would not think about it too much. In time they will get along, plus the soldiers are leaving in the morning to head back home. Things will settle once they are gone." I spoke with a mouth full of food not realizing it. The food was so good, it had to be the best thing I have eaten in years. The desserts all filled my heart with warmth. I dug into the chocolate mousse and a freshly baked cake. For a moment it was like everything was back in order, and I was back home. Enjoying my mother's fine cooking. No matter how much I ate, I could not get enough. I didn't even notice that Aerin stopped eating, or for how long I have been the only one indulging myself. I could not help myself though. In my defense, the food was so well prepared.

Aerin stood up and quickly took a piece of meat to go, and I followed him. The letter really seemed to be bothering him. I wanted him to be happy, I wanted him to feel that moment of peace no matter how long it would last.

"I will take care of it, Aerin. I will send the men home early. I promise you things will go back to normal." He stopped walking and turned to face me.

"What if they don't, what if things don't ever just become peaceful?" He was filled with all different emotions, and for the first time since I can remember, he was showing them all at once.

"You can't dwell on what might be. Focus on what is." I walked to him and pulled him into an embrace. "Let's try and focus on what we do have. Like each other, our family, your kingdom. Everything will work out, trust me." He went onto his toes and kissed me gently.

"How do you always know what to say to help me relax?" I smiled at him and took his hand. We walked to the city garden together and found Sylas roaming around. He was wearing another new outfit he picked out from the local tailor. It was different shades of red. He was practicing his magic, and when we got there he was casting a fire circle, and somehow not killing the local wildlife. He was manipulating the fire itself to not burn him or the plants around him. I was completely shocked by how fast he has been able to master the new powers.

Aerin walked to Sylas and was completely trusting him to not burn him alive. As he got closer the fire did not part, instead I heard Sylas shouting to Aerin to walk through. That he could control it. I still swallowed hard and grabbed his arm preventing him from walking into the flames. Aerin understood and did not walk right through. Instead, he put his arm inside the fire. I watched as it was completely engulfed in flames, but his face showed no sign of pain. He reached back for my hand and pulled me through the fire with him.

As I entered the flames, I could feel their heat, and the temperature rose about 100 degrees. But there was no sign of pain, I looked at my arm still being tugged by Aerin, and saw the flames dancing on it and was in complete awe. I could remember when I was his age, all I wanted was to be gifted like Aerin. My magic, however, was never strong, I could only tap into it when I was a complete ball of emotions about to burst. We walked to Sylas and he downed the flames. He turned to us smiling, awaiting our praise. Aerin jumped right in and was amazed by how fast he learned. We spent the rest of the day in the garden together as a family, Aerin spent most of the time pointing out different flowers what kind of powers they held, and what they could be used for. I lay in the grass with Aerin on my chest and watched the clouds making shapes out of them.

Once the sun started to set we ventured our way back home and settled in for the night. I was afraid to fall asleep. I held Aerin wondering if he would be off on another adventure tonight, unable to control his power and visiting his sister. I fought the sleep that was starting to weigh on me, and just watched as he slept peacefully in my arms.

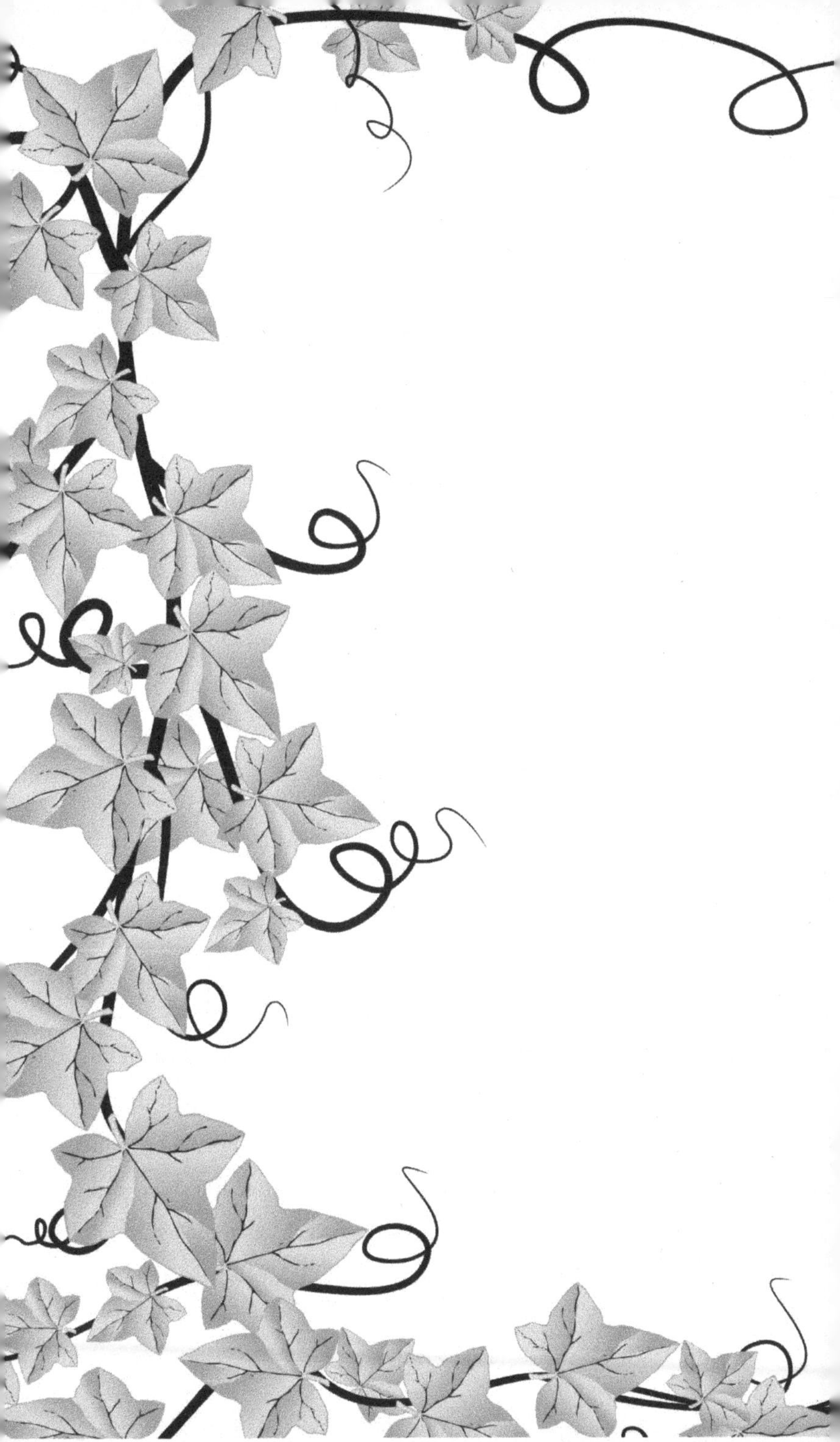

CHAPTER 23:

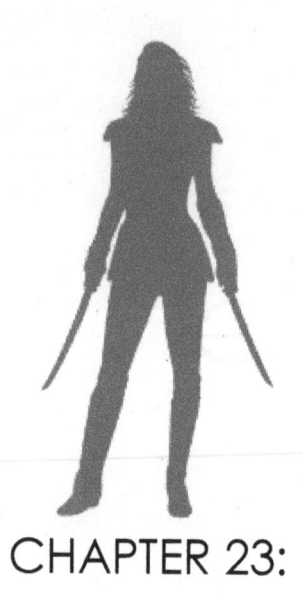

Aerin

I woke up and turned to face Thorne who was already out and about for the day. He was sending the soldiers home, which to be honest was doing my mental health a favor. The King would be protected, and peace could finally start here. I dressed and walked to the window. Looking out I could see Thorne walking back and forth in front of the men, and speaking to them. The men stood proud, as they received the message from him. I saw them salute him before turning and marching off.

I quickly ran to the mirror and fixed my hair. I settled with the usual braid over the shoulder that I have grown accustomed to since being here. As I was wrapping up my braid Thorne walked into the room. He knelt behind me and wrapped me in his arms. I smiled at the warm embrace.

"Are you ready for your city of peace to begin?" I turned and leaned down to kiss him. I was ready to see my dreams in action, but I also had a horrible feeling in the pit of my stomach. Part of me felt that we should have gone with the soldiers to make sure they returned to the king safely. Morgana's threats still haunted me. I had to figure out the truth behind her plans and fast. I had to keep everyone I loved safe, I had to keep my kingdom safe. I tried to hide the doubts from my face and thought I did a pretty good job at it. That was until Thorne grabbed onto my arms, and looked me dead in the face.

"What is troubling you?" Thorne asked me, trying to get into my head. I blocked him out though.

"Morgana, we don't know her next move." It hurt to say, and admit I was scared. Sure he still did not know everything I knew, but he knew enough.

"It does not matter what her plans are, Aerin, we will defeat her. Don't dwindle on that, think about your people, and how amazing this time of peace will be." Thorne was trying his best to help me relax. I could tell he did not like the idea of me being so lost in my own mind, but I couldn't help it. I only just got him back, and she wants to take him away. My hands started to shake as I was thinking about it. Thorne took them in his and gave them a squeeze before gently holding them against his heart. I could feel his heart racing. It snapped me back to reality, and he was right. I had to focus on right now not on what might happen.

He stood up, walked over to the shelf on the wall, and grabbed the elven crown I had not put on yet. He walked back to me, placed it on my head, and grinned. I looked in the mirror at the golden crown on my head. The vine wire looked amazing, and the color of the crown looked good on my hair, and made it look brighter–I loved it. The crown had no magical powers to it and I was a little disappointed to learn this, but with it on my head, it all finally clicked in. I am king of the elves, it is my job to keep them all safe.

I stood proud in the mirror swallowing the task that would be at hand. I turned to Thorne and took his hand leading him out of the room. We met up with Sylas on the stairs and went down into the city together. Thorne was right that the city was more peaceful. I saw men helping the elves, with building houses, and a group of kids playing in the clearings. We passed a bard telling a story of his adventures across the sea and children sitting on the ground listening to him. Sylas stayed there to hear the stories while Thorne and I continued on our way. We walked through the city enjoying the quietness of the city. It was the first time we noticed the large tree in the middle of the city. It had yellow petals on it with beautiful golden leaves.

We sat down on the ledge next to it and leaned against the tree. I pulled Thorne close to me and wrapped my arms around him. I was so happy to be with him. It was the life I always wanted. I had him, and the whole of elven kind again. Things were finally starting to look up for me. This was a much-needed change. I looked up at Thorne, who had a cocky smile glued to his face, and smiled back at him. Could this really be my life? Do we just forget everything else, the King's mission, forget the realm of men and just be here? I knew it was never going to happen, but it was nice to dream. I lowered my head onto his shoulders and took a deep breath in.

****

When I exhaled through, I was in the darkroom again. I could see Morgana pacing back and forth.

"Where are they? It should have been done already." She continued to pace back and forth. She was growing anxious. She walked over to the table and swung her arm over it breaking various glasses and vials. The ones that did not break shattered once they hit the floor. She paced a little more, but quickly turned her sight onto the table and flipped it over. Once there was nothing left for her to attack she created a ball of dark magic and flung it in my direction. I panicked a bit and flung my hand up and my dark fog absorbed the magic. I quickly noticed what I had just done and looked up at her.

"Aerin, are you spying on me?" I could feel my heart starting to race. Fuck! Wake me up, Thorne, bring me back. "I know you're there." She spoke walking towards me. My heart was about to beat out of my chest. Don't tell me Thorne fell asleep now. I need him to wake me the fuck up before she kills me. My magic works differently in this form. I put my hand down by my side and realized I had no weapons either. I was at a loss here. I backed up till I felt the wall behind me. This way at least she couldn't show up behind me. I felt my breath becoming fainter as she inched closer to me. My hands were shaking, where was Thorne?

"Your Majesty," a small gremlin voice called out to Morgana. Luckily for me, she stopped dead in her tracks and turned around.

"The King's men?" She stared back at the goblin.

"Some yes," I swallowed hard while listening in. "We cut them off, but they were strong, Your Majesty. They killed many of my troops and we had to retreat." I let out a quiet sigh of relief, most of them made it back to the King. I knew we should have gone with them, but what good would we have been for a surprise attack?

Morgana's anger knew no bounds as she walked to the goblin and started to strangle him. "What do you mean some of them, I wanted all of them." As she screamed at him her hair stood on end. "It doesn't matter," she started laughing and released his neck. "The King will soon meet his end, and I will take my place on his throne." I felt a hit in my chest. I wanted to forget about her plans, but every time I start something new it reminds me of them. The men are not my issue, it is my job to protect the elves. But Thorne, if anything happens to the King, he will return to the realm of the men. I can't lose him. I walked to Morgana and the goblin, and as I did I noticed a small blade on the floor. I grabbed it and quietly made my way behind her. I swallowed hard and raised my arm. I swung it down and felt her blood on my hands.

****

"Aerin," Thorne called out as he shook me. I opened my eyes and looked at my hands. They were still covered in her blood, and they were shaking really hard. Thorne grabbed my wrists, avoiding the blood, and inspecting my hands to check for cuts. He dipped my hands in the river nearby and pulled them out, once he saw I was okay he hugged me. "What happened?" He asked, holding me close.

"Morgana, she attacked the troops, she is planning on attacking the King." I paused for a moment to see how the news would register for him. There was no emotional change on his face. "Morgana is intending on taking the throne of men." I felt his hands grasp onto my shoulders and work their way down to my biceps.

"Are you okay?" I nodded and he hugged me. "If she is after the King we should warn him." I agreed with him, but I was not ready to face Morgana again. Just the thought of her name made me start to shake, I knew there was no way I could face her right now. I must have let my guard down because before I knew it Thorne was inside my mind. "You can face her, you are not alone anymore." He placed his hand under my chin forcing me to look up at him. I swallowed hard but nodded.

"But we only just found a new happiness, Thorne, I wanted to enjoy it a little more with you before we had to go on our next adventure."

"Every day with you is an adventure, whether we are here living happily or on the battlefield. Every adventure with you, I would not trade for the world." He took a deep breath. "I love you, Aerin, nothing will be done alone anymore–we are in this together for better or worse." I nodded to him and he hugged me tightly.

"What about Sylas, are we going to bring him with us?" Thorne shook his head.

"Someone has to be here to look after the city and keep everyone in line. Without some kind of ruler, the city will fall into chaos." I looked at him worried. I knew Morgana wanted us to separate, if we grouped around the king she would turn back and go for Sylas.

"Is that really a good idea?" I asked him, thinking about the worst that could happen with us away from the city.

"With your power of the shadows and my strength, we can take her down. This time it will be different. We will defeat her, and Sylas will be safe here inside his barrier. If he leaves, the barrier will fall." To be honest I did forget about that small detail. Even if Sylas wanted to come with us he couldn't, our only option now is to separate and be fast about it.

"Okay, but we should be swift about it, I don't want to be gone from here too long. Promise me we will return together."

Thorne took my hand in his and looked me in the eyes. "I promise we will return together, and we will have that happy ending." I really liked the sound of that; getting to come back here and be with him forever, grow old together, and raise Sylas in a time of peace. What better life could I ask for? I squeezed his hands together inside mine.

"Thank you," I whispered to him.

****

That night Thorne and I sat Sylas down and told him everything that was going on. I told him about the threat from Morgana.

"But you guys need me to defeat her, Aerin said himself." He was twisting my words against me. I hated it, but deep down I knew he was right.

"You are staying here, Sy, there is no fighting it this time. The barrier needs to stay up, we can't fight a war on two fronts." Thorne was kind of hot, putting his foot down like that. I can't lie, I was kind of turned on.

"Plus, Sy, this is a good test to see if you will be king

one day–the elves will need a ruler when I get old and gray." Sylas laughed, I could tell he was picturing me with gray hair, and the thought of it honestly scared me. Gray hair, as if I will get that old.

"Oh, so you already want me to be your successor?" He was getting a bit too cocky, but I knew if I wanted him to stay behind I would have to play along. I took a deep breath.

"I do–Lord knows Thorne would kill someone or blow a gasket the first second something went wrong."

"That is true, we both know how he can be. Fine, I will stay behind, but you both better come back." Thorne and I looked at each other and smiled.

"We will both be back, I will keep your brother out of too much trouble."

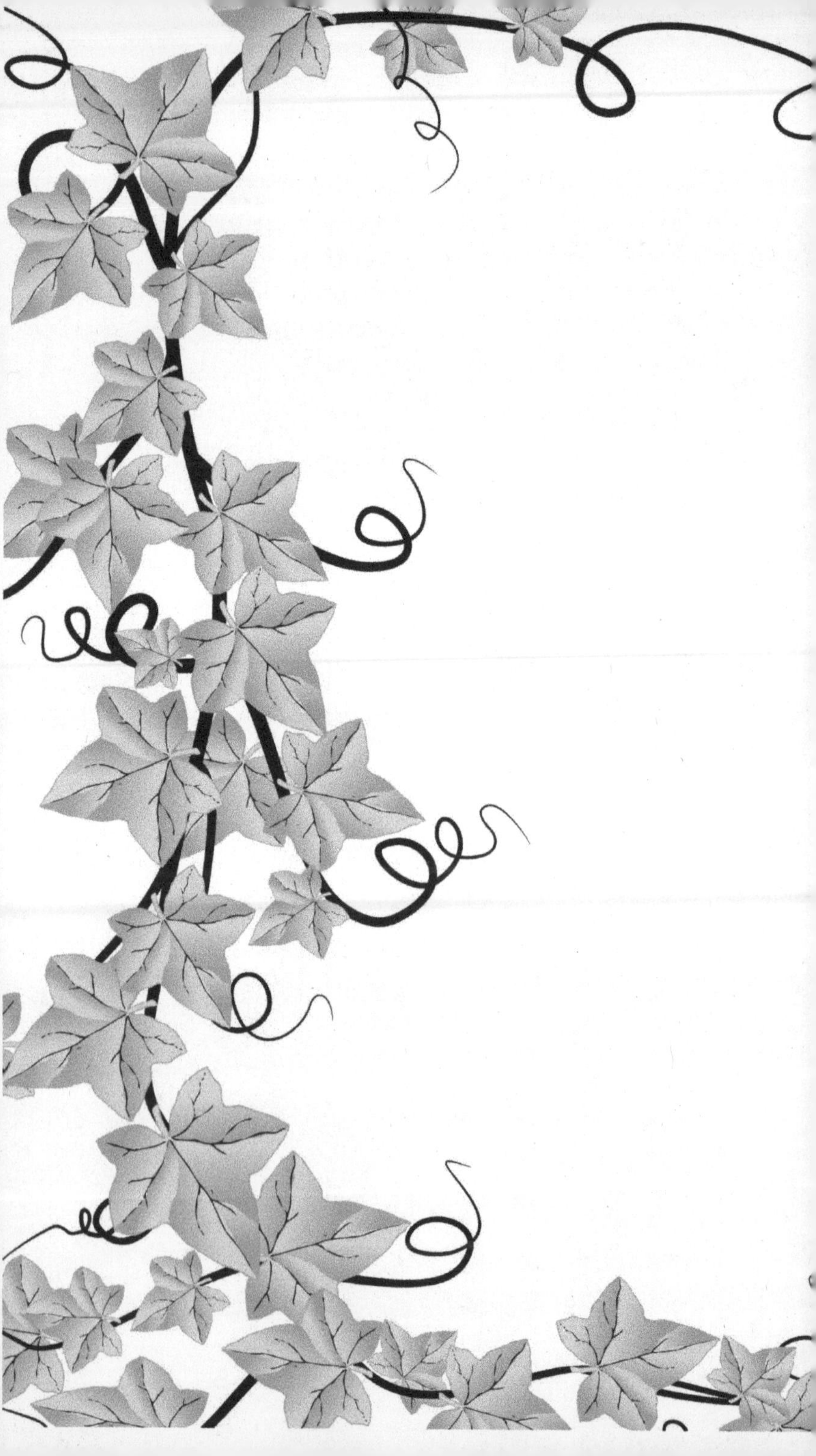

CHAPTER 24:

Thorne

I woke up the next morning before Aerin. His hair was pressed behind him perfectly, I never understood how he always looked so good even after a long night's rest. He had a smile on his face, and I was hoping that he was dreaming of me. I leaned over and gently pressed my lips against his. He blinked awake before wrapping his arms around my neck. I leaned in and kissed his neck a few times, squeezing in a few nibbles and smiling slightly at the erection he had growing under me. Though now was not the time, it was still nice to know that his body longed for me just as much as mine longed for him.

We both grabbed our clothing and snuck down the stairs and into the river that was close by. I couldn't wait for the dip, I did not know how long it would be before I had that chance again. Another bonus to this dip was getting to see Aerin naked even longer. I watched as he walked to the river, admiring his curves, and plump rear. I ran up to him and grabbed a handful of his ass, he turned to me.

"If you are going to keep on teasing me, you better be ready to act on it," Aerin threatened, but I was more than ready to fulfill my end of the bargain. I swept him off his feet and carried him the rest of the way into the water. I held him as he let his head dip back into the water. His hair flowed so naturally. Aerin's eyes were shining bright, and I was no longer able to control myself. I balanced him on my arm. My free hand traveled up his thigh. "Take me, Thorne" Aerin let a slight beg slip, and who was I to deny him? After all, he is my king.

We made love there in the river, and I'm sure half the city knew because Aerin was having a hard time keeping his moans quiet. Our legs shook at the same time, and our hearts matched a face pace as we both reached our release. We cleaned quickly as we lost a lot of time during our little escapade, and needed to gather willing elves and be on our way. After we dried off and dressed, we made our way with my arm around Aerin's waist to the great hall.

Sylas was there waiting for us, he had on prince robes that Aerin had laid out and had custom-made. "Aerin, Thorne, are you guys ready to call the meeting?" I looked over to Aerin to see his answer and nodded to Sylas. I took a deep breath as he held my hand walking up the stairs to the podium. He nodded again to Sylas who waved his hand, and a gust of wind blew from behind him. The bells in the room started to chime. It was a magical sound, the bells were not loud but rather elegant.

After a short wait, the room was starting to fill up with all the elves choosing to stay behind and ones set to follow Aerin. This was not going to be an easy task for him. He had to ask the elves to give into mercy and forget the revenge of the past lost loved ones to go protect the man that tried to kill off their kind.

Aerin stood up from the throne that was carved out of a tree and walked to the edge of the stage. He took a deep breath and looked over at his people.

"Today I ask you one of the hardest tasks. I ask that you let go of the past, and look to a new future. I know this is no easy feat, and I understand if you can not overlook the things the King has done. But he is in danger and is a changed man. I ask for your aid in protecting him." Aerin stopped speaking, and the room became a hostile place. The elves were shouting at him, calling him a traitor among other things that I wish not to repeat. They were about to completely revolt against him. I pushed him behind me and prepared for the worst, but I still had hope that they would see it from our perspective.

"Silence!" I shouted at them in elvish. The room went quiet and fast. "Aerin feels your pain, he has felt it more than any of you. He has felt the fires and heartbreak that the King has brought upon us all. But he was not alone in doing that–my father betrayed his own kind, he betrayed all of us." I looked over to Sylas. This was the first time he was hearing the truth about our father. Judging by the look on his face, it was not fazing him at all. I guess deep down he knew his father was not a good person. "I have spent my life trying to atone for his sins, I learned that I can not change the past." I took Aerin's hand in my own. "It can not be done. We can not change the past or bring back those we lost, however, we can protect those we have now. And I will not let anything happen to my happiness. Who among you is ready to lay down your lives to defend what is most important? We are not asking you to fight for the King, but to fight for a brighter tomorrow." There were some hushed voices from the crowd, but no one was still willing to lay down their lives in defense of the King.

"My father died in that fire, I have put my past behind me and forgiven those who have wronged me. If I did not do so, we would not have our great capital. We would still be a lost kind, traveling the world like beggars. We are elves, it is our job to keep balance in the world. The King has done us wrong, but if he dies now, Morgana will take over and be back stronger and with more men. We ask you to join us in this battle to defeat her. This will not be the final battle, that I am sure of. We ask for only those brave and strong enough to forget the past and look towards a new future. I ask that you follow in your king's footsteps, and move to fight for peace, and to find a new happy ever after." He took my hand and kissed it softly.

"And who is to be here to defend the capital, or our families for that matter?"

"I am entrusting Prince Sylas with this task. He is the one who defeated Morgana last time, and he will be able to protect your family now. Those who are willing to fight by my side are to join me at the gate in one hour. Those who wish to stay behind are welcome to and have my blessing to do so. It will be your task to make the capital strong again. Find a way to protect the capital as it once was. Cloak it to the eyes of mortal men. You are free to go." Aerin took a seat on his throne and put his head in his hands once the elves left the room.

I walked over and knelt down before him. I placed my hand on his leg and he looked up at me. His eyes were glossed over, but he was holding it together. Sylas walked over to us and placed his hand on my shoulder.

"I am going to go up and eat something." I nodded to him and he left the room. Once he was gone, Aerin finally started to speak.

"Are they going to show?" he questioned me, hoping I

would have the answer he wanted to hear. And sure, I did, but I was not going to lie to him.

"You are their king, you did not order them. You will see, Aerin. I am sure they are faithful, and will show up. I took his hand and stood up. "Let's not focus on it though. Let's go upstairs, and rest for a bit longer." He came with me willingly, and we went up to our room. There was food on the table, and we sat around it. We enjoyed some light elven bread and fruit before crawling back into bed. Aerin inched closer to me and laid his head on my chest. He closed his eyes and fell asleep. I stayed awake though keeping an eye on him, he was in a mix of emotions, and when this happens to me my powers go wild. I could not risk him venturing off to Morgana again, not in his current state.

****

Aerin and I sat on Alatar's back at the main gate. As we waited we noticed in the distance an elf riding in front of hundreds of other elves. Aerin smiled proudly, and I hugged him from behind.

"I told you they would show."

"King Aerin, we ride by your side–live or die with you. My King, we are ready to fight." Aerin bowed his head slightly, and the man retreated back to his formation. They rode out with Aerin, their banners soaring. I reached into my pouch and pulled out his crown, placing it on his head.

"You ride as their king." He smiled and led the army

out of the city. Behind us, we heard women and children cheering as we left. The sounds shortly died out, and we were alone with the troops. We rode most of the day through the rain. It was so hard to see through, I was glad Aerin was at the reins instead of myself. I would have called the march a long time ago. He truly is the more stubborn of us both. The sun had set some time ago and we were traveling by sheer willpower, the rain would not allow for lanterns or torches either.

"Aerin, I think we should call it for right now. We can finish our travels in the morning," I suggested to him. He raised his hands and we stopped to make camp. The elves set up a large tent for him, and he took my hand leading me into it. I was in complete awe by what I saw, the elves set up tables with fruit and snacks. The room had a small bed in it as well. I couldn't help but wonder who was the one carrying all this. Aerin started a small fire in the tent and we stripped, hanging our clothing over it. The cool air was harsh on my skin, and it was still damp.

I grabbed the fur that was on the bed and walked over to Aerin. If I was this cold he must be even colder. I had more body weight and muscle to keep me a little warmer. I wrapped it around him and pulled him into me. We fell onto the bed and he sat on my lap looking at me. We both smiled, and he leaned in to kiss me. I fell back on the bed, allowing him to cover me completely. With our bodies pressed this close together, I was no longer thinking about the cool breeze. We made love once more before cuddling close for the night. Again, I was too afraid to fall asleep. I wanted to make sure I was there if Aerin needed me, and I knew I could sleep on the trip since he would be steering Alatar. I lay there with the love of my life in my arms, his breaths were soft and warm, and with each breath, my heart fluttered a little more.

We woke the next morning and ate as the elves took down the tent and packed Aerin's belongings. Once everyone had their fill of rations we settled up and were on our way. We had half a day of travel left before we would arrive back at the kingdom, and I would have to face the King again. At least we will be able to sleep in a house again and not a tent. I looked forward to having the house with just us in it. I climbed up behind Aerin and we took off. I rested my head on his shoulder and was asleep before I knew it.

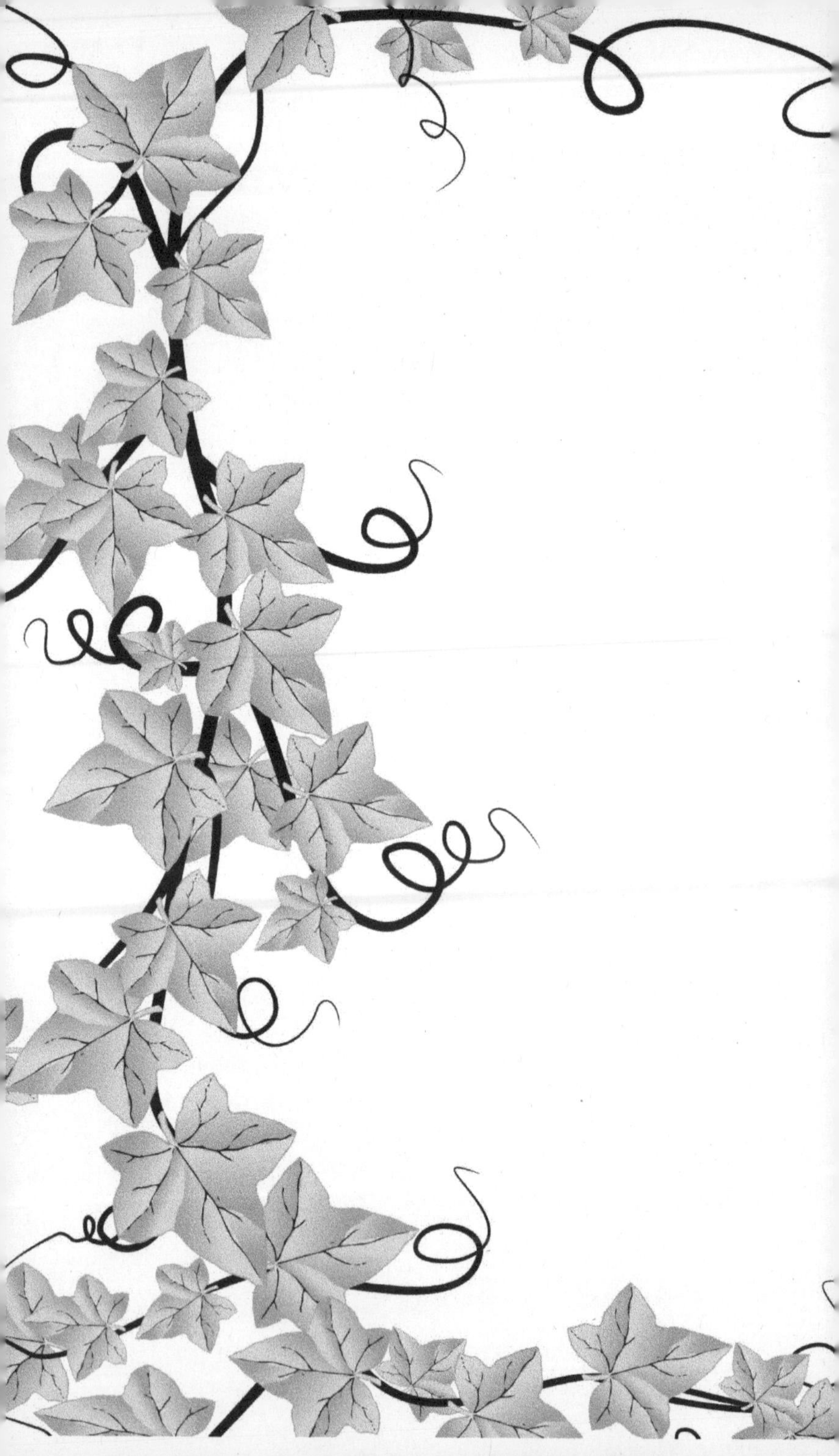

CHAPTER 25:

Thorne

I woke when Alatar came to a halt. I opened my eyes and saw that we were standing in front of the gates. I must have slept longer than I realized. I was trying to get my bearings as it's not often I wake up on horseback. I could not get enough of Aerin's scent and was happy to be holding onto his waist. I let go for a moment to rub my eyes to help myself adjust to the sun. The guard out front waved us into the city. As we entered, everyone was quiet. The city was different, but it was hard to explain. The merchants were not out, and the streets were bare. Aerin signaled the men to find a place to set up camp and they left us.

We went to the tavern and took a seat together. The tavern was also empty, there was not a single person in there. Sam came out of the back room and looked at us. He forced a smile on his face before offering us some drinks. He was not his usual self. He didn't try to flirt with me or offer me sex. I knew something was definitely not right around here. I carefully sipped my drink and rested my hand on Aerin's inner thigh. He jumped a bit from the motion, and I nearly spit out my beer.

"Sam, what is going on here?" I was getting worried that something awful had happened.

"The King is very ill, it seems that the water supply has been poisoned. Business has been slow since it started, everyone is afraid to leave their houses. Many of them have already died, we can't keep up with the dead and they are starting to pile up on the outskirts." Aerin's eyes darted to me, and he took a deep breath.

"What kind of poison, do we know?" As I was asking him questions to find out more information Aerin whistled and three elves came running into the tavern. Aerin met them at the door and spoke to them before they nodded and left the building.

"They are going to check the water supply, see if they can cure it. They should be able to cure the King as well." I nodded to him but turned back to Sam.

"When did this all start?"

"About three days ago." I watched Aerin gasp as we both remembered that was the first time he lost control of his powers and ended up in that room with Morgana. Did he not tell me everything the first time? No, he wouldn't do that. I looked at Sam and was questioning if he had the date right on when it all started, but the look in his eye was very sure.

"Thorne, Sylas, and I knew she was planning an attack on the King three days ago but we thought it was an actual attack, not a cheap tactic. I'm sorry."

"It's fine, but we need to go and see the King at once." Aerin nodded to me. We both knew we had to face him and see how much longer he had. The thought of that worried me, I don't want the crown if it is going to pull me away from Aerin. Part of me wanted the crown so badly, but I would sacrifice it for him. I would sacrifice everything. Lord knows I really hoped the King was okay for now. We both downed the remainder of the drinks and were on our way.

****

Aerin and I were escorted into the King's personal chambers. He was lying in bed, unable to move. I walked over and placed my hand on his head, he was hotter than any flame I had felt. His skin was whiter than a fresh snowfall. I knew he did not have much more time. There was a bucket of water next to him, and a sponge in it from his last bath with a glass of ale next to him. I took a knee next to the bed and bowed my head to him, Aerin stood in the doorway.

"Your Majesty, can you hear me?" I spoke softly. I took the King's hand in mine after dipping mine in the water. I tried to cure him, but the poison was beyond my magic. I knew Aerin could heal him, but I can't ask that of him. If he heals him he will take in the poison instead, I can't ask him to give up his life if there is no cure. What should I do? I'm not ready to become king. I started to tear up a bit, not because the King was dying, but because if I became the king I would be apart from Aerin. He must have a sixth sense for this kind of thing because he walked over and knelt next to me.

"Are you afraid of being king?" I couldn't talk. I knew if I did I would lose control of my emotions further. Instead, I just shook my head. "Is it because you are afraid of being away from me or losing me again?" I shook my head again, and he placed his hand on my own. "We would make it work. Make a united kingdom if that was the case." His words were sincere, but how would something like that work? I mean how in the hell would we make a joint kingdom, the elves barely even wanted to come to help the King and he thinks they would welcome a united front. "We could use the city of the elves as a base and have a legislature here, rule from both, and build a united front for that peace we both want." I finally understood what he meant. We would rule from one kingdom, travel back and forth, and be together. To be honest that did not sound bad.

"Thank you, I don't know what I would do without you." I squeezed his hand and laid my head on his shoulder. In return, Aerin laid his head on top of mine.

"Your Majesty, the elves are here, they said they know of some kind of cure."

I turned to see the guards standing in the doorway and Aerin went over to them. The elves came into the room and started to chant around the King. I stood back in Aerin's arms and watched in silence. Once they finished the King opened his eyes, and his breathing became normal again. I smiled as he sat up in bed.

"Thorne, you found the elves?" the King asked, coughing up a little bit of blood. Aerin walked next to him and smiled.

"We found them." The King nodded and looked directly at me.

"Will they return me to my youth?" I shook my head, that was too much to ask them. He took everything from them, I was not about to ask them to give him another life. He sighed and looked out the window. "Then I fear my time here is not long."

"Everything comes and goes at some point," Aerin chimed in. "We are not masters of death, it is not in our power to change it, or grant a longer life."

The King nodded and he knew Aerin was right. He reached over to the table next to him and took the ring off it and handed it to me. "Then Thorne, you are to be king, the city is yours. Protect it."

"I will." I took the ring and put it on my pointer finger, I was not about to remove the ring from Aerin and it was the only finger the fat ring would fit on. I stood and the knights behind me bowed. I would like to travel to your kingdom once more, Aerin. Should you allow a frail old man to join you on your travels?" Aerin smiled and bowed.

"We would be honored by your visit."

If I was to be king now, he should know about our plans, but it's not really the best time to tell him. Would there be a better time, I am sure he would have to have someone he thinks would be a good leader to rule under me. The only person I really knew that well in the city was Sam, would he really be a good leader though? I had to ask him and find out his thoughts.

"Your Majesty, it is my plan to rule a joint kingdom with Aerin, I need to know if you have one in mind that would be a good fit to rule under me and keep the city in harmony." The King did not answer right away but was giving it some thought.

"A knight would not be a good fit, however they would not need any training. If I was you I would pick someone who understands the people, someone who is able to put themselves in issues that everyone else faces." I smiled and nodded to him, I understood what he meant. I knew exactly who to entrust the city to, and my first thought was the correct one. I wrote down a message to Sam and handed it to the guards to deliver. I turned to Aerin and nodded towards the door. He extended his arm for me, and we left the King to recover.

****

Sam walked into the throne room, where he knelt before me and Aerin. He changed his outfit from earlier and was wearing some of his better clothing.

"I have been crowned the new king. He shall live, but the goblet has been handed down. It is my goal to lead the people from Aerin's kingdom. I will need someone here I can trust, to lead the people under my command. I have decided you should lead them. I need someone I can trust, but also someone who understands the people." Sam stood up and walked to me and Aerin. He looked at Aerin and smiled.

"So, this is the person you were so butt hurt over." He looked Aerin up and down. "I can see why, but you better protect him." Aerin smiled and laughed at this. I, however, felt a strong blush coming on. I wouldn't say I was butt hurt, but he was right–it did weigh me down a bit. Okay, I know it weighed me down, but I thought I did a good job of hiding it. I cleared my throat before speaking again.

"Will you accept and lead the people here, I will travel to the kingdom often, and guide you along the way."

"I do accept" He smiled, and I stood up from the throne and let him take a seat. He sat down and shivered before getting back up. "I don't need to live here though, do I?" I laughed but knew what he meant. It was stuffy here, it just didn't feel like a home.

"No, you can conduct business from the other room, and go on with your everyday life as the barkeep if you want."

"Oh, thank god," He joked back to me. He bowed before leaving, with a skip to his walk. I turned to Aerin, and he sat on my lap.

"Well, Your Majesty, what are the plans now?" he asked me, staring lovingly into my eyes.

"I thought we could go back to my house, and see where things go from there." I knew exactly where things were going to go, and if they did not I would make sure they did. I was going to take him today, I could not resist the temptation growing inside me any longer. I hungered for him and was ready to ravish him. Aerin smiled and stood up.

"Well, then let's go."

We made it back to my house, and we walked in holding hands and laughing. But that shortly came to an end. There, sitting at the table was my father. His blond hair had turned gray, and his expression was that of pure anger. He slammed the glass of beer down on the table and stood up. I felt like a little kid again. I was shaking and found myself ready to run out of the room. I could not slow my heart rate either.

"Where is Sylas?" He walked closer to us, and I found myself with my back against the door. "I told you when I returned you better both be here in the house." He raised his hand to hit me, and Aerin stepped between us. He took a deep breath and blew. The wind picked up out of nowhere, and my father went flying into the table. "I see you are still protecting him. I told him you wouldn't always be around to save him. I guess they missed one."

Aerin's hand snapped to the side, and a fireball formed in it. His hair was on fire. Did my father lie to me, did he really choose on his own to betray the elves? I did not want to believe it, but it sure looked that way. My anger was getting the best of me, and I really wanted to let Aerin toss the fireball at him.

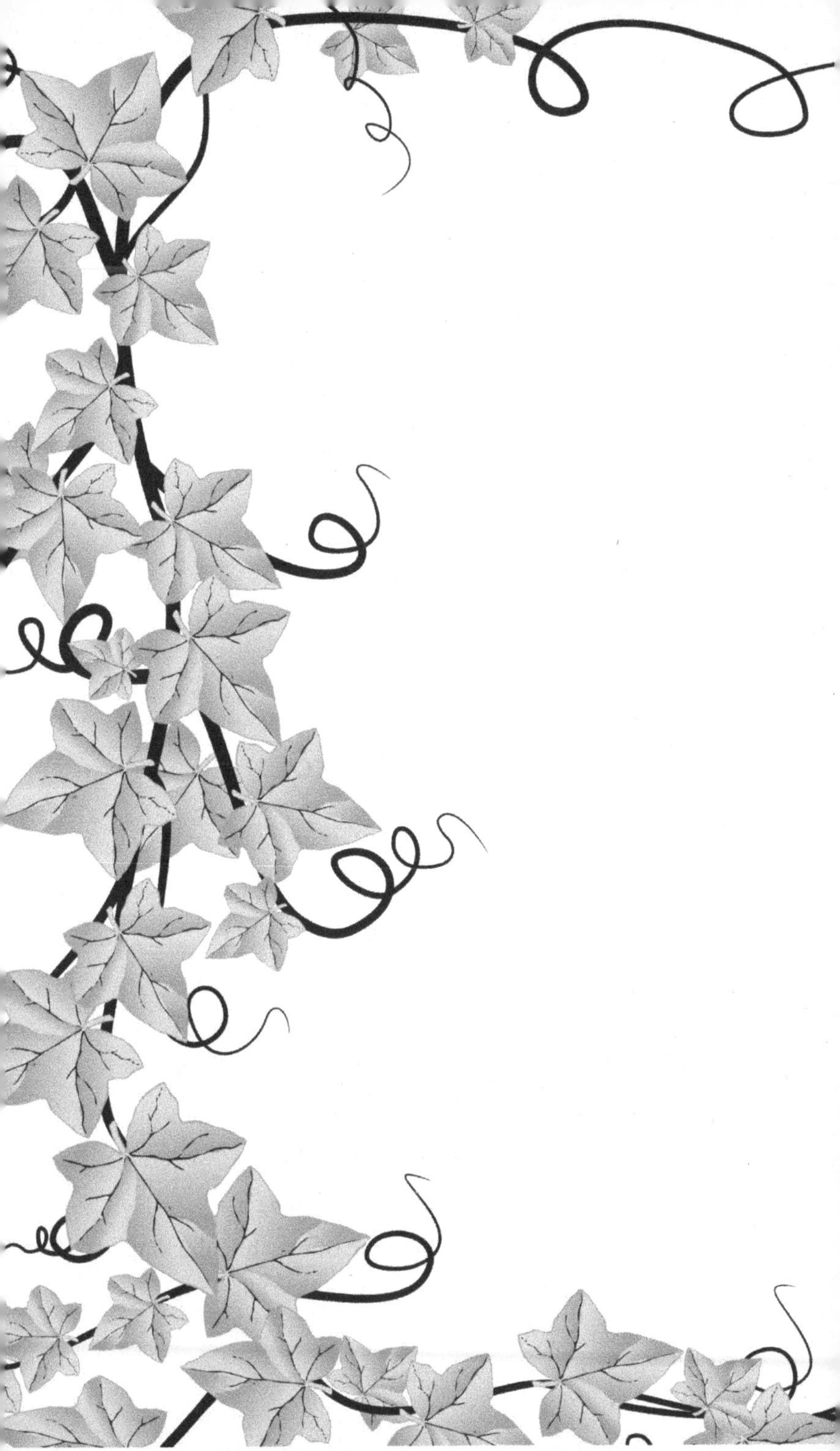

CHAPTER 26:

Aerin

I was about to melt Thorne's father's face off. I held the ball of fire to his face and watched as he cowered below me. I was waiting for Thorne's blessing, I did not want to take away his family as he did mine. Thorne, however, was frozen in fear just like when we were younger.

"You will bow before the king of men and the king of elves." I watched as his eyes went wide. "That's right, you failed–we are just as strong as we were before. And I will always protect Thorne. I protect those I love, unlike you. Now bow before your kings." His father did as I asked of him, he was basically kissing the floor at our feet. I put out the flames and walked back to Thorne. I took his hand and pulled him to his room. He sat on the bed still shaking. I placed my arms around him and pushed his head onto my shoulder. "It's okay, take a few deep breaths."

I sat next to him, and he laid his head on my lap. It was a shock for him to see his father again. Part of me wanted to kill him right there and then but Thorne did not want that, even with all the pain he has caused him. Deep down he loved him still, he was not a bad father to him when he was sober. Sadly though that was not often.

Thorne started to relax a little bit and kissed my cheek. "I am so glad you are here with me, and now that I know he is back here, I can't wait to leave." We realistically could leave, the old king is okay and Thorne has the throne; there was nothing left here keeping us. It isn't like we were stuck.

"Whenever you are ready to leave we can." Thorne nodded at me and lay down in his bed. He closed his eyes and took a deep breath. I lay next to him and kissed his head. I loved him so much, and his father was not like this until we got together. He never got along with my father, and always thought that he could do a better job at leading the elves. When he was turned down by the tribe, he started to drink more.

I laid down next to Thorne and kissed his head again. I pulled him close to me, and he let his hand run up and down my exposed abdomen. It sent shivers down my spine, and I was trying to keep the fact that I was getting turned on to myself. His hand stopped and we both fell asleep together. I was woken by Thorne removing my pants, and letting himself swallow me whole. I whimpered softly as he bobbed repeatedly, and before I knew it my legs went stiff and I released inside him. I returned the favor and enjoyed every second of it. I enjoyed his taste, his smell, everything about the moment. I did not want it to end. But just as fast as it started it ended, I must be better than I thought at this. I chuckled to myself as his hips buckled, and released.

We rested for a bit and managed to catch our breaths again. He looked at me with a worried expression. "What is it?" He glanced away, and then back to me.

"Can you tap into your powers again, and see what she is planning?" I could tell he hated to ask but he was right, we had to know her next move and see if it was safe to travel back home.

"Will you watch over me, don't leave for anything, promise? Last time was way too close." He nodded and handed me one of the fighting knives. I held onto it tight and lay down in bed.

****

I opened my eyes, and I was on a horse, riding with an army. I looked around but was not sure where I was.

Morgana was in front of the army riding as their leader. I could not hear her but was able to overhear a couple of people around me. They were talking about a fight they could not wait for. Others were talking about how it was time for Morgana to take back the crown. I looked down at my hands and noticed I still had my fighting knives. I pulled the horse back a bit and started to blend in with the soldiers. There were all different races riding with her, even the faeries were flying overhead.

I knew I had to be careful, with so many eyes here it would be so easy to spot me out. I ducked down and pulled up my hood. It was time to go back to the Shadow Hunter. I started to slay those around, and they fell to the floor. I took out about 100 of them in stealth and noticed the castle in the distance. Thorne, it's time to wake me up. Do it before she gets there. While I waited, I continued to kill all those I could. I lost count of how many I wounded or killed before the army came to a halt.

"Brother, I know you are here. Where are you?" Morgana started to ride through the army looking for me. I dropped off the horse and spun my daggers waiting for her to get closer. As Morgana inched closer I could feel my heart racing. She stopped for a moment and turned away from me. That was my chance. I spun my knife before tossing it at her. I watched as it struck her in the back, and she let out a scream.

****

Thorne woke me up, and I informed him of her plans. We quickly dressed and raced out the door after telling his father what was happening. We arrived at the castle before Morgana, and Thorne sat on his deserved seat. He gave orders to the guards. The elves did not need any command from me, as they could feel her presence as she got closer. They set up posts around the city and awaited her arrival. I stood next to Thorne as we waited inside the castle. I looked out the window to see the city filling with purple fog, and the elves and men fighting together to defeat the enemy.

The room started to fill with the same fog, and I hid against the wall by the door, and Thorne remained on his throne. Morgana appeared in front of Thorne with a few goblins around her.

"You are on my throne," she spoke softly.

"You have no throne here, Morgana."

"I killed the king with no child, I am here to take what is mine. The time of men is over."

"The time of men will never be over, Morgana," Thorne spoke, not moving. The goblins started to walk closer to him. I kept my back against the wall but drew my bow, trying to get a clean shot. As the three were in front of him, I pulled back the string and fired an arrow. It shot cleanly right through the three of them, and they lay dead in front of his feet.

"You are outnumbered, Morgana," I shouted to her, the big room made my voice echo. Morgana laughed as she spun around the room trying to find me.

"You two are no match for me. Did you forget I am The Lady of Darkness, The Queen of the Fae, The Bringer of Death?" she spoke proudly of her titles.

Thorne stood, drew his sword, and swung at her neck. Morgana dipped back and dodged the slash. She created a shadow blade in her right hand. I noticed her left hand still had blood from the knife I threw in her back. As she spun around I saw it still sticking there. My hair ignited, but under the hood, it was kept dark still. I inched my way closer to her and reached for my blade. She spun and her dagger clipped my hood. I was just able to duck under the swing. Morgana held out her hand and pushed Thorne back into the wall, but he was quickly back on his feet and charging at her. I watched as he spun in the air, the sword transformed into a bow and he fired shot after shot at her. I matched him by hurling fireballs at her.

The sound of clashing echoed in the room. We managed to hit her as she was unable to keep up her guard with only one hand. She flew back into the wall, and we moved closer to her. She was hunched over holding her stomach. Thorne spun again, turning his bow back to the sword, and held it to her. Water flew out of it, and chained her hands against the wall.

"This is where we say our final goodbye sister," I spoke as I spun my dagger around and held it to her neck. "Any last words?"

The door flung open, and Thorne's father raced in. Thorne was caught off guard and the chains were released. Morgana used energy and blew me across the room. She reached behind herself and pulled the dagger out of her back. She hurled it at Thorne. Before I could say a word, his father jumped in front of it and it stabbed through his chest. Thorne dropped to his knees and held his father's head. Morgana let out a loud cackle and started to charge towards him. I blew down letting the wind whirl below my feet launched at her and met her mid-jump, tossing her back into the wall. I swung my blades, and she was able to deflect each one.

She was getting faster and started her own attack. I was unable to dodge every blow and ended up with cuts along my arms and chest.

"Thorne, I could really use some help here," I called back to him. I glanced over at him, and he was losing control of his emotions. The sword in his hand started to glow blue, and the room filled with water. Morgana laughed as she vanished from the room, I was unable to cast a fog as fast as she did. The room was turning into a whirlpool, I was being sucked down into the current, and could not catch my breath.

"THORNE," I called out to him, but he couldn't hear me. The current picked up, and I was about to be sucked under. What should I do? I started to reach out to him, and my hand brushed against his arm. He managed to snap out of it, and the water left just as fast as it formed.

"Aerin, I am so sorry."

"Me too, Thorne, is he okay?"

"He's gone." Thorne removed the knife and cleaned it before handing it back to me. "We had her, this was almost all over." I hugged him tight and nodded.

"Soon, Thorne, it will be over."

I looked outside and noticed that the fog had lifted as well. The army was gone, and the men and elves cheered. This war was far from over but another victory was granted to us, if you can call it that.

****

We gave his father a proper send-off and returned to his home. Thorne went straight to his room ready to call it a day. I gave him some space and cooked a small meal for us. I know what it is like to lose your father, and it's a curse I wouldn't wish on anyone. I wonder when we are going to tell Sylas, or do we leave him thinking that his father is still out there somewhere? It wasn't my place to tell him anything, that would be up to Thorne–I am sure he will make the right decision.

I cleaned the kitchen and brought the food into Thorne's room. He sat up and sipped on the broth. I kissed him softly before lying down in bed with him. I closed my eyes, and drifted to sleep, wondering where our path would take us next.

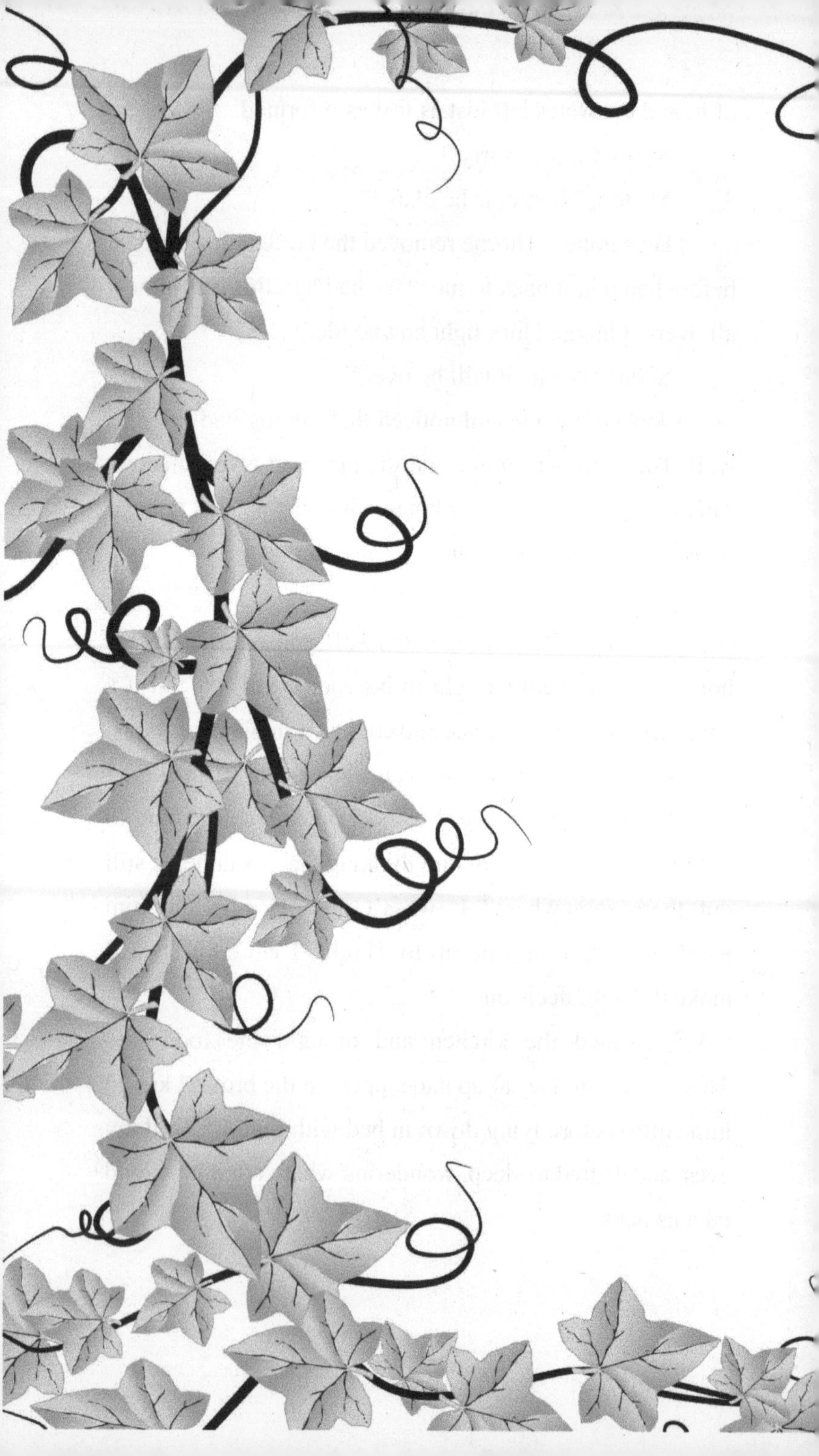

CHAPTER 27:

Thorne

We arrived back at the homeland in the morning, Sylas was at the gate waiting for us to arrive. I guess he received the message Aerin sent ahead. I hopped off Alatar and helped Aerin down. Sylas ran up to us and gave us both a huge hug. He nearly knocked me over. He was excited to tell us about the changes they made to the city, and how some of the buildings have been repaired while we were gone. He showed us around the city as if we were familiar with the area. Many of the run-down buildings were built like they were brand new, and statues that were torn down have been fixed. It looked amazing.

The city finally looked like it was never attacked, it looked just as I remembered from centuries ago. I turned to see the King smiling ear to ear. Sylas finally noticed him when we arrived at the dining hall.

"Your Majesty," Sylas spoke, bowing to him.

"No, no not anymore, he is the king now." He spoke, holding his frail arm out to me. Sylas turned and smiled at me.

"You mean my brother is a king?" He was so happy to hear the news.

"Yes, and that makes you a prince." Hearing that made me panic a bit. I had to protect him at even more costs now. One day, Aerin and I will be gone, and it will be up to him to protect and rule over each kingdom. It was a lot to ask, and a lot more for him to take in. He froze for a moment. I connected to his mind, and he was thinking the same thing I was.

"Don't worry, little brother, that will be a lifetime away." I placed my arms around him and gave him a big hug. I watched as the King looked around in complete awe and for the first time since I met him, he was left speechless. There were platters of all different kinds of food in the middle, and the sun was shining through the painted stained glass. The King sat next to Sylas, and Aerin and I sat across from them. I was glad we finally made it inside, I could sense the tension the elves felt now having the King in the city. Part of me was right there with them, he seemed almost too eager to be here. He is probably hoping there is some elf here that is willing to cure him.

I shrugged the thought off and reached across the table for one of the baked goods. It was cocoa-based with chips of chocolate and a chocolate custard. It was enough chocolate to send someone in shock, but I could not resist myself. It has been a week since I had something sweet, and this had everything I needed in one bite. Everyone shortly after followed my lead and started to fill their plates. I was more than happy to only eat this, but my stomach wanted so much more. I quickly gobbled down the pastry before loading my plate with all other kinds of food.

I can't lie, I was getting a little tired of eating the same thing over and over again. It was always steamed vegetables for me. The smell of the cooked meat was making my mouth water. It has been years since I have eaten any kind of meat. I watched as Aerin slid slices into his mouth, and it made me want it even more. I leaned into Aerin and whispered in his ear asking if I could try a small bite of whatever meat he had on his plate. He smiled before cutting it smaller and held the fork up to me. Without hesitation, I opened my mouth and his fork slid in. The meat was tender, yet soft and juicy. It was perfectly seasoned as well, it had me wanting more. Aerin cut another slice and held it up for me, and I dove right into it. It was like someone else was taking over me. I leaned back over the table and filled another plate with the different meat options.

We finished our plates, and the sun was starting to set. I felt the travel weighing on me as I was fighting to keep my eyes open. I did notice that there was something a little off with Aerin. I wasn't sure what it was, but he seemed a bit distant after we finished eating. I knew that now was not the time to talk about it in front of everyone. I would wait till we were alone in our room.

****

Once I closed the door behind me and I was alone with Aerin, I sat him on the edge of the bed and looked deep into his eyes. He was blocking me out of his mind, and it was the first time I could tell how hard he was trying to keep me out.

"What's wrong?" I asked him. His eyes started to fill with tears before he spoke.

"If I was to surrender myself, Morgana would leave everyone alone." Hearing those words struck me right in the chest. How could he even think such a thing? Has he lost his mind?

"That is not an option." He took my hands and let his tears flow.

"If I join her, I can keep you all safe."

"But think about what you would be losing." Did he even think about it, losing me, his kingdom, Sylas? All of this would have been for nothing. I was panicked inside my own mind, how could he think this would be the answer?

"Along the way here, she spoke to me in my mind. She promised to recall her troops if I joined her. She said all the suffering could end–there would be no more war. I can protect the ones I love and my kingdom. I could keep you safe just like I promised I would, Thorne."

"At what cost, we only just found each other again. I spent a century of torment worrying about you, how can you ask me to be okay with that again?"

"Thorne, please, this is not easy for me either." If this bastard thinks I am going to just lay down and let him join Morgana to save me, he has another thing coming.

"Then don't do it. We can find another way, we always do."

"There has been too much bloodshed already." Aerin laid down in bed facing away from me. I lay next to him, trying to pull him into my arms. He didn't even inch back into me. He was already starting to pull away–his mind was made up.

"Please, Aerin, give me time. We will figure this all out, let me help you. Don't turn your back on me and Sylas." He rolled over and met my gaze.

"I am not turning my back on you, I'm saving you," His voice was chokcd with the bottled-up emotions he was facing. I took his hand in my own and kissed it.

"Give it some time, Aerin. We will figure this out,

promise me that much."

"I promise, Thorne, but if it comes down to it, I will join her to protect you. I thought it over, and as long as you are safe and can protect Sylas...well that is all that matters."

"A last resort, okay? Until that day comes, you remain here by my side. Promise me, Aerin." I felt myself getting choked up. I could not hold back the emotions any longer. He was asking me to let him kill himself, I would never. I would find a way to keep him here with me no matter what. I felt a new fear growing and knew that I would have to fight for him. I will have to fight to keep him where I need him, by my side.

I will find a way no matter what it takes. I am not going to lose him again. If we find out where she is hiding, we can plan a united attack. Bring the fight to her, let her face all the deaths. End this once and for all.

Aerin leaned into me again, and I felt my mind clearing from the confusion of what to do. I smiled again and stroked his hair. I want to take him on a date. Something he will never forget. I sit up for a moment, write a long message to my brother, and hand it to the guard standing outside to take to him. I turned back to my lover who was stripping and getting under the covers. I did the same and walked to him. I needed to remind him that we were supposed to be together, and my plans for tomorrow will do that. I lay next to him and we spoke about the past, and the dates we've had. It was nice to see him smiling again and relaxing a bit with me holding him.

"I love you, Aerin."

****

Aerin sat in my lap as I unpacked the picnic basket I had Sylas make for us. I held up some grapes and Aerin enjoyed eating them from my fingers. He spent a little longer than needed sucking on them as well. The sun was rising over the mountain, and the wind was blowing softly. Aerin's hair blew behind him gently and he looked amazing. This was so perfect and felt just like we were back home spending the day together.

Sylas joined us a bit later and brought dessert. I watched Aerin indulge in the fudge. I smiled as I wiped a bit off his lips. I ran my finger across them. I was admiring how soft they were, and how they glistened in the sunlight. I closed my eyes and leaned into him. He met my gesture, and our lips connected. The kiss was soft and sent shivers down my back. My free hand was in my pocket toying with the ring my mother gave me so many years ago. I stood up and helped Aerin to his feet. I dropped down to one knee and looked up into his eyes.

"Aerin, you make me so happy–I love you more than anything. It might not be the right time to ask you this, but I can't wait any longer." I took out the ring and looked up into his green eyes once more. "Will you marry me?" Aerin could not get words out through all his tears falling. He eventually nodded, and I slipped the ring onto his finger. I stood and he swung his arms around my neck then kissed me. It was the happiest I have been in a long time. Sylas ran and gave us a group hug before he walked away to give us some privacy.

Aerin took my hand and led me to a secret tunnel in the mountain. He held out his other hand and lit the way for us. We came to an opening where the sun shone in, and there were diamonds reflecting the light all around. In the center was a small body of water that was crystal clear. It was breathtaking, I found myself left speechless with how amazing the view was.

"After you left, I found myself here." He let go of my hand and walked out into the water. I followed behind him and stripped down. The water was warm, unlike the rivers around the city. I found myself enjoying the heat as it relaxed all my muscles. I also felt my magic being charged. I felt stronger than before. I shook the feeling away and moved closer to Aerin.

"What did you do here?" He kept walking and showed me a picture he painted on the wall. It was of us, lying in the snow. It melted my heart. How long was he here? How many nights did he spend alone? I could not think about that. I pulled him into me and kissed his forehead. "Well, we will be together forever. Never to be parted."

"I like the sound of that, Thorne."

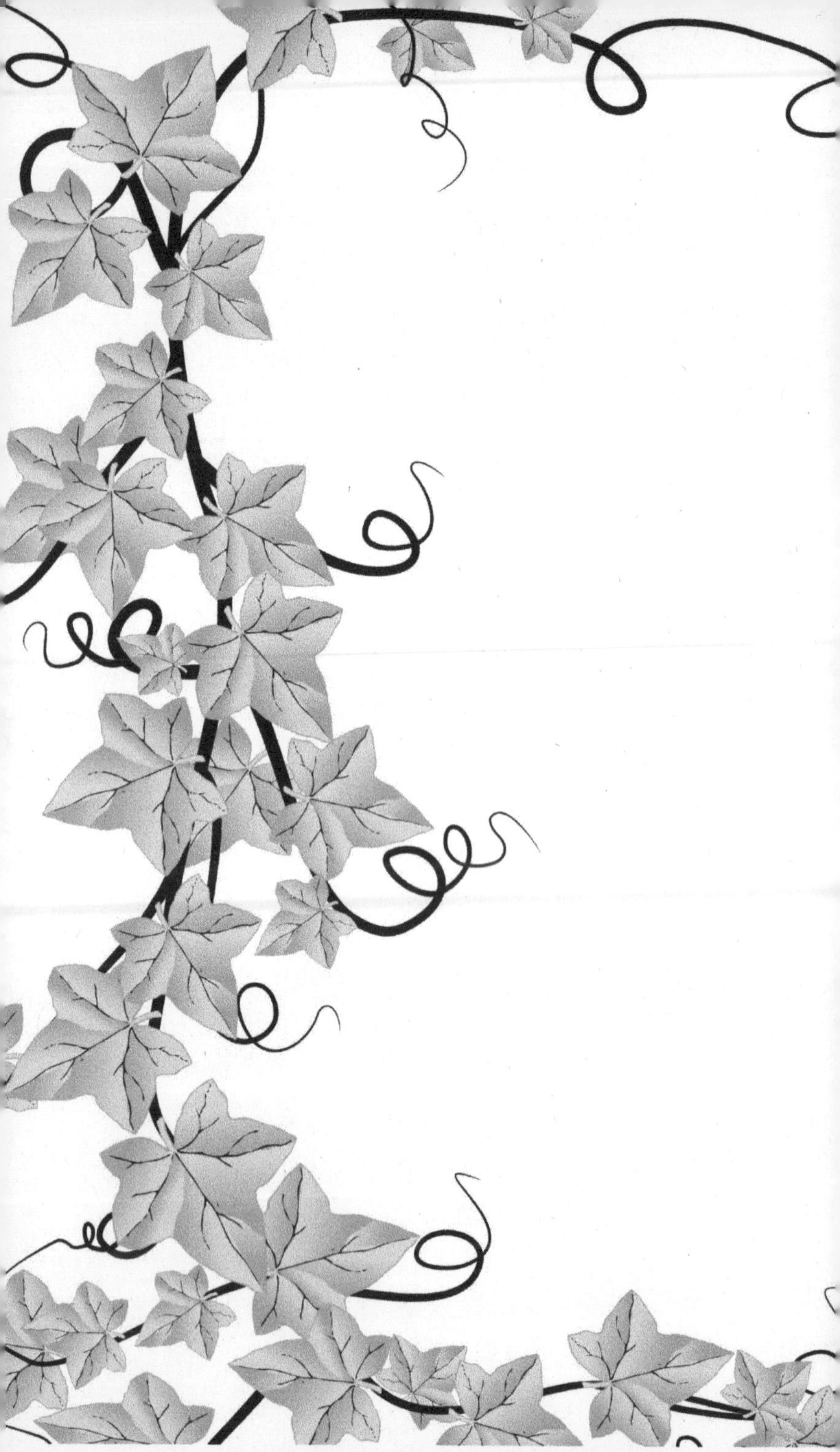

CHAPTER 28:

Aerin

I had a dream of many different weapons. Ones that I have never seen before, and I was wondering if it was something we could use against Morgana. I woke up earlier than normal, and Thorne was still out cold. I kissed his head gently, and squirmed my way out of his arms, careful not to wake him. I made my way down to the dining hall and started to draw the ideas I had. I've never heard of a machine that would fire exploding arrows, and I'm not even sure how we would do it. But with the brain power of Sylas and the other elves, there was no doubt we could figure something up. I drew for what felt like ages. There was a pile of papers stacked next to me crumbled into little balls. Nothing I drew felt right, it was starting to feel like no matter what I drew it was never going to work.

I, however, kept at it, I did not want to sacrifice myself. I wanted to live forever with Thorne and now that we were engaged, it was consuming my mind. I spent most of the morning there, and at some point fell asleep at the table. It was not until Thorne came in and placed his hand on my shoulder that I woke up. I was startled a bit and nearly fell out of my chair.

"What's all this?" he asked, trying to reach for some of the crumpled papers. I swatted his hand away and looked up at him.

"I had a vision of sorts. I guess you can call it an idea. But it is never going to work so it doesn't matter." I quickly covered the scraps of paper with the tablecloth, resting my head in my hands. I was trying to hide the defeat I felt. Thorne uncovered the papers and unfolded them looking at my sketches. He smiled, and rested his hand on my back, rubbing it softly.

"A machine that fires exploding arrows?" He thought for a moment and then shot me a smile. "This could work." He sat down next to me uncrumpled a bunch of my drawings and took the quill from my hand. He started to doodle his own sketches based on mine. He kept the same shape, but adjusted the size and positioning, then adjusted the hole and how the arrows would fire. He drew a path for a line that would be ignited. He turned it to me and smiled. "How's this?" I took it from him and grinned. "This could definitely work." I felt a sigh of relief coming on and I nodded to him.

Sylas joined us in the room and sat down waiting for the elves to bring out breakfast. Thorne covered the crumpled papers again with the cloth and put his drawing into his pocket. Sylas smiled at us as his stomach growled and echoed in the big room. The elves must have heard it because right after they started to bring out the food, they stopped for a moment seeming a little shocked because we usually are not here when they bring it in. They put the food on the table and smiled at me then bowed before leaving.

I made a plate for myself of some pastries and started to make one for Thorne when he asked me to put some eggs and smoked meat on his plate. It kind of caught me off guard. I never thought he would eat meat. But he was changing and he wanted to share everything with me. I really appreciated it. It was going to be a bit easier this way for me as well. I always felt bad eating meat in front of him. I laid my head on his shoulder and looked out at Sylas.

"Are you feeling smart today?" Sylas put down his fork and folded his hands, nodding to me. "Show him the sketch." Thorne took out the sketch and passed it across the table to him. He nodded looking at it. I could hear the gears grinding in his head. I waited for him to reply.

"I think we can do it." He finished eating and took the sketch with him.

****

Thorne and I went to the garden to sit and talk and I was enjoying the alone time with him. We joked about getting married and how it was going to be. Overall we agreed on a lot of things, and that made me extremely happy. He picked a small flower from the garden, placed it in my hair, and rested his hand on my cheek. He leaned over and kissed me softly. It was an amazing day. That was until a messenger arrived. They handed him a note; he read it and told me he had to handle this. He kissed me and left without providing me any more information. I was not liking the secrets between us. I knew it had to do with his kingdom, but part of ruling a joint kingdom is to do it together. Not keep secrets from each other. I hated it, and it was really eating at me. I had to do something to keep my mind at ease.

I made my way to the archery supply store. I walked in and took a look at all the arrows they had available. They were all pretty standard except a few different types of wood used to make them. Some of the arrowheads were oval, but nothing really stood out to me. I knew I would need something stronger if I was going to fight Morgana again. Something that she would not see coming. I would need some kind of magic arrows. It would have been nice if my father ever wrote down anything about this bow. If I could somehow tap into the power it has, everything would be easier.

I took the bow off my back and took a good look at it. Something had to give away how it works. I looked the bow over, and it just looked like a handmade bow with vines carved into it. There was nothing special about how it looked. I ran my hands over the vines and thought about the magic it could hold. I thought about Thorne and Sylas and how I wanted to figure this puzzle out. I wanted to be able to protect them from harm, I wanted to be with them for a long time. As I was thinking about it, the bow came to life. The vines wrapped around my arms, and sat gently against my skin. I looked around and took out an arrow. I fired a single bolt into the scarecrow. After the arrow struck, the vines flew out of the bow and wrapped the figure up before pulling it into the daggers on the bow.

I could tell my smile was huge because my face started to hurt. That makes one part of the mission done for defeating Morgana. Now, to figure out if I can make some kind of special arrows. I have no idea where to even start. Sylas was already busy so I was on my own. I kicked the dirt around me and noticed how it fogged up. I wonder if I could use that. I bought a couple of containers and carried the dirt back to the palace with me. I ventured up to my room and set to work. I made a couple of test arrows, and many more duds were piled up on the floor next to me. I managed to control my anger and did not turn them all to twigs. I figured I could maybe change up the models, and make them work as intended.

I grabbed my bow and was about to head back out to the garden when the door swung open nearly taking off my nose. Thorne slumped into the room and plopped onto the bed. He did not notice me at all. He ignored my very being and that hurt. I didn't let it get me down because I just made a huge breakthrough.

"Thorne, I think I figured something out that will help us," I spoke excitedly, I was like a kid in a candy store.

"Cool," he spoke back, not even turning over to look at me. I walked over and sat on the edge of the bed.

"What's wrong?" He didn't answer me and still refused to look at me. It felt like a stab in my chest. "Thorne?" There was still no answer from him, and now I was getting annoyed. I huffed and left the room, slamming the door behind me. Fucking asshole, how are we supposed to rule a joint kingdom when he closes off like that. It felt like he was pulling away from me, and it was starting to eat at me. I was so afraid of losing him again, that is why I did not let him in right away. Now, it feels like I am–maybe being the king is too much for him. Maybe being with me, at the same time, is not going to work.

I noticed that I left the arrows in the room, but I was not going to go back in there with my blood already boiling so I made my way down to the sparring ground. I met with some elves there, and some of Thorne's soldiers. I knew I could defeat any of them blindfolded, but I needed to let off some steam. I just feel bad for whoever I am against.

One of the stronger of the bunch stepped into the circle and pointed at me. He was challenging me. He's either stupid or brave. Either way, you asked me, he was stupid. I stepped in, and the sparring captain nodded. I waved him on, and he charged at me. His arm pulled back before swinging wildly at me. It was too easy to dodge. I laughed at him, and quickly spun kicking my feet out from under me. I should have seen that coming, but I was too focused on Thorne and his silent treatment. Did I do something wrong? He got a few good kicks on me, and I heard a snap. My rib was fractured or broken–I knew it. The captain nodded and the man walked back to the soldiers and was the hero among them. Everyone was cheering his name. When I did not get back up, he walked over and extended a hand to me. I reached up for it, but quickly pulled my hand back. Not to be rude, but the pain was bad. Two elves carried me back to my room. Before they were able to open the door, I told them to put me down and leaned against the wall.

I pushed the door open and walked into the room. Thorne was sitting up in bed now and looked up at me the minute the door opened. He quickly got to his feet. He ran over to me, and I walked to the bed using anything I could find to hold myself up. He looked at me and frowned. His hand rested against my eye which I knew was black and blue, I could tell from the stingy pain that he bruised it. I pulled away from his hand, I was still furious about the silent treatment. He had no idea how it left me in a state of worry. I thought I did something wrong. All he had to say was that he didn't want to fucking talk about it.

He grabbed some water and put his hand in it and the other over me. I pulled away again, I did not want him to touch me. Not right now. I called for the healers and they came in and healed me. Thorne sat on a chair on the other side of the room and watched. I was not having it. They finished their job and left the room, and I sat up in bed.

"Aerin, what happened?" I was about to explode, but took a deep breath.

"I went to the sparring grounds. I should have been able to put anyone there down and you know it, but my head was not there." He got up, walked over to me, and sat on the edge of the bed.

"You were thinking about me, and how I treated you?" I did not have to say anything, he already knew. "I'm sorry, I didn't want to worry you about the kingdom, you have enough to worry about here."

"That's the thing, if we are not going to talk about the issues the kingdoms have, how are we supposed to rule a joint kingdom? If we are going to rule like that, then wouldn't it be easier to go back to your kingdom and do it from there?" As I was afraid that it was too harsh, I took a deep breath before continuing. "I do not want that but

Thorne, is it what you want?" He took my hand and scooted closer to me.

"It is not what I want, Aerin, I'm sorry. I promise no more secrets." I nodded to him, but deep down it did open up some old wounds. I found myself wondering how long it would take before he left again. How long until I am alone in the world once more? I knew I couldn't think that way, but it was how I was feeling. He leaned in and kissed me softly–a tear fell from my eye hitting his cheek.

"Aerin, I'm truly sorry, I love you. I want to be here with you. You're right, no more secrets." He told me what his silence was about, and I felt bad for him. The civilians over there feel betrayed and left, he is not sure what to do, or how to handle it. We spent most of the day there talking about ideas, of what we can do to make them feel included.

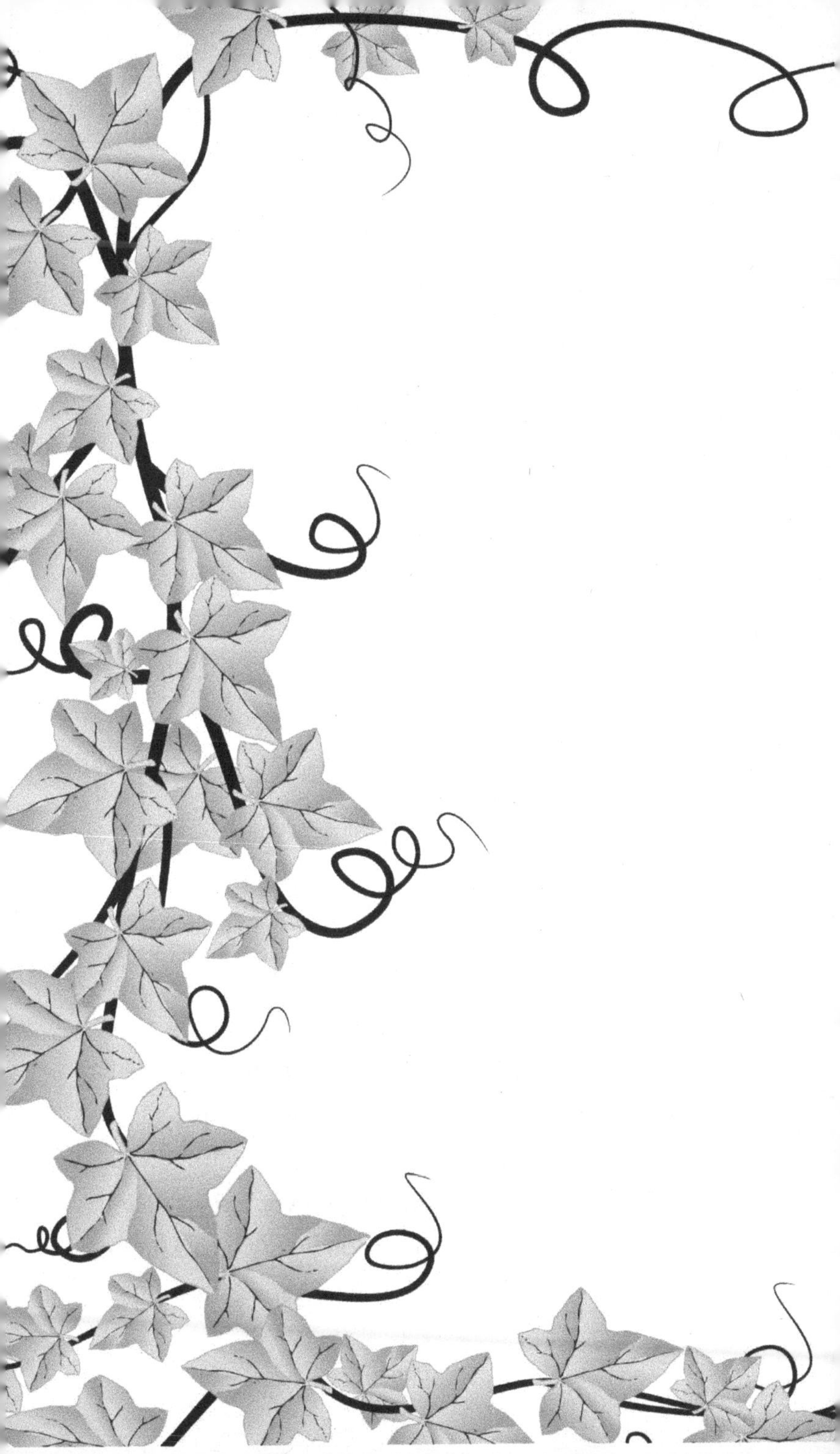

CHAPTER 29:

Aerin

It has been a long month, and while most days were pretty good, there were still others that were horrid. As the month wrapped up, a lot more of these days were getting worse. Thorne and I were pulling apart from one another. He did not feel it, but deep down I did. There were various times I thought about breaking us up. Letting him go back to the world of men he was so stuck in, and getting on with our lives before we hurt each other. Yet, every time I started the conversation, my heart cried out for his touch. It was not something I could do, not at the moment.

I have not been to the workshop where Sylas has been practically living bringing my sketches to life, and he was very keen on not giving out any information about how it was coming along. My guess was to not upset me, that my dream would never be a reality. I have sent elves out to the neighboring cities with different treaty options for the towns and cities around us. Offering some trade options, our steel and weapons for food and cotton. I still have not heard back from them, and it was getting a bit worrisome. They have been gone for days and should have returned a lot sooner than this.

I had a lot to worry about–Morgana was still around and part of me feared that the elves were attacked while on their mission. I'm not sure if I would forgive myself for that. I knew there were a lot of risks of sending them out while we were still at war. I took a deep breath to ground myself and sat up in bed. I rolled over trying to clear my head and become nothingness, but the minute Thorne woke up and sat up on the edge of the bed, my heart said fuck that idea.

I moved closer to him and kissed the back of his neck.

"Good morning?" I asked rather than spoke to him. He turned back to me and I could sense the love in his eyes. Every morning was like this, we would wake up together and the love was there. It was always during the middle of the day that we would grow apart. I think that if we did not share a bed, it would have been over a long time ago. He and Sylas would be out of my life for good. The thought of that stung beneath the skin.

"Good morning," he finally spoke back and kissed me gently. Our lips barely pressed together, and it was those kisses that made my heart beat a thousand times faster. "What do you say we make a surprise visit to Sylas today, and see how he is coming along?" That was his way of saying I'm done waiting, and losing patience. He wanted answers on how much longer until we could bring the fight to Morgana. To be honest, I was nervous and excited as well. I wanted to bring the fight to her and end this war. I wanted to let the peace rain over our little world that we were working so hard to build. It would also make things a lot easier between Thorne and me.

We had breakfast together, and it was anything but silent. Thorne was talking to me about the issues his kingdom was facing. They had a lack of food much like we did, with most trade being cut off thanks to the endless attacks from Morgana's army. Everyone was so afraid to leave their own towns. I tried again to convince him to move everyone here and point out that the united front would be easier to start at one location. He met my opinion back with the usual why here and not there. I know he meant well and was looking at it from the mindset of his people. He did not mean it as to why from the world of elves it would be better, but every time I heard it, it felt like that was what he was saying.

I told him I would send some more elves out with rations for his people, with what little we had to spare, it was going to be hard to send much to them. However, we are in this together, if one kingdom starves so does the other. He smiles at me and looks down at the table. It was no longer large feasts, but rather small amounts of bread and some fruit. I felt like I was turning into him only eating this. I needed my protein. Luckily, Thorne was more than willing to provide that at night.

****

Thorne held the door open for me to the secret lab Sylas and a bunch of elves created together, and I ducked my head avoiding the door frame before entering. I let my hand drape along his waist as I entered the room. He closed the door quickly behind himself and whispered to me.

"Keep that up, and we are going to have to make a stop at some point today to fix this damn issue you are starting." That to me was nothing more than an empty threat and I turned to him, pinning him to the wall and grabbing his balls gently. I gently massaged them in my hand and looked him right in the eyes.

"We could always come back later, why wait?" I

spoke, whispering in his ear. His head jerked back a little which exposed his neck to me. Sure, he did not notice, but it was ready for me to bite down on. Before I had the chance, he put his hand over mine and smiled at me.

"We are already here." I let him go and shrugged, walking down the hall swaying my hips a little more than needed to just tease him more. I could hear his heart racing, it was one of the perks of my elvish hearing. He joined next to me, unable to control himself watching my ass sway in front of him. He curled his fingers around mine and we composed ourselves before he opened the next door.

Once the door flung open and I could hear the banging of hammers, the smell of wood chips filled my nostrils. It was a nice smell, and one that I missed along with the smell of campfires I used to sleep around. We walked over to Sylas, and he nearly ignited us when I placed my hand on his shoulder. He quickly doused his flames. He seemed very on edge, and Thorne crouched down to him. I didn't notice what he was saying to him, I was too fixated on taking Sylas in. His eyes had bags under them, and he looked pale. How many days has he been working non-stop? I heard his stomach growl and handed him the loaf of bread I was saving for later. He dropped the saw he was holding and quickly snatched it from my hands.

Thorne looked at me, he didn't have to say a word. We were sharing the same thought. He needed a break, he needed to just relax for a moment and sleep. Once Sylas finished the bread, he turned back to us and showed us around the room. His desk in the room was covered in papers and books. If he hadn't take the desk from my room, I would have thought the books were being held up by magic. He led us to a trapped object and stood in front of it smiling at us. He pulled the covering off and exposed his work. My dream was a reality, this was the kick we needed to gain the winning hand.

I was in complete awe of it though and found myself walking around and admiring the craftsmanship. Over a thousand arrows sat inside the machine, ready to take flight, and it had vine work around it that matched my bow. He took some inspiration from the bow as well and added blades to the front of the machine. I smiled at him, and he smiled back pointing in front of the machine. I looked past it and saw about five more machines he made the same way. No wonder we have barely seen him.

I ran over and swept him up in a hug. I was so proud of him, it was amazing. The only trouble now is how we are going to get these big machines out of the room.

"They can be disassembled and reassembled easily. I wanted to make the elves and men have no issue when it comes to moving them." He really was smart, he thought of everything, and as quick as he was to invite us to see his work he was faster to shoo us out of the room. "I will see you guys tonight, I am working on the last one."

****

Thorne and I were walking back to our room to take care of what I had started earlier when my name was cried out from behind us. I froze since I knew the voice. It was one of the elves I sent to get the treaties signed. I squeezed Thorne's hand and he squeezed mine back. We turned around to see the man by himself. His breath was heavy, and he had some cuts on his face. I knew something happened. I knew this was all a fucked idea.

"How far out was the attack?" I asked before he could say another word. "Where were you when it happened?"

"West, we were along the boundaries. We tried our best to avoid them like you said." I swallowed hard. "I only survived because I played dead, I was a coward–please forgive me."

"You were no coward, you were smart. Morgana would have killed you as well."

" Lord Aerin, it was not just Morgana. We were attacked by her men and some soldiers." Thorne stopped him and looked him dead in the eyes. "My men would never betray their king," he shouted at the man. "You lie."

"Not your men, Your Majesty," the older elf paused for a moment. "I'm not sure whose men they were, but their armor had a sun on it and some clouds." Thorne turned away from the man after apologizing to him. His face grew pale, and he looked ready to be sick. He knew something but did not share it in front of the elf. The elf handed me some treaties that they managed to get signed before the attack, and I thanked him for his hard work. I put them in my pocket to review them later and rubbed Thorne's back. After he was sure the man was gone and out of earshot, he looked at me.

"Those are the men the King warned us about. Remember when he said to stay away from the West? This is why. The King always had trouble keeping him in line. I guess he got word that I am the king now, and has joined Morgana in her thirst for power. He always wanted to be the true king, the one that all men answer to." Thorne punched a pillar that was standing next to him. "I begged him time and time again to launch an attack against him before it was too late. The King wanted peace though." I took his hand and quickly healed the broken fingers before they had time to swell. I kissed his hand and held it tight in my own.

"It's not your fault. It's mine for sending them out, I knew the risks and still did it. It's my burden to bear not yours, Thorne." I took a deep breath and held it for a moment before letting it back out. I wanted to cry and scream, but I was holding it together for Thorne. He hugged me and took a handful of my hair twirling it around his fingers.

"It will all be over soon." He whispered to me before kissing my cheek.

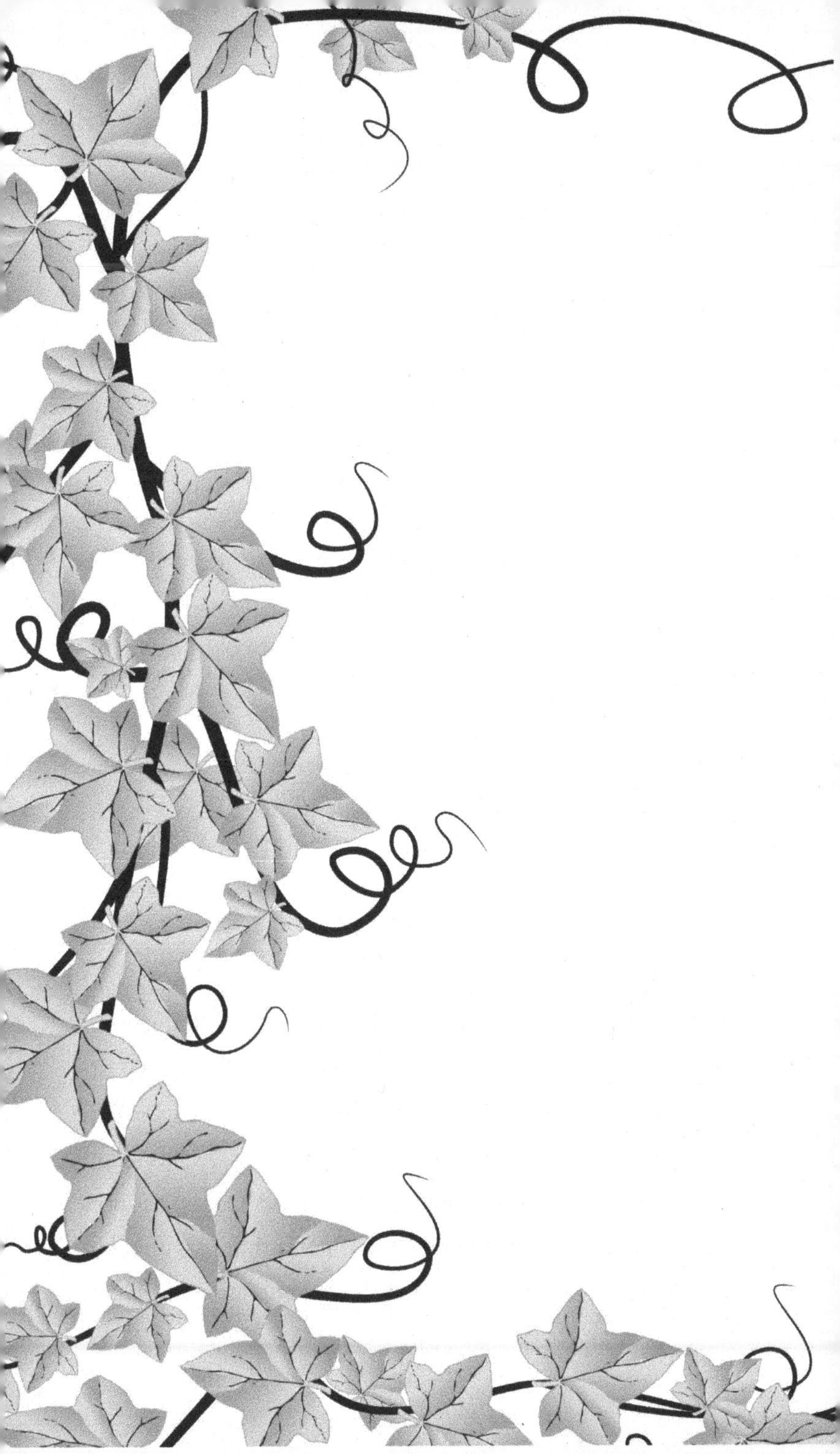

CHAPTER 30:

Aerin

Sylas was feeling drained, and Thorne and I both knew it. The barrier that protected the city had fallen, and every last person was on high alert because of it. We waited for the full power of Morgana to rain down on us. Sylas has slept for about a week, he has not left his bed and Thorne has not left his side. Not that I blame him, I don't think I would be able to leave either if it was him in that condition. Sure, he was healed, but there is only so much the elves can do. The rest is up to him; he needs to recover his magic from the exhaustion of creating the arrow launchers, and keeping the forcefield up for this long. I could not be prouder of him. I don't think I would be strong enough to accomplish half of what he has.

The week has been a long one, and I have been wandering around my city like a lost puppy without my lover by my side. This morning was no different. I awoke early in the morning to an empty bed and felt the stabbing in my chest return. Some days it felt like we never found each other, and I was still the same Shadow Hunter. Unlike the rest of the days, today had an eerie vibe to it. I turned, grabbed my cloak, and slicked my hair into the hood. I lifted it up to cover my head. Today felt like the Shadow Hunter is exactly what we need. I made my way down the hall to Sylas's room, hoping that he was awake.

I gently opened the door but saw him still passed out. Thorne was hunched over the bed clinging to his brother's hand. His head was lying on the bed next to his brother's side. He was so worried about him, and I was too. But we couldn't just sit in the room waiting. The kingdoms need us. I walked over to Thorne and sat him up gently in the chair before he woke up with a sore back that I would need to heal later, and gently pressed my lips against his cheek.

"I will be back later. I love you," I whispered into his ear. His eyes did not open and he shifted gently in the chair, getting comfortable. His hand grabbed mine and gently squeezed before he let go of his strength, and he was back asleep. I crept my way back out of the room and gently closed the door, careful to not make a sound. I returned to my room and grabbed my arsenal of daggers, the fighting knives Thorne purchased for me, and some arrows. I knew that today had to be the day Morgana made her move. I was going to be ready for her, she would not make it to them. She was not going to make it to my loved ones, no matter what. I will be dead before that happens. I peeked my head in the room one last time and saw Thorne still passed out, and closed it again, sneaking off.

****

Unlike normal, I hide in the shadows while traveling around town. I wanted to get a true feel for the people of my kingdom and understand what they truly needed from me as their king. They would never tell me the truth to my face, and that kind of ate at me. I did not hear too many complaints, other than the elves who were ready to fight being impatient. That warmed my heart a bit knowing that at least I was doing one thing right. I was keeping the kingdom safe the best I could.

I was walking near the edge of town when the purple fog started to roll in. I ran back into the city and rang the bells to prepare the elves for the fight of their lives. It was now or never. They quickly formed formations behind me and walked to the front gates ready for the battle. I kept my hood drawn tight over my face to hide me from any attackers, they would charge me first if they spotted me. I waited, hidden among the elves. The fog rolled to the gates and then vanished, exposing men in shining silver metal suits, and goblins. I wanted to be sick, seeing the men willing to fight beside those creatures.

No one moved, neither side made the first attack. The tension between us was growing. The elves drew their bows but waited for my command to fire. The goblins stood in front of the men like a wall, ready for us to fire. They were given metal shields that most of them could barely lift over their heads. The attack was desperate, and not well thought out. This should be an easy fight.

I was about to yell the command for my archers to rain down arrows when the fog appeared once more. Five trolls appeared, and Morgana showed herself on a horse made of smoke. She had the most devious smile glued to her face. I found myself in a temporary panic, and I let my mind wander around the city. I astral projected to the back and made sure she was not using the same tactics I did against her. I noticed nothing out of the ordinary and returned to my body.

"FIRE," I shouted and the elves lit their bows on fire and rained down their arrows on our enemy. I watched as they bounced off the men's armor, and killed most of the goblins. One of the trolls ran in front of Morgana and took over a hundred arrows for her. He started to swing back and forth before falling forward and crushing a good amount of their soldiers. I smiled cockily knowing this fight was basically over. Once the dirt cloud faded, I saw Morgana smiling still, as more goblins and men appeared. My smile left my face as I shouted to the elves to charge her.

Arrows still flew through the air, and they raced beside me still cloaking me from her sight. Morgana however did not move; she stayed in the exact same spot watching, waiting, and searching the battle ground for me.

I pulled out the daggers from their holsters and started slicing into any goblin I saw. The daggers quickly became too slick with blood for me to keep a hold of so I tossed them all into the same goblin and watched as he fell to the floor. I pulled out two more daggers and slowly made my way to Morgana, killing any goblin that stood in my way. The trolls must have gotten the command in their head because Morgana did not say a word out loud yet they began charging through the lines. They were swinging their clubs around sending my troops through the air as if they were feathers.

I was ready to tap into my powers and show myself. My eyes were turning red and my hair burnt hot enough to singe my cloak to ash. I caught a quick glimpse of Morgana as her head turned and she stared at me. One of the trolls changed direction and began to charge at me. He was larger than the last three trolls and was faster as well. Before I could react, he was at an arm's length to me.

The smell from him was enough to make anyone sick. That smell could be a weapon of its own. I turned off my mind and started to breathe out of my mouth in order to stay standing and not pass out from lack of oxygen. I grunted hard when his club smacked into my gut but managed to cling to it for dear life. Once the club is over his head, I jump off it, and land on his neck. I pulled out every dagger I had and one by one stabbed them into his head. The troll let out a groan for each stab and I was amazed that he was still standing after that many blades pierced into his head. I ducked down dodging his club as he tried to smack me off of him. I pulled out my fighting knives and looked back at the tall tower where Thorne was sitting with Sylas.

I could really use his help right now.

I spin the knives before stabbing both into his skull. He let out a sad groan and the other trolls stopped fighting and looked at him. That was it, the final blow. I tried to catch my breath as he swayed back and forth. He fell hard on the ground, and a bigger cloud of dust appeared. I was getting tired from all the fighting and stood on his back catching my breath. I hunched over and removed my knives from his head. I looked up and noticed that I was face to-face with Morgana.

I looked around and saw the forces were evenly matched. For every man that died here, an elf lay beside him. I met her gaze and the wind started to pick up around us. Our hair blowing wildly, mine on fire, and Morgana's looking like a fog. She got off the horse, and it vanished. We stood there for a moment circling each other before she finally stopped. She whipped her hands down to her sides and two short swords appeared out of the fog.

"Is this the best you can do, Morgana, I thought you were all-powerful," I spoke while still catching my breath and it was not working. I was so winded. "Are you that scared of me that you can't fight me without your army, without someone or something to have your back?" Morgana cackled before she stood straight up. Her head tilted back, and her eyes went black. I knew she was searching the battlefield looking for Thorne.

"Like you can talk, where is your precious Sylas or even Thorne for that matter? Are things not so happy for you?" She cackled again once she knew there was no sign of either of them, it was just her and myself. She also knew very well that she hit a soft spot. I could not hide the pain that was being caused by the lack of them both in my life.

"No, thank you for meddling every time we are happy." I feel my blood boil, and a second wind comes over me. My hair is even hotter now, the sound of Thorne's name from her mouth has completely set me over the edge. I was seeing red, and she was going to die right here. I twirled my knives, charging at her. The battlefield grew quiet as everyone stopped to watch us. Our blades were evenly matched as they clanged against each other. Sparks flew from the clashing metal, and our arms swung away from each other from the recoil. We both meant to kill the other. One of us was not going to walk away from this fight. We both knew it. We were fighting for our lives. Fighting strictly on instinct. I was very surprised that she didn't tap into her magic either. This was so far a fight of pure skill, and we were evenly matched.

She tapped into her old elvish magic and was moving faster than the naked eye could see. I pressed on my heels and kicked off them, tapping into a slight part of my magic. I recalled a moment from my past when my father was drunk and bragging about how I was always faster than Morgana, but I was also easier to anger and had a harder time staying calm. Was he ever right about both of those statements? I was barely even tapping into my powers and still kept up with her. I charged her again and smiled, deflecting a dagger and slicing her cheek with the other. She slowed for a moment and held her cheek. I waited to see her next move, and was ready for anything that she might throw at me. She took a deep breath and screamed. A shockwave flew out of her, but it did not rock me. I was standing my ground. I was routed in place, and ready for her this time. The time away from Thorne paid off, along with the nights I spent at the sparring camp. I knew this fight was far from over, and was wondering how long I could keep this up before I fell over being completely drained of my magic.

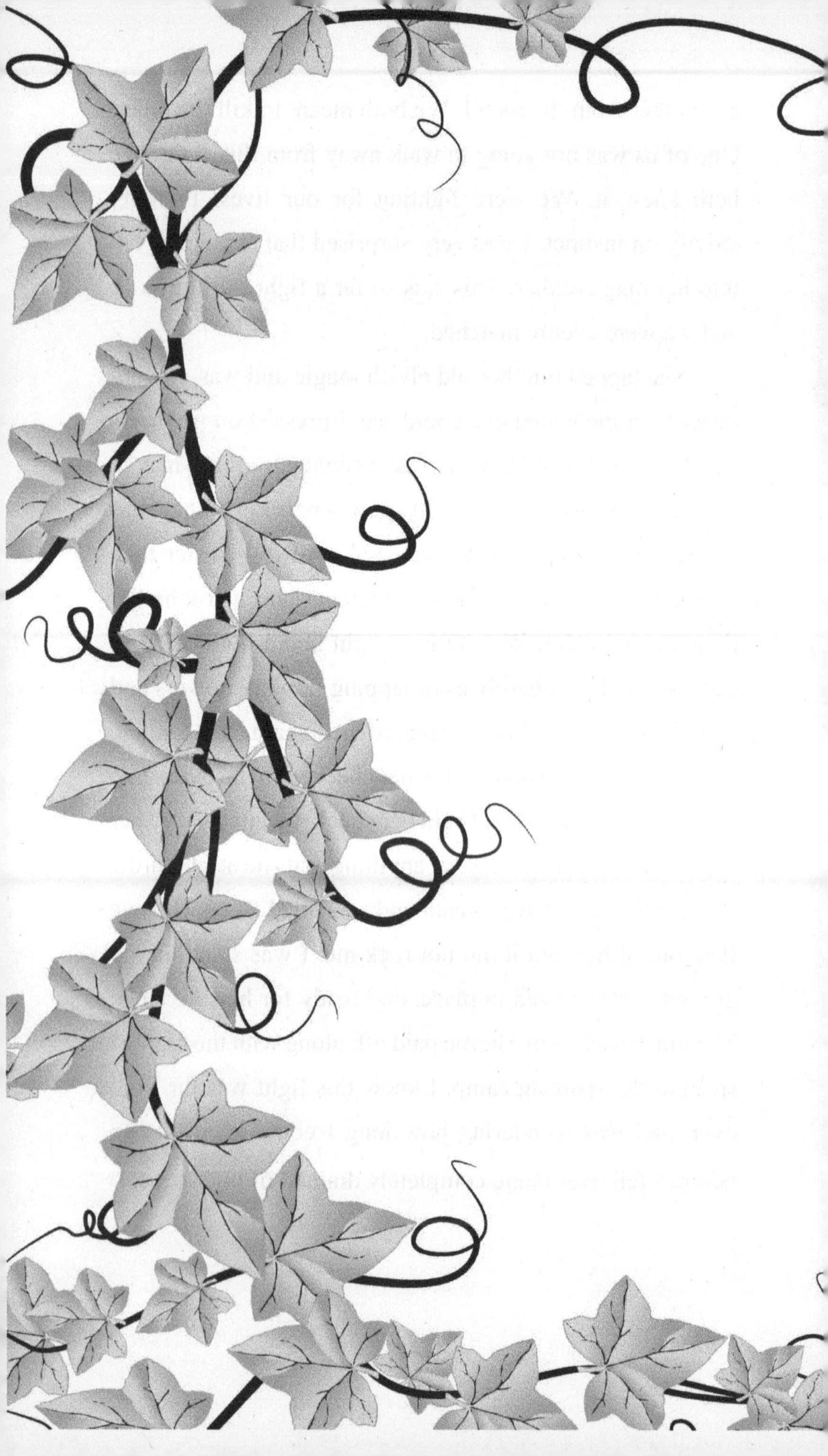

CHAPTER 31:

Thorne

I sprung to life when I heard a pounding coming from the door. It busted open shortly after and one of Aerin's personal guards stormed into the room. He was out of breath and hunched over slightly, his spear the only thing holding him up. I felt my heart drop to the floor, Aerin gave them strict orders that this room was off-limits. The only reason he would break a direct order is if something happened to Aerin. I stood up fast and the chair flew back from under me.

"Where is he?" The guard pointed out the window, he was still out of breath and unable to get any words to leave his lips.

I raced over to the window that overlooked the city. I looked out, I could not see much other than purple fog being met with black fog. I raced to our bedroom and grabbed my sword. My heart was pounding and felt like it was ready to beat right out of my chest. I ran as fast as I could to get to him. I was so slow, that I removed my armor as I got closer to pick up my pace. I shoved my way through the crowd of elves, men, and goblins alike. I tried to get close to them but was forced back by the wind they were causing. I could not see them clearly as they were too fast for me to keep track of.

What do I do? I can't just stand here, he needs me and I need him. I need to save him, I need to help him. My heart would not stop racing and I could hear the beating it struck through me. Fireballs and shadow balls started to fly out of the funnel of mixed fog. The elves and men backed up to avoid being hit by any. I watched as the remaining goblins were hit and vaporized. They were going to kill each other. That was their plan, wasn't it? Someone was not walking out of there alive. Soon after the fireballs stopped, so did the shadow balls. They were replaced with shadow weapons and lightning bolts.

I wish I could see what was going on. I tried again to charge into the middle of them but was pushed back again.

They were moving faster, they had to have been because I was not only pushed back but sent flying. I landed a few feet away and on my ass. I stood back up and ran back to them again. I finally heard Morgana shout and the current stopped. I raced into the midst of them and found Aerin. He was holding onto his stomach and hunched over much like Morgana. They had matching wounds. Were they evenly matched? Aerin collapsed for a moment into me. He flashed me a smile and I kissed his head. My hand was warm as it became covered in his blood.

"Oh look, there's the man of the hour." I heard Morgana call out from behind me. I turned to her and readied my stance. Aerin nearly fell over and I dropped my sword to catch him.

What do I do here, I can't fight her and bring him to safety. I turned back to Aerin whose eyes were flickering between their normal green and their magical red. He was nearing the end of his magic. He can't keep fighting like this, it's too much. No one should be able to.

"Are you ready yet, dear brother? Are you ready to die, or join me and live?"

I swallowed hard after hearing that. She brought it up again, joining her. I looked down at Aerin and shook my head no. I helped him to his feet only for him to push me to the side. A ball of pure darkness struck into his chest and he was sent flying back. I whipped my head up and saw his legs wobbling as he tried to stand. He walked slowly back over to us and stood in front of me.

"Haven't you learned yet, brother, love is weakness. It will only leave you burned."

Aerin did not say a word, he only looked back at me and smiled. How could he smile at me through the pain he is in?

"What would you know about it, Morgana? You don't know what love is." In a blink of an eye, she was in front of me, and Aerin was thrown across the battlefield.

"I have felt the sting of love." Her face showed the truth even though it was burnt to a crisp. She lifted me by my neck, and let go after her fog was wrapped around me–choking me. I was unable to move as it bound me in the air. I forced myself to look over at Aerin and felt tears rolling down my face. I was fearing the worst, they were both right–someone was not leaving this fight alive and I feared it was me. She was going to use me to turn him. Aerin swallowed the pain and stood back up. He limped his way over to his sister and dropped his weapons. My vision started to blur but I could make out him dropping to his knees in front of her.

Morgana had to use a tree to keep herself standing as well. They were both badly beaten. The fog dropped me and I fell to my knees choking for air. The world was spinning around me, but I started to crawl to Aerin. As I approached him, one of the trolls lifted his leg and brought it down on Aerin. Morgana's cackle echoed through the city. I winced hearing the snapping sounds of Aerin's legs. I wanted to cry out for him, but that would make it easier for Morgana. The other trolls stepped on me to keep me in place as Morgana tied a rope around his legs and summoned her horse again. I reached for him as he lay lifeless on the ground in front of me.

I was helpless. I came out here to help him, instead I might have cost him everything. If I was more gifted, if I was stronger, I could help him. But I'm weak, I am not strong enough to protect him or Sylas. Morgana saddled her horse and held onto the rope. Aerin picked up his head once the troll removed his foot. He mouthed the words I love you before he passed out from the pain or blood loss. Whichever took effect first. What have I done, I killed the man I love. I tried to crawl out from under the troll's foot but could not move. I was forced to watch as Aerin was being dragged behind Morgana.

A bright light formed from behind me, and a voice shouted.

"You will go no further, Morgana." I watched as Morgana and her horse ran into a wall.

The weight from my back was lifted and I turned to see my brother. He was floating in the air. It was not just my brother, the light around him was in the shape of Rillifane, the outline surrounding his own body. Rillifane was tall and muscular, and his hair was long and dragged behind them. Every elf there stopped and fell to the ground, bowing to him. Rillifane was not only the god of the wood elves but also the leader of all elvish gods.

Morgana froze in place and did not turn around. I watched as Aerin's body floated in the air and came back to me, resting in my arms. He lifted his hand and touched my cheek gently before passing back out in my arms. I felt for a pulse, there was one but it was faint and his breaths were shallow.

Morgana turned slowly and for the first time, I could see fear in her eyes. Tears fell down her cheeks as she walked closer to him.

"Rillifane," she spoke softly but I was able to pick up on it.

"Morgana, I have given you so much, and look what you have done with that power." She looked past him to the bloodshed left behind.

"You walked away from me, you left me scorned and alone," she shouted at him, the fog forming behind her.

"No, Morgana, you chose power over love. You chose this, it was you who walked away." Sylas and Rillifane held out their hand and a light shone down onto Morgana. Sylas fell to the floor and landed softly, and Rillifane was standing before us in a mortal form. Morgana fell to her knees crying. She looks like she has seen a ghost. It was the same reaction Aerin had when we first reunited. Were they lovers? Exactly how old is Morgana? This opened up a can of worms I wanted to seal fast.

"Morgana, I loved you but now you leave me no choice. I am taking away the remaining elvish powers you possess. You turned your back on love, peace, and everything you once stood for. I am renouncing you as an elf–you belong to the dark fae now." Rillifane turned back into a small light that was absorbed by Sylas's body and one of the elves ran over to pick him up, bringing him back over to us. He knelt next to me holding my brother. The goblins and men that were once mixed in with us vanished in retreat, and the trolls were turned to stone. Morgana was alone. She screamed out as her face was no longer young, her skin wrinkled, and the burns were exposed to us all. The purple fog quickly formed around her and she was gone.

****

The elves were nice enough to carry Sylas's bed up to our room and put it against the farthest wall. I managed to heal Aerin to the best of my ability, the wound on his stomach was no longer there but he still didn't wake up. Sylas was still out like a light as well. I sat in a chair between the two watching as they slept. I never left the room even for a moment, afraid of not being there if something went wrong or if they didn't wake.

The sunset and the room were only lit by a candle the elves lit when they dropped off dinner for me. I haven't eaten for days, I couldn't and had no appetite left. My eyes were getting heavy and I crawled into bed with Aerin. I took great care not to move him as I inched close enough to feel his breath on my neck. I closed my eyes and cried myself to sleep like I did every night, and questioned everything. Was my love for him the cause of all this pain? Was it the reason he was defeated, he was fine until he learned I was there. I am not strong enough to be with him. If I stayed, was it going to be the reason he died? I could not risk that. I need him alive, I would rather never see him again knowing he is alive than be his downfall.

I gently pushed my hand under his head and rubbed his shoulder. I laid on my back staring at the ceiling. I was hoping that he would open his eyes. I needed to hear him say that everything was okay. I needed him to give me a reason to stay.

Is love really a weakness?

"Don't you dare think that," he whispered to me. "Love is strength. It is because of my love for you and Sy that I was able to fight her for so long."

Aerin slid his hand into mine and rolled onto his side groaning a bit from the pain and nuzzled into my neck. "Everything will be okay, what was it you told me? You can't dwell on the what if." He stretched his neck and kissed my cheek.

I could not look at him. He was finally awake, I was happy as could be but I could not bear to look over at him. If I didn't try to play hero this would not have happened. If I had just stayed put, and let him handle everything. His burns, the scars, the cuts, all of it is my fault. I need to be stronger. I need to protect him. I felt my chest warm up and watched as a shield formed around Aerin. Was I finally learning my true Elvish gift? Will I be able to protect him?

"You're so warm, Thorne," Aerin spoke to me without opening his eyes. "It's nice."

I love him so much, and I am so very afraid of losing him. I wish someone was around to tell me what to do. Every ounce of my being wants to be here with him, to help him with anything. But there is a thought in the back of my head screaming to run, get as far away from him as I can. Every time we get close something happens and I lose him.

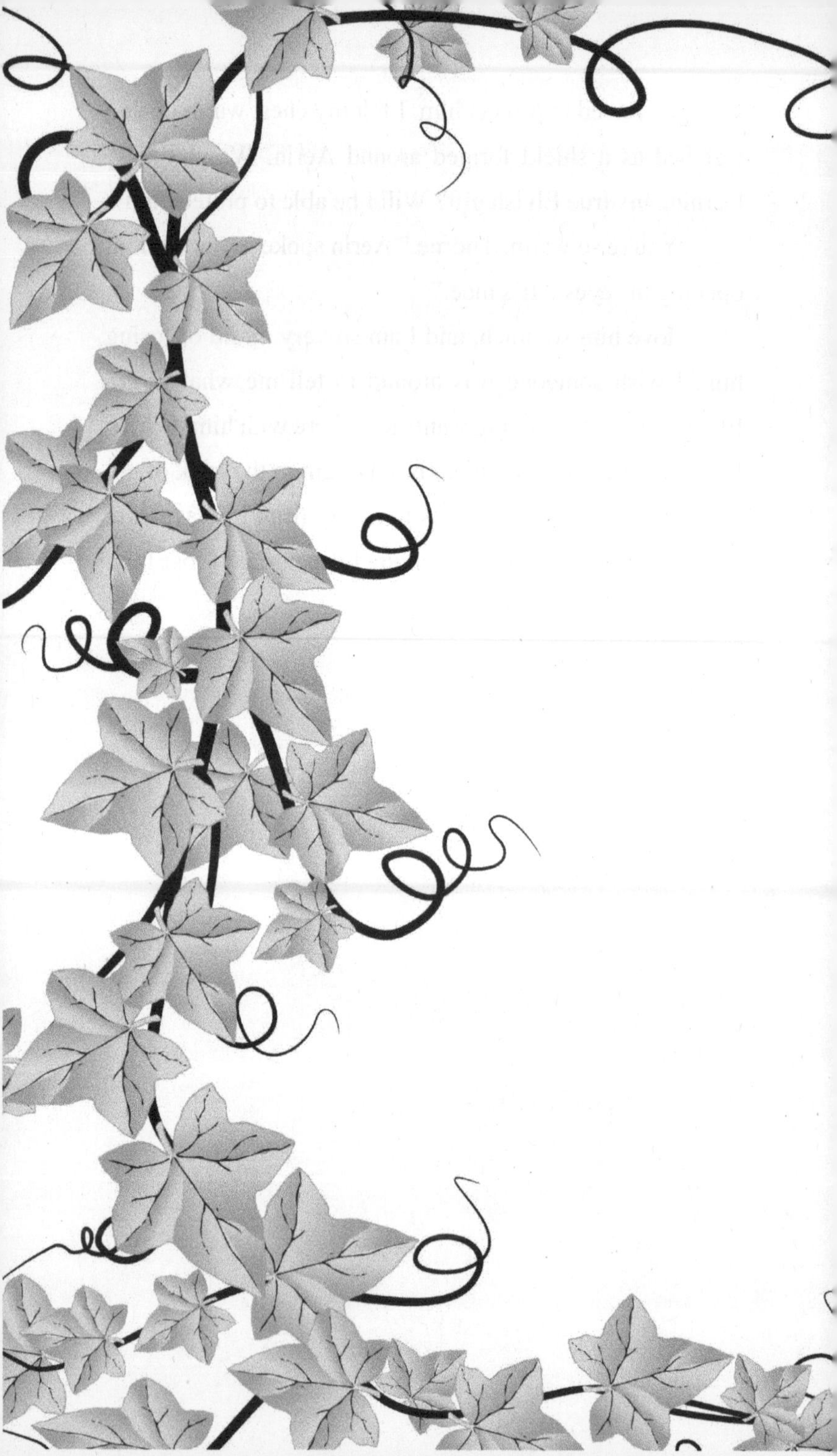

CHAPTER 32:

Thorne

I woke up early the next day. I was able to feel Aerin's cock hard as a rock pressed against my ass. I wanted it, I wanted to be close to him again. It felt like it was years since we last connected. I gently moved my hips back, grinding up on him. He groaned at me and told me to not tease him so early in the morning with Sy in the room. I forgot that Sylas was in our room now until he woke up.

Sylas was still not waking up. Did the use of his

powers mixed with Rillifane take a toll on him as well? There is nothing we can do, there is nothing to heal. All we can do is wait for him to wake up. I pushed myself up in bed and looked down at Aerin whose head was resting on my chest. I tried to calm my own morning wood down, but it was hard with Aerin so close to it. His hand gently laid on top of my leg. It was so close to my inner thigh and brushed against my balls. I swallowed the whimper I was holding in and moved my leg up to adjust his hand.

I slowed my breathing until I looked down and saw the tent in the blanket receding. I felt accomplished until Aerin fully woke up and kissed my cheek. I smiled at him and lifted his chin kissing him.

"How are you feeling?" I asked him, wondering if he needed more healing. I can only do so much when someone is awake, and even less when they are out cold.

"So much better now that I am in your arms. I really missed this." He smiled at me and looked at his hand that was lying on my chest. His ring was shining from the sun that was peeking in from the window. He sighed, and I knew it was because he was daydreaming about our wedding again. It was something I often found myself thinking about as well. I loved him more than anything. I swallowed hard before looking over at Aerin again and took a deep breath.

"How much do you remember from the last fight?"

"The last thing I remember was giving up, dropping to

my knees, and giving myself over to make sure you were going to be safe." Aerin's eyes started to fill with tears, and I held his face in my hands. I rolled over to face him and kissed his head. "I am so sorry, I know we agreed but I had nothing left. It was the only way to make sure you were kept safe. Has Sylas woken up yet?"

I shook my head and explained to him what happened after he passed out. He nodded to me, understanding why Sylas was still asleep. I was a little surprised that there was hardly a reaction after hearing the truth about his sister.

"So, you mean she used to be with a god?" He was kind of a mix of surprised and dumbfounded.

I nodded to him and he just laid his head back down trying to circle around all the facts that made no sense.

****

Hours had passed and I was enjoying having Aerin in my arms. I would've laid there forever holding onto him. It was time to get a move on and at least show his men that he was alive and well. I pried him off me, and he growled at me slightly but agreed it was time to get up. We dressed and he went to leave the room. I quickly grabbed his hand and pulled him back into me.

"You're not leaving without me." He smiled as I held the door open for him. As he walked out the door, I gently patted his ass and he jumped slightly unexpecting it. He walked out into the city, and I was standing close watching everyone as they bowed to him. He walked to the families that were in tears offered his condolences and welcomed them to join him in a grand feast tonight in their honor. Many of them agreed to this. He was a great leader just like I always knew he would be. I knew he would be the king that I would follow no matter what.

We made our way through the whole city and worked up an appetite. We walked into the small soup shop and took seats at the table by the door. I pulled the chair out for Aerin and pushed it in as he sat down before taking my own seat. I smiled at him from across the table and took his hands in my own. We sat in silence, just staring into each other's eyes. Every second that passed made me love him even more.

We ate the soup before heading back to the palace to check in on Sylas. I swept Aerin off his feet and carried him up the stairs and into our room. I pushed the door open and plopped him on the bed. I walked over and sat next to Sylas.

"Sy," I spoke softly, smiling at him. There was no reaction from him though. All the healing was done, and I hunched over the bed starting to tear up. I was beginning to lose faith that he was ever going to wake up again. Aerin walked over to me, rubbed my back gently, and kissed my cheek. He held his hand on Sylas's forehead and looked at me.

"He still has brain function, relax, he will wake up. I promise you."

I nodded and sat back in the chair. Aerin sat next to me on the floor and leaned against Sylas's bed. His legs spread, and I crawled down from the chair and took a seat in between them. He wrapped his arms around me and I rested my head against his shoulder. I love him so much, just being with him makes everything easier. It reminds me that I do not need to face everything by myself and that I have someone to share everything with. Whether it be pain or pleasure.

Shit, I should not be thinking that. I find myself becoming rock-hard again. Aerin wraps his arms around me and gently rubs my arms. His touch was not helping with the issue. I stood up and dragged Aerin out of the room, I had to have him. I could not hold it back anymore. I had a thirst and hunger that I needed him in order to get rid of.

I closed the door behind us and looked up and down the hall, when I saw no one around I pinned him to the wall. The rush was amazing, and the thrill of being caught made it even more exciting. Aerin bit down onto my shoulder to keep his moans to himself, and it encouraged me to thrust harder into him. I wanted to hear those moans, I wanted everything.

****

The table was set with hundreds of plates, and extra tables were brought into the dining hall. The elves pulled out all the stops. There were mountains of food on the table. Platters filled with meat, fruits, vegetables, and bread. My mouth was watering. I needed food so badly, especially after the workout I just had with Aerin. Aerin took a seat at the head of the table and I sat next to him. He took my hand gently below the table as we waited for the others to join us. It was not long before the room was packed with all the elves and their families. A younger elf sat next to Aerin, and I did not appreciate the looks he kept giving him.

He kept staring at him, not in any kind of threatening way, he had the worst look of lust glued to his face. I wanted to jump off the table for the looks he was giving him. I wanted to punch him till every ounce of lust left him for the rest of his life. Aerin must have either noticed the looks or the fact that I was about to lose control of my magic because he reached under the table and gently rubbed my knee. He was trying to keep me calm, but it was not working.

Aerin was my lover, anyone who hurt him or looked at him like that deserved to be knocked down a few pegs. Aerin removed his hand and took mine above the table. He gently kissed it before making his plate of food. I smiled at him and kissed his hand back, keeping my eyes on the young elf. I watched as his face fell to the table, and the lust left his eyes. I sighed and slouched back down in my chair.

I looked around and watched as everyone dug into the feast around them. Aerin stood up and smiled at the guests. He picked up his glass, starting to clang it with the fork he was using to eat.

"I would like to thank you all for joining Thorne and

me for dinner tonight. We can not thank your families enough. We eat together tonight remembering everyone whose lives were cut short. This is not going to be the last fight with the dark fae, they have been our enemy for longer than time itself. We have always stood against it, but I will no longer require any of your families to do so. You all get the choice to fight. As your king, I want you to know that I will keep you all safe." Aerin sat back down and the elf next to him stood up. I had to bite my tongue as he looked at Aerin before speaking.

"Lord Aerin, I speak for all of us when I say there is no other king we would rather follow. You have proven yourself. You have shown us you will die for us, and we will do the same for you."

He reached down to take Aerin's hand but he quickly pulled his hand away and rested it on his lap. The elf frowned and took his seat again. The elves cheered not noticing, but agreeing they were ready to fight with Aerin. Everyone finished their food and went on their way back to their homes. The boy was the last to leave and my eyes never drifted away from him. It was just us three left in the room, and I was about to explode. Aerin cleared his throat and looked at the boy.

"I am engaged, I am happy, please do not look at your king in that matter. Thorne nearly leaped over the table. You need to remember to keep your emotions in tact especially if you plan on taking your father's place in my army. I can not be worried about a surprise appearance in my tent. I can't help it if Thorne takes you out because you can't keep yourself in check."

I shot him a cocky smile and leaned back in my chair, raising my eyebrows at him.

"I am sorry, Lord Aerin, please forgive me." I could tell he meant every word he said. I was trying to remind myself that he is young and that he is also just getting through puberty. He might be over a hundred, but was still young. I kept my eyes on him still until he left the room. Once he was gone, I finished the food on my plate and Aerin grabbed some extra dessert.

"Thank you, Thorne, for keeping it together." I smiled at him and nodded.

"Luckily we were able to have that quickie before dinner or I am not sure I would have been able to. I winked at Aerin but found myself thinking about Sy. I was wondering if he would wake up tomorrow. I wanted this fight with Morgana over, and that could not happen until he was awake again. I also just wanted my brother back—I wanted to hug him, I wanted to tell him how proud I was of him. I wanted our family back. Aerin noticed my thought change and he grabbed my hand again.

"I have an idea to wake Sy up. If he is not awake soon, I can dream jump and bring him back to us."

I swallowed hard. I knew the dangers of dream jumping. I knew that he could be lost forever, but if it all worked out he would be able to wake him up. He would be able to understand what is keeping Sy asleep. I squeezed his hand and shook my head. I was torn between letting him sacrifice himself or waking my brother. That was a decision I could not make, nor did I even want to think about.

"I am not asking, Thorne. He is my brother too, I am going to bring him back to us."

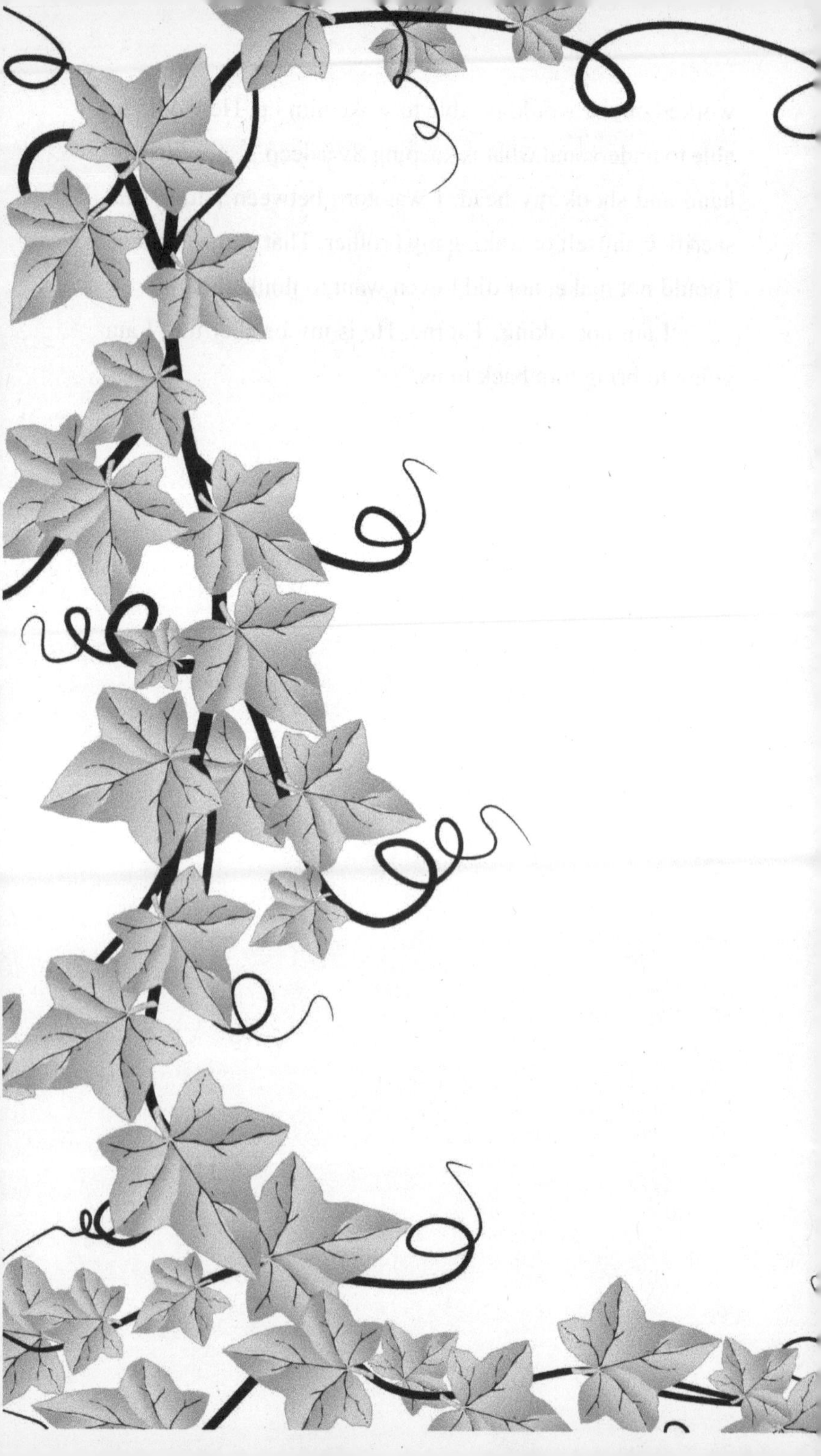

CHAPTER 33:

Aerin

The next morning I woke up and walked over Sylas's bed, there was no change in him. He was still asleep, his breaths were the same as before. I took a deep breath and walked over to Thorne. He was still passed out. I leaned over kissing him awake. He woke up and pulled me down onto his chest. I chuckled and listened as his heart skipped a beat. He did not open his eyes but held me tight.

"Is Sy awake?" he asked me while still keeping his eyes closed.

I did not answer him, instead just laid there with him in silence. He sighed because he knew my mind was already made up. I am going dream jumping. Thorne sat up and rested his back against the bed frame. The blanket fell down to his waist, and though I have seen his body so many times, his muscular chest rising and falling made my mouth water. I wanted his arms around me. I wanted him to hold me on his chest again. I swung my leg over him and he pulled me down into him.

Mission accomplished.

I lay there on his chest listening to his heart beating. I looked at the candle next to him and ignited it with my mind. I looked up into his eyes and he smiled softly at me. I slowed my breathing and lowered my heartbeats.

"Don't let me go, promise." He smiled at me and nodded. "I need you to keep me grounded while I am gone."

He leaned down and kissed me. "Don't worry I am not going anywhere. I will be right here when you both come back home."

I shifted my eyes away from him and back to the flame. I felt myself drifting into a trance, as I watched the flame grow and shrink. The flame grew and turned purple, and I found myself in pitch blackness.

I could no longer feel the warmth from Thorne, I

could not hear his heart beating. I was alone. I called out for Sylas and was pulled by a force into a forest. It looked like my old home. It was a spitting image of it. My house looked exactly as I remembered. There was no one around, and it was quiet. There was no sound of animals or anything. The swing my father built was still hanging, I could see the rope that held it from over the bushes. It was swaying to and fro but there was no wind here. I walked over to it and saw Sylas sitting on the swing rocking his feet planted on the ground.

I walked over to him and started to push him on the swing. I let him enjoy the time for a little before I spoke to him. He was laughing like a kid enjoying the moment of childhood he wished he had.

"Higher, Thorne, higher," he called out before turning around to see me there.

"Why are we here, Sylas?" I asked him.

"Thorne always talked about this place, I wanted to see it for real. I come here often in my dreams. He is right, Aerin, it is so peaceful here. I really wish I was born when you both lived here."

I smiled at him and found myself happy as well. It was nice to be back here.

"It was nice, Sy, you would have really liked it." I pointed out to a tree across the way and he followed my finger as I pushed him higher. "Over there is where I first told Thorne I loved him."

"What was Thorne like when he was younger?" Sylas wanted to know everything about this place and about his brother.

"He was very handsome, and the reason I woke up every day. He gave me strength I never knew I had. He was always a great protector. I never felt safer than when I was in his arms. Everything was perfect here, Sy, or so I thought." Part of me wanted to stay right here and with Thorne again. I wanted things back to how they used to be so bad. I always did.

With me here in his dream world, the world started to shift. Elves appeared and the town came alive once more. All of my memories came to life, and Sylas hopped off the swing when a younger version of myself appeared before us walking to the tree.

A young Thorne popped his head around the tree and talked to the younger version of myself. I knew exactly what day this was. It was the last time I saw him. I watched as the two cuddled beneath the tree and talked before Thorne carried me to the swing. He gently pushed it and Sylas took my hand in his.

"You two were so happy, you both look so much in love."

He is right we were very much in love. I was so happy. Nothing could hurt me when I was with him. I wanted this again. I wanted this same feeling. I had to fight every urge in me to race over to him and tell him about what was going to happen next. If I intervened at all I would be stuck here. As I watched the scene in front of me, the sun started to set. I felt tears falling down my face because I knew what was next.

"Sylas, we have to go. Now." Sylas looked up at me and crooked his finger to get me down to his height. I bent down and pushed away the tears.

"What happened here? Thorne always talked about this place, and how happy he was. And boy do I see why, you two were so in love. But what happened that it all ended?" Right as he asked, the entire forest was engulfed in flames. I did not want to relive this. But I had no choice, I could not leave him here alone.

"Sylas, listen to me. You need to stay very close to me, there is not much time." The fire grew closer to us, and I watched as a younger me ran out of the house screaming for Thorne. I felt my heart being ripped out of my chest. "You need to wake up, Sy, your brother needs you—we can make a new peace, a new happiness." The sound of elves screaming as the flames devoured them grew louder.

I blinked for a moment and Sylas was gone. I knew he woken up, but I could not. I watched and waited for Thorne just like before. I followed the younger version of myself around the forest searching for him. Our voices matched as we shouted for him. Right before the flames swallowed me whole, the day restarted. This was the nightmare I lived with for centuries. I knew exactly how it played out every time. The pain I thought I put behind me was now back and stronger than ever.

When the scene replayed I was no longer watching a younger version of myself. I was inside my house, I looked in the mirror and saw a younger me looking back.

****

I sat against the big tree waiting for my lover. I was hoping he would be able to sneak out of his father's house again to visit me.

"Aerin," I heard Thorne's voice from behind the tree as he popped his head out. He sat down next to me and laid his head on my lap. We were so young, so stupid, and so in love.

"I was thinking about your offer, Aerin. I would be happy to move in with you. But on one condition." I smiled up to him and nodded for him to go on. "I get to hold you every night."

"I don't know, Thorne. You draw a very hard bargain there. Hmmm. I don't know, being held in the arms of the elf I love more than life itself doesn't sound like something I can live with forever," I spoke cocky and sarcastically.

Thorne sprung to his feet and turned to pick me up. I draped my arm around his neck and kissed his cheek.

"My strong elf. If you had your way I would never walk again." He flashed a bright smile at me and placed me on the swing. He walked behind me and gave it a push.

"Higher, Thorne, higher." I turned to see him and

he was gone, the sunset again. I was in my house laying in bed waiting for Thorne to join me with his belongings. I told him we could unpack tomorrow, and for him just to climb in bed when he gets here. I was losing control of my own mind. I was going to be stuck here, living this day until I drew my last breath.

I woke from a dream about Thorne and smelt smoke. I looked out the window and saw people running around on fire, the smell of burnt flesh was filling the air and I wanted to be sick. I raced out of the house. "THORNE!" I shouted and searched the forest for him. There was no sight of him, and his father's house was one of many already burnt to the ground. When I could not find him, I felt my heart being ripped out of my chest and stomped on the ground. I fell to my knees and screamed. I could not take the pain of losing him. I lost myself there that night and nothing has ever been the same since.

I punched the ground hard and broke my hand which never healed properly either until Thorne healed it centuries later.

The scene replayed time and time again, I could not stop it. I was trapped. I wanted to die every night, but every morning I wanted to stay there. I was trapped in the endless cycle of love and hurt. My biggest fear was replayed over and over. I was losing Thorne, and I could do nothing but live it again and again. I started crying every morning when he picked me up because I knew moments later he was going to be gone. I reached the point where my mind was about to break. I was shaking uncontrollably. I knew I could not wake myself back up. I knew that this was going to be how I died.

That next replay of the memory, I found myself walking through the flames and standing in them. I wanted to die. I could no longer take the pain of my heart being ripped from my chest. I felt my skin start to burn and I smiled. It was all over. Before I felt the grasp of death's hand, I was pulled back to the morning again. I was crying, looking in the mirror. I could not go numb as every morning I felt the exact emotions my younger self did. With the only exception of the pain of losing Thorne added in.

I was sitting against the tree again and Thorne laid his head on my lap.

"I thought about what you asked me. I would be happy to move in with you Aerin, on one condition." I nodded again and forced myself to smile through the tears I was holding back. My heart was pounding a mile a minute. "I need you to wake up and come back to me."

"What did you say?" I asked him softly.

Thorne picked me up placed me on the swing and gave a strong push.

"I need you to wake up. I need you back with me. Please wake up, Aerin." It was Thorne, my Thorne, not the memory. He was calling out to me. The memory vanished and I was left in complete nothingness again.

****

I closed my eyes and when I next opened them, I was back in my body. Thorne was rocking me and I turned to him. I pulled him close to me and cried on his shoulder. He continued to rock me and held back his tears trying to be the strong one here.

"Thorne?" I asked, while my arms were clenched to him. "Am I still dreaming? Are you going to leave? Please stay, don't leave me. I can't... I can't..." I was losing it. My mind was fried, I was so terrified and I hurt so much. I could not tell what was real, and what was fake anymore. Everything was a blur in my mind.

"Aerin... look at me."

I shook my head, I was too afraid to look at him. I was afraid that it was just another younger version of him. I was terrified that nothing changed. He turned me onto my back and leaned over. "Open your eyes, Aerin." I shook my head again and he leaned down and kissed me softly. "Please look at me, Aerin."

I slowly opened my eyes and looked up at him. I was back, but my mind was still living in the nightmare. I could not move past the pain. I could not bring myself to realize that I was back and I couldn't stop crying.

Sylas came back to the room and raced over to me. He had a mouth full of food and looked at his brother.

"What happened?" His voice panicked, it echoed in my head.

"I don't know. He woke back up like this, I got him to calm down."

I felt Sylas connect to me using his gift. He fell to his knees, his young mind and heart could not bear the pain I was feeling. He looked up at Thorne, crying.

"He relived it ten thousand times. He lost you ten thousand times, Thorne." Sylas could not be in the room with the pain, he could not control his gift around emotions so high. He ran out of the room and called for healers. Thorne turned on his side and laid in bed next to me pulling me in close to his chest, and running his hands through my hair.

"Thorne, where are you? Thorne, don't leave me alone. Thorne," I shouted out to nothing. I could feel his tears rolling down his face and hitting my own, but I could not stop. I was in so much pain, I was so lost.

"Aerin, I am so sorry. I had no idea this would happen, I had no idea that fear weighed on you so hard. I wish I could go back and change it. I wish I was there for you, I always have," Thorne whispered to me.

"Thorne, come back. I need you," I shouted. "I love you, don't leave me."

I was trapped in the fire. It was no longer repeating the day, but the fire and pain felt so real. Every time I saw this memory, it piled all at one time. I could not break free. I could not break the grasp the memory had on my mind.

"THORNE, SAVE ME," I called out.

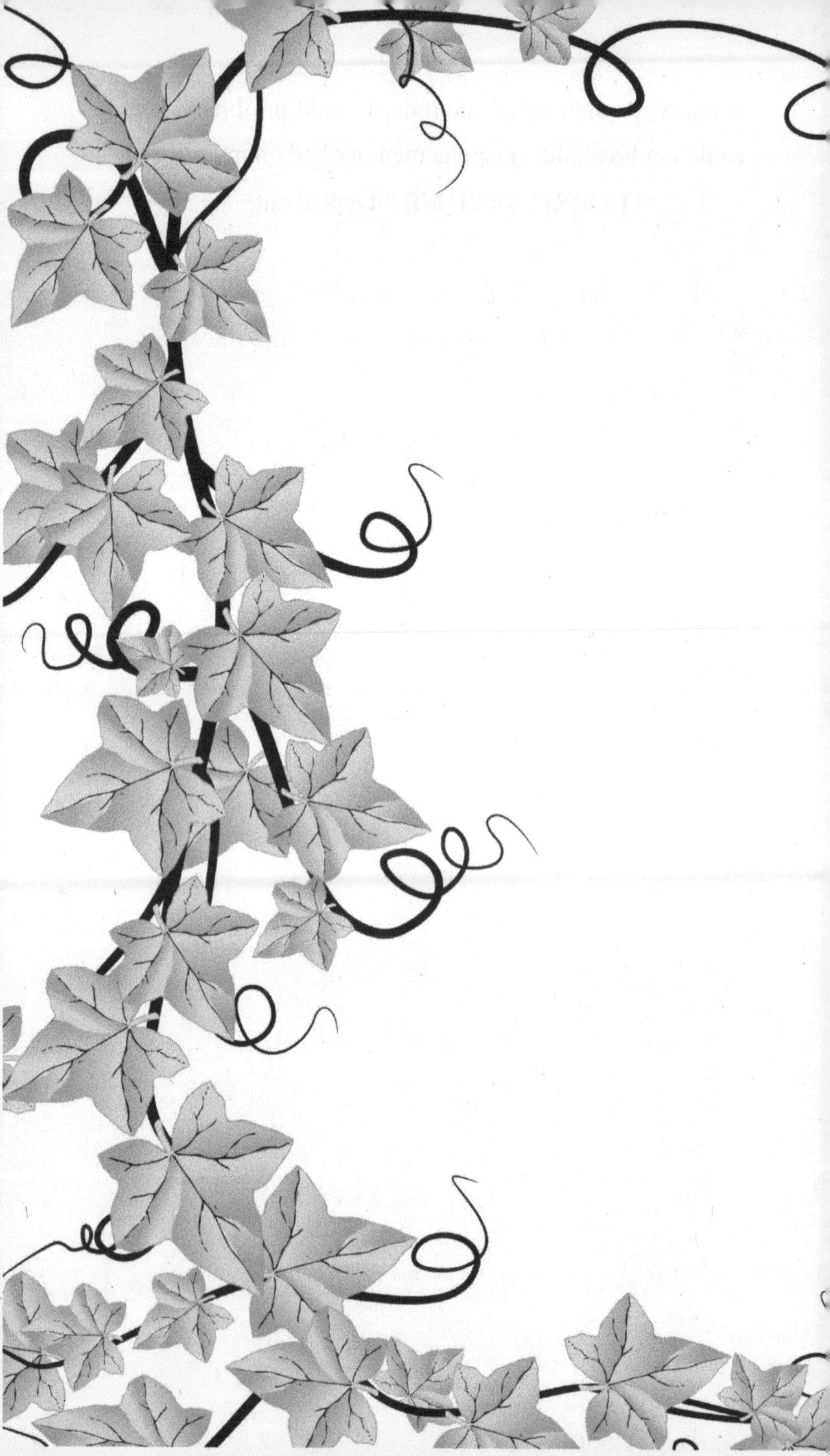

CHAPTER 34:

Thorne

The healers could not get here soon enough. I was falling apart while Aerin broke down. There was nothing I could do for him. I rolled him over and gently kissed his lips. I held onto him as tight as I could. I wanted to shield him from this, I wanted to bring him back to me. I needed him here. All of him.

I turned him onto his back, and he still would not look at me. I pulled him in close and kissed him again. Our lips touched, and he started to cry harder. I closed my eyes, recalling that day like it was yesterday.

"Aerin, I thought about what you asked me." I watched him as he finally opened his eyes and looked up at me. I shot him a warm smile. "I will move in with you on one condition." Aerin nodded to me. "I get to hold you every night, just like I have for the past year. I get to be the one you love forever."

Aerin did not scream, he did not pull away. He stared at me as if I was a ghost. I closed my eyes and let my gift take over. My mind wandered into his. I was there with him. I could see the flames and our homes being burned to the ground. For the first time, I was living in a great fire. I raced around the village calling out for Aerin. I could hear him shouting my name and I raced to him.

He was covered in soot, and his red hair was completely black. I had to swallow my emotions as I walked to him. He dropped to his knees and started to shout out my name, begging me to not leave him. I knelt next to him and scooped him up.

"You came for me," Aerin spoke, crying out. He buried his face into my shoulder, and my emotions took over. I never want him to feel this pain again.

Never.

My eyes turned deep blue, and clouds formed overhead. They opened up and doused the fire. The memory changed and it was just us left in the city.

"I will always come back for you, I will always protect

you. I love you, Aerin." Aerin blinked a few times before he kissed me passionately. His arms draped over my shoulders and around my neck, pulling me into him. He finally stopped crying and smiled at me.

"My hero, like always. You always know what to do or say. Thank you." Aerin vanished from my arms, and I took a quick look around the city. I wanted to die, everything we'd known and loved was gone in a flash. Aerin had to live this over and over. I will make this up to him one day. I swear to it.

I closed my eyes and when I opened them back up, I was in bed again holding Aerin. He was quiet and cried a little more into my chest. I ran my hands through his hair trying to relax him. I never want him to hurt like that again. I never want him to go through something so painful. I had to protect him and myself, we are going to get the life we both deserve. We will be together, and we will be happy.

****

We sat at the dining hall table, I was unable to take my eyes off Aerin for even a moment. I made my plate and ate without looking away. Sylas joined us and made plates of food as well. He must have been so hungry after not eating for so long. I could see him chug water by the pitchers as well. Aerin only picked at the food on his plate. I grabbed onto his elbow and squeezed it. I shot him a smile, and he smiled back at me. I wanted to take it all away from him, but I can only do so much. It was times like this that I hated being a useless half-elf.

"Thank you so much, Aerin, for coming to get me," Sylas finally broke the awkward silence in the room. Aerin smiled at him and nodded. "How long was I out for?"

"Almost a month," Aerin whispered to him. I watched as Sylas's eyebrows raised.

"Well, I really appreciate it." Aerin reached over the table and squeezed Sy's hand.

"You are my family, and I will always protect you and your brother." Sy smiled at him and looked over at me.

"You were very sweet when you were younger, Thorne. You were so love-struck by Aerin. It's kind of cute seeing that soft side of you," Sy joked with us.

Aerin laughed at his comment and I felt my face start to turn red. But it was nice for Aerin to be laughing and smiling again. I needed that, and it helped me relax a bit.

"Do you remember anything from the time you were asleep?" I asked Sylas, wondering if I would need to explain what we all say to him, well I guess Rillifane does. He shook his head and I took a deep breath filling him in on all the fun details. He smiled knowing that he was the host of our god and that he shared the powers with him. He felt powerful, and rightfully so.

The room fell silent again, but this time it was a good kind of silence as we all finally dug into our food. It was nice eating together as a family once more. I smiled at them both and took their hands.

"I love you both," I kissed Aerin's hand. "When this is all over, we will be a strong family together–you will see how happy we will be." They both flashed me a smile and finished their food. I was dreading what was going to come next. We had to plan our attack on Morgana, the sooner the better.

****

We went back to our room and looked down at a map of the country. Aerin used anything he could find to lay out our plan of attack. He sounded like a true leader and was ready for anything that Morgana might throw at us. The battle map looked perfect, it looked like there was no way we could lose. He placed two candles for where Sy and I would be alongside the army leading the attack. But when I looked closer I noticed there was no sign of where he would be.

"Where are you for the fight?" I finally asked and he looked at Sylas. Sylas took the hint and left the room.

"We need someone on the inside, we need a spy. You can connect to my mind, and we can learn Morgana's plans and be ready no matter what." I looked at him, not completely understanding. "I am going to give myself up to her; I will be the inside man, we can not ask that of anyone here. You know that as well as I do. I am going to give myself up to her, I will become her prisoner, and face whatever comes with that. I will communicate with you. This will be the last fight, Thorne."

Aerin took my hand and dried my eyes. I hated this

plan. I was no longer on board with it. Sylas came running back into the room and hugged Aerin.

"You can't do that," Sylas shouted at him, squeezing him tight. "What if she..."

I knew what he was going to say next, and it was the same fear I had. He was not doing this.

"What if she just kills you, Aerin, what if she sees through you." Aerin smiled at me, and I knew he was scared as well.

"Then you and Sylas will run away–don't fight, go with the elves back across the ocean where her magic can't reach you. And live your lives, be happy." He looked away from me for a moment, and then back at me again. "You need to do that for me. Promise."

I nodded my head, but it took every ounce of my strength. I could not live without him. How can he think I could ever be happy without him by my side?

"There has to be another way," I shouted. "There has to be a better plan than a suicide mission."

"Thorne, I thought about everything. This is the only way to make sure this is the last fight. We can't keep asking our men to give their lives. It is not right for their families." I walked over to him and pulled him close to me. I felt my true gift come out of me again and a red aura only I could see wrapped him up as I cried. Sylas left the room to start taking apart the machines he built and getting them ready for the trip, leaving me alone with Aerin.

"If this is your wish, then I will do as you say. I really don't like it, but I know there is no changing your mind. I just wish we were not going to be apart. I wish that I could do something, anything." I was starting to think about how I was again useless, and cursing myself for being a half-elf. Aerin looked up at me and smiled before pushing me down onto the bed.

"If today is going to be my last day with you, I want it to be just about us. Not about Morgana anymore, not about our kingdoms. Just us like we used to be."

I forced a smile onto my face and opened my arms for him. He jumped down onto me and nuzzled into my chest. I stayed strong for him, but inside I was a wreck. I hated this plan, I hated everything about it. Why couldn't we just march together and storm her? Why did we have to separate? I curled my fingers through his and looked deep into his loving eyes. He was right, and if this was going to be the last day we were together then we were going to do it right.

I sent a message down to Sylas and waited for his answer. I spent the day holding onto Aerin and dreading the morning when he would be away from me. My heart tearing in two, but I still kept the smile glued to my face. I enjoyed the day with just us, and it was so nice to lay in bed with him. I felt our hearts melding together, as they once did. His eyes shone the way they used to, and it melted me into a puddle of love.

"I love you, Aerin. More than anything. Marry me." He looked at me confused.

"I already said yes." He kissed me softly.

"No, I mean now. I want to marry you right now." He looked at me still confused and I stood up walking with him down to the big gazebo in the middle of the city.

There were elves everywhere around, and Sylas stood in the gazebo waiting for us. I looked down at Aerin and he smiled back up to me. We walked into the gazebo together and stood in front of Sy.

We were an arm's length apart, but our hands never faltered away from each other. I squeezed his hand and looked deep into his eyes. They were the greenest they had ever been. I love this elf and I want to be with him forever. Aerin knelt down to Sylas when he cleared his throat, and he placed the elvish crown onto his head. I did the same and put the crown of men on my head.

Sylas started speaking but all the words were lost to me. I was hypnotized by Aerin's beauty. I was lost in his eyes, and reliving every moment with him. Aerin started to blush because of my loving gaze, and we both smiled. I picked his hand up, gently letting my lips press against it.

"Do you, Aerin, take Thorne to be your husband, to be with him no matter the outcomes of wars, sickness, till death do you part?"

"I do. I love you, Thorne. Even after death, we will never part."

"Do you, Thorne,"

"YES. HELL YES," I blurted out, unable to contain my emotions.

"Then by the power invested in me, I pronounce you husband's–you may kiss the groom."

I pulled Aerin in close and spun him, holding him down. His eyes sparkled with the stars shining in them as he looked up at me. I closed my eyes and leaned in close to him, kissing him softly. I picked Aerin up in my arms and walked back to our house. I leaned into him and whispered,

"Now, the fun part of the wedding night." I watched as his face blushed before he buried it into my chest again. It was going to be a night we would both remember for sure.

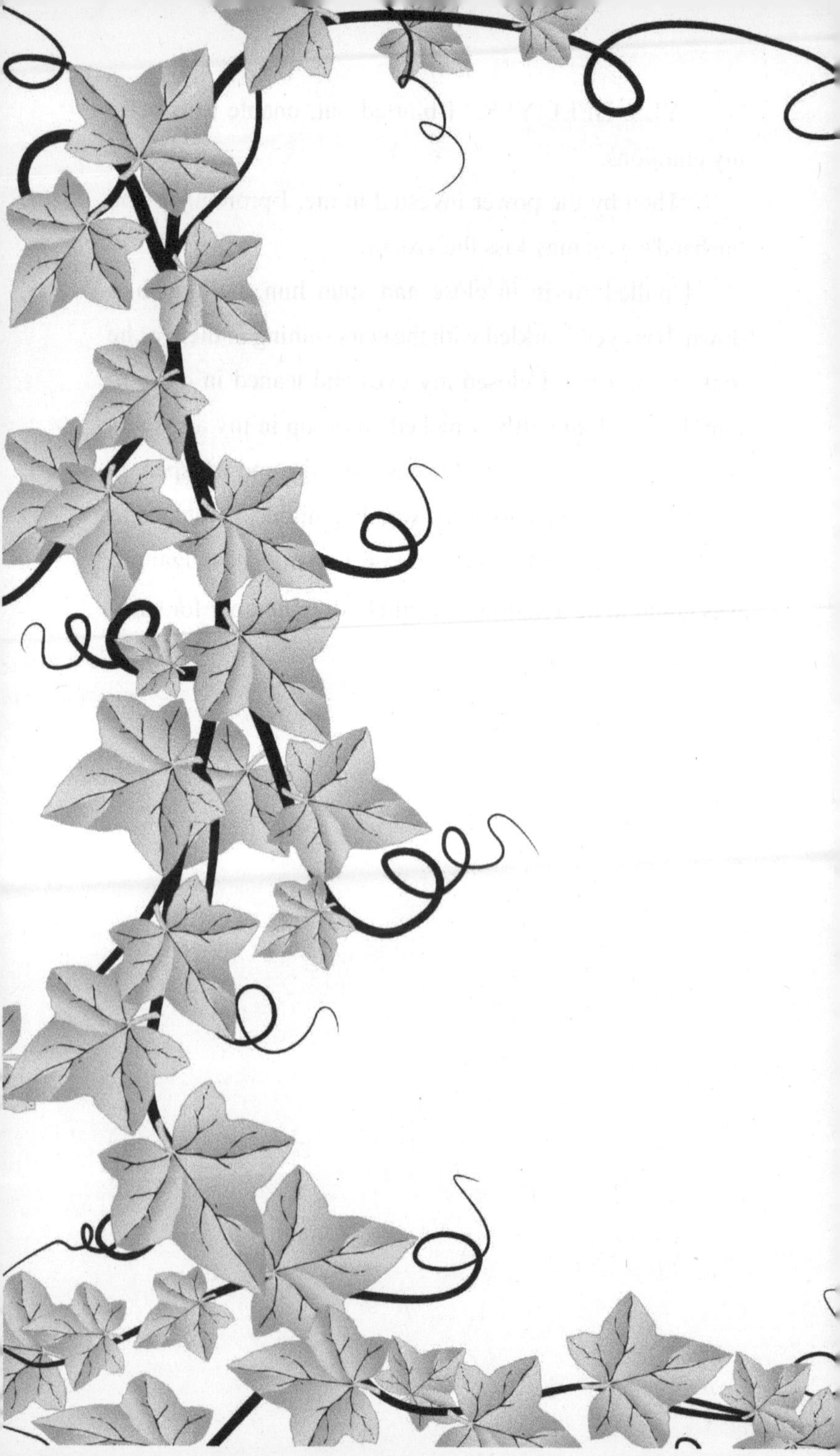

CHAPTER 35:

Aerin

I woke up to being pulled into Thorne's chest. I smiled and took a breath of his scent. I wanted to remember this. I did not know when I would see him again. His eyes were still closed, he must be exhausted from all the fucking. I smiled to myself thinking about last night. My legs were still numb from the pleasure, and I could not lay flat on my back without constantly adjusting myself. My ass was throbbing, but I still wanted it. I wanted more of him.

I kissed his pecs before nuzzling into them. I kissed down, lower and lower till I was at his waist. I gently bit down on his skin, leaving a beautiful bright mark. Thorne's hips bucked up to me, but he remained asleep.

Now would be the best time to leave, it would only be harder once he woke up. I knew it would be so much harder actually. He would not let me leave. I gently climbed out of bed and wrote a note before placing it on the table next to him. I dressed quickly and turned my back to him. My black fog filled the room and I was ready to be in front of Morgana. Before I was able to disappear, Thorne's arms were around me squeezing me into him. I felt a tear roll down my cheek but I did not turn around to face him.

"You were going to say goodbye, right?" I rubbed his arm and he spun me to look at him. "Are you sure about this?" I nodded to him and forced myself to smile for his sake. I wanted him to be happy.

"It's a day trip, we will only be apart for two days. We can do this." I watched as Thorne closed his eyes and kissed me. I hugged him and laid my head on his shoulder. My fog wrapped around my body. His eyes were still closed.

"I love you, Thorne," I whispered to him before I was transported away. I felt my heart being ripped out of my chest as the fog tore us apart.

****

My dark fog left me in the middle of an alley. I looked

around quickly before pulling my hood over my head. I felt Thorne in my mind seeing everything I was. I did not have much time so I raced around the town, allowing him to see everything. All the allies, where to attack, and how to prepare for this battle. I noticed there was not a single child or woman around, only the soldiers, and Morgana's creatures. To be honest this was a huge relief, I did not want the death of innocents on my hands. I continued along the way taking in every inch of the city while I walked up to the palace that made the old kings look small. This guy was definitely overcompensating for something.

I walked to the doors that were solid gold and used all my strength to crack it open. I walked down the halls until I found the throne room. I slipped inside and stuck to the back shadows. I listened for a moment. I could hear the voice of the king and Morgana talking. I took a deep breath and lowered my hood walking towards them. I felt Thorne with me, and it gave me the strength I needed to keep my feet moving. I felt warm as though he was there with me, hugging me.

As I inched closer, Morgana stood up and let out a horrifying cackle. She walked down to meet me face-to-face. I swallowed hard and looked right into her eyes.

"Brother, what are you doing here?" she asked me, tilting her head and giggling to herself.

"Promise to not hurt Thorne or Sylas, you will leave

them alone." She laughed again and looked back at the king.

"I told you, love is useless." She looked back at me again, "I will not attack them, but if they stand in my way it can't be helped."

"Then I give up Morgana, you win–I can't keep doing this anymore." Morgana inches closer to me looking me up and down. I came to her without any weapons, and I cleared my mind blocking Thorne out for a moment. I knew she was checking to see if it was a trap. Rightfully so, I would have done the same because this was way too easy.

She turned back to the king and walked to her throne next to his. She practically skipped knowing she won the battle. She turned back to me before taking a seat and swung her hand. I was sent flying into the wall hard and a statue fell onto me, keeping me pinned to the ground. I could not wait to pay her back for that. Two guards walked into the room and tied up my hands and feet then dragged me out of the room. I felt Thorne again in my mind. I wished he wasn't there as I was dragged down flights of stairs to the dungeon.

"Morgana wants to make sure you are weak when she comes to visit and take your magic. So we get to have some fun now," one of the guards spoke to me, I could hear the amount of pleasure he had in his voice as he grabbed one of the whips off the wall and cracked it onto the floor next to me. Out of instinct, I flinched knowing it would be crashing with me next. I could feel Thorne's anger brewing inside me. I tried to block him out, but I was not strong enough. The other guard grabbed me by the neck and tossed me into the wall chaining my hands above my head. I faced the wall away from them, the cowards dared not let me see their faces, they knew that if the Shadow Hunter escaped, they would be the ones to die first.

The whip cracked against the floor as the guard raised it over his head and snapped it on my back. I felt my skin rip open, and I could feel the blood dripping down my back. All of that from one slash. They better kill me because when I get out of here they will die slowly.

"Elf trash," he shouted as he brought it back down onto my back again. I held in the screams of pain because I was not going to let Thorne know how badly it hurt, and I was sure as hell not giving the fuckers a chance to hear it and get some sick pleasure from it.

When they got nothing out of me they grew angered and unchained my hands before tossing me onto a bench and chaining my hands below it. They shoved my head into a mesh bag and started to pour water over my head. I could not breathe for a moment, and my body started to panic. All I could see was pure darkness. I heard the guard walk away and grab more buckets to fill up with water. I could still smell the leather from the whip that was close to me. As he brought it up, it crashed into my chest. My body clenched up into the whip, but I still did not make a sound. They were not going to break me. I would not let it happen.

Bucket after bucket was poured over my head, and I wanted badly to scream but couldn't. I could no longer block Thorne out.

"Aerin, what's going on," his voice echoed in my head. I focused hard on the sound of it.

Suddenly I smelt flesh burning as they pressed a metal rod that was sitting on fire against my stomach. I could hear the sizzle of my own skin, and the pain was a lot to handle. I could no longer hold in my scream and shouted out. They started to whip me again and again in the same spot they just burned. They were enjoying every second. They removed the bag from my head, and the guard who was delivering water to me pulled a dagger out of its sheath.

"I have always wondered what makes an elf tick. Let's see if we can find out what it is." The guard spoke tracing the dagger against my jaw.

"Aerin, if he... So help me." I could hear the anger brewing in Thorne's voice. He cut my top open exposing my chest, and the dagger's icy metal traced down to my waist. I swallowed hard again as I tried to slow my breath.

The guard tilted his head to the side as the tip of the dagger pierced my chest just enough to cause me to bleed. I knew they had done this before. They enjoyed bringing pain. I closed my eyes as the dagger moved along my body, slicing into me over and over again. I was starting to become numb to the pain. This is not good, I need to feel, I need to stay awake. They picked me up again and hung me from a nail in the center of the room as if I were a dead cow.

"Once Morgana is done with you, we can really have fun." He ran his dagger against my face hard, slicing my cheek clean open. Being stuck up like this, gravity was doing its work. I could feel my blood rushing out of every cut on my body from his dagger, and the whip. I was engulfed in pain again, but it was nothing–I could handle this. I can do it.

"Aerin, fucking answer me." I felt the warmth from Thorne again and heard his gasp. He now knows the extent of what I had gone through. I could feel him crying and punching the wall.

"I'm okay," I thought loud enough for him to hear me. The whip was brought back down against my chest. The force of it made me spin as the two took turns whipping and slicing into me.

I blacked out at some point during the brutal beating. Either from loss of blood or the pain becomes too much to bear. When I woke up again, I could not move. They sliced so many nerves to make sure I would feel it. The pain was agonizing, but I looked around the room seeing what I could find, trying to plan my escape. The room was barren, nothing but the pails and a few benches remained in the room after they left. There was a rope that I thought about using to hang myself, stopping the pain. But I would need to figure a way down first. I had no strength to kick let alone pull myself up to unhook myself. It felt like I was walking the line between life and death. The room started to spin and I blacked out again.

I was woken by a sharp pain in my side. I groaned slightly when I looked over and saw Morgana sticking a finger in one of the wounds. I bit my tongue to hide the pain it was causing as she wiggled her finger and ripped it back, tearing more of my skin.

"Doesn't love just suck. We give so much for it, for what?" she asked as she walked around me to look me in the face. She slapped me, and I spat blood onto the floor in her direction. "I never thought I would see the day when I would prove our father wrong. That I was a stronger child." I looked up at her and tried to make her out but everything was still a blur.

"Just do it, take my powers. Kill me, get it over with already," I spoke to her with what little voice I had left.

"Now, now, where did all that fight go, brother? This is no fun, no–we will get to that soon enough. I did promise the guards they could have fun with you after all, and I am a lady of her word." She snapped her fingers and the guards returned with snakes. They held the snakes up to me, snapping their jaws at me. They were going to poison me and watch me die slowly. I should have known.

"I should have known my sister was a coward." Morgana snapped again and the men left the cell.

"I am what?" she screamed at me.

"A coward. You couldn't stand that Dad chose me and you ran. You lost your powers and you ran. You had love and you ran from that, too." She slapped me hard enough that the inside of my cheek was bleeding again. "You can't even face me on your own. You, my dear sister, are a coward." She screamed and sent me flying into the wall before turning and slamming the cell door shut again. I landed on the floor and smiled.

Well, at least I'm off the hook now.

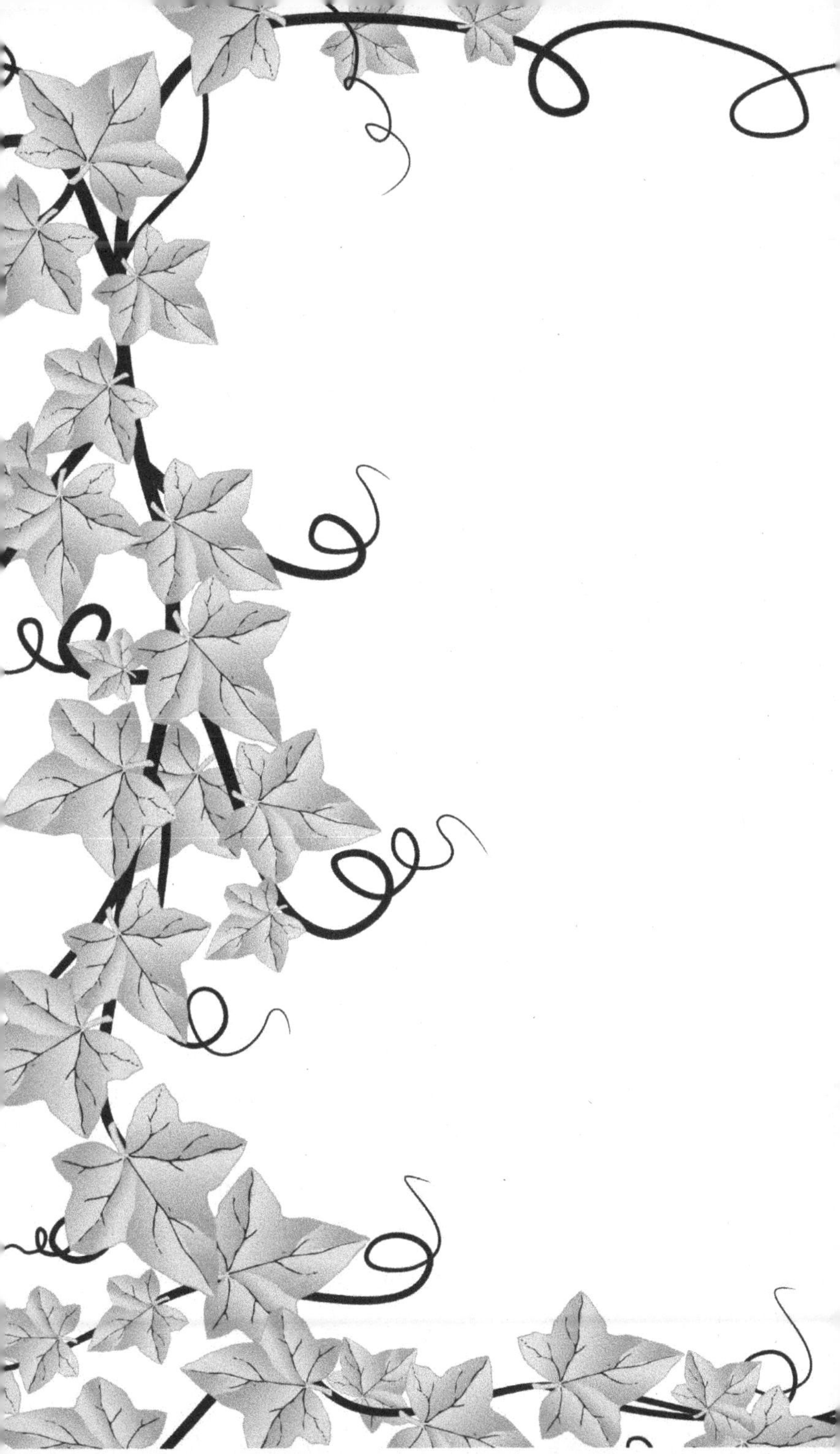

CHAPTER 36:

Thorne

I could feel each crash of the whip as it met with Aerin's flesh. Allowing my mind to be there, I was able to take some of the pain away and feel it myself. I looked down at my chest and had various cuts on it. The pain made it hard to ride Alatar alongside the army but I stiffened my back to avoid anyone noticing, especially Sylas, and rode along.

The trip was long, every minute seeming like a century to me being apart from Aerin. Part of me could not wait to make camp so I could hide in Aerin's tent and just cry. I wanted to release all the pain and emotions I had building up. Morgana was going to pay for this, and I was going to make sure she would feel the exact pain my lover did.

We stopped at the clearing that was less than an hour's ride to where Aerin marked the battleground. I raised my hand and all the elves stopped moving. The message I sent to my kingdom arrived, and they were already there waiting for us. I smiled at the sight of our reinforcements. We easily outnumbered the troops the king had in his army. This was going to be a fast victory, I hoped. I wanted it to be fast so I could rescue Aerin, and bring him back home.

It was a sight to behold as the elves were sitting together talking around campfires. It was a sight and dream that Aerin had hoped for. We did it together, we united them. I could hear the mixture of elvish and men singing battle songs. Everyone had their own way to prepare for the battle ahead. It melted my heart and gave me the strength needed to move on. I just really wished that Aerin had been here to witness it.

The elves finished setting up Aerin's tent, and the men had one set up for me. I walked towards Aerin's tent though. I wanted to be as close to him as I could. I laid in the hammock bed they set up, and turned on my side. It felt like Aerin was there with me. I could see him lying next to me covered in blood. I knew he wasn't really there, but with our minds connected it felt like he was.

"Lord Thorne." An elf bowed before coming into the tent. I snapped back to the reality that I was there alone and turned to him.

"Yes?"

"The elves are worried about Lord Aerin. We can sense that he is in pain. Is he going to make it?"

Those were not words I needed to hear–not now–not ever. I had to take a deep breath to give myself a moment to think.

"Lord Aerin is very strong. He will pull through this. He will join us with a new flame burning for the end of this war. You'll see. He will be okay."

The elf bowed to me and walked away from the tent. I was not sure if I was trying to convince myself or him that Aerin was going to be okay. He has to be. I hated not being able to step in, not share the pain more. I hated knowing more that he was on death's doors. I could not tell anyone that though. I had to be strong for everyone, I had to put on a brave face. My emotions were going wild, and I could hear a storm brewing outside. I punched through the table in the middle of the room, releasing most of my pent-up aggression and the storm stopped.

"Thorne, what is going on?" Sy asked as he pushed the curtain open and sat on the chair in the corner of the room. "I know something is troubling you, talk to me."

I wanted to tell him everything, and before I could even stop myself I started.

"Aerin is in trouble. We are here doing nothing, and he is paying the cost of it. I can feel the pain, Sy. I don't know if he can make it. It's a lot, I can't focus on my thoughts anymore. I can't think straight. All I can hear are his screams." I paused for a moment and looked back at the hammock. "Morgana's won, she broke him. We can't defeat her without him, but we will die trying. I don't want you to fight, Sy."

I turned back to see Sy sitting in the chair next to me. He was glowing, and the image of Rillifane was around him. It was his voice that spoke back.

"Thorne, you sound like you have already given up. You need to hold on to your love. It is what will bring you victory." He walked over leaving behind Sylas asleep in the chair. He held his hand on my forehead, and a warmth ran over me. I felt stronger. I felt like I had a huge magical refresh, and that I could do so much more. "You have always doubted your abilities, but you have such a strong gift. You can protect those around you, just like you always wanted. You control the balance of life. Water bends at your will. Don't you ever forget that you are one of my chosen children? You are not just a half-elf, you are pure of heart and you will save Aerin."

With that, Rillifane was gone and Sylas woke up. He walked over to me and hugged me.

"You seem different," Sylas spoke softly to me. I held my hand out and the water in the air turned into a spear. I smiled looking at Sylas. I walked to the opening of the tent.

"I will be back tonight. I am going to save Aerin."

"Thorne, wait! Is that really the best idea, would Aerin be okay with that?" I ignored him and whistled for Alatar.

"If I am not back by sunrise, lead the troops to the attack markers." Sylas nodded to me knowing there was no changing my mind.

****

The spear I held turned to ice as Alatar led me into the city. I stabbed my spear into any guard that stood in my way. I made my way to the palace, and Alatar took off. I turned and pushed the doors open, sneaking around while making my way down to the dungeon. It was not too hard with everyone asleep and the occasional guard left to stop me from leaning against the wall falling asleep. I was amazed by how many weapons I was able to pull out of thin air and found myself enjoying the powers.

I made my way to the last door, and my heart started to pound. I was close to him, I could tell once my heart was crying out for him. I kicked the door down and pushed both my hands out in front of me sending a wave into the room before I entered. The two guards that were standing against the wall were sent crashing into the back wall with the wave holding them there for a moment.

I raced over pulled the rusted bars down and pushed

my way to Aerin. I knelt down by his side and cupped his head in my hands. He opened his eyes and smiled at me. I smiled back at him as I healed his wounds. His eyes closed once more until I was finished. I helped him to his feet and he turned to the men leaning against the wall.

He pushed his hands out and the men were sent through the wall, the sound of their bones shattering echoed in the room. He walked over to them, his hair was complete fire and he held a fireball in his hand. He hunched down over one of the guards and removed their helmets, holding the fire to his face.

"Remember burning me? Now it's my turn." The man shouted as his skin sizzled. It was a darker side of Aerin I had never seen before. He reached down to the man's side and pulled out a dagger, raking it across his cheek in one fast movement. Cutting his face then cauterizing it with his fire before it had a chance to bleed. He was keeping him awake so he could feel every slash. I walked over to him and pulled him off the guard. He turned to me and his eyes were black, not their usual green or red when he used his powers. It was the shadow dagger's effect, the dark magic was so strong due to his emotions.

He held the dagger to my neck and I took a quick breath before holding it in.

"Help me," he whispered and dropped the dagger before passing out in my arms. I picked him up and raced out of the palace before anyone had time to get us. I knew someone had to have woken up from the sound of the wall breaking or the palace shaking from the sudden structural change.

I carried my lifeless lover out and whistled for Alatar. I laid him over her back before hopping up myself and racing out of there and back to the safety of our army.

****

I gently laid Aerin down in the hammock before climbing in next to him. I was afraid of waking him, he needed to rest. He needed the time to get his emotions in check.

I placed my arms around him and kissed his head. He did not move or make any sound, but at least he was here in my arms. As I started to drift to sleep, I felt an aura around us both. I opened my eyes to see the red shield around us. My power of protection. Nothing was going to harm my love tonight. I kissed him softly and fell asleep with him.

I was awoken by Aerin's soft lips pressing against mine. I blinked my eyes open and saw one of the elves putting food down near us before leaving. I pulled Aerin tight into my chest and took a big breath in, drowning myself in his scent. I was so glad he was okay, his eyes had returned to their beautiful green hue and I knew he was back. Aerin sat up leaning his weight onto his arm and looked down at me.

"Thank you for coming to get me, Thorne." I smiled at him but he still looked worried. "How did you, how did you do all that?"

I knew exactly what he was talking about. He wanted to know how I learned to control my magic so fast, how I became so much stronger in such a short amount of time.

"Rillifane granted me a gift, he appeared in my head showing me how to use it and how to control my abilities. Also, when you are in love–you do some stupid things without thinking. Like running into the enemy with open arms and no plan to save someone so special to you."

I watched as Aerin hid his face from me, I knew he was turning all different shades of red. He got up and pulled me off the hammock. He handed me a plate of food to eat. It was filled with eggs and meat.

"Just eat it please, Thorne. You will need your strength for the fight." I was not going to fight with him, I took up the fork and dug into the food. I had not eaten in two days so he was right, I did need to eat something. It was a nice moment together, and Sylas joined us to eat some food, too. I knew that soon this would all end, I would be on the battlefield fighting for not only the freedom of the elves but for my life and the life of my family. I looked around at the two of them and pulled them both into a hug. I kissed Aerin and smiled at them.

"I love you both." Sylas smiled at me, his mouth full of food and Aerin kissed my cheek.

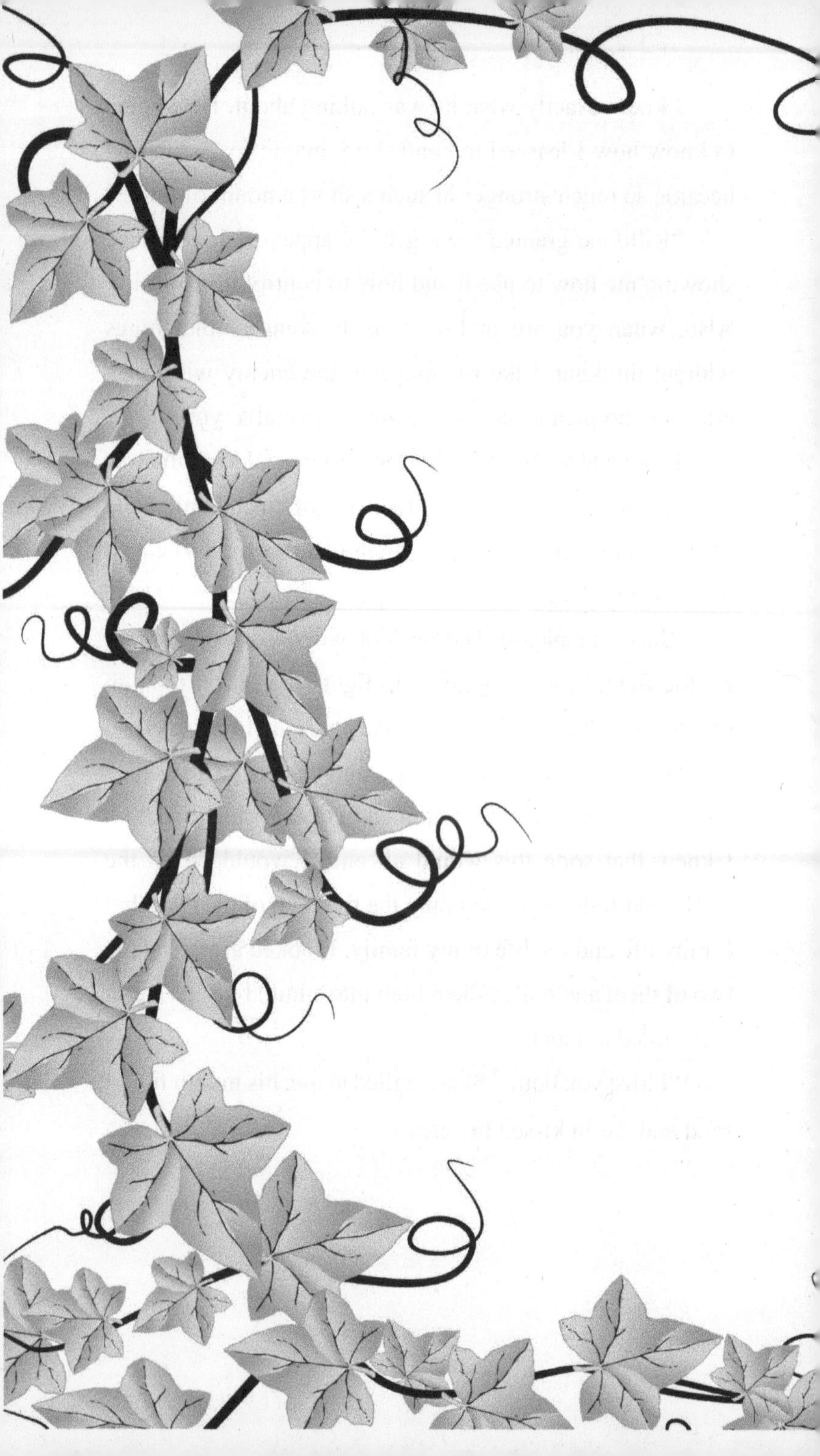

CHAPTER 37:

Aerin

I met Thorne's loving gaze as he held onto me almost too tightly before I stood and changed into my armor. I grabbed my daggers and placed them along my body. My fighting knives were sitting firmly in the arm gauntlets I bought. I moved to grab my bow and tighten it to my quiver when Thorne grabbed my arm from behind me. I knew it was him, I knew his loving touch. I felt a shiver crawl up my arm and my heart jumped. He spun me around to him and he kissed me gently while handing me a new quiver. It was the deepest green I have ever seen and had all new arrows in it, including the ones I created.

He smiled as he slipped it over my shoulder and I spun for him to attach the bow to it. I turned back around and kissed him. I was not sure what the quiver was made out of, but it was much lighter than my old one even with everything inside it. I really enjoyed how it felt, and the freedom it gave me knowing that it would not slow me down. Thorne smiled, watching me trying jumps and maneuvers to make sure the quiver was on tight enough. I walked over and punched him gently in the arm.

"Well, what do you think?" he asked, folding his arms and waiting for a reply. I jumped into his arms and kissed him hard.

"EWWW, come on. You two are so cringy," Sylas called out to us as he left the room. I turned to him and stuck my tongue out before turning back to Thorne and gently kissing him again. He hesitated to put me down but did. I got my footing and watched as Thorne walked over to grab his chest plate. I helped him tie it behind him and stuck his sword into its sheath.

"So, Mr. Big Bad Elf. What is your gift? I already know you can manipulate water, but what is the warm sensation you keep shooting over me?" I asked him, completely intrigued to find the answer.

"I think it is some kind of shield. It lets me share the

pain with someone, but also protect them," he spoke, hugging me tight and his gift completely surrounded me. I felt warm again. Is this the reason I always felt so safe around him? Why was I able to just be myself and let my guard down? Was it his gift? "I guess the gift fits me though because I want nothing more than to protect you," he spoke, rubbing my arm with his thumb. I wrapped my arms around his neck and kissed him patiently.

****

I walked back and forth in front of the elves and men with Thorne by my side. The camp was still set for us to return to, but it was time to march forward. Before we did I knew one of us would have to give a speech, something they all needed. They were scared and rightfully so. You did not need a gift to see it. They all shared the same fear of never seeing their families again. I looked at Thorne, and he smiled.

"It should be you, Aerin, you're the better speaker between us. I whistled for Alatar and took my place on her back. I rode back and forth in front of the army and prepared myself.

"Elves, men, we are about to embark on a battle your descendants will talk about for centuries. You will go down in history. I do not ask you to fight for me or Thorne, and I do not only speak to the elves. We ride today for the ones we love. Our children, wives, husbands, and grandchildren. We fight for our freedom, to not be enslaved by darkness.

This is not a fight between elves and their enemy. It is a fight between us, all of us, and our enemy. We will defeat them today and guarantee a peaceful life for us all. We will shine, united as the brightest light anyone has seen, and charge into the darkness. We will expunge it from our land. Are you with me?"

The army wasted no time and cheered louder than I had expected. The army was pumped, they knew the realism of the battle and I hated it. I hated knowing that so many of my friends and kin would die here today. If I could, I would prevent each of the deaths. But it was a challenge I would need to face later, something I would have to deal with for a long time. I extended my hand down to Thorne and pulled him up onto Alatar with me. His arms wrapped around me as we rode to the kingdom of darkness.

****

We stopped the ride about five minutes from the city. The elves quickly got to work helping set up the machines. I could feel my heart pounding as I attempted to prepare my mind for this battle. Sylas ran up to me and told me they were ready to fire. I looked at Thorne over my shoulder, who took my hands in his and gave them a squeeze. We both took a deep breath.

"Once we do this, there is no going back," I spoke softly, my heart crying out for the way things used to be.

"I am ready to face anything as long as I have you by

my side." He kissed my cheek and provided me with the strength and courage I needed.

"FIRE," we both shouted.

I turned to the machines and saw the elves igniting the ropes attached to their machines. Three seconds later, a loud boom sounded and arrows started to fly over our heads. I watched with excitement as the sun was darkened by the arrows. My idea came to life thanks to my family. Sylas was jumping up and down with glee that his craftsmanship actually worked. I had forgotten that we never tested them so I guess you can say we lucked out there. The sun shone again above us and the arrows continued on their flight.

It was not long before we could hear explosions from the city, and see clouds of smoke forming over it. I clicked my heels into Alatar and she took off towards the city. The war cry from my army could have shaken the ground below us as we charged. We made it to the gates and I held my arm up to stop the troops. I looked around seeing nothing but rubble. The city was left in shambles. I could hear the cries of pain as I looked around. I was not proud of it, I know we have injured so many who are just slaves to the king and Morgana. They were forced to fight out of fear. Not every single person was a bloodthirsty killer like the guards I had to deal with.

Was this really the price of peace? Would thousands have to die on both sides? I wondered if there was another way we could have had our happiness.

As I looked around, I saw more people racing around trying to put out the fires and others jumping into the well to save themselves from being burned. I found myself breathing heavily at the sight of pain, death, and panic. Was I any better than my sister?

Thorne reached around me and hugged me.

"You are nothing like her, this had to be done. They would have killed us all without a second thought. We both know that. You are not a monster, Aerin."

I hopped off Alatar and once Thorne did the same, she galloped off into the distance leaving me to wonder when I would see her again. Thorne took my hand for a moment and Sylas held the other. I took a deep breath before giving the command to charge.

I watched as our mixed army ran into the city, and took it over. Blood was spilled on both sides and then just as fast as we were winning, Morgana showed up. Her dark fog showed and our troops retreated. Although we could not see her, we could all hear her laughing.

"My sweet, sweet little brother, you are just like me." I could hear her voice inside my mind, she was only speaking to me. "You have led these men here to die for you. How sweet. Look what you've done, so many pure hearts lay dead at your feet. Look at how blood-stained your hands are."

I looked down and saw my hands covered in red, and I

started shaking. Morgana was playing off every weakness that I had been feeling already.

"Maybe you are ready to join me. Maybe I thought too little of you. How does it feel? The dark magic coursing through your veins. Doesn't the power feel good?" Her voice was getting louder inside my head. "My brother, the Shadow Hunter, how many lives have you cut short? Let's find out."

I closed my eyes trying to clear her out and when I opened them back up, I saw a bloody battlefield. My army was all dead. The millions of people I killed over my lifetime laid in front of me. I fell to my knees and looked around more. The pain I felt in my chest was nothing compared to the pain I felt when I saw Thorne with a sword sticking out of him. Then I heard Morgana laugh again, and the bodies all vanished.

It left me on my knees next to Thorne. I screamed and a black fog engulfed me like a typhoon. I screamed again and it grew in size. I was a monster, everything I never wanted to become. It was all true. Everything she said was true. I was no better than her. I am a monster.

I screamed again and the wave of darkness knocked my troops away, leaving them on the ground hundreds of feet from me. I could see what was happening, and it only made it worse that I couldn't stop it. I was useless, I was trapped. All I could do was cause pain.

I felt a warmth from behind me as Thorne wrapped

himself around me, Morgana's voice was gone and all I could hear was Thorne inside my head.

"You are not a monster, Aerin. You are kind, gentle, and loving. Think about all the people you have saved. The old baker still talks about you with smiles glued to her face. My brother looks up to you. He idolizes you. Aerin, people love you, I love you. You are nothing like your sister, you are stronger. You have friends and so much love. You will never be alone like she is."

I felt the fog retreat back into me as Thorne spun me into him. He gently kissed me and looked into my eyes. I knew they were still black because everything I saw was nothing more than a foggy haze. He pulled me in tight to him and hugged me.

"Come back, Aerin. Come back to me." I heard him calling out to me and I opened my eyes to see that there was no fog this time. I was unable to smile or speak but tackled him, hugging him tight.

"I'm so sorry you're stuck with a monster."

He shushed me and kissed me softly. "No one thinks you are a monster here, Aerin." I just held onto him, gathering myself. Sylas came over and hugged my side.

"You are my friend, Aerin." Sylas chimed in reassuring me. "I would never be friends with a monster." I smiled down at him and tousled his hair as Thorne helped me back up to my feet.

"I love you, Aerin–remember that and nothing she

throws at us matters, we have each other." I nodded to him and turned back to the city.

"CHARGE," I shouted as I ran into the city with my army.

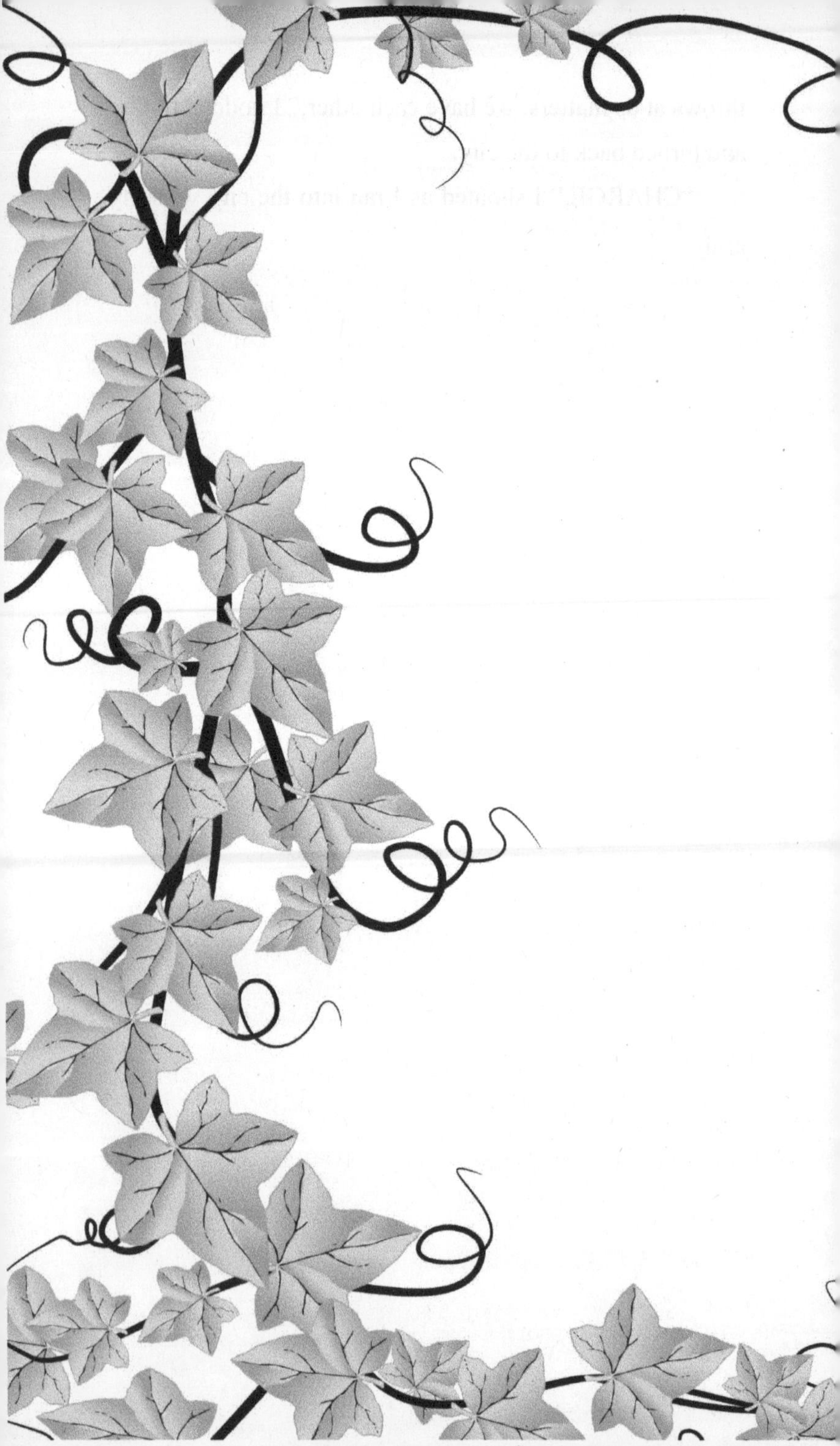

CHAPTER 38:

Thorne

I watched worriedly while Aerin charged onto the battlefield. I was worried if he was really in the right mindset to fight Morgana after losing control of his power like that, as well as the torture he faced only a day ago. I was wondering if this battle was happening at the right time. Part of me wanted to grab him by the arm and get him out of there. I wanted to bring him home and fight another day. I knew it was an idea he would never agree with, but it was a dream I guess you could say.

I had two short swords formed from water, one in each hand. I stood back to back with Aerin as we fought off the enemies. Sylas stayed close to my side and we protected him from every attack. Sylas was not allowed to fight–orders from me and Aerin alike. He was to stay close to us until we found Morgana. It was the only way we would be able to focus on the battle and not be completely worried about him. I glanced back at Aerin to see him attacking with his fighting knives. He moved swiftly and the old baker was right, watching him fight you would think he was dancing around the enemies. In one move he would spin and his knives would pierce everyone around. I was amazed that he somehow had the time to move his blades before they cut into my own neck.

I pushed my hands out and the short swords went flying into two knights in front of me. I quickly formed a glaive that immediately turned to ice. I smiled at the new weapon for a moment before spinning it and slicing one of the goblins in half. It was lighter than you would expect for being so big, and with it, I was able to cover way more ground. I knew that I would need to create some kind of path if we were ever going to move forward.

I continued to spin the glaive, either knocking whoever was in the way out or taking good chunks out of them. Sylas must have seen what I was up to because he got Aerin to follow behind me. I cleared a path through the battle and into the heart of the city. We managed to break away from the fight for a moment, and I turned to make sure both Sylas and Aerin were okay. To my surprise, luckily, neither had a scratch on them. I let out a huge sigh of relief and hugged them both.

"Where to now?" Sylas asked, looking up at me and Aerin.

"Morgana is too scared to fight without her elvish magic, she feels weak right now," Aerin chimed in. I pointed the glaive to the golden doors, before speaking.

"She is in there, no doubt about it–her and that traitor of a king."

Aerin and Sylas nodded to me and we made our way to the doors. There were a handful of guards that Aerin made short work of firing arrows into the weak spots of their armor. I really need to keep that in mind and change the armor my men wear. Because god is a large target.

"Aerin, remind me to change the armor when this is all over," I called out as we charged the doors.

It took all three of us to push just one of the doors open. We walked in and were surprised by three more guards. I drew my sword and managed to raise my arm in time to block the attack. Sylas was startled more than Aerin and I were, and his powers came out to protect him. He flung his arms above his head and the three men were turned to dust. Part of me was terrified at the amount of power he has now.

He was getting stronger every day. I hid the fear deep inside me, but that made it hard to.

"I'm sorry, I panicked," Sylas spoke softer than a whisper.

I pulled him to the side and smiled at him. "Think you can do that to Morgana, and make this really fast?" I said, trying to cheer him up. He shook his head.

"She is too strong, it will take a lot more than that to defeat her."

Even inside the building, I could hear the fight from outside. I hoped that my men and the elves would be okay without Aerin or myself out there, but we needed to be together for the next fight. I took a deep breath and stood back up from Sylas. We made our way down the long hallway, heading to where Aerin had confronted Morgana before. We pushed the doors open, and the room looked to be empty. Aerin went in first and searched around the room. He turned back to us to meet my gaze. He flagged me over and continued to walk backward. I noticed his foot go down a bit as he stepped on a tap.

Arrows flung out of the wall, and I held my arm out to him. Aerin quickly readied himself for the impact knowing he would not have the time to dodge them. The arrows ricocheted around him as they collided with the barrier I was able to surround him in, just in the nick of time, too. I took a deep breath in and looked at him fiercely.

"Watch where you are going!" I shouted to him, a bit

annoyed that he fell for something so simple.

I picked up Sylas and followed behind Aerin as he carefully made his way through the room. There was a small wood door behind the throne room that we made our way to. After putting Sylas down, I carefully opened the door. There, sleeping in a bed, was the mighty traitor of a king. I quickly pulled out my sword and went to walk to the bed. Sylas grabbed my arm and shook his head, it left me questioning why he would stop me for no reason.

I looked around the room and saw that it was covered in trip wires and before I knew it Aerin was making his way along them. He stood over the king with his knife to his neck. I pushed Sylas back towards the door, shielding him from the bloodshed about to unfold before my very eyes. I took a deep breath and watched as the king woke.

"Where is my sister, we have unfinished business?" Aerin spoke, waking the king further.

The king went to sit up but immediately threw himself back onto the bed once he felt the steel of Aerin's blade. He scowled at Aerin, and I noticed his hand roaming around under his pillow.

"Aerin, look out."

He looked back at me and I pointed to the king's moving arm. Aerin quickly spun his blade before driving it deep into the king's arm pinning him to the bed.

"I wouldn't do that If I were you. It might have been Morgana who told the men to torture me, but they are your men. Give me a reason to kill you, I dare you."

As Aerin spoke, the black fog began to pour out of him and fill the room. I could hear his voice becoming deeper, and demonic sounding. The king screamed out in pain and fear.

"I will not ask again, where is my sister?"

"I'm out here, dear brother, come and get me." Morgana cackled from outside the room.

Aerin turned to the door and slit the king's throat in the process. I turned to see Morgana holding Sylas hostage, her hand over his mouth. He was trying to break free from her grasp, but the purple fog made that almost impossible for him. Sylas bit down on her hand and she quickly pulled it away from his mouth.

"You little brat, someone needs to teach you manners," she shouted at him as she backhanded his face. I went to run to him, but she quickly formed a dagger and held it to him. "Move and he gets it, we are going to talk."

I dared not move and was blocking Aerin from her view. She moved to the side to see past me, still keeping Sylas against her. I tried to flag Aerin to relax as the room was filling more with his dark powers. I could tell he was close to the breaking point. I looked down at my brother and swallowed hard.

"And what do you want to talk about?" I shouted to her.

"A simple trade really, one of you for him."

"No," I shouted back but it was drowned out by Aerin.

"FINE. Let him go first." I turned back to Aerin and widened my eyes. As he walked by me, he spoke softly so only I could hear, "His life is worth more than mine."

As Aerin walked through the door frame, Sylas's hands began to glow. He spun shooting fire into Morgana's face and he quickly started to run over to me. Her fog wrapped around his leg and dragged him back to her. It held him upside down in front of her. Aerin bolted to Morgana but was too late. A black dagger stabbed through my brother. I dropped to my knees and felt my heart being ripped out. I immediately lost vision of the room from the tears welling in my eyes.

"Told you to learn manners," Morgana shouted as she tossed his lifeless body to the side.

I tried to stand but my legs gave out from under me. My brother was not moving, and it was hitting every last nerve of mine. I crawled my way over to Sylas and picked up his head. He opened his eyes and looked at me, smiling. He coughed and blood filled his mouth. I knew he did not have much longer to live. I looked back at Aerin whose darkness had completely filled the room. He was in direct combat with Morgana now. I was frozen, I had no idea what to do. I was not able to cure such a deep wound. I was not a healer. I was too slow to protect him. I knew this would happen if he came along. What kind of brother am I? That should be me lying there, not him.

"Thorne?" he asked, resting his hand on my cheek.

"Can you tell me about the old village again?" Sylas asked me and I nodded to him, telling him about the trees and houses and my love. His breaths were starting to slow down, and his eyes kept closing.

"Don't you dare, Sy, we can heal you. You have to be strong," I shouted at him, begging him to stay with me. "AERIN." I needed him to stay alive, I needed my family.

"Yes, Aerin, what is it going to be–save your little friend or your army?" Morgana cackled and vanished.

Aerin stood in the middle of the room, lost in his head. She just gave him the hardest choice. He would have to pick between our troops, the hundreds we brought with us, or my brother. He had to pick between his family and the lives of so many. She truly was a monster, making him decide. A blackness filled the room to the point where I could no longer see again, and Aerin shouted louder than ever before. Every window and glass object shattered. I laid over Sylas protecting him from the shards.

I turned back to him and saw the glass whirling around him, and just as fast as it started it vanished. I heard people outside screaming and I guess they were being chopped up into small bits by the glass, and then I heard Morgana scream. I looked up at Aerin, and he turned to me. His eyes were green, but filled with tears as he ran over and dropped down next to me and Sylas.

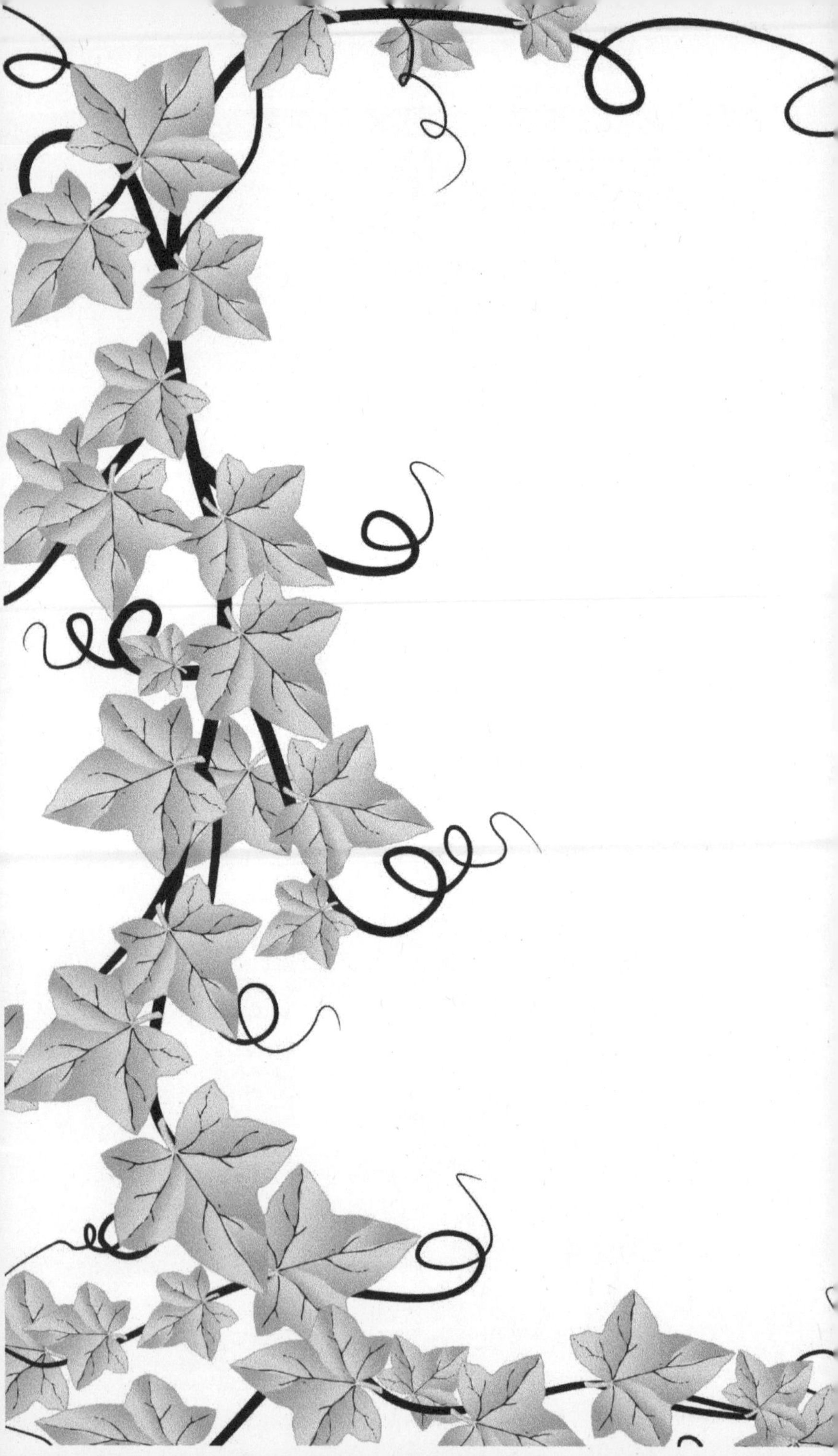

CHAPTER 39:

Aerin

I knelt beside Thorne who rested his head on my shoulder. I looked over Sylas for a moment before I pulled the dagger out of his gut. Sylas screamed from the pain of the blade being removed, but I had no other option. I held my hand over him and a bright red beam shone over him. I had to see the damage before I could heal him. The blade pierced a good bit of his organs, and I frowned without realizing it as I was inspecting the wound.

"Well, can you heal him?" I looked over at Thorne and nodded.

"I can, but he will be mortal. He will still have his powers, but won't be able to be healed again. I will be taking away his elvish life. He will be cursed as a man."

I watched as Thorne's face went blank, he was lost. I looked back at Sylas, who was fighting to stay alive.

"Sylas, I need you to listen to my voice. Focus deeply on only it. I can heal you, and you can live. Do you want to live a mortal life?" I watched as his head nodded and I began to chant.

The wound started to close below my hand, and Sylas coughed before sitting up. Thorne quickly hugged him close and kissed his head.

"Are you okay?" he asked Sylas before pulling me into him and Sy. I smiled, but knew what that meant to have him living a normal life. Whenever he uses his magic he will feel weakened, it will take a toll on him like it used to do to me. And now that Rillifane was using him as a host, it could also kill him. I am sure Sylas knew this, but Thorne would not.

I grabbed Thorne by the arm and looked him straight in the eyes.

"When we leave the room, you are to get Sylas back to camp and stay there with him. Promise me, you will get him to safety."

Thorne's eyes flicked back and forth taking me in for a

moment before he nodded in agreement. "But the fight, the plans."

"The plans are still the same–Morgana dies today, it will just take a new strategy is all."

I stood up and walked to the main doors followed closely by Thorne who was carrying Sylas. I used my fog and made a path for Thorne to run through. I pushed each person, not caring who they were, to the side parting them. Once Thorne was out of sight, I lowered the fog and began my hunt for Morgana.

****

"Brother, have you come to play?" she asked as I looked around seeing the soulless bodies surrounding her. It was my men, Thorne's men, and even her own. It was just proof that she didn't have to care for who she killed to get what she wanted. It was going to stop here.

"Morgana, your power grasp stops now. You die today. No more tricks. It ends here."

She spun around to meet my gaze, and she smiled.

"You're right, no more tricks. This all ends now."

She charged me with daggers in hand. If it was a dagger fight she wanted it was a dagger fight she would get. I bent over backward and dodged the blades that were aiming for my neck, spinning around to look at her. I tossed one dagger in the air before pulling another from its sheath.

I watched as Morgana stared at the falling blade as I kicked it at her. She was fast enough to dodge it, but it took off a chunk of the little hair she had left. She did not take too kindly to that as she charged me again. Our daggers met between us and she smiled.

"Do you know why I like to use daggers?" I squinted at her. "It's so I can get a good look at the faces of those I kill. Tell me, why do you use them?"

I did not answer, instead I pushed off my back foot and caught her off balance. She spun away from me making sure I was unable to lunge at her. She was not getting in my head this time, no matter how hard she tried. I was going to keep a calm mind, and not let her have that upper hand.

"Tell me, Aerin, did Sylas die with his eyes open or closed?" I felt my face squint a bit, and she knew she struck a nerve.

Well fuck!

There goes my whole game plan out the window but if it is the monster she wants so badly, maybe it's time to give it to her. Maybe that is what it would take to bring her to her knees. I took a deep breath and when I exhaled everything was clear around me, I could see all as if it was moving in slow motion. I was tapping into the darkest of my powers.

"You want a monster, Morgana, well you got one." I charged at her and was faster than I was before. I found myself teleporting through the fog and appearing at all different sides of her. Each time I reappeared, I would slice into a ligament and leave the blade behind. This repeated until she dropped to one knee. I looked around to see if anyone was coming to her rescue but instead, they all just stopped and looked around.

No one was bothering to step in; they were just watching in awe. No one could believe that I bested my sister, and to be honest I could not believe it either. I was about to deliver the final blow and slice her neck when she vanished and reappeared behind me. Before I even had the time to gasp, I was shoved against a wall by her magic and held there by chains of fog. I tried to break free but was unable to move my body an inch.

She cackled as she walked closer to me.

"Did you really think it would be that easy? Did you?" she asked as she pulled one of the daggers I left in her out. I noticed there was no blood on the blade. She either healed it extremely fast, or she is not human anymore. A simple blade is not going to kill her, it would take magic. Do I even have that much magic to kill her?

She moved closer to me, enjoying herself. I fell right into her trap and I was alone. No one would try and stop her, and I don't blame them. We all know she would not waste a second killing them before they even got close. She was an arm's length away from me and leaned in.

"I am going to enjoy this," she said as she flicked the dagger and it sliced part of my earlobe. I took a deep breath in but was not going to make a sound. She was already far too happy. "Do me a favor, will you?"

I did not answer and instead spat into her face. She did not let this bother her though, she knew she already won.

"Tell our father hi for me. Ask him if it hurt when I killed him." I gasped and my eyes went wide. "Oh, you didn't know?" She walked away from me, toying with the knife before turning back to me. "The night the fire started, do you know who started it? Why nothing you stupid elves worked would put it out. Sure, Thorne's father betrayed you and told the King where to find you but," she waved a hand over her face and it transformed into the King. "Do you really think he knew what he was doing? The old man already killed his wife, I had so much time to plan this that he didn't even see it coming."

"You lie, the King's men were there. I was there that night, Morgana."

"I tipped the King off, and he sent his troops. It's so easy to play men. Once the fire was set and the men stormed in, I was able to keep to the shadows. Our father tried to save his sweet innocent little baby boy. He was blinded by love and walked right into my blade. It was so easy." Morgana turned and jumped at me landing right in front of me. Her hand squeezed my face while she held the dagger to my neck. "A mistake I will not make again, dear brother." She pulled the dagger back to her waist ready to stick it inside me. "So, are you ready to die?"

It's funny when you're about to die your life does not

flash before your eyes like everyone says it does. You instead hear the voices of the ones you love. I could hear Thorne and every time he whispered I love you. I could hear Sylas laughing. I looked deep into Morgana's black soul and smiled at her. Although I was going to die, I was not going to die alone. I have love, and I have a family. I was never like her.

"You're not a monster," I heard Thorne's voice echoing in my head mixed with the whisper of I love you. I was not ready to die, I wanted more time with him but if this is how I have to protect him then I am ready and accept it.

Morgana thrust the blade into me. I closed my eyes and prepared myself for the end. I opened them back up and looked at her questioningly. I was not in pain, all I felt was the tip of the blade against my skin. Was she having a change of heart? Could she not kill me? She pulled her arm back and tried again, this time I did not feel the tip of the blade at all. Instead, I heard it shatter before it hit me.

"Morgana, you are so wrong. Love is strength, and we will show you just how strong it could be."

I could not believe Thorne came back, but I was so glad that he did. A water chakram sliced the fog that was holding me back, and I kicked Morgana hard enough to create space between us. Thorne ran over to me and caught me moments before I fell to the floor.

"We have to stop meeting like this," I joked with him and kissed his cheek.

Morgana was furious, and the area around us was filled with her dark purple fog. Thorne helped me to my feet and looked at me. He took my hand for a moment while Morgana was still trying to figure out her next move.

"Are you ready to finish this?" he asked me and I nodded in return.

"Till death do we part."

Morgana charged at us hurling balls of pure darkness, we jumped apart dodging the ball, and stood to either side of her. I saw Thorne create a glaive, and start twirling towards her. I quickly drew my bow and nocked an arrow, lining up a shot. Thorne was fast and he was able to keep up with her various attacks, thanks to the reach of his weapon. I finally had a shot once Thorne managed to trip Morgana with the dull end of the glaive. I let loose the arrow and Thorne jumped away from her leaving the glaive behind. Just as I knew she would, she caught the arrow with her fog but the moment it connected it exploded. The explosion was strong and sent her through the wall of a small hut. Thorn ran over to me and patted my ass.

Fucking men.

I nocked my next arrow waiting for her to get up.

"Thorne, it will take a lot more than we thought to kill her. Weapons are not going to be enough. We need magic."

"Then I guess it's a good thing Sy refused to stay behind, too. He has already started his part of the plan as well." I nodded to him, I knew we would have to keep Morgana distracted if this was going to work.

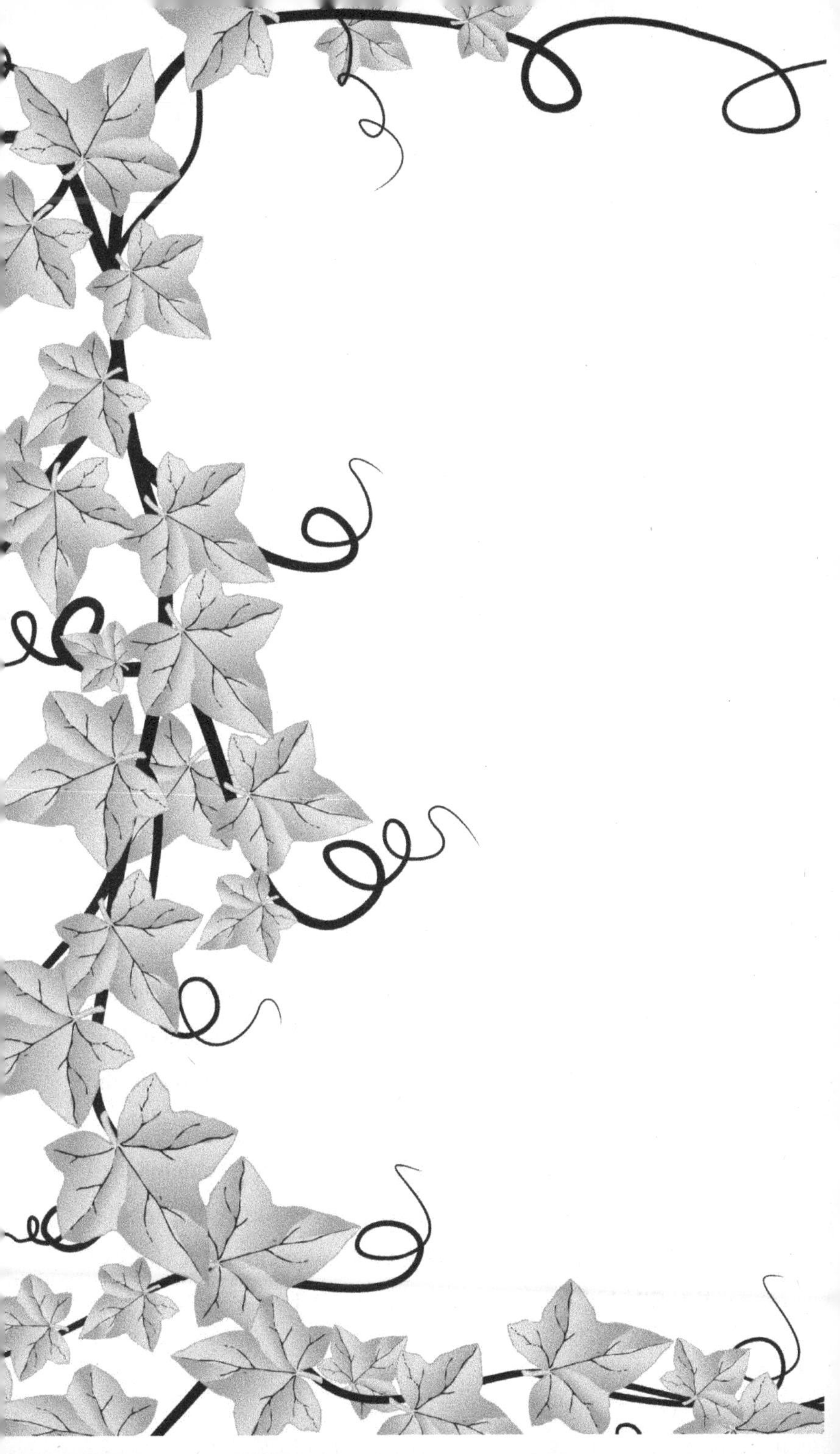

CHAPTER 40:

Thorne

Aerin and I waited for Morgana to crawl out of the rubble she was launched into. Instead, she appeared behind us grabbed me by the back of the neck, and tossed me to the side.

"When did you learn how to do that?" She demanded from Aerin,. Who did not answer but instead pulled another arrow from his quiver and shot it between them. A cloud of dirt filled the space between them. I was able to hear

Morgana shout about her eyes. Aerin raced over to me and helped me to my feet.

"I'm fine,." I whispered to him.

I looked up to where Morgana was still standing, cleaning her eyes as the dirt cloud vanished. I quickly created two water-short swords that turned to ice and readied my stance next to Aerin who readied his next arrow.

"So many little tricks, how long do you think you can really keep this up before you both meet death's icy grasp?" Morgana asked as she pulled two more daggers out of herself and charged at us. She let out a blood-curdling screech as she spun before getting to us, spinning her daggers wildly. Aerin and I parted and she stood between us once more. "Nope, not that again!" She called out teleporting behind Aerin and using the butt of the daggersmacked him in the back of the neck. He fell hard to the floor and I charged her.

Aerin nodded to me, and I used his back to leap up higher bringing both of my Iice blades down towards her. She had no issue deflecting them with the small daggers and quickly lunged back at me. I fell back onto the ground and the tip of the dagger just grazed my nose. It stung, but it was just a nick. I spun getting back up to my feet and managed to trip her with my shin. As I stood, she fell to the floor.

Just as fast as she landed though she teleported again. I knew Aerin was right; this was going to be a lot harder than we thought. I took a deep breath and raised my sword to block her incoming attack. She flew off the blade, and she nearly cut it right in half. I glanced over her shoulder at Aerin, who was starting to shake, he could not get a clean shot. If he fired now, we would both be struck by the arrow. I dropped my free blade and created a small ice shard in my hand. I stepped back and turned on my heel digging the ice shard deep into the ligament on her ankle.

That should hopefully slow her down.

I watched as she quickly healed herself as if nothing happened. The ice shard fell out of the skin and hit the floor shattering. At the same time, she kicked up hard, and with enough force to send me flying. I bounced off the floor while landing and got up rubbing my ass. I looked back at her.

"So, Thorne, you wanna play cheap? We can do that."

She charged at me and was only stopped when one of Aerin's arrows pierced through her chest. I watched as her eyes went black for a moment before returning to normal. She quickly turned to Aerin who had been chanting in elvish. Vines whipped off his bow and flew at Morgana. They wrapped around her body dragging her slowly to Aerin. She was unable to break the spell or fight her way out of the vines no matter how hard she tried. I had to bite my tongue because it was quite the site.

Morgana tried to pull them back towards me, and I grew tired of the tug-of-war game they two were playing. I swept her legs out from under her and she hit the ground hard. I almost felt bad because her head bounced off the ground since she was unable to defend herself. That was until the blood smear disappeared from her healing herself. I folded my arms walking behind her as we got closer to Aerin.

He held his bow firm and vines started to bind with the bow once more. The blades on the bow grew larger and before I knew it Morgana was impaled by them. I watched and winced as they pierced through her back and out her front. Aerin yanked the bow out of her and ran over to me. She lay on the floor for a moment as her black blood poured out of her. That was the first cut, wound, anything that actually made her bleed. She lay there on the ground clutching her chest.

I put my arm around Aerin for a second while we waited for the next move.

"You fools you can't kill me, The spell will keep me alive." She stood up, her wounds still gushing blood. I drew my sword from its sheath, and spun on my left foot jumping, the bow transformed and I fired arrow after arrow of magical lightning at her. Many of the arrows– to my surprise–- were actually connecting with her, and I could hear the sound of thunder crashing at the same time the arrows connected. Aerin followed my lead and started firing some arrows from his bow. He, however, was more careful about firing at will. Not that I really blame him, he has a cap on the amount he can fire. Nothing special happened from his arrows.

That was until Morgana started to quicken her pace. She was charging faster than my eyes could keep track of. I was sliced in several ligaments. My nerves were pinched and I found myself on my knees.

"You both want to fight dirty, so be it." Morgana raised her arms and the ground shook below us. Zombies started to climb out from the depths of what seemed to be hell. The ground split apart and I could see fire below us. I looked at Aerin and saw him starting to shake. He met my gaze and quickly calmed himself. We were outnumbered one to a hundred. I looked at Aerin who fired an arrow at the center of them. It stuck in one of the zombies and exploded. It took out a good few of them, but there were so many. What were we going to do?

Aerin put his bow away and twirled his fighting knives waiting for them to get closer to him. I continued my onslaught of arrows, each arrow managed to take out one, but I was not a fast shot. I knew soon I would have to transform the bow back to the sword. I fired as many arrows before they circled me and transformed the bow back to the sword, taking off a few heads in the process.

Sy needed to work faster, it was getting hard to keep up the fight. I felt the fatigue starting to kick in. I fell to one knee to catch my breath and looked over to Aerin. He was still going, he was dancing around the zombies taking their heads off one by one. I have no idea where he gets the willpower to keep fighting. Then I saw what Morgana had been planning. She was conjuring a great amount of power. She pushed it forward at Aerin and killed every zombie in its way. I reached my hand out to him and got my gift to him just in time.

Aerin still flew back, the blast was too much for my new gift. He hit a wall, and I raced to him. He was unconscious for just a moment. When he opened his eyes he flashed that stupid smile of his and kissed me.

"My hero."

Morgana screamed, annoyed that he was still alive.

"Why don't you just die?" I turned to her, lowering my head and smirking before speaking.

"Because Morgana, we have something to live for. Love is strength." I extended my hand down to Aerin.

Aerin took it getting back to his feet, and Morgana was losing control of her powers. It looked so much like when Aerin did. A purple funnel formed around her, and the clouds started to darken. The sun was completely covered, Aerin put his hand in front of me pushing me behind him. I looked over and saw his eyes were black, he was using his dark powers to see.

"Get behind me, Thorne." His voice sounded different and he was not playing around.

I did exactly what he asked of me, and stood directly behind him. Aerin's hands were gone before my eyes;, his dark fog formed around them, and before I knew it he was completely engulfed in fog, but still kept his human shape.

"Do you really think your magic is stronger than mine?"

"It is when I have something to protect."

Aerin shouted at her as they charged towards each other. I could not see a thing as the fog collided and made a bang louder than any thunder I had ever heard. Lightning struck down from the sky, and looked like it was being used like a weapon. I could not tell who was being hit, and all I could hear was the wind that picked up as it circled them.

I closed my eyes trying to clear my mind, I extended myself into Aerin's mind and held my gift around him. It felt like I was hugging him, but being there inside his mind, I was able to see everything. I could see them both tossing the lightning at each other, I could see Morgana breathing just as heavily as Aerin was. From what I could see they were evenly matched. Neither looked tired, and they were both giving their all going all out. I could only assume that though. I was just watching, and protecting. At least I was able to help a little bit.

We needed a break, we needed Sylas's power. What was taking him so long?. I kept my gift on Aerin but connected to Sylas's mind.

"Sy, how much longer?!"

"Almost done, not much longer." I looked through his eyes, and he was just about completed moving the machines in closer. I returned to Aerin's mind and told him it was time.

Aerin pushed all his magic out to Morgana and pinned her to the wall for a moment. Before I could blink, his arms were wrapped around me and we were teleported out.

"FIRE!" Sylas called out and he ignited the rope.

The clouds opened, and light shone through them, as the arrows rained down over where Morgana was. As they flew in the air the elves started shooting them with fire and we heard explosions as the arrows landed. I watched as the building that was next to her started to crumble. The arrows still rained down over her. I am not sure how many arrows were in each machine, but each one fired hundreds of arrows over her. Each arrow is charged by an elf's magic. This had to have been it.

This had to have worked.

Once the arrows stopped, Aerin teleported me back to see if Morgana was finally dead. The rubble was quiet, there was nothing to be seen. I turned to him and hugged him tight, gently kissing his lips.

"We did it," I said, kissing Aerin's cheek. But he did not look at me, he just continued to search the rubble for her.

"Did we? It seemed too easy." I took his hand and we turned around to walk back to Sylas.

The sound of rubble moving filled my ears from behind filled my ears. I quickly turned around to see purple fog slipping through the cracks. Aerin drew his bow again and readied an arrow. I pulled my sword back from its sheath and waited. The rubble exploded open and Morgana slowly stood up cracking her neck.

"So true Aerin, that was too easy."

"It was not enough magic, are you kidding me right now?. Hundreds of arrows, all charged, was not enough to take her down?." I was completely frustrated. " What do we do now?"

"Now you die!" Morgana shouted back.

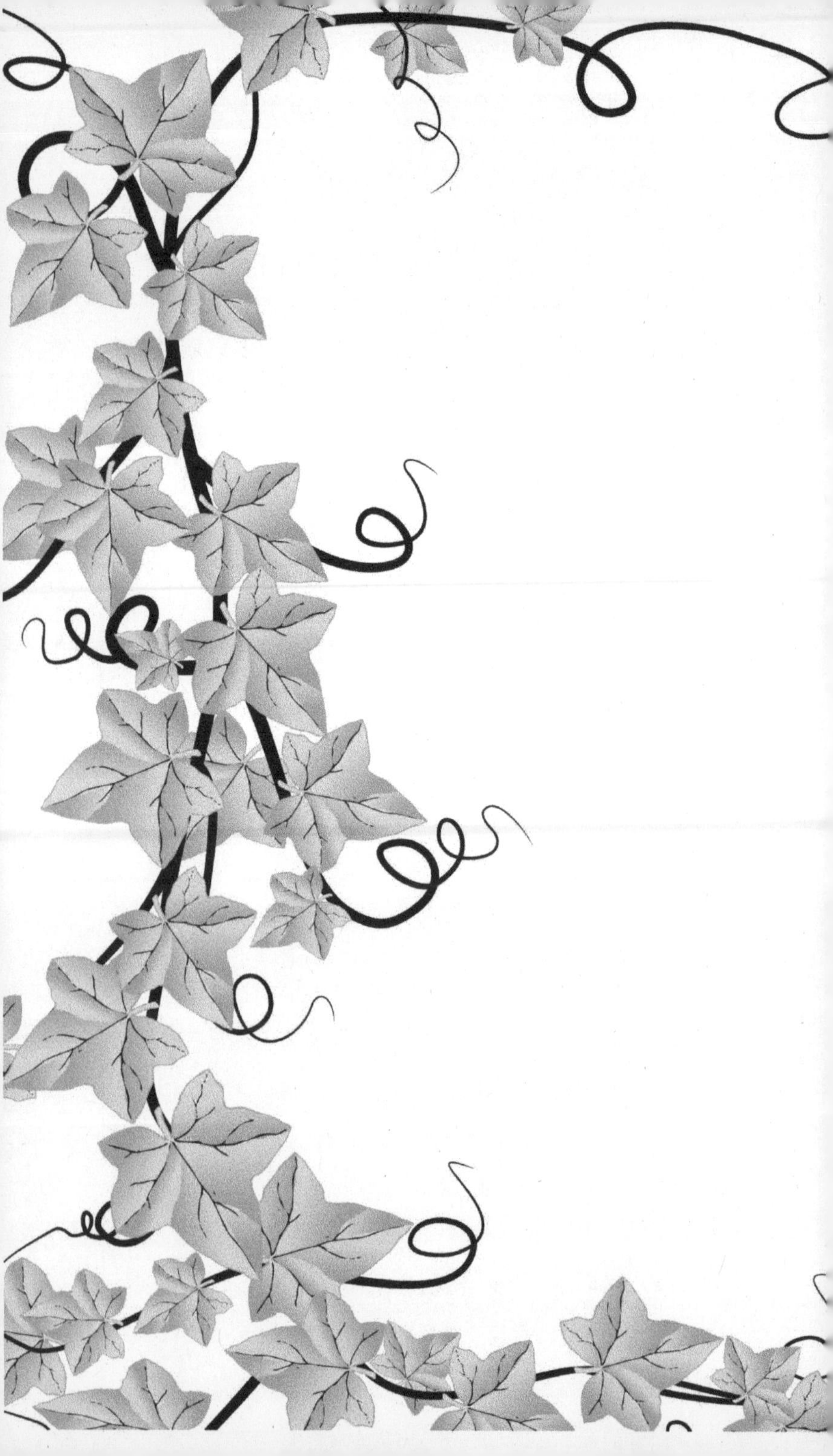

CHAPTER 41:

Aerin

"Thorne, look at her, not one arrow hit her. She dodged them, and most of them hit the building,." I shouted to him, and he nodded back to me.

I shot a fireball into the air signaling we needed backup. That was probably not my best idea either because I heard the clashing of steel start again. Morgana laughed as she slowly walked towards us and created two dark energy balls in her hands. She waved them together over each other and it grew in size with each wave of her hands. I swallowed hard, knowing this was definitely going to hurt if it did not kill us.

Morgana hurled the ball towards us. Thorne turned to me and pulled me in close to him. He kissed my head before closing his eyes.

"I love you, Aerin."

The ball stopped when it hit a golden wall that appeared in front of us.

"Morgana, you have met your match,." Sylas shouted to her.

Sylas slid down the rubble till he was standing next to me and Thorne. I looked down at him Sylas, who did not seem phased at all by the amount of magic he was using. I squinted at him, wondering how that could be. He lost his mortality, he should be feeling every drop of magic he spends.

Sylas held his hands down by his sides, and two beams of golden light shone out of them and hit Morgana in the chest. She flew back into the rubble. I quickly shot an arrow and it hit her arm. Good enough for my bow to work its magic. I quickly started to chant and vines wrapped her up. As it pulled her closer to us, I saw Sylas twirling around and fire mimicking his motions around him. He held his hands out and clapped them down. The fire spun around him and flew at Morgana. It looked like a dragon's mouth. The mouth was over her and it clamped shut. Her scream echoed through the city, over all the clashing steel. Then it went quiet. There was not a sound from the army, not a sound from Morgana. The vines continued to pull her into my bow.

The vines forced her body to stand again and she was impaled by the bow. I pulled the bow free from her, and she fell to the ground. I knelt down beside her body and rolled her over. Her eyes were closed, and it did not look as though she was breathing. I put my bow down to feel for a pulse, and right as my hand touched the cold skin, her eyes opened.

I fell backward, and my bow bounced away from my reach. She quickly sat up and grabbed my arm and held me in front of her like a shield. She walked backwards and I could hear her breathes quicken as her heart rate increased. She was scared, I could feel it.

"Not one move or he dies,." She called out to Sylas and Thorne. Thorne fell to his knees and dropped his sword, and Sylas did the same. I looked up and both armies were looking down at us watching everything unfold.

Thorne could not look up at the sight of me being used like this, and Sylas was shaking with anger. Thorne punched the ground out of anger, but I noticed that when he did a small stream left his fist and was making its way over to me. It was small enough that it would be hidden from anyone who was not looking for it. I followed it with only my eyes, and it stopped next to Morgana and me. It slid between us, and before I knew it, it had risen up separating between us. Morgana lost her grip on me and I pulled away, turning back to look at her.

The water formed into an ice wall and Morgana was frozen. I gave it a good kick and sprung off the wall landing next to Thorne.

"Quick thinking,." I shouted as I landed. I pulled out my fighting knives, and let my black fog cover them. If magic is the only thing that can harm her, then I will use shadow blades. Thorne followed my lead and ran his hand along the blade of his sword and water formed over it with the occasional lightning flash. Sylas created fireballs in both hands. We were ready, and this would be the final fight.

The ice block that Morgana was frozen in shattered, and she looked more pissed than before. I looked around at all their eyes peering down at us and noticed that the men she once had on her side, were ready to retreat. They were just waiting for her to fall. Sylas made the first move and tossed one fireball at Morgana, and she had no issue reflecting to the side. Thorne and I leaped together and brought our blades down towards her head. The purple fog wrapped around her hands and she grabbed onto the blades and tossed us to the side. Her eyes were glued to Sylas.

Sylas took some steps back but soon found his back against the wall. There was no more room for him to run.

"I killed you,." Morgana croaked at him. "How are you

breathing?" She tilted her neck, walking towards him. She extended her hand reaching for his neck. Morgana screamed suddenly and pulled her hand back away. Sylas was standing in front of her with a pillar of fire coming out of his mouth. He was breathing fire. This was something unlike ever seen before by an elf. I looked over at Thorne puzzled and he shared the same expression.

"Are you sure he is half-human?" I whispered to Thorne, who just shrugged his shoulders.

Sylas pushed his arms out at Morgana and she was propelled back to me and Thorne by his flames. I don't think I will ever get that smell of burning flesh out of my nose. I quickly stabbed my shadow blade into her hand, pinning her to the ground, and Thorne held his blade to her neck. Sylas walked over to us, his mouth still had small flames dripping from it. Once he got closer I could see his pupils had turned to small slits. I read about that before, and I knew I would have to talk to him and Thorne about it.

Sylas stood over Morgana and created a large fireball in his hand. He waved his hands in a clockwise motion and the fireball grew in size. He held it above his head and looked down at Morgana.

"This all ends now." As he spoke, Rillifane showed over his body again. His body was almost invisible due to the bright light.

"Morgana, remember you brought this onto yourself."

"Rillifane, this is just the beginning., I will undo

everything you have done."

Purple fog filled the area, and the glow quickly faded back to only Sylas. He fell back, and Thorne quickly rushed over to him. Thorne looked him over and let him lie down gently. Morgana pushed me away with her fog and removed the dark blade. She stood up and looked at the three of us.

"This is far from over."

Sylas sat up and his eyes glowed golden, and a beam that matched them shot out and stuck Morgana pinning her to the wall. I quickly turned and moved my arms in front of me in a counter-clockwise motion before shoving my arms out and shooting a beam of dark magic at her. Thorne looked at us both and did the same shooting out a beautiful crystal blue beam. The three beams met and entered her chest.

"No, you can't do this,." Morgana shouted at us. As she fell to her knees. "This is not the end." She held up her hands and the purple fog left the area creating a funnel above her. It extended as high as the eyes could see and down to her hand. She was sucked up into it, and it smacked into all of us until she vanished from sight.

I sat up looked around and crawled over to Thorne who was still next to Sylas. I took his hand and he looked over at me. His eyes lit up, as he looked at me. I could feel the amount of love he had for me in them. He scooped up Sylas, whose body still looked like Rilliafane.

"Is it over?" Thorne asked me then to squeeze my

hand.

"No, like she said– it is only the beginning,." Sylas spoke to us as the voice of Rillifane. "I don't sense her here anymore, she has left this realm but she will be back,.." His voice spoke softly as the light faded and Sylas was left in Thorne's arms, unconscious.

I let out a sigh of relief hearing that and looked up to the elves and men who fought beside us. I smiled at them as Thorne and I slowly climbed our way back out of the chasm. I stood on a large piece of rubble.

"We leave today as to the victors. Our families are safe." I looked around at the many who lay on the ground dead. "Let us not forget those who have died today, they are part of the celebration as well. Their families will feel this war the most, it is our job now to comfort them. We must come together as one family, one united front. We will overcome this hurdle. We will leave behind one of the machines, and bring the bodies back with us. We will give them a proper send-off. Every Elf and Man grab one of the fallen, and we'll ride back to camp."

I stepped off the rock and whistled for Alatar. Thorne gently placed Sylas in my arms while he hopped up onto her. He took him back and leaned down to kiss me. I held onto his hand for a moment extending the kiss. It is finally over for now. I could have my family again. I can make this all work.

"I will see you soon., Be careful out there Morgana

might be gone, but her army is still here, I can feel it." He nodded to me and kissed me again before commanding Alatar to leave.

I assisted in picking up the bodies of the fallen and placing them gently into the cart before I saddled up on one of the horses. We rode back to camp. There was something about the air that felt lighter, and the atmosphere felt peaceful without Morgana's dark magic interfering with everything.

It was nice.

****

We made it to the camp's site and I was so glad we did. I needed to lie down. I was feeling the aftermath of using so much power, let alone the amount of pure strength. I needed to just crawl up in bed next to Thorne and close my eyes.

I hopped off the horse and rubbed my ass. The horse did not ride nearly as smoothly as Alatar, and god, that made the trip a lot longer than it needed to be. I patted the horse, still thanking it for the ride, and turned to my tent. I pushed open the flaps and Thorne raced over to me. He picked me up and spun me around, and gently pressed his lips against mine.

"How are you holding up?" He was still holding me, I wrapped my legs around his waist.

"I am holding up, how is Sy?"

"He is good, he is resting in his own tent.," Thorne placed me on the hammock and smiled at me. "We did it!"

"We did, but at what cost?. We have to say goodbye to so many tonight. The elves are searching the area for tinder, and logs." Thorne frowned a moment.

"It is hard, Aerin, but remember we all knew the risks of this. We all knew we were fighting for peace. And can't you feel it?"

I smiled at him as he got in the hammock next to me. I took his hand and kissed it gently...

"I definitely can." I inched closer to him and laid my head on his heaving chest. I listened to the sound of his heart beating and soon found myself fast asleep.

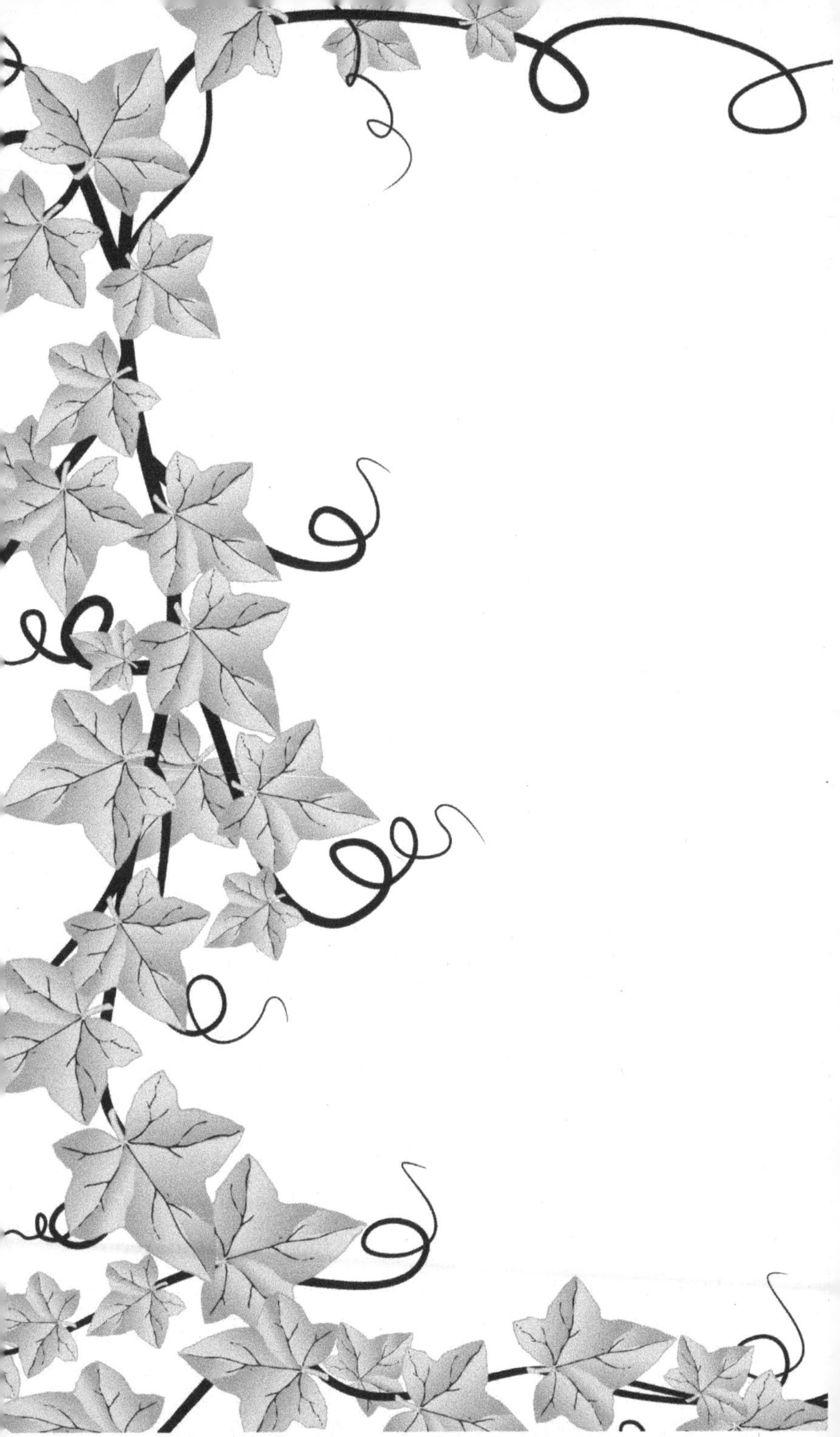

CHAPTER 42:

Thorne

I held my adorable elf while he spent the hours sleeping. I could not help but feel more in love with him. My heart was ready to beat right out of my chest. I wanted this moment to last forever. One of the elves came to the tent flaps. He parted them and peaked his head in, clearing his throat.

"We are ready,." He said speaking softly, I could hear the pain of all the loss in his voice. I closed my eyes and nodded to him. He left the tent, and I looked down at Aerin. I knew this was going to take a lot out of him, but he would want to be there for his men. I gently kissed Aerin's head.

"Aerin, it's time." Aerin slowly opened his eyes and kissed me. I rolled off the hammock and helped my half asleep off lover, off the hammock. I took his hand and looked back at our weapons. For once we were able to leave them behind, and that felt amazing to me. I squeezed his hand before we walked out of the tent, and pulled him into my chest. His hand laid gently on my pecs, and I leaned down to kiss him. "Remember, Aerin, this is not your fault., You are strong, and I love you."

He forced a smile onto his face and went up on his toes to kiss me again. I hugged him for a moment and did not want to let go, and I could tell neither did he. We separated and walked out of the tent.

The elves and men were crying, as they stood together as a mixed bunch. The dead were laid together on a bed of dried branches and logs. Aerin walked beside me as we moved to the wooden beds. He turned back to the army and smiled at them.

"We remember those who have given their lives. Our kin, our friends, our families. Know they have not died in vain. They died heroes."

Aerin held out his hand and one of the elves brought a bow and arrow to him. He nocked strung the arrow and ignited it. He drew back the string and fired it into the center of the beds. They slowly burned, and the bodies were cremated along with it. Aerin handed the bow back to the elf and walked back to me. Our fingers interlocked as we watched the fire. Aerin rested his head on my shoulder, and let himself cry once his back was to the army.

"So many are gone, Thorne. It's not fair, how am I going to face their families?"

I turned Aerin to face me and brushed away his tears.

"So many more are alive thanks to you. So many have a chance to be happy again. So many have a chance at peace now."

I pulled him in close and kissed the top of his head.

"I love you, Aerin."

"I love you too, Thorne,." He mumbled into my chest, trying to gather himself, before he looked up at me or the army. I looked around and the army had dispersed and were starting to cook food. The sun was setting, and the stars were starting to shine through. I stepped away from Aerin for a moment and took his hand, dragging him to the edge of a cliff. I sat down and patted the spot next to me.

Aerin took the hint and took a seat next to me. The cliff overlooks a river that flows through trees. We could see deer galloping through the trees, and all different animals drinking from the river. I pulled Aerin to me again, so he could rest his head. He smiled watching the wind blowing through the treetops.

"We brought back peace,." I spoke to him. He pushed me back and laid on my arm. We looked up at the stars for a bit. I rolled over and looked down at him. It was exactly like when we were kids. His eyes were once again glistening, and the stars danced in them. I leaned over him and kissed him. I laid back down next to him and pointed up. "I can see Orion's belt."

"What, no you can't!" He called back to me. I pointed up and tried to show him the three stars and the figure of the person in the sky. "I don't see it."

"Follow my finger, Aerin, and you will." His eyes shot up and he smiled before looking back at me and kissing me softly.

****

Aerin and I sat on the small chairs that were in Sylas's tent and waited to see if he would wake up any time soon. It was quiet in there, we tried to contain our hormones which let me tell you was no easy task. All I wanted to do was to take Aerin. I wanted to properly celebrate our victory.

I stood up and walked over to Sylas, opening his eyes to see his pupils, remembering how they looked during the fight. I looked back at Aerin and sat next to him.

"You did not seem surprised about the eye change or him breathing fire. What was all that? I've never heard of an elf doing that before. Rillifane's power wouldn't do that either."

Aerin took a deep breath before standing and sitting next to Sylas.

"I have read about it before–, when Sylas was born, do you remember if he had any kind of issues?" Aerin asked me while looking at Sylas.

I thought about it for a while, trying to remember that far back.

"When Sylas was born, I remember my father and his mother never leaving his side. They prayed over him every night. Then one day it stopped., I was allowed to see him, and talk with him."

"If I am correct, he was dying. Your father brought him to a dragon, who blessed him with life. In doing so, part of that dragon's life force joined him. One day he will be able to become a dragon if he chooses. He will be unkillable, and will only die of old age. It's a gift and a curse. If he taps too much into his dragon abilities, he can end up losing his memories, and slowly turn into a full dragon. He can do small things if he chooses once he learns how to. Things like controlling the fire the way he does, controlling what it burns, but also flying."

This was a lot for me to take in. My half-elf brother was really a third human, a third elf, and a third dragon? I thought dragons were only a myth. Now I am hearing that my brother has to be careful because at some point he could turn into one. Aerin had to be pulling my string here. I looked over at him, and he finally met my gaze.

"He will be okay, as long as he controls his powers."

I nodded to him, but still could not believe this new information. That was until I looked back at Sylas, and he was levitating over his bed. I nearly fell backward in the chair. I got up and walked over to Sylas. I said his name and he fell back into the bed. His eyes sprung open and he looked around panicked.

"Where is she?"

"She is gone for now, Sy. We did it." Sylas laid back down and let out a sigh of relief. He flagged us over to him and he pulled us into a group hug. Aerin gave us some alone time and went back to his tent. I looked down at Sylas and explained to him everything that Aerin had told me about his powers. He took it better than I thought, especially when he told me he had a feeling that his powers were stronger than normal. He really was so smart, he had the wisdom of fifty elves all trapped inside his little head. I smiled at him and gave him a hug.

One of the guards came in with a plate of food for him, and he dug right into the food. I laughed at the hunger he had.

"You did great today, Sylas, get some rest., Aerin is going to want to head home at first light."

Sylas smiled at me as I left his tent and returned to Aerin. He was sitting down at the small table that he fixed for me, breaking it. I walked in rubbing the back of my head.

"Sorry for breaking that.?" Aerin chuckled and patted the seat next to him.

We ate in silence, enjoying each other's company. Once his plate was cleaned off I grabbed his hands and pulled him to his feet. I kissed him softly, removing his top. I looked over his body, and smiled, biting down on my lower lip. I was glad there were no cuts, it just meant I could get to the fun part of the night sooner. He jumped up and wrapped his legs around me. I kissed him deeply and pressed him against the support beam in the middle of the tent. I put him down for a moment so he could take off his pants. He turned away from me pulling them down and teasing me, knowing that I was ready for him. He walked back over to me and stripped me before jumping back into my arms. I pushed him back against the beam and slid inside him in one long thrust.

He bit down on my shoulder to muffle his moans. We both didn't have the audience of the army checking in on us. I could still hear the musical sound, and it just made me want him more. I was not going to end after one release. This was an important moment, and my body wanted him so badly. I moved him to the hammock and it was amazing– the swinging from him made it all more exciting.

We made love until the sun came up. We both lay in the hammock breathing heavily and clinging to each other. It felt amazing, and we both wanted to go longer but did not have the time. We would have to wait until we got back home. Aerin covered us in case anyone came in, and we stared into each other's eyes. I could feel his love, and I was intoxicated by the feeling. He looked at me the way no one ever has, he is the best thing that ever happened to me.

Aerin nuzzled into my neck taking deep breaths and enjoying my scent. My heart was racing faster and harder than before. A mix of exhaustion and my love for him was pouring out of me. Sylas came into the tent and smiled at us.

"Someone was busy last night. Did you two even sleep?" He asked, looking away from us, giving us a moment to dress. "Don't be so embarrassed, Aerin, it's part of life, nothing to be shy about, but maybe next time, sleep a little."

Aerin was as red as a tomato and hiding behind me. Sylas was able to pick up on his emotions as if they were being screamed at him. Once he was dressed, he hugged me from behind and peeked over my shoulder. Sylas smirked as he looked around the room.

"So, when we get back, what's the plans?"

"We will have to break the news to the families and remind them they are loved, and that peace is finally with them," I answered him before Aerin had a chance to speak and get worried about the same thing. I held onto Aerin's arms that wrapped around me. I raised one hand and gently rubbed his head.

"I love you," I whispered to him and Sylas made a gagging sound mocking us. I walked over to Sylas with Aerin still glued to my hips and tousled his hair.

"Let's get a move on, the army won't wait forever." I let the two out of the tent and we sat by a small fire eating breakfast while the troops took down our tents. Once everyone finished eating we started to get ready to move out.

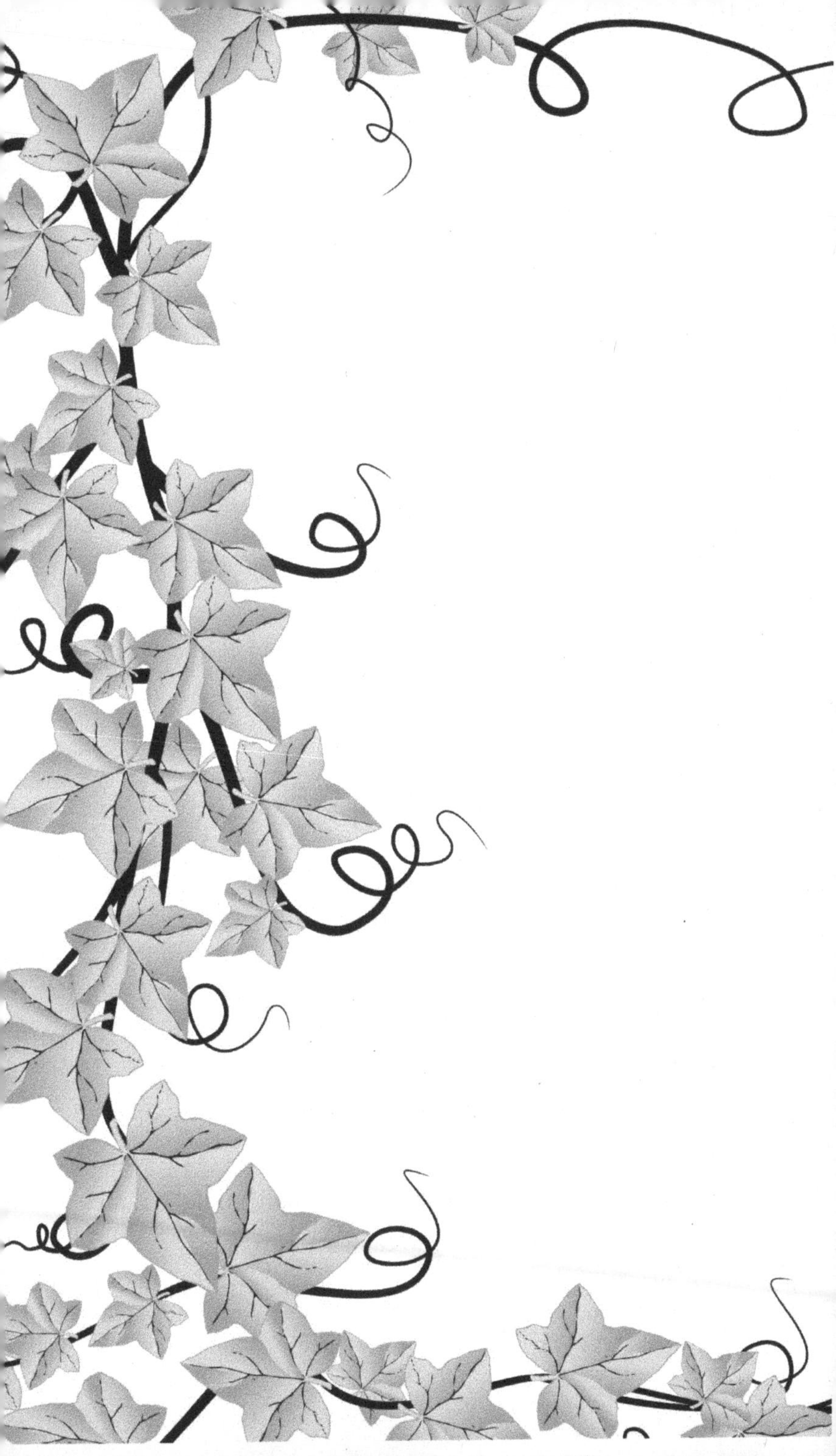

CHAPTER 43:

Aerin

Thorne was wrapped around my waist, and I was trying to control my breathing as we grew closer to the city walls. I could see the many families that gathered there waiting. I found myself wondering how many nights they spent waiting for our return. Thorne was holding on tight to me and kissed my cheek trying to calm my nerves.

"I can't do this, Thorne., I can't face all of them,." I

spoke softly without turning around trying to make sure that no one noticed other than him.

"You have fought the strongest dark fae and won, you have survived for centuries. You can do this, Aerin., You are strong, and I will be right beside you." He kissed my cheek again and gave me a slight squeeze.

I wanted to just turn Alatar around, I could live in solitude again–, it wasn't that bad. Before I had the chance to do it, I heard someone call out 'There they are', and the elves started cheering. I knew I could not turn back now, no matter how badly I wanted to. I held my chin up high and rode Alatar proudly to the gates. The army came to a halt at my command, and they quickly got off their horses. And there was a lot of commotion as the families looked for their loved ones to reunite.

At first, it was a very heartwarming sight. A picture that will always be in my heart is a young elf no more than a hundred years of age, dropping to her knees when her lover stepped down off his horse and removed his helmet. How fast he picked her up and spun her around, made my heart melt.

Thorne held his hand out for me to take and helped me off Alatar., One of the stable workers took her back to the stable, and Thorne hugged me close. His arm wrapped around my waist holding me against him, he leaned into me and kissed me deeply, slipping his tongue in as well. I pulled away from him smiling and smacked his chest.

"Not here."

Thorne chuckled and slid his hand down to my ass and gave it a squeeze., I sucked my lips into a smirk pout and broke free of his grasp. I took his hand and walked him into the city.

****

I took my seat on my throne next to Thorne and Sylas. We waited in silence for a bit before I nodded to Sylas and he rang the bells to summon them. It was not long before the room was packed with the elves. I stood up and walked to the edge of the platform. I looked over them all. Some of them were in tears clinging to the remainder of their families, while the others were grasping their loved ones who managed to return.

"Thank you all for your effort in the battle. We have come out victorious. Morgana has left the realm… We can start our time of peace. I look around at all of you today as a proud leader, and although we have lost so many,. They died for what they believed in. They have granted not only their families a chance at the life we elves once had, but all of us a chance of happiness. King Thorne and I have taken precautions, and those who have lost family, know we are here for you. We have food on its way, your families will be taken care of." I took a deep breath before continuing, there was a lot of emotion and I could tell Sylas was having a hard time coping with it.

I connected with Thorne's mind. *Get Sylas out of here, it is too much for him.*

"Take your time to grieve those you have lost, and remember them not only as your family but also as heroes. We are all one family here, we all feel the pain of the ones lost. Don't forget that you are not alone, and the palace doors are always open for anyone who needs a place to stay, or food to eat. I am here for anyone who needs to talk. We will get through this together."

I watched as the room cleared out, and once it did I could hear my heart racing. Thorne came out from behind one of the pillars and walked up to me. He kissed my cheek and helped me to my feet. He tilted his head slightly and stared into my eyes. I jumped into his arms and kissed him.

"Let's get ready for this time of peace."

Thorne smiled and carried me to our room, where he gently laid me on the bed. He slid my pants off and bent down to remove his. I slipped out of my top and lay on the bed sprawled out naked, the sun hitting my skin. I was ready for this. I wanted it so badly. I wanted his skin pressed against mine. I wanted his lips to touch every inch of me. I wanted Thorne more than ever;, I wanted the reminder that we are together, and happy, and there was nothing stopping us from this.

Thorne climbed into the bed and ran his hands up my legs. I did not bother hiding my smile, as they traced up to my inner thigh. My breath was getting hard to grasp as his fingers lightly slid up my waist and followed it back towards my cock.

"Stop teasing me," I demanded as he gave in to demand.

****

It's been a week now since the big fight with Morgana. To my surprise, everything was still peaceful. There were no attacks from her lackeys left behind, or even any word from any city of her dark powers. I was so relieved that the thought of Morgana only lived in the very back of my mind now. Things finally picked up where they left off and Thorne and I were happy as can be.

I sat up in bed that morning and Thorne was already gone. It was like most of the days, he always was the first one up. After all, I need my beauty sleep. I stretched my body out and quickly dressed. Every night was amazing with Thorne, I was very glad that he was all man below the belt. He had enough to go around if you catch my drift. I had to snap myself out of it and stop thinking of his rock-hard dick before I got too worked up again.

I quickly dressed and made my way down to the dining hall to find something to eat. Thorne was in there waiting for me, the minute I walked in he stood from his seat like a good gentleman. I ran over to him and he hugged me, picking me up and kissing my lips patiently. It was our morning routine and I loved every second of it. I never thought I would find this happiness again, and it felt amazing having it back in my life. I love this elf more than anything.

We took our seats ate breakfast together, and waited for Sylas to join us. He trotted in wearing his usual star outfit and took his seat. His eyes flickered between human and dragon for a few moments, and he dug right into the food. His appetite has changed since he learned about his new gift. His inner dragon demanded more food, but it completely made sense why he looked so young. He has the aging of a dragon and an elf mixed in. It was a little worrisome that he would be alone for many years to come. But that is for another time.

Once Sylas found a moment to stop stuffing his face full of food, he smiled at Thorne and me.

"We started on new plans for different machines, and ideas to help us if Morgana or anyone tries to attack us."

"As long as you are staying out of trouble." Thorne smiled at him.

"Me? Trouble?, I think you have that the other way around." Sylas barked back at him.

"Don't worry, that is my job to keep him in line now,." I chimed my way into their conversation and rubbed my hand along Thorne's leg. "I have my methods to make sure he is well-behaved."

Thorne tensed at the wording I chose there, he knew it had two meanings behind it. He knew the kind of bedroom games I liked. Sylas shook his head and finished his plate of food before running out to go about his day. Thorne and I stood and he took me in his arms.

"And what do you want to do with your day?" He asked me with his cheesy smile glued to his face.

"Why don't we go for a little dip in the lake?" I proposed to him, and he was all too eager to get there. He took my hand and we made our way down to the lake. "Are you excited for a swim or just getting to see me naked again?"

"Why can't it be both?" He called back, jumping into the lake.

I shook my head at his lame answer and stripped down. I much prefer being naked anyway around him. Hell, I loved it. I gave myself a running start and jumped into the lake next to Thorne. I swam up in front of him and wrapped my legs around him. I held onto this neck as I dipped my hair into the water looking up at the sky. The clouds were blocking the sun from blinding me, and it was nice. Thorne leaned over me and kissed my chest. I shuddered from the softness of his lips. I leaned back up into him and kissed him.

"You know she is coming back right? This is not over,." I whispered to him. For some reason, I could not get her out of my head today.

"I know, but when that time comes we will defeat her again." He pulled me closer to him, bending his legs to let more of our bodies into the water. "Let's not think too much of that today. Instead focus on what we know, dear. Focus on my love for you. Focus on being together."

I nodded to him and he walked us to a large rock., He pinned me against it, kissing me gently. I felt my love growing for this man every day, and this is why. He was so romantic, and caring. He was a catch, and I was never going to throw him away, not after everything we have been through.

Thorne kissed my neck, and I found myself lost in whimpers. I could feel myself getting stiff as well. I had to think of other things just to keep my lust in check. He whispered in my ear how much he loved me, and as his breath lingered there I could feel it there was no doubt anymore. I knew he was not going to leave me. I knew that we were in this together, forever. It warmed my heart, and I felt like there was nothing we couldn't do together.

I leaned up into his neck and kissed it softly.

"I'm glad you came back to me, Thorne." I took a deep breath. "I am even more happy that our dreams came true no matter how bad it started off."

"Me too, Aerin. I love you more than life itself."

I kissed him and held him close to me.

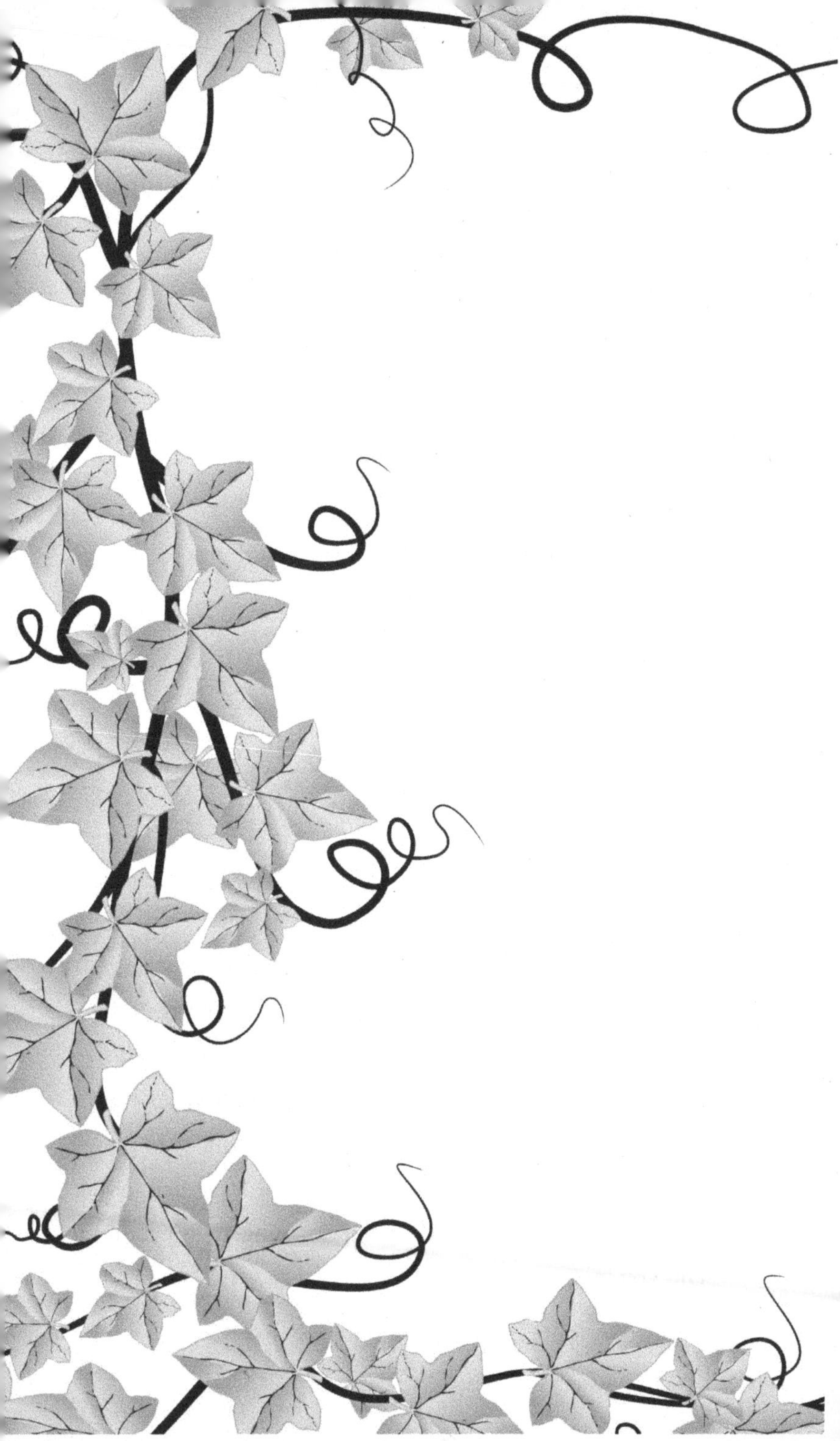

Epilogue:

Aerin

I shot up in a cold sweat. I saw Morgana, she is coming back. I know it. I rolled over and scooted into Thorne, I did not want to wake him since it was just a dream, but it felt so real. Part of me knew she would be coming back to fight again. The next time I promise she won't be so lucky to get a chance to leave.

"AERIN,." I heard Morgana shouting in my mind. "Did you miss me?"

I opened my eyes again and looked around the room. I sat up in the bed and looked down at Thorne. This is really it. She is going to be back before we know it. I walked over to the window and looked at the sun rising over the mountain. I saw the mixed-race city below bustling with the townspeople. I smiled and took a deep breath as a tear rolled down my cheek. Thorne walked up behind me and wrapped his arms around me.

"Good morning, beautiful." I turned to him and he saw the tears. "What is it?"

"She is coming back, Thorne., I heard her in my head., I could tell she was stronger, are we really ready for when it happens?"

"We are ready for anything as long as we are together." He kissed me softly. "I will be your shield and protect you."

"And I will be your dagger, nothing will get close to you." I smiled at him and hugged him close.

"I can't lose you again."

"You never will.,"

"Thorne, you are my everything."

"And you are so much more to me, Aerin."

"I love you, promise to always be by my side?." I begged him, looking into his eyes.

"Always, I promise to never leave you. I love you, Aerin."

I laid my head on his chest and took a deep breath. We

will win and find our happy ending. I swear to it. This is not how it ends, it will end with Morgana's blood on my hands. But my family is safe. I love Thorne, and I am going to protect him no matter the cost.

About the Author

Austin has followed his dream and published his first book. Austin enjoys writing romance novels of all kinds. Austin's goals are to keep writing romance novels of all genres. When Austin is not writing is crocheting or enjoying time with his dog Skittles. He spends the days with his loving husband, and other fur babies Void and Mirku. Austin enjoys watching television and dreaming of his next books. Austin can often be found lost in thought thinking about the characters and how they would react in todays world.

Milton Keynes UK
Ingram Content Group UK Ltd.
UKHW041431261024
450247UK00006B/41

9 798330 493241